Praise for

C.E. MURPHY

and her books

The Negotiator

Hands of Flame

"Fast-paced action and a twisty-turny plot make for a good read...Fans of the series will be sad to leave Margrit's world behind, at least for the time being."
—*Romantic Times BOOKreviews*

House of Cards

"Violent confrontations add action on top of tense intrigue in this involving, even thrilling, middle book in a divertingly different contemporary fantasy romance series."
—*Locus*

"The second title in Murphy's Negotiator series is every bit as interesting and fun as the first. Margrit is a fascinatingly complex heroine who doesn't shy away from making difficult choices."
—*Romantic Times BOOKreviews*

Heart of Stone

"[An] exciting series opener...Margrit makes for a deeply compelling heroine as she struggles to sort out the sudden upheaval in her professional and romantic lives."
—*Publishers Weekly*

"A fascinating new series...as usual, Murphy delivers interesting worldbuilding and magical systems, believable and sympathetic characters and a compelling story told at a breakneck pace."
—*Romantic Times BOOKreviews*

The Walker Papers
Coyote Dreams
"Tightly written and paced, [*Coyote Dreams*] has a compelling, interesting protagonist, whose struggles and successes will captivate new and old readers alike."
—*Romantic Times BOOKreviews*

Thunderbird Falls
"Thoroughly entertaining from start to finish."
—Award-winning author Charles de Lint

"The breakneck pace keeps things moving...helping make this one of the most involving and entertaining new supernatural mystery series in an increasingly crowded field."
—*Locus*

"Fans of Jim Butcher's Dresden Files novels and the works of urban fantasists Charles de Lint and Tanya Huff should enjoy this fantasy/mystery's cosmic elements. A good choice."
—*Library Journal*

Urban Shaman
"A swift pace, a good mystery, a likable protagonist, magic, danger—*Urban Shaman* has them in spades."
—Jim Butcher, author of The Dresden Files series

"C.E. Murphy has written a spellbinding and enthralling urban fantasy in the tradition of Tanya Huff and Mercedes Lackey."
—*The Best Reviews*

"Tightly plotted and nicely paced, Murphy's latest has a world in which ancient and modern magic fuse almost seamlessly... Fans of urban fantasy are sure to enjoy this first book in what looks to be an exciting new series."
—*Romantic Times BOOKreviews*
[nominee for Reviewer's Choice Best Modern Fantasy]

C.E. MURPHY

WALKING DEAD

BOOK FOUR: THE WALKER PAPERS

www.LUNA-Books.com

Recycling programs for this product may not exist in your area.

WALKING DEAD

ISBN-13: 978-0-373-80301-9

Copyright © 2009 by C.E. Murphy

First trade printing September 2009

Author photo copyright © by C.E. Murphy

www.LUNA-Books.com

Printed in U.S.A.

AUTHOR NOTE

Welcome back to the Walker Papers!

It's been five books in two different series and a handful of short stories and comic scripts for me since I've written a Joanne Walker story. That made coming back to Jo and her world a little strange—would I still know how to write her?

Some things, it seems, are like falling off a bicycle. I hope you enjoy the return to the Walker Papers as much as I have, and by the way, if you haven't, stop by my Web site, http://cemurphy.net, and read "Rabbit Tricks," a Walker Papers short story that fits between *Coyote Dreams* and this book.

Catie

This one's for Frank Darcy,
who taught us all to raise a glass to life

Acknowledgments:

Sarah Palmero, Nicholas Whyte, Paul Knappenberger (better known as "Trent" in these acknowledgment pages), Cameron Banks and Katrina Lehto read early drafts of this book in hopes of helping come up with a title, and, since they were doing that anyway, gave some helpful feedback on the shape of the story. If I missed anybody in that list, I beg forgiveness, but I think it was just those five. Also, Laura "Soapturtle" Denson helped me keep my blog software up-to-date when I had no brain left for such things myself. Thank you all tremendously.

There are the usual suspects who need thanking: my husband Ted, who does a remarkable job of maintaining sanity when I'm in the worst of writer-modes, and both my agent Jennifer Jackson and my editor, Mary Theresa Hussey, who inevitably make my books more worth reading. Cover artist Hugh Syme and Harlequin art-department wizards Kathleen Oudit and Fion Ngan also have my undying gratitude for giving me such a beautiful, beautiful book.

I would also like to thank the dozens of people who kept e-mailing me to ask if there was going to be another Walker Papers novel, and when it would be out. Here you go!

CHAPTER ONE

Saturday, October 29, 9:45 p.m.

My wig itched like a son of a bitch.

I wanted to say I didn't know how I'd gotten myself into it, but the truth was, I knew exactly how I had: Phoebe Kostelis, normally my fencing teacher. Tonight, however, she played the part of my short Sapphic sidekick, working the crowd outside the party hall like she'd been born to it. They looked happy to be worked, since she wore only slightly more clothing than I did and had a body that even I coveted in a strictly Platonic sense.

I hadn't thought this much about ancient Greeks since college, which probably meant I wasn't having enough fun. Phoebe, on the other hand, was having a blast, wheezing with laughter as she clutched the arm of a cop I didn't know. At least, I thought he was a cop: he was dressed as one, anyway.

But then, Phoebe was dressed in a scrap of cloth wrapped

around her breasts, a very short skirt and a blond wig that suited her even more poorly than long hair suited me. At least my wig and my natural hair color were the same: black. Phoebe's hair was also black, and being blond did her olive complexion no favors. On the other hand, she was having fun, though I wasn't convinced it was *more* fun than she'd have as a brunette. It didn't matter either way, as long as she kept everybody's attention off me.

I should have known better than to let her choose my Halloween costume. The last time she'd dressed me I'd ended up in an itty-bitty gold-lamé shirt, and jeans that stopped somewhere several miles south of my navel. This time she'd put me in a midriff-baring, boob-enhancing, hip-riding leather-pleated-skirt thing with ass-kicking boots and a variety of increasingly useless-looking weapons. I'd flat-out refused to wear it without a mask. Phoebe insisted that particular outfit didn't have a mask. I insisted there was no way on this earth she could get me out of the house with my face—not to mention other body parts unfamiliar with seeing the light—showing. She'd finally given in and provided me with a golden mask "from season six" that left my mouth and jaw exposed, but hid more recognizable features, like my slightly too-beaky nose. Between it and the wig, I hoped nobody would know it was me.

I walked through the doors a few feet behind Phoebe, who cleared the way with a quarterstaff taller than she was. I didn't really think she needed the quarterstaff: one glower from beneath Phoebe's Frida Kahlo eyebrow was enough to quell *me,* and I had an eight-inch-height advantage over her.

Of course, it was a party, which meant the glower wasn't

really in place. Instead of skedaddling, people grinned, and then they got a load of me. A wolf whistle broke out, followed by a smattering of applause and a cheerfully bellowed, "Damn, Joanne, your legs go all the way up, don't they?"

So much for not being recognized. I had a peace-knotted sword on one hip and a round yin-yang thing on the other. I loosened the yin-yang and shook it threateningly, but no one looked even slightly threatened. Someone *did* start a betting pool on whether Phoebe or I would win a fight. I put ten dollars on Phoebe and made my way farther into the room.

The noise was astonishing. Phoebe and I had been there all afternoon setting up, only leaving an hour or so earlier to go change into our costumes. Since then, an easy two hundred people had jammed into a hall meant for maybe a hundred and fifty, and enough of them were cops that somebody really should've taken the moral high ground and called the fire marshal. Instead, people were dancing, laughing, shouting at each other, waving red cups of cheap party drinks in the air and generally looking as if they were having a good time. I'd never helped throw a party before, much less one people came to by the hundreds. I felt all proud, and felt even better when Thor the Thunder God came through the crowd to stop in front of me with a smile. "Can I get you a drink?"

I looked him up and down, like he had to pass muster before I decided he was worthy of fetching refreshments. He did. In fact, at a guess, there was nobody more mustery at the party. He wore a tight-fitting sleeveless blue shirt with half a dozen shimmering circles set in two rows down his front, and jeans, which made him a rather modern god. Still, the loose blond hair and the goatee he'd grown out over the last few months went a long way toward the look. So did the sledgehammer he'd strapped across his back. It looked like a much more effective weapon than either of the ones I was carrying, and I was briefly jealous. He'd forgone a traditional Viking helmet, but since the man looked like Thor in his day-to-day life, he really didn't need it to pull off the costume. His smile broadened, becoming more godlike as he looked me up and down in turn. "I thought you didn't do Halloween."

"I thought so, too," I said dryly. "Phoebe thought otherwise." I tugged the mask off and rubbed my nose. If people were going to insist on knowing who I was, at least I could indulge in breathing. Besides, I'd been kidding myself about being unrecognizable. Phoebe'd chosen the outfit because I had the physical stature for it: in bare feet I stood half an inch under six feet tall, and had the breadth of shoulder that came with working on cars most of my life. Or, I guessed, if I was going to stay in character, with swinging a sword all my life. I'd actually only been doing that for about six months, which was a lot more than I'd ever imagined doing. Anyway, Seattle's North Precinct police department wasn't littered with women my height, so even though the point of a costume party was disguise, I probably would have had to arrive as a short bald man to actually be mistaken for someone other than myself.

Thor was still grinning at me. "I think this is one matchup they never had on the show. We should get our picture taken."

"You're seriously deluded if you think I'm going to let anybody take my picture in this getup." Thor waved at somebody as I spoke, then turned me around. A flash went off in our faces and I tried to lurch two directions at once: toward the camera to destroy it, and toward Thor, possibly to destroy him, too. Our photographer squeezed away through the crowd, leaving me to bonk my head on Thor's shoulder and groan. "Thanks a lot. Anyway, I never saw the show. Why would she be running around with Thor? I thought she was, like, Greek."

"How could you have never seen it?" Thor asked incredulously. "Don't you ever just turn the TV on and watch whatever's on?"

I shrugged. "Not really, unless I catch a *Law & Order* marathon. I don't watch a lot of fantasy shows."

"Mmmph." He considered me a moment. "Maybe I wouldn't, either, if I were you. You want that drink?"

All of a sudden, I did. Thor's reminder wasn't enough to get my panties in a bunch the way it would've a few months ago—which was good, since there was no way to discreetly debunch panties under my teeny-weeny skirt—but an outloud mention in public was a tad on the overwhelming side. *Overwhelmed* must've shown in my face, because Thor pushed off through the crowd, people making way for the thunder god without thinking about it.

A dippy little grin edged its way across my face as I watched him go. He was a good guy, probably better than I deserved. Certainly better than I'd treated him as when we'd first met and I'd saddled him with the *Thor* nickname. I mean, yeah, he was tall and blond and gorgeous and had shoulders slightly wider than the Grand Canyon, but I'd been pissed off that he'd replaced me as a mechanic at the cop chop shop, and had given myself license to call him whatever I wanted.

I'd been, if you wanted to get right down to it, a bit of an asshole. I hoped I was starting to improve, but in the meantime,

Thor—whose real name was Edward—had admitted that as nicknames went, Thor wasn't bad. I wouldn't have expected him to put on a costume and run with it, but people surprised me all the time. Sometimes I surprised even myself.

Like now. I popped up on my toes to gain another inch in height, and for once I ran with it and gave myself permission to see a little more clearly.

Not just see, but See. Edward had an aura that suited the nickname I'd given him: it was all stormy grays and blues, with shattered bits of white crashing through it. He was, by nature, good-humored, and those sparks of brilliance were usually wit, but I expected if he got his dander up, they'd be as deadly as the lightning Thor was supposed to be able to call.

For a few seconds, the entire room danced with light. Everyone was in high spirits, obvious from not only the laughter and ribald teasing, but the warmth and camaraderie of people feeding each other's energy and keeping it going in a positive cycle. It felt good to revel in that energy, but watching it constantly made the real world harder to see, and despite it all, I still preferred the real world.

It'd been nearly a year since I'd been laid out in a parking lot with a sword in my lung and a smirking coyote offering me the choice between death or life as a shaman. In all my waking hours I'd never thought of wanting any kind of mystical gifts or healing powers, but I'd wanted to die even less. It had occurred to me once or twice since then that even in the absolute worst of circumstances, there were choices to be made. The sticky bit was that we tend to think of choices as being one good thing versus one bad thing. When the available options all suck, you took the one you could live with.

In my case, that was a very literal *what I could live with*. It'd taken me the better part of six months to chin up to the responsibilities I'd agreed to, and finally doing so had changed the shape of my life. Now the least of my esoteric skills was turning second sight on and off, letting me see more deeply into people without so much as a blink.

A party was not the time to be dwelling on my unnatural skill set. I did blink, even if it wasn't necessary, to clear away the glimmering colors, and moved to lose myself in the crowd. Edward would be able to find me; I was taller than almost everyone in the room, and he was taller than I was. I squirmed by a pair of clowns whose eyes were on the level with my breasts. The one with his nose in my cleavage looked entirely too pleased. I threatened him with the yin-yang thing and his companion had the good sense to turn his face away. I moved in the other direction, hiding a laugh. Being amused by people ogling my chest seemed out of character for my leather-clad persona, never mind me.

A big chunk of a man in a blue satin evening gown with a matching bolero jacket edged through the crush, trying not to step on anyone. I escaped the clowns and waved my mask in greeting. "Hey, Billy. You look great."

Billy Holliday, paranormal detective extraordinaire—he saw dead people—my work partner, and overall one of the solid, reliable linchpins of my life, looked me up and down and said, "You look surprisingly naked."

I covered my bare stomach with the mask and wondered if a blush could start as low as the xyphoid process. It felt like it. "I don't think that was the response I was looking for."

Billy, without a hint of genuine repentance, said, "Sorry,"

as his wife appeared at his elbow. "I've just never seen you quite so, um."

Quite so *um*. There were probably worse compliments a girl could get, but overall I think I'd have preferred better. Then again, married men probably weren't supposed to open with a salvo of *you're surprisingly naked* to begin with, so maybe I should take what I could get.

"Bill, you're not supposed to let the pregnant wife get lost in the madhouse." Melinda Holliday stood a full foot shorter than her husband, and wore a velvet tuxedo that properly squired his evening gown. Wonderfully long tails nearly dragged on the floor, and she adjusted a cummerbund stretched over a very round belly as she examined me. "Joanie. You look…"

I sighed. "Surprisingly naked?"

"Well," she said cheerfully, "yes. Fantastic, actually, but surprisingly naked. Who convinced you to wear that?"

I said, "Phoebe," in a voice that I hoped spelled her doom.

Melinda laughed, which boded poorly for my doom voice. "Half the force will thank her for it. Have you seen Michael?"

"Michael? Morrison?" I didn't know a lot of other Michaels, but I never thought of my boss by his first name, and found it bewildering that Melinda did. "Morrison's at my party?" I had a fair amount of experience with the world ending. None of it had looked anything like a costume party, or else I'd have put Morrison's attendance down as a sure sign of the apocalypse.

Melinda's eyebrows shot up. "You invited him, didn't you?"

"I didn't think he'd come!" Curiosity got the better of me as I craned my neck to look around. "What's he dressed as?"

"A cop, of course." Melinda sounded delighted.

I squinted. "He is a cop. That's not a costume. Unless he's in uniform, but that's cheating."

Billy, sounding every bit as pleased as Melinda, said, "Oh, he's in costume." I turned my squint on him, then peered around again. Morrison typically wore suits, except for when protocol demanded he pull out the full captain's dress uniform. I hadn't seen him in that since a funeral in June, and while he'd looked as handsome and solemn and reliable as a police captain should, I didn't think he should get away with it as a Halloween costume. Especially when I'd let Phoebe put me into some strategic bits of leather and a sword. I'd have died of hypothermia if the party wasn't a success.

Thor reappeared, bearing drinks and a look of amusement. "Have you seen the captain?"

"I don't even believe he's here." I took one of the plastic cups he offered and sniffed its contents—pink and foamy—suspiciously. "What is this?"

"I didn't ask. There were two choices. One involved dunking my head and apples. I took this one." He took a sip of his own drink cautiously, then made a moue. "Typical fruit-drink-and-soda party stuff."

Reassured, I took a sip, then coughed, eyes tearing. "You forgot to mention heavily spiked." I blinked tears away, then took another sip more carefully. Woo. Worse than the Johnnie Walker I'd gotten wasted on a few months ago. At least I expected that to knock me senseless.

Melinda heaved a melodramatic sigh. "Do they have anything nonalcoholic?"

"They better. I told Phoebe we had minors attending the party." I nodded at Melinda's belly. "You look ready to pop."

"I was ready to pop three weeks ago. I've forgotten what my feet look like. My children have taken to calling me El Blobbo."

"They have not," Billy said equitably. Melinda beamed at him and he said, "They call her La Blobbacita," which earned him a sudden reversal of the beam into a credibly injured pout.

"When's the big day?" Thor took a swig of the pink drink and made a face.

Melinda let go of her pout to sigh gustily. "November sixth."

"Well, that's not too bad, right? Only another week."

Spoken, I thought, like somebody who's never been pregnant. I didn't say it out loud because it opened up a whole bunch of questions I had no desire to answer, but the look Mel gave him pretty much said what I didn't.

Billy grinned. "She's doing jumping jacks every morning to try to hurry things along." He bent to give her a kiss, promised, "I'll find you a drink," and cleared a path through the crowd. Evening gown or no, he was by far a big enough guy to do that easily, though it closed up behind him again.

Melinda, beaming, called, "My hero," after him, then folded her arms across the top of her tummy and looked around. "Good party, Joanne."

"Thank you. From shut-in recluse mechanic to partying shamanic police detective within a year. You too can get on this ride if you're over this tall." I waved a hand near the top of my head, then took another hasty swallow of my drink. Apparently it was more potent than I'd realized, if it was taking me from wanting a drink so I didn't have to think about my mystical power set to babbling about it.

Melinda, bless her, snorted and stood on her toes in an attempt to reach the required height, while Edward leaned forward to knock his forehead against the side of my still-lifted hand. He had a good three inches in height over me, and his voice dropped somewhere around his, um, knees, as he murmured, "I wouldn't mind getting on that ride."

This time I was sure a blush could start around the xyphoid process. His smile turned into a grin and he watched that blush go all the way down, which only served to enhance it. I whispered, "Stop that," but not with any particular conviction.

He brought his gaze back up to my face and leered, then laughed and stepped in against me. I elbowed him with even less conviction than I'd scolded. He slid an arm around my waist, looking pleased with himself. "You brought it up, so now I get to ask something I've been dying to."

I said, "No dying," semi-automatically. Too many people around me had died, or had had alarmingly close calls, this past year. I didn't like even joking about it.

Apology flashed through his blue eyes and he nodded, but he went ahead and asked, "Halloween's a spooky time of year. Does it kick things into overtime?"

I frowned, first at my drink, then at my date. "Why? Have I been acting weird lately?"

He and Melinda said, "No more than usual," in tandem, and he laughed as Melinda presented a high five for him to match. "Nah. I was just curious, and you don't usually bring it up, so I thought I'd seize the opportunity."

"That's not all you've seized." Billy presented a cup of water over Melinda's shoulder. She waddled around to give him a kiss of thanks, and he smiled broadly before remembering he was haranguing Thor. "Is this guy bothering you, Joanie?"

"Terribly. Help, help." I made a feeble attempt to escape, then blew a raspberry and leaned against Thor. "I haven't noticed any correlation between the time of year and the amount of weird in my life, no. Get back to me in five years and I might have a better…what do you call it."

"Survey sample?" Melinda suggested.

"Yeah, something like that. But I don't think it fluxes and rises with the time of year. I mean, what kind of mystical portent does the second week of July have?" Actually, everything that'd happened in July had been entirely my fault, not some kind of magic cosmic conjunction. I didn't feel it necessary to mention that aloud.

"Well," Thor said, "it had enough mystical portent to make me ask you out. That's got to count for something."

"No," Melinda said dryly, "what's mystical is she said *yes.*"

"I had to. It was Alan Claussen's band. I like them." I actually scraped up a few lines of lyrics, half singing, *"Ill met by moonlight, first kiss, stolen late at night,"* which got a round of applause from Melinda as Thor staggered back as far as the press of people would let him, a hand over his heart.

"I see how it is. I'm only wanted for my concert tickets."

I patted his shoulder, since he'd only escaped to about eighteen inches away. "Your concert tickets and your uncanny talent under the hood. There are worse things a guy could be wanted for."

Too late, I realized the error of my phrasing, and raised my voice to say, "He's a mechanic! *I'm* a mechanic! I like guys who are good with cars!" over Billy and Melinda's synchronized "OooOOoooh!"

"The lady," Thor said cheerfully, "doth protest too much. You're not helping yourself."

"Yeah, yeah, yeah, I know." I was too pink cheeked and laughing to get myself out of that alive anyway, so I took a swallow of my fizzy drink and reveled in the sheer simple fun of being teased by my friends.

"Jo!" Phoebe squished through the crowd and seized my arm. I straightened away from Edward, and Phoebe shook me. I went *agglty* while she said, "You have *so* got to get a load of your boss," and swung me around to face the door. Still rattling, I looked for Morrison and whatever costume had everybody I knew insisting I needed to see him.

Instead, the doors flew open and an entire cadre of zombies lurched through them.

CHAPTER TWO

It said something very disturbing about what I'd come to consider a normal life that the first thing I did was reach for the sword on my hip. The peace knot held, which gave me enough time to remember that this was a Halloween party, and that hordes of undead weren't unexpected at such festivities.

Still, loosening my fingers from the sword's hilt took more effort than it should've. Phoebe, more or less under my elbow, said, "Well?" in such obvious delight that I scowled at her, then looked back at the zombies.

"What? Morrison's a zombie?"

"No!" She thrust a finger out, pointing dramatically. I followed the line of her arm and still didn't see my boss. There were a pair of cross-dressed hippies, an Elvira being hit on by an exceptionally sleazy-looking vampire, an '80s *Miami Vice* look-alike and what appeared—from various blue skin, white hair and black leather costumes—to be the entire cast of a science-fiction show, but Morrison's distinctive silvering hair wasn't visible anywhere. I shot Phoebe an irritated look, opened my mouth to speak, and my gaze snapped back to Don Johnson without consulting my brain.

"Oh my *God*."

Morrison turned around at my high-pitched exclamation, and Melinda, gleefully, said, "Told you he was a cop."

I made a gurgling noise deep in my throat.

He had it all: the gradated cop sunglasses, which were not at all the right shape for his face; the pastel-pink shirt, unbuttoned far enough to show the world that Morrison had a very nice chest with what appeared to be the ideal amount of coarse, graying hair. The white blazer thrown over his shirt matched pale slacks and he wore loafers without socks. I stared at his feet, trying to wrap my mind around Morrison being that casual, then brought my gaze back up to the crowning horror.

"What did you do to your *hair?*"

Self-conscious wasn't a look I was accustomed to seeing on Captain Michael Morrison. He touched his head, then glowered at me. "What'd you do to yours?"

"It's a wig!"

At a loss for moral high ground wasn't a look I was used to seeing on him, either. "It's temporary," he muttered.

I laughed, and, without thinking, slid my fingers through the tidy brown cut. It wasn't a bad color. I just thought of the silver hair and the damn blue eyes as part and parcel of Morrison's aging-superhero look. Changing the hair made him look younger and more human. "You've even got stubble." Stubble no more belonged in Morrison's universe than, say, animistic-based shamanic magic did. It didn't stop either of those things from being in his universe, but they didn't belong. "Look at you, Morrison."

Instead, he looked at me, which made me notice I still had my fingers in his hair.

I said, "Shit," and pulled my hand back, focusing on his shoulder while I tried not to blush. It didn't work, and the best I could do was hope nobody called me on it. Hoping nobody'd noticed I'd been feeling up Morrison's head was asking too much. "Sorry. Is, uh, is that the color it used to be?"

"It was blond."

"Really?" Silver-shot suited him, and I couldn't imagine him with anything else. Even seeing it, I couldn't quite imagine it.

"Really," he said with a hint of amusement, then helped me get my footing back by saying, "Look at *you*, Detective."

I regained enough equanimity to give him a severe look. "I'm a princess warrior. You're the detective here, Captain."

"I'm in disguise," he told me. "You're not supposed to call me captain." He hesitated a moment, looking a couple inches up at me. My boots were heeled, giving me a rare height advantage. Unshod, Morrison and I were the same height down to the half inch, and I'd been known to wear heels just for the satisfaction of looking down on him. Not recently, though, so finding myself taller than he was disconcerting.

He let his hesitation out in a breath, said, "Looks like a good party, Walker. Thanks for inviting me," and reached past me to accept a drink from somebody.

I stayed where I was a few seconds too long, convinced he'd

been going to say something else entirely and still waiting for him to say it. Morrison, and the party, moved on, leaving me wondering just what it was I'd thought he'd been going to say, and what I thought I'd have said in return. Not that long ago Morrison and I had had a wholly antagonistic relationship. Like everything else in my life, it'd gotten more complicated lately.

No, that wasn't true. We'd drawn some lines in the sand, the captain and I, that was all. *I,* had drawn a line in the sand. I'd taken a promotion to detective instead of taking a chance on something else entirely, and Morrison respected the decision I'd made. Which meant whatever it was I thought he'd been going to say, he wouldn't have, and I needed to stop worrying about it.

I nodded, a too-visible acknowledgment that I'd given myself a firm talking-to, and turned around to find all my friends looking as if there were many, many unspeakably interesting things going on in their minds, and as if they would all very much like to speak them. Even Thor had a hint of that look about him, and while picking up on subtle social clues wasn't my strong point, I was pretty sure the guy who was more or less my boyfriend wasn't supposed to look like that with regards to me having a conversation with another man.

He, however, was also the only one who put aside that gossipy look and offered me a hand. "I have it on pretty good authority you can dance."

"I have it on better authority that I'm an embarrassment on the dance floor." I put my hand into his anyway and he tugged me through the crowd to a space where the pressed bodies played against each other in more graceful rhythms.

Music dominated that corner of the room, compliments of someone willing to play the parts of both Frankenstein's monster and DJ at Phoebe's party. It *was* her party; the fact that I'd invited half the police department and they'd showed up didn't make it any less hers. I wouldn't have known where to start in renting a hall or getting a caterer, but providing a significant portion of the guests defined me as co-host. The dance floor was a bit less crowded than the rest of the room, and I alternated between taking cues from Thor—I really wasn't a very good dancer, but I could manage to follow a lead, at least some of the time—and watching the room.

People were having fun. At my party. I imagined telling my fifteen year old self that a dozen years later she'd be what she'd have called popular, back in the day, and knew she'd never believe me. I didn't quite believe it myself. On the other hand, my plastic cup full of foamy pink stuff was gone, and having a cup of heavily spiked punch inside me made it easier to believe almost anything. I said, "Six impossible things before breakfast," aloud, and when Thor crinkled his eyebrows at me, snorted. "I need another drink. Water this time. Oi."

"The bar's over by the dunk tank. Lead on, MacDuff."

"That's *lay on*," I said, suddenly cheerful. A man who was into cars and misquoted Shakespeare was a good guy to be dating. I squirmed forward through the crowd.

Squishing through partygoers was good for my ego. People who could barely move in the crush did double takes and stepped back to admire the whole costume. I heard an *"Ow!"* and Thor's innocent whistle, like he'd maybe prevented a wandering hand from copping a feel. Overprotective boyfriends should probably be scolded, but instead I grinned and looked back to thank him even as I kept pressing forward.

All of a sudden the crowd disappeared around me, sending me stumbling. Thor let go of my hand, which didn't help at all, and I caught myself on the edge of a cauldron.

I said something clever like, "Buh?" and got a laugh for it, but I was genuinely surprised. I didn't remember us ordering up a gigantic pot—and it *was* gigantic, coming halfway up my thigh and an easy four feet across at its bulge—but Phoebe stood on its other side, looking pleased with herself.

Nervous instinct made me glance around for a third witch. I'd spent a bit of time in a coven, and had absolutely no doubt of their goddess-granted earth power, but I didn't have any particular need to hoe that row again, particularly at a party. To my relief, it appeared that it was just Phoebe, me and the cauldron at center stage. I knew I wasn't a witch and I was pretty sure Phoebe wasn't, so I straightened up and dusted my hands against my skirt, all take-charge and businesslike. The minor detail of not knowing what business made me stage-whisper, "Are we boiling somebody for dinner, then?" across the cauldron.

"Sure! Boil, boil, toil and trouble!"

Nobody ever got that line right. I muttered, "It's *'double, double toil and trouble, fire burn and cauldron bubble,'*" and the cauldron erupted.

My first thought, through the green smoke and the coughing and hacking, was that I really should've been allowed to complete the couplet and set the charm before anything exciting like an explosion happened. My second was to notice that the shrieks around me were turning to laughter, and my third was to notice I didn't seem to be missing any body parts. In the grand scheme of things, that was good.

The undead rising gracefully from the cauldron were less good. There was something inhuman about the way they came up: smooth, effortless, as if they floated instead of climbed like normal human beings. They didn't seem to be intent on flinging themselves at anyone in search of human flesh, but rather twined around one another, sensual in every move.

I didn't especially like horror movies, but I was fairly certain your average zombie didn't have abs of steel, or an ability to undulate the way the pair in the cauldron did. Zombies were more about body parts dropping off than rhythmic motions. I held off panic another few seconds, giving reality just enough time to set in.

Under the gray-green skin makeup and the extremely well-done painted-on innards rotting out, the couple in the cauldron were pretty much beautiful. The Sight swam into place, assuring me that nothing was untoward about their psychic presences, and swam out again, leaving me to see with normal eyes and grasp that the duo were, in fact, exotic-dancer gorgeous.

The music took a turn toward a spooky bump and grind, and they moved to it, nothing alarming in their dance, except that I was four inches away from pelvic thrusts. The pelvises in question moved higher, the dancers still rising toward the ceiling with inexplicable smoothness. I admired an especially nice pair of thighs before Phoebe lifted her hands to clap and hoot and sway along with the music.

As if she'd given the crowd permission, other people joined in, laughter turning to shouts and cheers of approval. A ripple effect went through the party hall, overhead lights shutting down while black lights and tiny, brightly colored spotlights sprayed across the teeming masses. The dancing zombies' knees came into my view and a solid click sounded, finally explaining how they were rising so smoothly: the cauldron was fitted with a rising platform. I gave it a weak smile and turned back toward the crowd, looking for Thor.

He was there with a smile that turned concerned. "Joanie?"

"My imagination's working overtime. Can we get out of here for a minute?" Even wearing as little as I was, my skin was sticky and overheated. Goose bumps washed over my arms in chills that counteracted the heat, and the hot-to-cold flashes made my tummy twist uncomfortably. The air thickened too much to breathe, full of body heat and scents ranging from heavy makeup to perfume to sweat. "I'm not used to this many people."

"Yeah, no problem." He went all big and solid and masculine, putting an arm around my waist and his presence somehow enlarging, so the crowd fell back from around us. The claustrophobic heat faded a little and I dragged in a grateful breath of slightly cooler air, feeling like I could make it outside to silence and safety.

That was when the screaming started.

CHAPTER THREE

In the future when I've got a bad feeling, it would behoove me to remember that, having been granted phenomenal cosmic powers, it's okay to trust myself when something seems off. I froze, in the sense of icicles down the backbone and prickles on the skin, but otherwise not as literally as I'd have liked. Almost before the shrieks became more than passionately indrawn breaths, I was turning, not wanting to see what was going on behind me but even less able to ignore it.

The cauldron dancers were rigid, all the grace and beauty flown out of their bodies. The part of me that didn't know anything at all about medical diagnoses immediately decided it was a petit mal seizure, with their eyes rolled to white and their teeth bared by lips stretched thin and bloodless. Their hands were clawed and every muscle trembled with strain. Cords stood out in their throats as they screamed, and even those sounds were shadows of what they should have been, given the effort their bodies were expending.

The part of me that knew better than to try to diagnose medical conditions with a degree in English and a few too many television dramas tore away the real world and gave me the lowdown on what I could do to help. At least, that's what it was supposed to do. The first part worked, anyway.

Their auras gave me nothing. They were spiky with distress, the reds and oranges of earlier delight now bleeding dark and terrified: sickly shades with the enormous strength of fear be-hind them.

Thin gray film rose out of the cauldron, sucking itself skin-tight against the dancers' contours beneath their clothes. I had the impression I'd been granted X-ray vision—or maybe M-ray vision, Magic-Ray—as the Sight ignored what they were wearing and honed in on the stuff racing over them, providing me with a totally non-titillating examination of their bodies.

It was even money on whether the spasms were from being cling-wrapped tightly enough to send them into some kind of hind-brain attempt to throw it off, or if the murk was ac-tually invading their bodies. It had already crawled to their chests and throats and sluiced toward their gaping mouths, and I had no freaking clue what it might be.

A smart doctor—maybe a smart shaman—would diagnose the damn problem first, but apparently the whole warrior-princess costume obliterated any kind of rational thought I might've indulged in. I vaulted onto the cauldron with a yell and slapped my hands over their mouths just before the gray stuff slipped over their lips and down their throats.

About six things happened at once.

First off, somewhere way in the distance, I heard Billy Holliday bellowing, "Joanne Walker, what in holy living hell!?" As far as I was concerned, that pretty much made up the soundtrack for everything else that happened. Time stretched, extending into slow moments that crystallized everything around me into clarity and allowed me to discard that which was unimportant. On reflection, that included music, calls to 911, some shouting and the start of a stampede, but right then, those seven words made up the walls of the world for a brief and horribly long eternity.

The good news was that the gray film leaped off the dancers, who collapsed out from under my hands. The bad news was, it leaped from them to me, and I had a sudden intimate understanding of just what they'd been enduring.

Enduring. There's a funny choice of words. It's not one I'd think would apply to a scenario that couldn't have lasted longer than five seconds, but under the film's tenterhooks it was the only one that seemed appropriate.

It *was* trying to get in, trying to invade. I felt my muscles seize and bunch and rattle in just the way the dancers' had, a million pinpricks of ice jabbing under my skin and trying to work their way beneath. I'd never been flayed and wasn't eager to try it, but I thought it might feel like this: burning pain that did its best to defy words and to turn me into nothing more than a scream.

A scream. Screaming was bad. Not because I didn't deserve to, because anybody being flayed probably deserves to scream, but because the stuff had a purpose, and thwarting flaying gray film was a worthy goal. I snapped my mouth shut and rolled my lips in, biting their insides to keep myself from indulging in the scream that would let the stuff in. Then I wondered if my nose was enough of an access point to let it in, and how I was going to breathe if I needed to pinch my nostrils shut, too.

Then again, if the hurting didn't stop soon, I wasn't going to care much about breathing. More or less reassured by the thought, I stopped worrying about it. Look, logic in the face of excruciating pain isn't one of my strong points. It worked for me, which was all that mattered. Meantime, my stomach, eager to add its opinion on agony, violently rejected the fizzy pink drink I'd indulged in earlier.

It was significantly worse coming up than it'd been going down, and it hadn't been good to begin with. Human nature trumped scary crawling gray stuff and I doubled over, expelling bright pink spew. The film retreated, apparently as disgusted by Technicolor vomit as I was. The lack of pain left me astonishingly clear-headed.

Clear-headed enough to see that more of the gray fog was bubbling up from the cauldron and flowing over its edges, hurrying toward the partygoers.

Toward people *I'd* invited to come have a good time tonight.

I forgot that I was probably the only one in the room who could see the goo. Forgot that I'd jumped up onto the cauldron like a madwoman and the two people I'd touched had collapsed, which, by any coherent standard, suggested I was dangerous. Forgot that my own magic had a visible component, and that I was in the middle of a very public place.

Or maybe I didn't forget. Maybe I just didn't care, because I'd had *enough* of innocent bystanders getting run over on my watch. Agony fled my bones, chased out by fury, and I smashed through sickness to call up the healing magic that was my heritage. I had no idea what I was up against, but that'd never stopped me before. Better to turn myself into a super-size McSnack for gray ooze than to let anybody else get eaten.

Silver power surged, its brilliant blue highlights making me feel like an electrical conduit. I could See it, blazing with righteous anger, and while I still couldn't hear much beyond Billy's shout, I'm pretty sure that was when the stampede started. Anybody in their right mind wanted to get the hell away from me. For a room as crowded as that one, it was amazing how everybody managed to jump back two feet and leave a circle of emptiness around me.

At least, I thought it was them lurching back. I had a certain amount of success with the idea of capturing things in nets, but a net wasn't going to hold goop in. I went the bubble-boy route, sending a physical flare of magic from my core into a sphere around me. It was wholly possible that I shoved everybody out of my way, although I didn't think that was very polite and shamany. Then again, a dead shaman had told me I'd walk a warrior's path, so maybe I had license to metaphysically bludgeon people once in a while.

Either way, they were a bit farther out of harm's way, and the cauldron-born ichor ran up against my sphere and began crawling upward, looking for egress and finding none. I figured it would take about two seconds before it reached the top and started dripping down on me. That meant I had about a second and a half to come up with a brilliant plan to stop it.

Time resumed its normal pace, two seconds blew by, and I was screwed.

There's nothing especially attractive about shrieking like a little kid and curling up in a ball with your hands over your head, but that's what I did. I didn't want to face that skin-peeling sensation again. Even the idea made my eyes hot with tears, and if falling down and sobbing kept it away from me for another half second, I wasn't too proud to grovel.

More than that went by before I realized my skin wasn't being pulled off. I peeked through my fingers at the shell I'd built around myself and the cauldron.

Man. I had no idea what it looked like from the outside, but from within, it looked like a Gaussian blur of hell. Formless gray surged and slid around me, a relentless ocean of potential danger and pain. Color bled in, but only at the corners of my eyes: if I jerked to look straight on at it, red and black faded away, as if something living didn't want to meet my gaze. Thin, bonelike hooks scratched at my arms and flinched back again. A sound crept in behind the small bones of my ears, something high and lost that reminded me of the banshee.

It made shapes out of the mist, emaciated wavering things with gaping eyes and mouths. They had the weight of age to them, pressing down on me as if, if they couldn't scrape their way in through my skin, they'd crush me into component parts that could be absorbed into the gray.

A little belatedly, it occurred to me to wonder why they *weren't* scraping their way inside my skin, and I stopped peeking through my hands to look at my fingers.

Seeing through your own skin is a bizarre effect. When my magic had first broken loose, there'd been so much to burn off I'd seen my flesh and blood as rainbows, shimmering with power. Over time that variety had faded to the silver and blue that I now considered to be mine, and right now that was what I saw: oil-slick pools of color burning in my veins and swimming through my muscles. All that magic had once been knotted up under my breastbone, making me sick with the need to act, but it'd become a much more integral part of me, almost always active to some degree, and ready to be called on in its full strength when I needed it.

Offhand, I guessed the gray slime wasn't down with shamanic power, and that a human body rife with it wasn't an appealing host. It had likely dared to attack me in the first place because I hadn't called my power up actively: now that I'd turned it on, I was unfriendly territory. That suggested I was probably dealing with some kind of death magic, because while shamanism had as much to do with death as life, I was coming to think of it as a more or less inherently life-positive kind of magic. Though if I found myself using phrases like *life-positive* very often I was going to have to life-negative myself out of humiliation. Nobody says things like that. Jeez.

The point, though, was that if the nasty gray slime couldn't get a foothold in me when I was topped up with blue glowy lifey goodness, then it probably had a big fat hold on death itself. In fact, me being a poor host was, in every aspect but one, excellent. It meant the bubble of power would keep the stuff in, and that I'd be perfectly safe as long as I could maintain it.

And therein lay the flaw. I'd been in the midst of a hideous gray blur for less than a minute and I was already eager to get out. I still didn't have any idea how. This kind of thing wasn't covered in the shamanic handbook. In fact, nobody'd given me a handbook, an oversight I felt was increasingly gross as I stumbled along this path.

Well, said a little voice inside my head, *you might not know how to get out, but you don't actually have to be stuck in the gray, you know.*

I hated that voice. It sounded just like me being sarcastic, which was bad enough, but it also usually had a very good point, which only added insult to injury. I was pretty sure everybody had a voice that made snide comments and that I'd had one before my world went magical and mystical, but I couldn't remember for sure. I was afraid to ask anybody else in case they said no. Being a shaman was challenging enough. Being an actually insane shaman would just suck.

Teeth clenched against mumbling imprecations at a voice in my head, I let go of the Sight so I could, well, see.

Only when the gray faded did I realize how weird it was I hadn't been able to See beyond it. Usually the Sight gave me layers upon layers: I'd looked through half of Seattle in the past, buildings becoming strong semi-visible constructs of pride and place, things that knew what they were meant to do and glad to do it. People were brilliant spots of color, and highways black-and-blue jagged smears across a natural land-scape. Other living things, trees particularly, were incredible with their light, but none of it blocked each other out like the gray film had done. I'd really only encountered something like that once, when a demi-god was trying to hide his exact location from me. It'd worked, and if that meant the cauldron was pouring cranky demi-gods out into my Halloween party I was going to have a come-to-Jesus meeting with the man-agement. Never mind that I had no idea who or what might constitute The Management in the complex spiritual world I'd been introduced to. I'd complain to it anyway. No fear, that's me.

No fear, or no sense. Sometimes it's hard to tell the dif-ference.

My sphere glimmered at a diameter too great for me to

touch with spread arms. Even without the Sight it was visible to me, and by the way people were scurrying for the doors, I guessed they could see it, too. I had to look bizarre, wearing that ridiculous costume and crouched in the midst of a shimmering ball of light.

Actually, I thought I might look kind of awesomely dramatic and theatrical, at least if I wasn't cowering. I straightened my shoulders, lifted my chin and put my fingertips against the cauldron's platform floor. I had no idea what other people thought, but it gave me an absurd burst of confidence, and an idiotic smile bloomed across my face. If that's what being an action hero feels like, sign me up.

Most everybody around me was moving away. From my action-hero pose I saw Thor and Phoebe holding their ground, though Phoebe's jaw was dropped and she held her quarterstaff as if she wanted to use it. I wished my sword wasn't peace knotted, then wished it was real, then felt a chill rush over my skin and knew that if I needed a blade to fight the mist, I'd have one. I'd earned or been given all the elements that made up sword and shield and armor, and even if I wasn't carrying them, they were an indelible part of my shamanic gifts now.

More certain of myself, I stood up to draw a silver rapier from the ether. I'd done it in the astral plains, and though the physical blade had been lying safe at home under my bed, its presence had been as real as anything else in the world between this one and the next. I was serenely sure I could reach through the intervening space in the real world, too, and have the sword I'd taken from a god materialize in my hand.

Billy Holliday burst through the mass of people running the other way and shouted, "Joanne, *don't!*"

★ ★ ★

All of my serene confidence exploded into little tiny bits. My fingers spasmed open, loosing any hope I had of seizing my sword, and the Sight flashed back on to give me a visual on the hair-raising sensation that the mist thought I'd shown weakness. Indeed, the sound-induced figures in the fog surged, clawing at my power, trying to break it apart so they could get inside me. The rest of the world went away, blocked out by the gray, and my heart seized up with the clenching panic of trying to figure out what I'd done wrong, or had been about to do wrong, that made Billy yell at me. Dammit, every time I thought I was getting a handle on things it turned out I was wrong. I'd have done anything to have Coyote and his lectures and interminable practice sessions back.

Billy said, "Don't move," and I knew from the sound of his voice that his teeth were clenched. I didn't know if he was talking to me or to Phoebe and Thor, but I thought maybe I'd just do what he said and find out why later. A moment later he stepped through the barrier of my power into the midst of the gray, and gave me a grim nod of approval.

Now, the sphere was meant to keep things in, not out, and if anybody could walk through my defenses it would be Billy, who'd shared enough psychic intimacies with me that if Melinda was the jealous type we'd both be in real trouble. I still wouldn't have expected him to do that in a million years. A combined demand of *what are you doing?* and *get out of here!* and *how did you do that?* came out as "Wblrdt," and Billy, to my utter shock, snapped, "Shut up, Joanne."

There were things I'd come to expect from William Robert Holliday. He'd turn up to off-duty events in women's clothes, for example. Tonight's ball gown wasn't an outrageous costume choice, overlooking the detail that Billy, like most people, didn't often have a chance to indulge in formal wear. So I expected that. I also expected him to take the mystical more seriously than I was constitutionally capable of doing. He was a True Believer, and had been since childhood when he started seeing ghosts after his older sister's death by drowning. I used to give him hell about it. Now I was grateful for his calm solid presence when the world went wacky.

And despite all the grief I'd given him, he'd never once responded with the kind of comeback I deserved, not even an *I told you so* when I found myself faced with irrefutable proof that the world contained a lot more than met the eye. I couldn't remember him ever telling anybody to *shut up,* much less me in the midst of a paranormal crisis.

I'd been functioning on "act now, think later," which had, as a rule, worked for me so far.

Now I was scared.

CHAPTER FOUR

My obvious impulse was to hiss, "What can I do?" but I'd just been told both to shut up and to not draw a blade on the mist. That left me with a big fat nothing in the easy-choices department, and every inch of my body was cold with indecision and worry. Moreover, I didn't take it as a good sign that the ooze slicked away from me and swirled around Billy, nibbling at the orange-and-fuchsia colors that made up his aura. They were as steady as I'd ever seen them, nothing in his psychic presence suggesting distress, but it bothered the hell out of me. I was supposed to take on all mystical comers, not let my friends step up and do the job.

Unless, of course, my friends had a better idea of what to do, in which case I should get over myself and help somehow, albeit without asking aloud what might be useful. Billy was almost obscured by the mist, nearly all of it having drifted from the perimeter of my sphere to surround him. My heart took up residence in my stomach and churned the remaining pink drink. I closed my lips on a vile-tasting burp and gave Billy five more seconds to tell me what to do before I went Grecian on the gray stuff's ass.

Billy said, "You don't belong here," so gently I flinched, first out of surprise at hearing his voice and then from childish insult. I wasn't the world's greatest shaman or anything, but I was doing my best. His vote of confidence meant a lot. Having it dismissed cut my legs out from under me.

"You should be resting." His colors strengthened, coming through the mist more strongly, like he was putting energy into what he was saying. Exactly like that, actually: from three feet away I felt soothed. Even the sweat beading under my wig and trickling against my scalp stopped itching so much. "I know it's easy to travel at this time of year, and that you miss your bodies, but they're gone. Long gone." Strain showed in his voice, and I finally clued in.

"It's dead people!"

The mist whipped away from Billy and surged at me, a high-pitched whine suddenly loud enough to make my eardrums ache. The gaping eyes and howling mouths came clearer to me, *much* clearer as one of the ghosts came at me like it wanted a kiss. Dull cold slid along my cheekbones, fingering a scar on one. I shuddered and stepped back, finding the edge of the cauldron with my heel.

"Joanie, stay still." Billy's voice was cold as the dead's.

I whispered, "They can't get at me. They don't like my magic. Just tell me how to banish them and get out of here."

"Joanne." Billy had four kids and a fifth on the way, but I'd never heard him employ a Daddy Voice before. Part of me seized up with resentment. My own father and I had an atheistic relationship, which is to say, he'd never quite believed he'd ended up with a child at all. I generally disliked anything that reminded me of that.

The rest of me just seized up because that's what instinct tells people to do when they hear a Daddy Voice. I stared at Billy, who kept his attention on the mist and spoke through his teeth. "They don't have to get in you. The longer you're around them, the more they latch on. The more you move, the more they notice you. The louder you are, the faster they come to you. So *shut up*."

I really, really wanted to do what I was told, but his volume had increased all the way through that, and by the time he was done, the party hall was visible again. My sphere contained a cauldron, me and a dense, almost-black cloud where Billy stood. There was no way I was letting him face that alone. I jumped down from the cauldron, took a quick look at the room beyond my sphere—it had cleared out, only Thor and Phoebe immediately visible—and forged into the dark fog that surrounded my friend.

His voice wrapped around me immediately, soft and cajoling, full of sympathy but very firm: he knew I was confused, that I was lost, that I didn't understand what was happening. All of that was absolutely true, so for a second I thought he was talking to me. At least the mist hid my blush when I figured out that no, he was still talking to the gray goop, and continued to in a gentle murmur. He knew he was a cipher, strange to the living world but safe to the dead, and that his presence gave them comfort.

Comforted wasn't the word I'd use for the agitation I felt in the fog. It—they—were becoming clearer to me now, easier to read, as though they were remembering more and more of what it was to be human. I could tell at least a few men from women, though the greater part of the mist was still formless, maybe having left their bodies behind so long ago they had no memory of a shape to fill.

I had met the newly dead before, but it was no preparation for meeting the oldly dead. The newly dead, at least the ones I'd met, were pretty cool and collected. It may have helped that they'd mostly been shamans themselves—in fact, the one newly dead girl I'd met who hadn't been a shaman had been pretty confused, now that I thought about it—but they'd had a sense of purpose and of self, and knew they only had a limited amount of time to impart information to me before they moved on.

The cauldron ghosts had only hate and fear to hold on to. They *desired;* oh, how they desired. They wanted flesh forms. They wanted vengeance. They wanted freedom, and would do whatever they could to obtain it. Thieving a body from a living soul would do: that's what the dancers would have provided, if I hadn't been there. I got a—no pun intended—ghost of an idea of how schizophrenic the dancers would have become, fighting for their own bodies with a plethora of spirits all determined to become the sole resident of their lithe forms. Only the strongest of the invaders would survive, but a few of the jettisoned others would cling to the surface, hoping for a chance to wrest control away. Even from without, their angry will could affect what a host body might do.

And right now they were trying to get inside Billy.

Not all of them. Some were listening to his voice, hearing the guidance he offered them. Those few could be put to rest, maybe because they were too tired of fighting to survive, maybe because they'd forgotten what they were fighting for. A few bits of mist separated from the dark cloud and dissipated, and I imagined I heard a sigh of relief. I shivered and wished them a good journey, wherever they might be going. Maybe to start again; a while ago Coyote'd told me that souls reincarnate. There weren't that many new ones, although apparently I'd been mixed up fresh: no history of mistakes to weigh me down, but as he'd said, no history of learning experiences to buoy me up, either. But these ones had held on to this world, to their most recent bodies, to *something,* so long that they'd lost cohesion. They were still energy, the way that spark that made life inside things was energy, but all that was left in them was a craving for a new body.

I couldn't help wondering if there were enough souls waiting to be reborn to fill all the people in the world, or if tortured ghosts like these left a handful of babies born empty every day. I hoped not. God, I hoped not, but just the idea opened a white-hot door inside me, through which poured the intention to help.

To my complete horror, the mist gave a sonic cry able to scour flesh from bone, and twisted toward that brightness.

The thinnest of it came first, like I'd put up a magnet that pulled filaments toward me. The weakest ghosts didn't have enough weight to remain firm, and flew through that burning door inside a blink. They hit a flash point as they went, turning from mist to flame and leaving marks on my soul, like the memory of paper curling and drifting to the ground.

Stronger spirits, carrying more resistance, followed more reluctantly, but an unburdened sense of relief swept me as some of them passed through into the brilliance. Once or twice an afterimage caught behind my eyes, like the echo of the life that had kept them there. I clung to those, and lost them even as I did: they left nothing, when they burned.

Murk slammed against the door in my mind and filled it, bellowing rage and refusal. The light faded away, blocked by a determination to hold on. Relief left me, joy left me; hell, even my power left me, slamming itself between the blackness and the white door in my mind. Triumph and fury sluiced through me in equal parts before the darkness fell away, and I had the shuddering sensation of a narrow escape. I mumbled, "Idiot," and staggered a couple of steps before cranking my head up to see how the party fared.

My sphere of protective magic was gone, eaten up by the retreat my power had staged. So was most of the mist, though a few dark clouds still clung to Billy, trailing him like residue from a smoke machine. Thor and Phoebe were still there, and the DJ's station blared "The Monster Mash," but the room, so crowded only a minute or two ago, now held only hangers-on, the moral equivalent of ambulance chasers, all staying a safe distance from the center of activity.

Phoebe said what everybody, including those who'd fled, was presumably thinking: "What in hell was that?"

"I don't know. I don't know." I dropped to my knees, then leaned forward on my palms, gasping against the impulse to upchuck again. I could feel ghostly willpower dissolving inside me, resistance to passing on drifting into ash in my bloodstream. More, I could feel the tremendous black weight of the one who'd blocked the door, and the protests of those who'd been left on the wrong side. I curled down even farther, hands made into fists that I rested my forehead against. I felt like crying, and I wasn't sure why.

Billy put his hands on my shoulders and gently pushed me back until I was sitting on my heels. His gaze was worried but calm, far more reassuring than the wide-eyed hollow look I felt aging my own face. "I haven't got your Sight," he said quietly. I could tell he was making his voice a lifeline, something stable to hang on to. Grateful tears welled up in my eyes. "All I see are the ghosts, Joanie, so I don't know what happened. Tell me what you did. It's going to be fine."

"She gave them the light," Melinda said out of nowhere. A twitch of conflicted gladness ran through me. I didn't want Melinda and her soon-to-be-born daughter anywhere near the dark magic flowing around me, but it was nice that my friends hadn't abandoned me when the smart money was on getting the hell out of there. "She opened a door to the light and guided them home."

"No." My mouth tasted terrible. I wiped a hand across it, but kept my gaze on Billy, who seemed solid and reassuring and safe. "I mean, maybe, but I didn't mean to. I just wanted to tell them I would help. Going into the light, that's just a load of crap—" confidence failed me "—isn't it?"

"A door." Billy's voice was terribly controlled, the kind of control that said unadulterated panic was one very fine line away from where he stood. "Joanne, listen to me. This is important. I know you use a garden as a metaphor for your soul. How do you enter the garden?"

I stared at him without comprehension for a couple seconds. I'd thrust my imagery of a garden on him when I was trying to heal him from a magically induced coma, but I'd had no idea it'd left him with an idea of my psychic set-up. I was beginning to think Billy Holliday could be very, very dangerous to me, if he chose to be.

"A rabbit hole," I finally croaked. "I almost always go in by a rabbit hole. Or a mole hole. I was a badger once."

Billy's shoulders relaxed fractionally. "All right. You're going to need to do a spirit journey and make sure that you didn't let the ghosts into your garden, but usually the mind sets up fail-safes. If you enter through the earth then probably the door didn't lead inside you."

"There's a door inside my garden," I said inanely. "But it leads to where people go when they're dying." It led to where I went when I was dying, anyway. "I don't use it. Much."

Melinda and Billy exchanged a glance that told me I didn't want to know what they were thinking. Instead of asking, I looked back at the cauldron, and noticed a leg sticking out from behind it. I crawled over and found both the dancers sprawled on the floor, breathing shallowly. I dropped my head, watching long hair brush my elbows. "Crap. I thought somebody would've gotten them out of here. I'm gonna need to…" I put a hand out, calling up silver-blue power, and Melinda came around the cauldron to crouch and catch my wrist.

"You can't."

"I can't? Why not? I think I can." I was a little engine that could. I tried to shake her off, though not very hard, for fear she'd weeble and wobble and then fall down.

"You need to check for ghost riders first. If any of them slipped into your garden, or are waiting on the other side of that door, they'll follow your power right back into these kids. Call 911 instead."

I lowered my hand, but kept looking at her. There were about eleven things I needed to do—make sure the bad things were gone, make sure the dancers were okay, come up with some kind of excuse for the partygoers, just for starters—but for a few long seconds all of that faded away while I stared at my friend.

I knew Melinda referred to her god in the feminine, and that she knew what a coven needed to be whole. I knew she and Billy had met fifteen or so years ago at a conference about the paranormal, and that her oldest son was casually confident about his own sensitivity to things that were Other. "You and Billy, Mel, where did you come from? You know all this stuff, you're so sure of yourselves, and I'm…" I gestured at myself. I was a twenty-seven-year-old cop in a leather bondage outfit, beleaguered by a destiny I could barely wrap my mind around, that gesture said. "I mean, did you *want* this to be real and just went and figured out that it was?"

Melinda's smile held real sympathy. "I'll tell you about my grandma someday, okay? They chased her over the border to keep her from hexing a bad man's cattle."

Phoebe, over our heads, said in a very small tight voice, "What exactly is 'this' that we may or may not want to be real?"

I looked up to find her still clutching her quarterstaff. Edward was just behind her, looking as if he wanted to hug me and wasn't yet sure that it was safe. I sighed and thumped down on my butt, drew my shins up and looped my arms around them. Too late, it occurred to me that my skirt was indecently short and I was probably flashing my panties to anyone who wanted to take a look. I groaned and dropped my forehead against my knees, wishing I still had my mask so I could pretend I was someone else showing off their undies, but I'd lost it sometime earlier. Maybe at the same time I'd drained the drink without noticing. I kind of wanted another one just then. "You remember that lung surgery I told you about when I started taking fencing lessons from you, Pheeb?"

"Yeah. You kept rubbing your breastbone. You said it was a genetic thing, not lung cancer."

The reminder made me want to rub that spot again. "I may have been a little misleading."

"She got stabbed through the chest with a rapier," Billy said, which was nice of him, because I wasn't very good at this confession. Of course, if my friends kept letting me off the hook, I wouldn't get any better at it.

Phoebe's silence rang out a few long seconds. "Don't any of the rest of you take this wrong, but I've seen you naked, Jo. You don't have a scar."

"I healed it." That came out surprisingly easily. "That genetic condition, it's… I'm a shaman. I can do magic." I looked up, because suddenly it was worse to imagine her expression than to actually see it.

She had that tremendously neutral look people get when they're trying to be polite about hearing something so outrageous they can't believe it's been said. She also had a stranglehold on her staff, knuckles practically glowing white.

I winced. "Healing's easiest, but I can send my spirit to the astral plain, and between what a lot of Native American mythology calls the Upper and Lower Worlds. Earth is the Middle World." I brightened a little, distracted by the details of my studies. "Actually, that's really pretty Norse, too. That

kind of world structure is more common than you'd…"
Phoebe's expression was getting more strained. I was not
helping my case by lecturing. "You remember the dead girl
in the locker room? Cassandra Tucker? You couldn't get me
to respond after we found her, even though I looked like I
was awake. I'd gone to the astral plain to see if I could find
her ghost and talk to her, but instead I got caught and was
bargaining…with a giant…snake…"

I put my hands over my face. I was doing my best, but it
sounded ridiculous. I honestly had no idea how to present my
life in terms that didn't sound insane, and I was once more
incredibly grateful for the handful of friends who either
believed to begin with, or who, in the face of irrefutable evidence, ground their teeth and accepted that my wonky reality
was in fact real. Demonstration was the only possible way I
could convince anyone I was on the level, because telling
them made me sound like a lunatic. I mean, really. Bargaining with giant snakes? I looked up again.

Phoebe's eyebrow was beetled. "Morrison got you to wake
up."

I nearly groaned. None of the rest of them had known
that, and Melinda's face brightened with interest. "I've
known him for years. I'd only known you a few months. He
had a more…"

"Intimate connection with you?" Melinda chirruped.

I muttered, "I'm sure the same thing would've happened
if Billy'd been there to wake me up."

Melinda widened her eyes and nodded sagely. I refused to
look at Edward, afraid doing so would somehow seem guilty.
Instead, I locked my arms around my shins and scowled at

Phoebe's knees. "You remember when the lights went out in January? Whole city blacked out for a few hours?"

"…yeah."

"That was me. I was, uh, fighting a god. Then when I passed out at the dance club in July, that was kind of the aftermath. Mark was sort of possessed by a god. A different one."

"A god. Two gods."

My shoulders slumped. "Yeah."

Billy, mildly, said, "She's telling the truth."

Phoebe eyed him, but before she spoke, Thor said, "So what just happened here?"

Billy, Melinda and I all said, "Ghosts," at the same time.

Phoebe threw her hands up, turned around and walked out.

I crashed my forehead against my knees. "That went well."

Thor crouched beside me and the sleeping dancers, jerking his thumb after Phoebe. "Want me to…?"

"No. I'll try to talk to her tomorrow." I pressed my eyes shut, then exhaled noisily. "Did somebody call the paramedics?"

"I did." Morrison spoke so unexpectedly I flinched all the way to my feet, gaping across the cauldron at him. He'd taken his Don Johnson sunglasses off and was frowning. "They'll be here in a couple minutes. You okay, Walker?"

I was better than okay. My chest was tight and my eyes were hot and so was my face, for that matter, but it turned out that for some reason, I was absolutely great. "I thought you'd left with the rest of the smart people."

His frown reversed itself, but only at one corner of his mouth. "Not when my people are in trouble. You okay?"

"Yeah." I pulled a tentative little smile up and nodded. "Yeah, I'm good, Captain. Thanks."

Morrison nodded, then glanced at Thor, who'd stood up beside me and was hovering protectively. "Take care of her, Johnson."

Edward slipped his hand against my waist. "I'm trying, sir. She's stubborn."

Morrison, dryly, said, "Really. I hadn't noticed. The paramedics are going to want to talk to you, Walker, so don't go far, but you look like you could use some air. Holliday and I will hold down the fort."

I said, "Thanks," again, and Thor shuffled me past the cauldron and the captain toward the door. I broke every rule in the book and looked over my shoulder as we walked out. I knew it was a bad idea. I'd only be disappointed when Morrison'd already turned away.

He hadn't. He nodded just slightly when my gaze found his, and I went out into the crisp October night wondering what it was I'd hoped to get from that momentary meeting of eyes.

CHAPTER FIVE

Thor slid his arm around my shoulders, surprising me with his warmth. He was wearing more than I was, true, but I'd have had to lie on the beach for six hours to radiate that much heat. He guided me through the lingering crowd—there were quite a few of them, given that it was only about forty degrees—and when we were a decent ways down the street, said, "I guess we're okay."

"Okay" wasn't one of the words I'd have chosen for much of anything right then. "We are?"

"Yeah, you know. Coworkers dating and all that. Gets frowned on, but the captain looked okay with it."

"Oh." I wasn't sure what I thought of Morrison being okay with me dating. I mean, obviously he shouldn't think anything of it, and I shouldn't think of him thinking anything, but—I cut myself off before I got caught in a recursive loop and said, "I guess so. How many people are staring at me?"

He twisted to look over our shoulders, then came back to me with a grin. "About thirty. Should we give them something to look at?"

"I think they've already got something." That sounded meaner than I meant it to and I gave him a lopsided smile of apology. I wasn't very good at having a boyfriend.

He squeezed my shoulders and put a kiss on my forehead. "You're not a freak show, Joanne. Don't worry about them."

My smile got less lopsided. "Yes, I am, but thanks. And thanks for staying, back there. I appreciate it. It was probably dumb and dangerous, but I appreciate it."

"You really know how to lay on a compliment, Walker." Thor sounded like Morrison, all dry and faintly amused. I made a face and he laughed before his expression faded into something more serious. "I can't run out when things get weird or dangerous if we're going to make this work. I want to be there to help. To keep you safe."

Warm fuzzies collided with bemusement to give me indigestion. "It's hard to keep me safe from things you can't see. I don't need that much protecting." It was true. Typically, what I needed was information, which—much as he might want to—I doubted Thor was in any position to provide. On the other hand, he really was making an effort to fit in to my life, and I didn't want to push him out just because the dangers I generally faced were one step removed from the reality he was grounded in. I nudged my hip against his, hoping I hadn't sounded ungrateful and that I didn't now sound patronizing: "But if I run up against Loki, you're the first one I'm calling, okay?"

"Sounds like a date, especially if you're going to wear that costume when you start fighting gods."

I said, "I'm usually in jeans and a sweater," without thinking, and he looked a little nonplussed. See, this was the problem with starting to accept my own surreality. It made me say things that sounded as if they'd been brought to you by the new brand of azure giraffe.

Sirens and flashing lights heralded the ambulance's arrival. I stopped beneath a leafless tree, trying to avoid drops of water from its black branches, and watched paramedics jump out of the vehicle and run into the hall. "I should go back."

"To give a report or to help?"

Only half listening, I said, "Yeah," and Thor slid his hand to mine and tugged my fingers, a shy and sort of charmingly little-boy action.

"You heard the Hollidays. You need to check for—"

"Ghost riders," I supplied, then ground my teeth. "Yeah. Okay, so to give a report, then, though I don't know what I'm going to say. Still, I…" I turned away, but Thor caught my hand a little harder and pulled me back. I looked up, surprised, to find his expression much like the gesture had been: shy and sort of charmingly hopeful.

"It's a kind of spirit quest, right? You've got that drum. Do you need somebody to play it for you?"

My heart and stomach took a quick drop toward my feet and left my cheeks burning. The question itself was fairly innocuous, but what lay under it ran a hell of a lot deeper. Thor had seen the skin drum that held place of pride on my bedroom dresser, and I'd seen his curious gaze linger on it more than once. He'd never touched it, apparently—and correctly—regarding doing so as an intimacy he hadn't yet been granted.

In fact, since my powers were so rudely awakened, only three people'd touched that drum: me, my friend Gary—who'd been invited to do so long before I considered using the drum as an intimacy at all—and Morrison, whose touch on the painted leather might have been fire on my skin. Part of me didn't want Thor touching the drum because it might not have that same sensual, completed feeling when he did.

The other part of me wasn't ready for him to handle it in case it *did*.

He didn't know that. He didn't have to. What he did know was the drum, and the out-of-body experiences it sent me on, were important, and that he hadn't yet been invited to participate in that. It was a glass wall, invisible but holding us apart, and all my rational bits thought I probably wasn't being fair.

My less rational bits—like my heart and stomach, which both still felt as if they'd fallen into the southern hemisphere—didn't give a damn about fair. They were worried about the right choice, and the lurchy feeling they left me with was way too much like a fifteen-year-old girl going against her smarts and having sex with a boy in hopes of getting him to like her. I'd been there, done that, got a lot more than a T-shirt, and like I said, I do at least try to make new mistakes. Edward was a great guy, but I wasn't anything like ready to ask him to drum me under on a spirit quest.

And he *was* a great guy, so as my heart resumed its regular place in my chest cavity, guilt swam in to fill the empty spots it'd left. There was no way out. I liked him too much to want to hurt him, but I couldn't give him what he was asking for, so of course he'd be hurt—not angry, because he was too decent for that, but disappointed, at least—and so up came the guilt, which made me think maybe I should, you know, go ahead and do what he asked anyway, and…

I didn't know if men ever went through that kind of thought process, but this was one of those emotional hatchet-job moments where I couldn't help thinking that being a woman really sucked.

And Thor, who really was a decent guy, didn't make me fumble my way through an apology. He just studied me while my face went stricken, then sighed quietly and nodded. "Maybe next time." He squeezed my fingers, then glanced toward the party hall and the paramedics. "Let's go see if they need your report, huh?"

"Edward." I didn't often use his real name, so he was looking back even before I pulled him to a stop, determined not to utterly blow a good thing. "I like you." Those were pretty simple words. It didn't follow that saying them should come out all shaky and nervous. "I like you a lot. This thing with the drumming, it's not…it's not because I don't like you or I don't trust you."

His eyebrows went up a little. "I like you, too, but you don't trust one of us, Joanie. I'm willing to bet on it being you, at least for a while."

I followed him back to the party hall, well and truly subdued.

The dancers were whisked away to the hospital suffering from severe electrolyte imbalances, which my mind insisted on processing as "severe acolyte imbalances." Once I'd been assured they'd be okay, I kept snickering at visions of little hooded figures singing Gregorian chants and stumbling around like drunkards. Thor looked askance at me, but apparently the joke lost something in the telling.

My report, like everyone else's, was all but useless, though in my case I had to explain why I'd clapped my hands over their mouths. A fumbling story about being afraid they'd bite their tongues got me more or less off the hook. Once the paramedics were gone, a startling number of people came back in to the party, but I gave Thor a kiss and slunk out to my car with every intention of heading home.

Billy tapped on Petite's window, catching me wriggling around trying to get my stupid little skirt far enough under my butt and thighs to provide some kind of barrier between bare skin and clammy leather seats. Petite was a beautiful car, the unquestionable love of my life, but she had a definite opinion about somebody wearing the kind of outfit I had on and sitting in her. My back stuck to the seat, too, and sent goose bumps all over me. I peeled away and rolled the window down. "Was I speeding, Officer?"

"It looked like you were doing something a lot more illicit than speeding, but Johnson's still inside. You heading home?"

"I think I've had enough partying for one night."

"I'd agree, except for two things." Billy leaned against Petite's roof and looked down at me. "First, I want to be there when you go checking for ghost riders, because you're not equipped to deal with them. They're more my specialty."

I opened my mouth to argue, considered his point and skipped the argument. "Fair enough. And?"

"And Phoebe's already gone, so Mel wanted me to make sure you realize that means you're the only host left for this party."

I put my hands on the steering wheel and stared straight ahead for a minute. "I hate my life."

"No, you don't." Billy pulled Petite's door open and offered me a hand. "C'mon. Mel and Johnson and I will stay late and help you clean up, and then we can get you cleared for duty."

"Everybody's going to stare at me if I go back in there."

"They'd stare at anybody who was as much of a long tall drink of water as you are in that outfit."

I cricked my neck and eyed him. "Did your wife send you out here to flatter me, Mr. Holliday?"

"My wife sent me out here to take whatever measures necessary to make sure she wasn't the one left cleaning up your party alone. Flattery first. Next I throw you over my shoulder and carry you back in. Your choice."

"All right." I kicked long bare legs out of the car and stood up. Hey, if he was going to make tall-drink-of-water comments, I was going to admire myself a little. "But if anything else out of the ordinary happens, I'm leaving. I'll just pay the damn fee for having the owners clean the place tomorrow."

I should have defined *out of the ordinary*.

It turned out worrying about my behavior had been pointless. Apparently most people thought leaping up onto the cauldron to help the dancers was kind of heroic, and enough alcohol had been imbibed that the light show around me had been largely written off as just that: a light show. There was a lesson to be learned from that, though by now I should've already learned it.

People were good at explaining away things that didn't make a whole lot of sense. Over the summer I'd been worried that I was foisting magic onto a world that didn't want it, but really, the handful of people who did want it believed, and the rest let themselves forget. A newly born waterfall at the

end of Lake Washington had been given the name Thunderbird Falls after half the city'd seen, well, a thunderbird fall into
the lake. By the end of August, though, if anybody mentioned
the gigantic golden bird at all, they remembered the astonishing cloud formations and sunset that night. I shouldn't
have worried, not then and not now.

By midnight nearly everyone had come back to the party,
even Phoebe, who ran a masquerade competition as if nothing
untoward had happened. I won a "Best Abs" prize that I don't
think had been on the original list of awards to be given out,
and the department-heavy attendees made Morrison walk
the stage three times before razzing him off with cheers and
laughter. A bunch of people told me I'd done good, trying to
help the dancers, and a bunch more dragged me onto the
dance floor or stole me away from Thor for the space of a
song. The booze ran out before the music did, and there were
maybe fifty people left, almost all of them dancers not quite
willing to go home, when Morrison tapped Thor on the
shoulder and asked to cut in.

See, I knew I should've defined *out of the ordinary.* Thor
bowed out and tried to steal Phoebe from a natural blonde who
didn't want to give up her dance partner. He ended up sand-
wiched between both of them, and I grinned before Morrison
put his hands on my waist and took up all my attention.

He said, "Sorry," perfunctorily. "I could've waited for faster
music, but I wanted to talk to you."

I flailed a bit and put my hands on his shoulders, which
were considerably more covered than my waist was. In fact,
although I hadn't thought anything of it when Thor's hands
had been in the same place, I suddenly wanted to hitch my

skirt up off my hips and settle it safely around my waist, where a proper skirt belonged. Except then my very short skirt would have become completely indecent, which wasn't a win at all.

Or maybe it was. I guess it depended on who you asked.

In an attempt to shut my brain up, I stuck my jaw out too far and bared my lower teeth, making a llama face. It was sufficiently embarrassing to take my mind off my skirt, so after holding it a couple of seconds I trusted myself enough to say, "No problem. What's wrong?"

Up. I should've said what's *up,* not what's *wrong.* Still, pretty much any time Morrison wanted to talk to me, something was wrong. His hands were warm, warmer than Edward's, and he smelled good. Like Old Spice, which I doubted was a *Miami Vice* cologne. And I was taller than he was, which reminded me of the clowns with their noses in my cleavage, although Morrison would have to look down to do that.

I made another llama face.

Evidently weird faces weren't enough to throw my boss off his game. "What happened earlier?"

"A bunch of angry ghosts spilled through the cauldron and tried to take over those kids." I said it without missing a beat. Somewhere along the line I'd decided to play it straight with Morrison. He didn't like my powers any more than I did, but he accepted I had something extraordinary going on, and if he couldn't deny it, he could at least do his best to make use of it. He'd made me a detective and partnered me with Billy so we could deal with abnormal cases when they came along, and what he was really asking right now was whether one had just fallen into our laps. "I don't know how or why. I think Billy and I chased most of them off, but he's still got some stubborn ones hanging around him and I might've let some latch on to me. We're going back to my apartment after we clean up here to check and give me the all-clear."

A bunch of minute things happened in Morrison's expression. Most of them had to do with tension and resignation, and said he'd asked and therefore deserved to get whatever outlandish answer I gave him. My face crumpled with apology. "Sorry. It's all I've got. Billy didn't seem to know what was happening, either, so—"

Morrison said, "Walker," making it sound very much like Billy's *shut up* from earlier, so I did. Morrison nodded, and that quick array of tiny changes flashed across his face again before he said, carefully, "Holliday'll watch out for you."

"Sure, he always does. I mean, I don't know, I guess…" I frowned at Morrison's brown hair, caught up in logistics. "It's going to be four in the morning before we get out of here. I can't really call Gary and ask him to drum me under, but Billy never has, and besides that he's going to have to go with me. I guess Mel, but—"

Morrison said, "Walker," again, and I clued in with a physical lurch that turned my ankle. Morrison's hands tightened on my waist. For an instant we were frozen in an awkward noir pose, the sort where the hero seizes the heroine's arms and pulls her close before kissing her like she's the most exasperating woman on earth. Except I was much too tall to be a noir heroine, even bent awkwardly while I tried to get my foot back under me, and for all the intensity of those old-movie poses, they never seemed to really have much in the way of bodies pressed together. There was body-pressing going on here. There had to be: Morrison'd braced me against himself so I didn't topple over entirely.

He did not, however, look as though he'd like to kiss me. He looked as if I'd stepped on his foot, and like whatever had prompted him to say my name had been a bad idea.

Intuition and me weren't the closest of friends, but I was still following the thought that'd led to my collapse. Morrison hadn't been asking if Billy would take care of me. He'd been asking if I needed *him* to. Bubbling gladness spilled through me, as though he'd offered an answer to problems I didn't even know I had. I wanted to hug him, or bury my nose in his neck, or something else unseemingly physical. I held it back to an idiotic beam and blurted, "Shit, I'm sorry, *yes,* that'd be—"

Morrison put me back on my feet and I looked over his shoulder to see Thor. Guilt that had gone passive surged back to life and my smile crumbled. Everything crumbled: I felt like I was shrinking, delight draining out and leaving bone-deep regret. I'd shut Thor down a few hours ago when he'd had the courage to ask if he could help, and jumping at the chance to put Morrison in his place, especially when the captain had been so circumspect in asking, seemed like a particular and special brand of cruelty. Thor'd been right: I didn't trust one of us in our pairing, and the fact that Morrison's offer sent my heart soaring where Thor's sent it plummeting didn't bode well for which one I didn't trust, after all.

Morrison turned us both so he could see where I was looking. His hands loosened abruptly and he fell back half a step, making room for the Holy Spirit between us. He took a breath and I knew, I just *knew,* he was going to issue a retraction. I grabbed his lapels hard enough that my hands ached from it, and he exhaled, words lost in surprise.

"I…" I wanted to say a million things. Most of them didn't

seem especially appropriate. I held on to his lapels for a moment longer, then let go and smoothed them, like doing so would help me keep my voice moderate. "I would be a lot more comfortable with you drumming me under than with calling Gary in the middle of the night and asking him to come over."

There. That sounded very reasonable. It didn't touch on why I wasn't having Thor do it, because that was none of Morrison's business. It didn't focus on the fact that Melinda would no doubt be perfectly fine drumming me under. It was also utterly true. I'd rather have Morrison, who was already awake, lend a hand, than get a seventy-three-year-old out of bed and ask him to help.

It in no way told Morrison, or let me acknowledge, that when my captain picked up that drum of mine, I felt magic.

Christ, I was doomed.

CHAPTER SIX

Phoebe and Morrison and half a dozen other lag-behinds stayed to help clean up, so we were out of there by half past three. Phoebe'd come over with me, but her eyes skittered away and she hailed someone else for a ride home. Worse, for the first time since I'd known her, she didn't remind me of our upcoming fencing lesson. Thor snaked his arms around me for a hug. "She'll come around. Give her a little time."

"To get used to me sounding like a lunatic?" I gave him a wan smile and glanced toward Petite. "I'm going to go home and get this ghost thing sorted out, okay?"

"Sure. Call me in the morning and let me know you're all right." If he resented being kept away, he did a good job of hiding it. I felt guilty all over again. Relationships were complicated. No wonder I'd stayed away from them all this time.

Amazing how the human mind will let a person rearrange

facts to suit her. That phrasing made it sound as if I'd made a deliberate choice to not get seriously involved with anybody since at least college. But if I was serious about the new Joanne-faces-reality lifestyle, it would be somewhat more accurate to say I'd buried my head in the sand and gone "LA LA LA LA LA" to drown out any possible chance of having to deal with romantic entanglements. Emotionally stunted, that was me. At least I had nice long legs to make up for it.

I nodded a promise to call, and Thor peeled off in his monster Chevy truck. It was black and chromey and had the worst gas mileage of anything this side of a Hummer, but it was also short-circuit-the-brain sexy, and I had a terrible soft spot for it. The wheels were three feet tall, and stepping up to the running board and the driver's seat proved Thor had some nice long legs his own self. I felt that same dippy little grin from earlier crawl into place. A girl could do a whole lot worse than her own personal Norse god.

He roared off, exposing Morrison getting into his top-safety-rated Toyota Avalon.

I burst out laughing. Morrison looked up—so did the Hollidays, for that matter—and I waved them all off and climbed into Petite, still grinning. If I didn't need my psyche examined, I'd have put my sweet little Mustang in gear and chased Thor down the road. Emotionally stunted or not, at least I could tell when a guy's car sense coincided with mine, and Morrison's never would. I reminded myself to give Thor an extra kiss next time I saw him, and drove home to find out what it was like to be part of a genuine ghost story.

Melinda looked like she'd swallow her tongue when Morrison pulled in to my apartment-building parking lot as

I climbed out of my car. I locked Petite, patted her purple roof and said, "I thought if we were going ghost hunting it might be good to have somebody who'd done it before drum me under," all breezy-like, as if it was no big deal. The weird thing was, right then it didn't seem like one.

Melinda unswallowed her tongue, coughed, "Sure," and gave Morrison a sunny smile. I figured stronger men than he could be hornswoggled by that smile. Billy wasn't bad-looking, but his wife was a knockout. If I ever needed to be a five-foot-two Hispanic woman, I wanted to be Melinda. Also, she could and did say, "Hello, Michael," like it was a normal thing to do, whereas I still couldn't imagine calling my boss by his given name. "I might've made Billy drive me home if I'd known you'd be here."

Morrison and I exchanged glances. It'd seemed awkward to me to mention he was coming over when I'd sent my boyfriend home, and I have no idea what he thought. Telepathy ought to come standard with psychic talents, although if I put any actual consideration into that, it sounded like a really bad idea. Morrison said, "I'm sure Walker will lend you her bed if you want to take a nap," and I gave a feeble nod of agreement that Melinda brushed off, clearly not too worried about it.

Billy gave first Morrison, then me, looks that said volumes, but kept his mouth shut. I made them climb all five flights of stairs to my apartment out of cheerful vindictiveness and the knowledge that the building's ancient elevator was both astonishingly slow and incredibly noisy. Only very drunk college students or heavily laden tenants used it, and the former had been known to fall asleep in front of its doors waiting for it to arrive.

Poor Melinda was pink cheeked and puffing by the time we reached my apartment. I had the grace to be ashamed of myself, but she flopped down on the couch and wheezed, "I'll try anything to go into labor. I could've protested in the lobby."

I scurried to get her a glass of water, and by the time I got back everybody looked comfortably positioned to perform a spirit journey. Billy was across from his wife on the couch, and Morrison'd taken up the entirety of the love seat, looking larger than life and extremely cinematic in his ridiculous pink shirt and pale loafers. I said, "I hope that stuff washes out of your hair fast. I have to change clothes," like they were related comments, and retreated to my bedroom. Back in January I'd discovered a draft blew in under the front door. No way was I sitting on the floor dressed in nothing more than a handful of leather bits.

Changing clothes also gave me a minute in private to nerve myself up to handing the drum over to Morrison. I pulled on sweats and a warm shirt, took my contacts out and washed away the kohl eyeliner before putting my glasses on. The woman in the mirror was unfamiliar, straight black hair falling around her face and catching in the glasses' earpieces. I pulled the wig off, dropped it on the toilet, and scrubbed my fingers through my hair, creating short messy spikes that made me look more like myself. The warrior princess was gone. It was just me, Joanne Walker, and I couldn't help thinking the other reflection made a much better hero type than I did. For one thing, anybody willing to run around in that outfit had meta-phorical balls of solid steel, whereas I only had an uncanny ability to keep staggering forward despite panic and uncertainty.

A bubble of warmth erupted in my belly, a reminder that I had a little more than a knack for keeping on against impossible odds. The damn magic could be comforting, sometimes.

It could also be bossy. I got my drum off my bureau and stood with it for a moment, running my fingers over its dyed surface. A raven's wings sheltered a wolf and a rattlesnake. Their bright colors were unchanged after half a lifetime, but the wolf looked smeared, as if the drum's surface had gotten wet. I wiped my fingers against it gingerly, worry making a pit of sickness in my belly. It didn't blur any further, and there was nothing in the leather's tension that suggested it had been soaked or damaged. For the first time I wondered if the figure was supposed to be a coyote, not a wolf, and if the smearing had something to do with my mentor's death. The sickness in my stomach turned to tears burning my eyes, and I clenched my fingers around the drum's edge, bone and leather denting my flesh. The polished beads that dangled from crossed lengths of leather holding the skin tight against its frame rattled, strain in my hands translating to the drum. It had been a gift for my fifteenth birthday, overwhelming and bewildering: I'd had no waking recollection of the dream-borne shamanic training I was undergoing. The drum was the first thing I'd ever had that made me feel welcome among what were technically, if not emotionally, my people.

My father was about as full-blooded Cherokee as you got in this day and age, and had been born with a wanderlust that'd sent him away from North Carolina and the Eastern tribe as a young man. He'd met my mother in New York, and she'd brought me to him when I was three months old. I took after her in most ways: fair skin and a smattering of freckles, green eyes and black hair, though hers had waves and mine was unrelentingly straight. In color, I looked Irish. In black and white, my bone structure stood out, and I was clearly Native American. The thing is, despite truisms like *kids don't see shades of gray,* what they saw when Dad took me home to Qualla Boundary was a tall gangly white girl with a perpetual chip on her shoulder. It wasn't their fault. It was how I'd seen myself, even though I'd been the one who insisted on settling down somewhere so I could go to high school in one place.

I don't think my father'd ever intended to go back to the Carolinas, but that was where he took me. We'd gotten by, me with an eternal defiant scowl and Dad with the air of always waiting to leave again. I didn't know if he was still there. I hadn't talked to him in years.

The more I looked back and thought about it, the more I knew my exile'd been largely self-imposed. My first memories were of Dad's big old boat of a Cadillac driving across the country, and my favorite memories were those of him teaching me how to work on that car, and then all the others that came along. We'd rarely stayed in any town long enough for me to make friends at the schools I'd gone to—six weeks here, six weeks there didn't do the job—and by the time we went to Qualla Boundary I had a hate-on at the world. It hadn't wanted me, so I didn't want it.

Truth was, in most ways, I'd only just started getting over that. I touched the smeary colors on my drum again, and, assured that it at least wasn't going to rupture if Morrison used it, took it out to the living room. Morrison stood up to take it from me, which seemed oddly respectful. I didn't know how to tell him I appreciated the gesture, and instead tried to steel myself against the vicarious thrill I expected when he took it.

To my supreme disappointment, I got nothing. Maybe I'd steeled myself too well. We both held on to the drum for a second, before Morrison said, "Stick?" in a tone that suggested maybe I wasn't too bright. I let go with a curse and went back for the drumstick, brushing my fingers against its cranberry-red rabbit-fur end before handing it over to my boss with far less expectation of getting a buzz. I didn't get one then, either, and sat down on the floor, telling myself I shouldn't be sullen.

Billy groaned. "Do we have to be on the floor?"

I blinked up at him. "I don't know. Do you even have to be in the same place I am? I don't really know what your plan is."

"You've never journeyed inside with anyone?"

"Is that a question that should be asked in polite company?"

Melinda laughed. "Good thing we're not polite company."

I wrinkled my nose at her, then shrugged at Billy. "Everybody who's turned up has just been there. I never invited anyone. I've done it the other way, kind of. Been invited in, or sort of fallen in." From the corner of my eye I saw Morrison's expression grow increasingly strained, and guilty recollection sizzled through me. "Or barged in."

Billy frowned. "You need to work on your sense of personal boundaries."

Guilt crashed right over into irritation. He was no doubt right, but this was a lousy time to bring it up. "I'm under the impression that I need to make sure my *brain* isn't *haunted*. Can we maybe worry about my crappy people skills later?"

Morrison said, "If I start beating this thing will they stop arguing?" to Melinda, and without further ado, did.

My world flipped upside down.

★ ★ ★

It might've been technically more accurate to say I flipped upside down. Or that I turned inside out. Either way, the floor went from below me to above me, leaving me sitting cross-legged on a roof of the earth with a tunnel burrowing down below me. I stayed there a couple of seconds, taken aback at how quickly the transition had happened. I knew Morrison could send me to other planes of existence with a touc… There was no way to get out of that sentence alive. The point was, he helped my transition from one world to another, but even so, I was used to the drumming settling into my skin before it transported me elsewhere. Just blinking from one world to another was disconcerting.

Billy presumably wouldn't have such a dramatically quick crossover, but that didn't mean I should stick—so to speak—around on the roof of the earth. I pushed off the ground and dived into the tunnel, squirming my way deeper. Almost instantly, I wasn't *me* any longer, not the way I think of myself, person-shaped with two legs and a torso and arms and a head. Industrious paws dug at the earth instead, pushing it aside with far more skill than my weak human hands could've done. I wasn't sure what I was; rodents weren't much for external awareness of what they looked like, but at least I was efficient.

I popped through to a sunlit garden in record time and staggered around on four feet, getting my bearings. A good shake got dirt out of my fur, and another one whisked me into my usual shape. I thought someday I might, like, get to just walk through a tunnel big enough to hold me, but so far when I'd come into my garden it'd mostly been as one form of vermin or another.

That was a thought I definitely didn't want to pursue. Instead I lifted a hand to block glare—apparently nobody'd told my inner sanctuary that it was four in the morning—and had a look around.

When I'd first come to this place, it was the most rigid, well-defined little plot of land I'd ever seen. The grass had been mown to a millimeter height, so dry and sparse the ground could be seen between blades. The benches had been austere, uncomfortable things, and the pathways had been narrow and very straight. A pond at the northern end had been shallow with a trickle feeding it, and the sky had been gray. In my defense, I'd been dying at the time, but anybody looking around might've guessed I'd been dead a long time already.

It'd gotten a lot better since then. It had nothing on some of the lush landscapes I'd seen representing my friends' souls, but there was some life there now. Moss grew on what had been stark walls, wearing down at their edges. The desperately precise footpaths were buckling a little as roots began to grow under them, and stone benches had turned to wood, far more inviting. The grass was richer in color and in amount, and no longer kept to a uniform height. There were even places along the walls where it'd grown into tall fat bunches with thick roots that would be difficult to loosen if I wanted to tidy up. The waterfall and pond bubbled cheerfully, and I could no longer see the distant southern end, where mist and trees obscured a door into the land of the dying. It was an altogether nicer place to be, and I was as proud as I was relieved.

Now, if I only had any idea how to let somebody else in. Coyote'd waltzed in and out as though it was his own territory, and the only other person who'd visited had taken advantage of my lousy shields and slipped in like a snake. My own pride wanted to make a better invitation to Billy than that, especially after he'd wounded it with his personal-boundaries comment. I wanted to prove myself.

I'd cobbled together my idea of proper shielding from *Star Trek,* and insofar as I imagined them at all, I imagined them rather like a big blue pearly bubble surrounding me and my garden. Presumably phasers set on "stun" wouldn't break through, and I trusted Billy wouldn't be shooting to kill. I curled my fingers in the grass, admiring how it was long enough to grasp, and tried to make a Billy-shaped hole in the pearlescent glow.

Billy-shaped, to me, meant a mix of a minivan and a police car. I liked vehicle metaphors, but usually I didn't get mash-ups. Melinda was a hundred percent minivan. Morrison was that damn gold safety-rated Toyota. I was Petite, which didn't work all that well if I thought too deeply about it, because a 1969 Mustang was a much sexier car than I was a person. Still, if anything'd been my heart and soul over the last decade, it was the purple Boss 302 I'd put everything into since I bought her out of somebody's barn. Even then, she'd been in better shape than I was, but like it or lump it, she was the shape of me in my head. Billy, though, got mixed up between the professional detective and the family man, at least when I thought of him. His own sense of himself, in car terms, had been more minivan.

An image formed within the shape of the doorway I was trying to make for Billy. It wasn't him: it was slighter and somehow more ethereal or feminine, though it shared the same general sense of gentle kindness I thought of being an inextricable aspect of my partner. I blinked, but it was gone before I'd even completed the action, so barely there I wasn't sure I'd seen it at all. I looked around, trying to find it again, and didn't notice Billy walking in. My first clue I had a visitor was his, "Huh," as he looked around.

Presumably "huh" wasn't supposed to get my back up, but it did. "What's that mean?"

"Tidier than I expected, that's all." He gave me a quick smile, and I blinked a few times, adjusting my mental picture of Billy to match his own.

They weren't violently different. He looked younger and slimmer in his astral projection, but I thought most people did. He also looked more delicate. Not fragile by any stretch of the imagination, but less burly than the guy I saw every day, and not in a way that a lower body weight accounted for. It was a more feminine aspect than I'd expected, despite knowing he often wore women's clothes off duty. He wasn't now, but his clothes were soft: a silk shirt with discreet poet's ruffles, and pants loose enough to flow with his movements. My long-standing theory had always been that Billy cross-dressed to exact revenge against parents who gave him the unfortunate nickname of Billy when their last name was Holliday, but seeing his mental image told me just what a jerk I was for being a smart-ass, even if I'd kept it to myself. I wondered briefly what I looked like to him, and decided not to ask. People contained multitudes. Apparently I contained multitudes of buttheads. I didn't want to know what that looked like.

"It's messier than it used to be." I got up and gestured toward the far end of the garden. "The door's down there. If I've got ghost riders, would they be hanging around the gate to death's country?"

"They'd probably be trying to get away from it." Billy slid his hands into his pockets and wandered down one of the pathways. My shoes vanished, leaving me to wiggle my toes in fresh grass as I walked beside him. "There were some things I wanted to tell you before Morrison drummed you under. Do you always go under that fast?"

"No." I left it at that. Anything more invited too many questions. They were probably all being asked anyway, what with Morrison volunteering to play little drummer boy, but at least I could pretend that wasn't beyond the norm.

Billy arched an eyebrow, then visibly put curiosity aside. "Right. Okay. My window for seeing ghosts is forty-eight hours, maximum. The gift doesn't run deep enough to see beyond that."

"Except your sister."

He gave me a sharp look. Not disapproving, just sharp. "Yeah. But blood's thicker than water, and Caroline and I were close." The air cooled, thin fog pooling around us as we walked down to the foot of my garden. This was my favorite part of it, new and full of promise. Ivy hung over the walls, making it look much lusher than the northern end, and I hoped the walls would keep fading farther and farther back, giving me more to explore. "My point," Billy said, "is that the cauldron ghosts were all older than that, so we're dealing with something I don't have much experience with."

"When you say 'much' you mean 'any,' right?"

He gave me that look again, though it was softened by the fog. "No, I mean 'much' because Caro is—was—an exception. If it turns out you've got a rider, I want you to step back and let me deal with it. Get out of here if I tell you to."

"Are you nuts?"

Billy stopped and looked down at me. Even with the delicacy added to his makeup, he was still bigger than I was. I quelled the urge to make myself a little taller in the garden of my mind, so I could measure up to the visitors. "If you've got a rider, it's someone or something strong enough to get a toehold in somebody brimming with shamanic magic. With life magic, Joanne. Of the two of us, if one is going to be possessed, it's a lot less dangerous for everybody if it's me."

There was a certain irrefutable logic to that. "What if you do get possessed? What do I do?"

"Get a priest and perform an exorcism." Amusement creased Billy's face at my expression. "I mean it. It's a violent way to send them over, and it'd be my last choice, but—well, you could say if it does happen, it *is* my last choice. Don't worry. It's not likely to happen."

"That doesn't reassure me at all." I forged ahead and crouched to pull the door key out from a little hole dug in the earth. A robin cheeped and I smiled, happy it was there. My garden wasn't exactly overflowing with wildlife, but there ought to be a robin to go with the hidden key to a secret door. "If we open the door and there's nothing there, I'm in the clear, right? I mean, if I've got a door between life and death, and that's where ghosts stay, then they should be here if they're here at all."

"Right." Billy took the key and I lifted ivy away from the door, sending a cool green scent across us. He fit the key into the lock and I held my breath.

"You said there were a couple of things you wanted to tell me. Did we cover them all?" Billy nodded and pushed the door open. It rasped with the sound of reluctant-to-move stone, and I turned on the Sight, more than half-fearful of what I'd see.

Nothing lay beyond the door except the enormous crater that had always been there. I exhaled noisily and shot a grateful look toward the crater's far-off rim. "Are we good?"

"No." Billy's voice sounded worse than the scraping door. I jerked to see his face graying and his jaw tense with concentration. He whispered, "Close the door," and I yanked it shut, but the tension didn't leave his face. He bared his teeth in a grimace of apology, and breathed, "Sorry, Joanie. I think I'm out of my league."

His eyes flooded black, then went hollow and gray, and the thing looking out at me was suddenly no longer Billy Holliday.

CHAPTER SEVEN

Too many late-night horror movies, or maybe just a sudden over-weening burst of confidence made me leap forward. I clapped my hand to Billy's forehead, and, with all the conviction of a revival-tent preacher, shrieked, "Demon of hell, I abjure thee!"

It would've been very dramatic if it had worked.

Sadly for all involved—except, I supposed, the unabjured demon of hell—Billy's jaw dropped and he let out a dry horrible laugh that sounded like a windup doll's little windup gears sheering out. It wasn't a human sound at all, and shouldn't have been able to come from his throat.

I was pretty sure this was the point at which Billy would be telling me to run, if he were in a position to do so. That left me with a conundrum: do what I knew he'd tell me to, or stay and fight for my friend.

Okay, it wasn't really much of a conundrum at all. I reached deep and seized hold of my magic as solidly as I knew how. It flared through me, and even here in my garden—maybe especially here in my garden—I felt myself go all see-through and powered up, magic flowing in my veins like blood. The light mist that covered this end of the garden burned away in blue heat, and sunlight flooded down on me and the thing that wasn't Billy.

It was trying to re-form his idea of himself. His skin bulged and split and came together again, mutating grotesquely. Brief glimpses of cadaverous faces melted into view, then snapped back again. His body weight changed, always turning emaciated before he pulled it toward his own more solid shape. Either the dead didn't have great body images or I was dealing with a supermodel's ghost. The second idea was more entertaining, but I'd put money on the former.

My fingertips were actually digging into his skull, like I was grabbing Play-Doh that'd been left out in the air too long. Flesh rupturing and reshaping under my palm felt like giant boils being lanced and rebuilding with living intent. It was utterly disgusting.

It was also, in those terms, a sickness, and sickness, I could deal with. Boils were poison, poison was something that didn't belong in the system…in vehicle terms, that meant water in the gas tank.

I'd used the idea before to drive venom from a thunderbird's veins. Water was heavier than gas, but in my analogy the healthy material was the weightier, mostly because it was easier to visualize pushing scuzz off the top than off the bottom. I wasn't, after all, actually draining a gas tank.

I dug my fingers deeper into Billy's squishy skull and poured silver-blue magic into him through those indentations. To my surprise, he acquiesced, ceasing his fight and permitting me to take it up. For an eternal instant he folded himself away, leaving nothing but my magic and the ghost rider in an echo of Billy's thought of himself.

The ghost scrabbled, fingertips scraping off my magic like it was made of glass, impenetrable to its touch. With Billy, it had been able to sink through, permeating all the parts of him. But magic became the water in the tank, too heavy for it to invade. Fear and fury whipped it around, but it didn't dare leave the sanctuary of Billy's thought-form; without it, the ghost had nothing, no shape, no hope of surviving, and it wanted to live more than anything.

Me, I wanted Billy to live.

My imagery seemed juvenile, and I was glad nobody else could see it. Blue magic filled Billy's lower half, just like he really *was* a gas tank, and the raging ghost swirled around his torso, a corrosive material that didn't belong. All I did, really, was let the magic rise, giving the ghost nowhere it could fit, and it spilled out with a scream.

I clawed my free hand into the mist that poured free, holding it with magic that I retracted, carefully, from Billy. It felt slow, because I was reluctant to abandon his thought-self until I knew he still had enough handle on himself to re-form properly. If he lost his sense of self I had a much bigger problem on my hands than what to do with a temperamental ghost. But he unfolded from whatever pocket he'd retreated to when I took over, and the idea of him stabilized with relieving rapidity. None of it took as long as an indrawn breath, but it seemed like much longer. Things that were important usually did.

As the magic spilled out of him, it wrapped around my captive ghost in a kind of safety net. It couldn't get into me, but I figured it couldn't dissipate, either, if I held it within a bubble of magic, and if it wanted to live, then within my power was better than nothing. And if I was going to find out what else it wanted, then it needed a voice, and neither nets nor bubbles could give it one.

I entirely blamed my subconscious for what happened next.

Magic took shape low to the ground, coalescing what I recognized far too early as a 1982 Pontiac Trans Am. The color was wrong, of course, because while my subconscious was a smart-ass, my magic was apparently content with remaining silver-blue. The ghost's dark gray roiled beneath the car's surface, making the "paint" seem changeable, even more so than Petite's carefully crafted purple. I put a hand over my face and dared a glance at Billy through my fingers. He was still pale, which was understandable: I doubted being possessed was a nice experience. But he'd fit back into his image of himself solidly enough, and looked, perhaps, a little more burly now, as though he'd beefed up the mental image to fight all comers. I didn't blame him.

He was also staring at the translucent car in my garden with a fair degree of disbelief while the corner of his mouth quirked. "So," he said in a voice so very neutral it didn't hide a bit of his amusement. "Was Michael Knight your first crush?"

"Don't be ridiculous." The *car* had been my first crush, but I was hardly about to admit that out loud. I was never, ever going to live this down as it was. I dropped my hand to the Trans Am's roof, rallied myself to magnificently ignore Billy and said, "You can speak now."

"S-s-speeaaaak!" Rage and desperation filled the drawn-out plea, spoken as though the thing had long since forgotten words and was drawing their shape from, oh, say, a logic-module voice synthesizer. Or maybe it was just echoing me.

"Who are you? What do you want? Why'd you fight against crossing over? I—"

"Joanie." Billy sounded tired but droll. "Maybe I should conduct the interview." He crouched in front of the Trans Am's hood and put his hands on it, evidently trusting that the magic I'd called up was going to prevent a second round of Billy Becomes Lunch. "There are at least three of you," he murmured. His self-image softened again, which I thought was fascinating. Next thing I knew I'd be wearing that leather getup when I wanted to be a tough girl on the psychic level.

"Three? How do you know? I—"

He gave me a quelling look. "The color, for one thing. Individual spirits turn pale gray as they fade away. Age doesn't blacken them. They have to be united somehow, to get that dark."

"Evil spirits aren't automatically black?"

He gave me another look. "This isn't the best time for a crash course in ghost identification."

I thought it was the perfect time, but I also saw his point. I bit my tongue against asking more questions, and he added, "Besides, I had them in me for a minute there. I might be out of my league, but at least I can tell when I'm dealing with more than one ghost."

I unbit my tongue. "If you're out of your league shouldn't I—" He didn't have to say anything this time. I bit my tongue again and Billy turned his attention back to the Trans Am.

All the color had pressed up against the vehicle's nose, under his hands, like it was trying to get out. In fact, I could feel it trying to get to him, but it was a minor nuisance, like a dull itch. I'd have to be rendered unconscious to loosen the hold I had on the ghosts, and I wasn't sure even that would do it.

"Something's holding you," Billy murmured. "Something strong enough to tie you all together. Family?"

"N-n-n-noooo." The cry sounded like a wailing child, angry and full of uncertainty. Unexpected sympathy lurched in my heart. Things trying to take over my friends were inherently bad, but lost things trying to find a way home were merely pathetic. I liked the idea of helping a lot more than banishing.

"The way you died, then." There was sorrow and certainty in Billy's gentle voice, like he was trying not to upset the already unhappy child. He whispered, "Shh, shh," to the uprise of misery that vibrated through the car, and I winced on behalf of the Trans Am's windows. It was magical, and the windows would hold because I wanted them to, but Ella Fitzgerald had nothing on the pitch the ghosts reached. "Violent death," Billy guessed softly and, this time to me, said, "It's what holds most spirits beyond their time."

Nervously, because I wasn't certain I was allowed to say anything, I asked, "How long would they usually stay? You see them all the time…."

"Not all the time. Just with murders. With an ordinary death, illness or age, they fade away as soon as the body dies unless they have some need for closure that's not related to their deaths. If they're victims of abuse, for example, or once in a while if they feel someone they love is in need of help or comfort they'll stay. There are people who say they feel the dead with them, even years after they've crossed over." He glanced at me. "Most of them are kooks, but some of them really do have spirits who stay with them, like Caroline did with me. There are mediums who can communicate with the long-dead, but my ability is shorter-term."

Beneath his quiet speech, the ghosts in the car twisted and howled, clearly too agitated by his question to give a straight answer. He ran his hand over the car's hood, soothing motion, but they still screamed and battered themselves against the cage my magic made. Billy ignored them, giving me more of that crash course in ghost investigations after all. I thought it gave the spirits something audibly soothing to latch on to as much as it educated me. "Even with a lot of violent death, like car wrecks, the spirit usually only takes a few hours, a couple of days at most, before it lets go. They usually have a sense of self still when that happens. Forms that you'd recognize as human, the ability to communicate."

He turned his attention back to the car. "These ones are old, Joanne. There's almost nothing left to them than the need to survive and earn vengeance. It's all right," he murmured, clearly no longer talking to me. Compassion deepened his voice, turning him into a gentle bear of a man, and tears stung my nose. I didn't think I had that depth of kindness in me. "I'm here to listen and to help. When you're ready you can tell me what you have to say."

Maybe it was worse for them to fear they might lose Billy's attention than to contemplate their stories, because despite his assurance he'd stay, their cries stopped and their halting, miserable voice searched for words. "S-s-s-sown, all s-sown."

"What," I said, "you reap what you sow? Does that mean you were murdered because you'd been murderers yourselves?"

Billy, over outraged spiritual screams, said, "You're really not helping," and I had the grace to feel a little abashed, especially since I'd just been admiring his compassion. "She won't say anything else," he told the Trans Am, and the steely note in his voice suggested to me that I'd really better not. I had vulnerable points Billy *didn't* know about, but he had enough of a grip on some that I probably didn't want to get in a fight with him, not even when I theoretically had the home-team advantage. He said, "Sown," when the ghosts had quieted and it seemed likely I wasn't going to open my mouth again. I could almost hear the gears grinding in his head as he worked through the possibilities of that word: "Buried in fields, or dismembered and scattered across fields? I wonder what was beneath that party hall fifty or a hundred years ago."

Frustrated rage gave the ghostly shrieks a new edge: "S-s-*sown!* All sown!" They swirled away from Billy's hands, filling the Trans Am with agitated gray, and beat at its windows and roof with blows that felt, to me, like human hands. I shuddered and told myself I was anthropomorphizing. These things hadn't been human in a long time.

They came back to Billy, and this time I could see I wasn't forcing human aspects onto nebulous bits of ether. Bony hands spread against the inside of the hood, matching Billy's, pressing like they'd reach through and slide their fingers through his. Their screams faded, turning into desperate intensity as they tried for words that had faded from their consciousness a long time ago. "Sown d-d-dead. *Dead.*"

Way in the back of my brain, a penny dropped, and my mouth said, "Sown dead. *Sowen,* the day of the dead. *Samhain,*" without filtering it through the active thought process in my mind. It was just as well: if I'd thought about it, I'd have never figured it out. *Samhain* was the Irish new year, falling on the same date as the western Halloween, and the next day was, in plenty of cultures, the day of the dead. I'd learned all about it from a precognitive anthropologist who'd predicted my death wrongly, and her own with depressing accuracy. To the English-reading eye, the word looked like it should be pronounced Sam-hayn, but in Irish, it was *Sowen.* "They all died at Halloween."

The ghosts erupted in a shriek of triumph, and Billy twisted to give me a good hard look before he said, "Nice job," without a hint of begrudgement. I didn't quite know what the look was for. It sort of made me feel as if I'd been holding out on having an encyclopedia of arcane knowledge to draw from, but I really didn't. I knew more than I had a year ago, but that wasn't saying much.

"It's a pattern." Billy was still looking at me, though the way his voice went calm suggested he was speaking to the ghosts. "It gives us a place to start. I want to make you an offer." He turned his attention back to the Trans Am. Faces were beginning to appear beneath the translucent hood. Not fully fleshed human faces, but something more than skulls. They reminded me unpleasantly of *The Scream* painting.

"We'll find your bodies, if we can. We'll find your killer, if we can. But I don't have the skill, even here, to draw your memories out clearly enough to learn everything we can from you." Billy sounded utterly at home with his talent's boundaries. I envied that, not because I wanted more power, but because I didn't know where the edges of mine lay. I'd read often enough that if you argue for your limitations, then sure enough, they're yours, but that wasn't what I heard in Billy's voice, or saw in the image of himself. He'd had most of a lifetime to learn what he could and couldn't do. The window in which he could see the dead had extended bit by bit over the years. In another thirty, he might be able to talk to ghosts a week dead instead of just a couple of days, but maybe not, too. Either way, I didn't get the sense he rested on his laurels, only that he accepted what his gifts were.

It wasn't a bad lesson for me to learn. Man, I was getting all mature and stuff. That couldn't be good for a person. Fortunately, the only person on hand to notice my leaps and bounds of maturity was Billy, and he was still talking to the ghosts. I rewound what he'd been saying—surprisingly easy, within the confines of my garden—and said, "Oh, no way, no how, hell no," to what memory informed me he'd suggested.

"I don't see much other choice." Billy stood up and faced me, broad arms folded over his chest. "They've got enough presence and opinion that they refused to cross through that door when you opened it, and I don't have the ability to usher them through. We need a much stronger medium for that, or to resolve their murders so they've got nothing left to hang on to."

"Yeah, but—"

He shook his head. "You can't risk having them here. One healing trance and they'll make a run for the short route out of imprisonment here and into someone else's body."

"I've got them pretty well wrapped up here!" I gestured toward the Trans Am.

Billy quirked an eyebrow. "Can you maintain that 24/7? Can you hold them apart from any healing you need to do? I watched how you pushed them out of me, Joanie. Eviction, then capture. You weren't splitting your concentration."

"Okay, yeah, but—"

"If I make them my riders voluntarily, it reduces their potential control, and right now they're willing to try it."

"The words *right now* in that sentence concern me, Billy. What if they change their minds? And you already have riders from the party. Not all of them detached from you." I looked around a little wildly, now that I'd remembered that. "Why don't I see them here?"

"They're not part of my self-image."

Indignant, I pointed at the gray mist inside the Trans Am. "They're not part of mine, either!"

"No," Billy said with exasperated patience, "but you opened up a door in your mind and invited dozens of spirits to pass through. The ones that refused to pass on didn't get rejected, just trapped. You said you'd had uninvited visitors before. Well, you more or less invited these ones. They're here whether you imagine them to be or not."

That made an irritating amount of sense. I glowered. "I still think it's a really bad idea for you to play host to a bunch of ectoplasmic parasites."

"I agree." Billy breathed a quiet laugh as bewilderment smeared across my face. "It's dangerous. But I think it's less dangerous than leaving them here. If you dissolve the car—" His mouth suddenly contorted as he tried not to laugh.

"The car just happened! I needed something the ghosts could communicate through, and he can talk! It's not my fault!"

"He," Billy said, and gave up trying not to laugh. My ears burned red and he whooped until tears came to his eyes, finally promising, "It's completely you," as he wiped moisture away. "Release them from the car and they'll come to me. It'll be fine."

I folded my arms, half sulking at being teased and half genuinely reluctant. I only had one argument to dissuade him, and I didn't like it much. On the other hand, but besides being persuasive, it struck me as a genuine concern. "Okay. Look. We know I can keep them locked in, if necessary. Can you? Because…what happens if one of these things changes its mind about hanging around on you, and latches on to the baby when it's born?"

I'd never seen Billy get so grim, which told me I was right: it was a legitimate danger. "We just won't let that happen."

"If Mel goes into labor before we get this thing resolved," I said very steadily, "I'm taking the ghosts back. I don't care what the other risks are."

"Yeah." Billy nodded, small tense motion that wasn't like him. "Yeah, okay. It's a deal."

We shook on it, and I released the Trans Am thought-form to infect Billy with the vengeful dead.

CHAPTER EIGHT

It jolted us out of my garden, me blinking the Sight on as soon as I realized we were back in the real world. Morrison stopped drumming, but his hand remained raised, ready to strike the drum again if necessary. His aura hadn't changed much since the last time he'd done this: it was still filled with rough edges of discomfort, purple and blue rubbing against each other wrong, but not badly enough to connote anger or fear. All too aware of the statement's inaccuracy, I said, "We're good," and Morrison lowered the drumstick to wait on those of us with more esoteric skills to tell him what had happened.

Billy's colors were grayed out, filmed over by his ghost riders. I could see varying shades, half a dozen or more soiling his presence. They amalgamated, darkening, and I imagined the ones he'd picked up in my garden were communicating Billy's offer of help to those he'd carried from the party himself.

Either that or they were staging a hostile takeover, the thought of which didn't reassure me at all. Mel sat up straight, her aura going bright with concern, though her daughter's was rosy pink and serene with sleep. "What did you do to Bill?"

"Walker?" That was Morrison, a warning note in his voice before I had a chance to say anything. Then Billy spoke, and I was grateful, because anything I *could* say would sound like I was trying to fob off responsibility. *It was his idea* just didn't cut it, even if it was true.

"It was my idea." Billy lifted his head wearily. His eyes were dull. "The hauntings that held on to Joanne were old murder cases, and I promised we'd get them to a stronger medium to see if we could help."

"A medium?" Morrison managed to keep the derision out of his voice, but he couldn't bury the disbelief.

Billy swung his head toward the captain, the motion too heavy, like he didn't have proper control of his actions. "It's what I am, Captain. I communicate with the dead." He didn't exactly sound challenging, but there was a note of undeterrable conviction in his words. I knew Morrison was aware Billy had an affiliation for the weird that allowed his homicide cases to be solved in record time. That was why he'd partnered us. Still, from their expressions, it was safe to say they'd never discussed it over a beer.

After a few seconds Morrison bared his teeth, though the look came and went so fast I couldn't have sworn I'd seen it. "Medium," he said, and if I wasn't sure his teeth had been bared, I was positive they were now clenched. "Shaman." He scowled at Melinda. "Anything weird you want to put a label on?"

Melinda gave him another one of those devastating smiles,

only this time tempered with deep sympathy. "Don't ask questions you don't want answers to, Michael."

It seemed like a bad time to mention *I'd* like those answers. Morrison pulled a hand over his face and nodded, then gave me a grim look. "Need anything else, Walker?"

"No, sir. Go on home and get some rest." I got up and thrust my hand at him awkwardly. "Thanks, Captain."

He shook my hand every bit as unnaturally as I'd offered it, nodded to the Hollidays and left without saying another word. All things considered, I thought that was the most rational choice. On the positive side, I didn't have any particular impulse to follow him out and thus avoid whatever peculiarities or arguments were about to arise. Maybe it was a little thing, but I was pleased with it.

With Morrison gone, Billy and I both turned our attention on Melinda, whose usual good nature had blackened. "You promised to find a stronger medium, *and…?*"

"And it was too dangerous to let Joanie keep the riders. If she needs to heal someone—"

"William Robert Holliday. Cut to the chase." Melinda didn't so much need him to as she wanted her ugly suspicions confirmed.

"I took them on." Billy held up a hand, stopping Mel's indrawn breath from turning into a tirade. "You're right. It's dangerous for me, too, and I'm sorry. But it's also four-thirty in the morning, and we're both—all—exhausted, which isn't going to help me keep my head with half a dozen ghosts riding me. Save the lecture until after we've slept, all right?"

Melinda got to her feet and put her hands on her waist. Or she would've if she'd had a waist, but pregnancy precluded that. It also precluded her from looking all that threatening. She looked a bit like a deranged penguin, really, what with the tuxedo and the tummy. "You just want me to mellow out," she snapped. "You know if I sleep on it I'll wake up knowing you made the right choice, even if I hate it."

Billy crooked the tiniest grin I'd ever seen. "I'm counting on it, baby."

Mel said something along the lines of, "Mrgnnmnmm grr grr grr," and waddled over to hug Billy hard. "You're a wretch."

"Yeah, but you love me." He got off my couch and tucked Melinda against his side, kissing her hair before looking at me. "There might be one thing you can do."

I said, "Anything," without thinking, but once I'd thought, it didn't matter. *Anything* barely began to cover what I'd do to help Billy or Melinda.

"Ever shared energy with someone? It's—"

He didn't have to finish explaining. I'd done it frequently with another friend, popping a bit of healing energy into a heart that'd been magicked into an attack. I stepped forward and put my hand over Billy's heart, calling up power.

Cheery blue-silver fireworks spat energy and comfort into his depleted aura. I'd drained myself damn near dry a couple of times early on in the year, but I got the impression that the more I accepted it, the deeper and more fundamental my magic became. If I had to go up against something huge, I might need to call in help from outside again, but even with the long night, I had more than enough juice to rev Billy's engi—

I really needed to get some different metaphors.

Fortunately, Melinda couldn't hear my thoughts, and Billy's colors strengthened, which released me from having to think anymore about how to describe what I was doing. I shot another pulse of energy into him, essentially imagining it as refilling a fuel tank, and he exhaled gratefully. "Thanks. I don't feel so worn down."

"You don't look so worn down," Melinda said with satisfaction. "The gray's fading out of your aura. You sure they don't have enough foothold to take over when you sleep?"

"I'm sure now." Billy hugged her shoulders, then nodded to me. "See you in the morning, Joanne."

"It's already morning. See you later. And not enough later, either." I gave Mel a quick hug and shooed them out the door before thunking my head on it.

To the best of my ability to count—and for all my various faults, that much I could still do—this was the third time Billy'd gotten into hot water thanks to me and my magic. I didn't know what his daily paranormal experiences were, but I was willing to bet banshees and comas and ghosts, oh my, had never been on the roster.

On one very practical hand, it made sense: Billy belonged to the Mulder subset of humanity. He wanted to believe, and because he did, he was usually on hand when the weird went down. That put him in a position of strength if he was dealing with his own particular branch of Other, but it made him vulnerable when he was dealing with mine. Realistically I couldn't keep him out of harm's way, but one of these times I wasn't going to be able to figure a way out of the crazy before he really got hurt. I either needed more friends to spread the risk around to, or fewer so I took all the scary stuff onto myself.

Billy would give me a swirly for even thinking that way. I gave up on trying to figure out how to save the world and went to bed.

Sunday, October 30, 11:57 a.m.

Somewhere out there in the big brave world there was an extra-grande amaretto coffee with my name on it. All I had to do was get through the three minutes until it was technically lunchtime, and I could break free of my desk and go in search of that beautiful, luscious cup of coffee.

I'd been a homicide detective for four months now. I was never in any way keen to put my detecting skills to the test, but for the last few hours, I'd have almost given my eyeteeth for a nice eventful murder. The morning had been filled with paperwork, some of it follow-up on a couple of cases we'd closed the week before, but more of it focused on trying to find anything about Halloween murders over the last hundred and fifty years in Seattle. I'd protested. I didn't think there'd been anything *in* Seattle that long.

Billy sent me to Wikipedia, where I learned that it'd been a Native American settlement forever. Well, okay, I'd known that, what with the whole Chief Seattle thing, but I hadn't known that white people had been there since the 1850s. Having been educated, I wondered if we should go back more than a hundred and fifty years. Billy said I was welcome to locate criminal records kept by a people who didn't have a written language, and wished me luck with that.

Pointing out that we didn't have any records that indicated people who *did* have a written language were being murdered on Halloween didn't go over especially well. Billy, who was as tired as I was, stomped off, and I'd started craving my amaretto-flavored coffee right about then. That had been almost two hours ago. I glanced at the clock. Ninety seconds. I could survive another ninety seconds.

A short slim man in a business suit and with an air of determination about him came through the door and stopped at the receptionist's desk, which was, by default, simply the one closest to the door. Technically, as the newest detective on the force, it should've been mine, but I'd bribed my way to three desks back and one to the left by doing expensive and time-consuming vehicle repair jobs for free. The guys I'd bargained with had saved a collective thirteen and a half grand, which had earned me two months' respite from the junior desk on each of their behalfs. I had another three months of no-desk-duties stored up, and a tingly hope that Morrison would hire another detective before my time ran out. Even if he didn't, at least I'd insinuated myself into the team and had gotten a chance to learn the ropes without being interrupted every thirty seconds by somebody coming in the front door.

Speaking of thirty seconds. I let out a sigh of relief and grabbed my coat off the back of my chair. It would take thirty seconds to walk to the clock and punch out. I could get my coffee. I'd even bring one back for Billy. God, I was swell.

"Detective Walker?"

The officious little guy called my name as I stepped away from my desk. My shoulders hunched around my ears and I pretended not to hear him. I made it two more steps before one of the guys whose car I'd fixed helpfully bellowed, "Hey, Walker!" making it impossible for me to sneak away.

I was going to pour sugar in his gas tank. I turned around with my best expression of seething discontent, hoping to both castigate the bellowing detective and scare off the suit.

Neither worked. The detective looked way too pleased with himself, clearly knowing he'd just ruined my lunch hour, and the fellow in the suit looked like nothing short of thermonuclear war would put him off the trail. He put a briefcase on my desk and reached over it to offer a hand in greeting. "Detective Walker? I'm Daniel Doherty with First Ally Homestate Insurance. I'm here to talk to you about your vehicle."

There are words which, when spoken, are intended to strike fear into the hearts of men. Anything involving the phrase "We need to talk" is gut-clenching territory, and when it comes from an insurance adjudicator, it's worse than that. My knees stopped working and instead of shaking Daniel Doherty's hand, I caught myself on the edge of my desk and admired the cold sweat breaking out on my forehead. The only reason I was sure I'd caught myself was that I wasn't on the floor: my hands were so icy I could've missed the desk entirely and I wouldn't have felt it. My heart hung between beats, and foul air filled my lungs with agony before I forced out a whispered "Is she okay?"

My inherent drama probably would've been better suited to hearing about a child's injury, but Petite was my baby. She'd been fine four hours ago when I parked her outside the precinct building. Short of a bulldozer rolling through the parking lot, I couldn't really imagine what might've happened to her, but I had visions of terrible things. Worse than tires slashed or roofs split open by swords or being helicoptered out of an earthquake zone, all of which were bad, but only the first hadn't happened to my poor car in the last year. We'd had a rough year, Petite and me.

"According to our records 'she' is." He gave me a smile that wasn't exactly oily, but I didn't have a better word for it. Slippery, maybe. He was nice-looking, if tiny—he was probably five or six inches shorter than me, very slim throughout, with curling black hair and chiseled features that verged on pretty. Not my type, even if he wasn't an insurance agent, and I didn't trust the smile. "But there've been some irregularities in your insurance claims this year, and I'm here to inspect the vehicle and spend a day or two with you so we at FAHI can get a better feel for your daily usage and what might be the appropriate insurance coverage."

I caught a "Like hell you are!" behind my teeth and kept it there. Belligerence rarely did any good with insurance adjusters. Or cops, for that matter. When I released the words, they were an as-polite-as-I-could-make-them "Petite's a 1969 Mustang and I consider her worth the cost of maintaining full coverage, Mr. Doherty. I'm pretty sure, in fact, that the premium I'm paying actually covers acts of God, so I'm really not sure why you're here."

"Your insurance is comprehensive." He managed to make it sound as if I should be given a gold star for knowing that. What a good little driver I was. "But you've had some extraordinary claims this year, have you not?"

"I have. My car was vandalized in January—" by a god, no less, but the insurance did cover acts of gods, dammit—not that I'd put it down as such in the paperwork, because that would be insane "—and I was unlucky enough to be at Matthews

Beach Park when the earthquake hit in June. Petite slid into one of the fissures and had to be winched out." With a helicopter.

"These things do happen," Doherty said with sympathy, except it didn't go anywhere near his eyes. "Curiously, though, you submitted no mechanic or bodywork invoices, and your driving record has been spotless up until this point."

That was because I was a very very good driver, and Petite could outrun any cop car you cared to pit her against. I didn't say that out loud. I gritted my teeth, pushed my face into a smile and said, "Actually, I did submit mechanic and bodywork-fee paperwork. I'm a mechanic by trade, and—"

Doherty looked at me, looked around the detectives' office I was in, looked at the nameplate on my desk with my name on it, and looked at me again, all with an air of mildly amused but polite disbelief.

I had six inches' reach on the guy, easy. I could break his nose before he even knew I'd thrown the punch, and then I could put a hand on top of his head and watch him swing like a little kid. I fixed my smile harder into place. "I'll show you my résumé, if you like. I only joined the force recently. Every other job I've had is as a mechanic, and Petite's my pet project." My face felt like it would freeze in its smile, which is presumably not what mothers all over the world meant when they gave that warning. "All of this is in the paperwork."

"I'm sure, but you understand that after such an exemplary record, coming on several expensive discrepancies in six months looks a little strange. We only want to provide you with the best possible service, Detective, and we need to have full and complete records to do that."

"It's taken you almost ten months to decide you needed to look at the case a little more carefully? I have full coverage. I don't see the problem. Perhaps I should be talking to your competitors instead of you, Mr. Doherty." My smile was getting a little strained. Maybe a lot strained. There was probably a rule against leaping on insurance adjusters and ripping their throats out with your teeth.

"You're welcome to, of course, although I think you'll find our rates are competi—"

His tone of utter reason did me in. My short fuse, let me show it to you. I leaned across my desk and his briefcase and snapped, "Oh, go to hell. I'm not scamming your damn company. I've submitted my invoices. I don't even charge for my own time—" Belatedly, I realized that could be the problem. "Would it help if I did? Would I seem more legitimate then? Would you be happier if I was asking for five times as much money? I thought I was asking for plenty already, but if you want to pay me for my efforts, I'm not going to object. Otherwise go away and cut me a check. There are people committing real insurance fraud out there. Go harass them." I wanted my coffee. I wanted dainty Mr. Doherty to leave me alone. I wanted all kinds of things.

It's good to want. Billy blew in through the front door—I didn't even know he'd left—and thrust a cardboard coffee cup in my hand, then grabbed my coat. "Drink up. We gotta go."

"What? Where?" I shot Doherty a look and put the coffee down to take my coat from Billy and fumble it on. Amaretto's distinctive scent rose from the cup and I nearly wept. "Thank you. This is manna from heaven. I'm unworthy of its gift, and yet I immerse myself in it." I got my coat on and scalded my tongue on the first blissful sip of coffee. "What's the rush? Where're we going?"

"The Museum of Cultural Arts. C'mon, you're driving." He threw the keys at me next, and I snapped a hand out to catch them.

"What, the café there has just opened a new coffee-and-doughnuts express line? I don't want to spend my lunch hour admiring old spearheads and meaningless blocks of color on contemporary paintings." I took a slow, glorious drink.

Billy scowled. "Good, because we're going to spend our lunch hour investigating the murder they've just called in."

CHAPTER NINE

The museum was a new building, funded by one percent for the arts and, much more helpfully, by a big fat grant from Seattle's favorite multiconglomerate powerhouse. I wished I thought that was noble and wonderful, but mostly I thought it a tax write-off. Still, at least some good had come out of the evil that corporations do.

I didn't consider myself much of an artist, but even my eye took in the curved sweep of the museum building with its slim arched wing rising into the air and grasped that I was looking at the architectural representative of a killer whale. It was white, not black, but it worked, and made for a very pretty modern building.

Inside was considerably more open and airy than I expected from a killer whale's belly. Billy'd read the museum's mission statement aloud on the way over, so I knew the left wing—

the tail—held the permanent Seattle display, with cultural material on loan from local tribes, fragile bits of the past preserved behind glass. I'd suggested, brightly, that if we came up dry with our research on Halloween murders, we could visit the museum's bits and bobs and try getting psychic readings off them. There were people who could do that, though Billy and I didn't number amongst them, and I'd probably deserved the dirty look he gave me.

We were met by the museum director, a tall man who looked more like the rugged-adventurer type—scruffy, slightly battered clothes, good solid boots, that kind of thing—than a behind-the-desk fund-raiser. He introduced himself as Saul Sandburg and ushered us into the right wing, the killer whale's head, and I suffered a moment of *one of these things is not like the others.*

Actually, two of those things did not belong. The second was the security guard lying on the marble floor. His head had lolled to the side, showing clearly how the back of his skull was broken in. Blood had caked on his ears, making his head seem even more mis-shapen, but worse, it was smeared in a wide brownish circle around a display unit. I was pretty certain bits of bone and brain were squished through that smear: he'd pretty clearly been dragged around the whole room. Everything stank of blood and other body fluids.

The first thing that didn't belong was the massive, gaping hole in the display unit where something was obviously missing. It was *so* obviously missing that it somehow overshadowed the dead man and the huge bloody smear around the room.

An enormous variety of supplementary material surrounded the gaping area: glass-encased books, a few manuscript pages, bronze and iron swords, a tattered remnant of leather armor. I was too far away to read the information docket set slightly to one side, but I had no doubt we'd get to it.

I exchanged glances with Billy. He nodded, which told me there was a ghost, and I put away my curiosity to give him space to work. My part of the esoteric investigation was less pressing: ghosts faded fast, and their ability to communicate depended on how fresh they were. Billy'd told me that before, but the previous night's experiences had hammered it home. I took Sandburg's elbow and directed him a few steps away from the dead man, partly so he didn't have to look at the body and partly so Billy could do his thing.

"What's he doing?" Sandburg looked over his shoulder as Billy crouched beside the corpse. I turned him back toward me as gently as I could.

"Preliminary investigation. The forensics team's on its way, but I'd like you to tell me what happened in your own words. Then I'm going to need you to help calm everyone else down so we can talk to them individually. I know it's a lot to ask." That was true. It was a lot to ask. However, many people—especially men—seemed to function better if they knew they had a specific and helpful task to perform. If I could make him an ally who felt important in the investigative process without actually getting in our way, it was good for everybody.

Sandburg bucked right up. He was holding it together pretty damn well as it was, but his posture straightened and his gaze cleared as he pulled his thoughts together. "We open late on Sundays, not until noon. There's twenty-four-hour security, but the first staff don't come in until eleven to set up."

"Are you among that staff?" It seemed unlikely. Directorial bigwigs didn't typically do the drudge work alongside their minimum-wage employees. I was flummoxed when Sandburg nodded.

"The museum's only open for four hours on Sunday. I work so I don't feel wholly divorced from the day-to-day running of the facility. Besides, sacrificing a few hours of my time means someone else can spend a weekend day at home with their family. I don't have any myself, but I appreciate its importance."

"That must make you popular. So you're here every Sunday?"

"It helps me avoid the pointy-haired boss label, at least." Sandburg offered a brief smile, then shook his head. "Three Sundays out of four. We usually have two people on, one for reception and ticket sales, the other to give guided tours every hour. The first one begins at twelve-fifteen." He looked at his watch like he was already running late, and his features crumpled. I gave him a few seconds, waiting to see if he'd recover on his own. After a couple of long breaths, he did.

"I did the usual morning routine, which is to glance at the security tapes, count the till, that sort of thing. Meghan came in at a quarter to twelve. She's the one who found the—" He broke again, then drew himself up with a shudder. "She found Jason when she went to check the security ropes around the exhibits. It's always the last thing we do before we open. Security does it, too, obviously, but children like to play on them and they get knocked out of place, so we double-check to keep it tidy. Appearances, you know…" It was a strange comment from a man with scruff and cargo pants, but I could see where he might lend a certain romanticism to a cultural arts museum. It probably needed all the romance it could get.

"What time did the deceased arrive at work?" Jason. Jason

Chan, who was twenty-four years old and who would never be twenty-five. It didn't help to think about him in those terms; *the deceased* was much easier, and in some ways, much worse.

"Six last night. Our security works twelve-hour shifts, six to six. Jason and Archie just worked Friday, Saturday and Sunday nights," Sandburg replied. I nodded and wrote it down—I'd been writing everything down, in a semi-comprehensible shorthand that I'd be able to read later because what Sandburg was saying was too hard to forget.

"Archie. That would be Archie Redding, your missing guard?" I knew he was; it'd been in the hysterical call that had brought us to the museum, but I'd learned two things as a detective. One, if your witnesses start babbling, listen, because they might say something important, and two, try to deal with one subject at a time when talking to them, even if it's all interconnected. It was the focus thing again: chances were their thoughts were already fractured and running amok. Asking them to deduce concurrent events was asking for trouble.

Right on cue, Sandburg sagged, as if the thought of another crisis was too much to bear. "Yes. He was a lot older than Jason, in his fifties—"

"Was?" I put too much emphasis on the word, but couldn't stop myself. "Is there another body, Mr. Sandburg?" I shot a look at Billy, wondering if he had more than one ghost to chat up.

Sandburg turned a bleak expression on me. "No, but isn't it just a matter of time?"

"Not necessarily. If Mr. Redding is missing but there's neither blood nor a body, he may have been kidnapped. We can hope our perpetrator has no reason to resort to more violence." Perpetrator. I felt all official, using words like that. I could've said perp, but I'd realized that made me feel like I was in a Chicago crime story, so I stuck with the multisyllabic version.

Sandburg's face didn't lighten any. "It's a thin hope, though, isn't it?"

"I'm afraid so. Still, I'd rather assume the best." We went through another round of routine questions before I finally bit back a sigh and brought my attention around to the elephant missing from the room. "What's been taken from the display, Mr. Sandburg?"

I'd been avoiding asking for two reasons. One, I wanted to get the details about the dead and missing men out of the way before moving on to missing property, which, in my opinion, wasn't as important. Two, I suspected whatever had disappeared was a lot nearer and dearer to Sandburg's museum-director heart than a couple of security guards, and I'd been afraid letting him focus on it would wipe out any details he might remember about our victims.

I was right. Sandburg very nearly moaned, not at all a sound I expected from a hale-looking man in his late fifties. If he'd sagged when I mentioned the second guard, he deflated now. "The Cauldron of Matholwch."

Billy looked up from his conversation with dead people and said, "The *what?*"

So did I, but when I said it, it was with bewilderment, and when Billy said it, it was with dread and amazement. I'd spent a lot of quality time online and in libraries the last few months, reading up on shamanism and the occult, but all it took was one phrase to let me know just how far at the back of the class I still was.

Fortunately, Sandburg didn't seem to expect that I'd recognize the name. "You might know it by its more common name, the Black Cauldron. It—"

"Wait! Wait! I know this one!" I bounced and waved my hand in the air, then remembered there was a dead man not fifteen feet away and tried to pull together a little decorum. "Like from the movie, right? I saw it when I was little. There's an army of undead in it, right?"

There's an expression of betrayal that I associate with deceptions on the magnitude of learning there's no Santa Claus. It says, *You have taken my childhood and crushed it utterly. There is nothing left in this world for me to remember kindly, or to hope for in the future. I am lost, and you are dead to me for all time.*

Billy and Sandburg both had that look. My hand sank and I looked between them, finally venturing, "No?" in a small, apologetic voice.

Sandburg recovered first. From Billy's expression, he might never recover, and he would definitely never forgive me. "That cauldron," Sandburg said a bit frostily, "originated from the true Cauldron, which belonged to an ancient Welsh king called Bran, who gave it to the Irish king Matholwch as a wedding gift when Matholwch married Bran's sister, Branwyn. The dead could be resurrected into undying warriors by placing them in the cauldron. It was reputedly destroyed in battle between Matholwch and Bran, by a living man climbing within it."

I held my hand up again, a finger lifted. "Battle between the king who gave the cauldron and the one he gave it to?"

Sandburg lost a little of his despondency, obviously enjoying the chance to lecture. "Matholwch mistreated Branwyn, and so Bran invaded Ireland to rescue her." He brightened further, adding, "Of course, there's no way of knowing for certain that this is Matholwch's cauldron. It was found several years ago at an ancient battlefield and gathering place in Ireland, with the remnants you see there." He gestured toward the display. "All of the artifacts are Celtic in origin, but compositional and artistic differences in the pieces suggest some are Welsh, while others are Irish. Combined with the cauldron's presence, it lends credence to the legend, and makes a wonderful story and artifact to draw audiences to museums. It's on tour."

His pleasure faded again and he looked at the empty space where the cauldron had been. "We must recover it, Detectives. It's insured, but there's no way of realizing its true value in monetary terms. It's a piece of legend and of history."

"How big is this thing?" I asked dubiously. "Big enough to put a dead man in, I assume. And made of iron?" A full-grown man could fit into, say, a fifty-five-gallon barrel, though not comfortably. I looked at the gaping spot in the display, and at Sandburg. "Even empty, that's got to weigh a ton."

"Some seventy gallons," Sandburg said, "and made of oak with iron bands. It's not quite a ton, but it's very heavy."

I stared at him a moment before questions poured out in the order of least relevance: "How long ago was this supposed to be? Wouldn't oak have rotted away? Wouldn't you have noticed somebody waltzing out of here with a seventy-gallon barrel bumping along behind them? Wouldn't the security cameras have footage?" No wonder Billy hadn't let me interrogate the ghosts.

"It was preserved in a peat bog." Sandburg got all bright-eyed and enthusiastic again. "Two partial bodies were recovered, as well. They're considered too fragile to travel, bu—"

"Sorry, Mr. Sandburg." Billy came over with his best wryly sympathetic look. "I'd love to hear about the bog men sometime, but right now Detective Walker's questions have to take precedence. Could I see the security-camera footage? Walker, you can oversee the forensics team." We'd been working together long enough that I understood the code in the simple phrase.

It meant I could oversee the forensics team.

All right, all right, it also meant he'd gotten what he could out of Jason Chan's ghost, and that it was my turn to study the crime scene on the supernatural level.

I'd consciously decided not to use the Sight when I first walked in. I'd done it first thing on at a few scenes, and I'd learned it superseded the real world too much. I could never quite see things the way they were supposed to be seen once they'd been tainted with the colors and emotional impact the Sight brought along. It was worth more to me to go in clear-headed and then move into the unusual. That, and Billy couldn't turn his off; if there were ghosts, he'd see them, so one of us seeing the unadulterated world while the other studied the magical one seemed like a good idea to both of us.

I took a look at Sandburg on his way out. He was agitated, darkness and discomfort whirling through what were otherwise very mild colors: for all his adventurer-clothing style, his aura was made up of pastels and whites. If I'd looked at him that way first, I'd have called him lily-livered, which wouldn't have been fair at all. Billy, beside him, looked much richer in color, which pleased me. I'd need to remember to give him another energy boost, just in case, but it looked as if his ghost riders weren't gaining any toeholds. The men disappeared around a curve, and I turned to look at the crime scene.

Knowing Billy saw ghosts made me surprised that I didn't, especially when I knew one was there. But aside from last night, my only experience in seeing the dead had been on a different plane of existence. I called it the Dead Zone, a vast purgatory-like nothingness. I'd told Billy the door in my garden led to a place people went when they were dying. The Dead Zone was where the already-dead hung out, at least briefly. I was absolutely terrible at calling them to me, and had very nearly gotten myself killed trying. My mentor, Coyote, had saved my sorry ass more than once. I missed him.

I sighed and pulled myself back to the job at hand. No ghosts for me. That was okay. There were plenty of other things to see.

Foremost was the cauldron. Even gone, it left a mark of darkness in the air, intense enough where it had rested that I had to move in order to see some of the artifacts. A general malaise hung over them, their energy—because everything had energy, which I'd eventually learned was one of the tenets of shamanism; all things were inhabited by a spirit of some sort, one that lent the object purpose and definition—their energy drained to a dull tarry brown. Well, they'd been buried in a peat bog for who knows how long. I'd be brown and sticky, too.

But it was more than that, at least where the cauldron had rested. There was—I hesitated to call it *evil*. Evil was a human conceit, and I wasn't sure an object could be imbued with it.

But there was death there, intense, concentrated death. I walked forward cautiously, half-certain the thin tendrils left behind would spring to life and draw me in.

They only wrapped around me, cool and uncomfortably inviting. I hadn't seen a death aura before, and if I'd been asked, I'd have guessed it would be terrifying, an unknown slash of black and fear. This glimpse made me think the auras surrounding illness were worse; there was fight left in the sick, and what encompassed me now had moved far beyond that.

I backed up, uneasy with the accepting nature of the cauldron's remnants. If its shadow took away the edges of pain and the sharpness of worry, the cauldron itself would be much more potent. If it offered that kind of peace to everyone, I didn't think a living body diving in would be the charm that broke it apart. It'd be an easy suicide, climbing into that thing. I shuddered and took another step back.

With distance, and maybe with my rejection, the cauldron's shadow lessened. The books and manuscript fragments burned away most of their murk, as though they'd been freed of the cauldron's touch. They were gorgeous, ciphers standing out in gold against creamy backgrounds. I edged closer, peering at the display-case information to learn what was oldest, and turned to the piece—barely more than a sliver of parchment—to see what ancient knowledge looked like with the Sight. I had the idea that if I could hold my gaze just right, then a picture or an answer would leap out at me, like a magic-eye optical illusion.

For a while the gold cipher on the page simply wavered at me. Then it twinned, a scarlet streak racing through it, and dizziness made my eyes cross. The Sight vanished, and I clapped a hand over my face, muttering. Aside from turning the Sight off, that was basically what the magic-eye illusions did to me, too. I should've known better.

My cell phone buzzed and I slipped it free, glad of something real to focus on. Billy's voice came over the line, exasperated but not surprised: "The security tapes have been looped. We've got nothing. Is forensics there yet?"

I looked toward the entryway, where the team was just moving in. "Yeah. Look, did you get anything?"

"We'll talk about it in the car. You?"

A frown creased my forehead as I turned the Sight back on, looking toward the forensics team and the museum's entrance. Wisps of black tar caught against the floor, minute smears I wouldn't have seen if the cauldron hadn't tried to draw me in. The forensics team walked over them, smearing their slight presence into even less, and I started to jog down the hall, cell phone still at my ear as I passed the team. A few seconds later I charged out the front door, Sight still blazing.

"Yeah," I said. "Yeah, I think I did."

CHAPTER TEN

Seattle was built on myriad hills. We'd driven up a bunch of them to reach the museum, but I'd been too intent on getting inside to stop and appreciate the vista when we'd arrived.

Now it was marred. Smears of black spread out like contrails, as if the cauldron had been broken into pieces and dragged across the city. I doubted it: thieves bothering with a reputedly magic cauldron would presumably be after the magic, and wouldn't risk breaking its power by taking it apart. That, and destroying a seventy-gallon wooden tank banded by iron would leave a bunch of debris behind, so either we had the world's tidiest killer on hand, or the cauldron was still in one piece.

Which, judging from the way the trails of its death-mark were spreading, meant the city would eventually be cloaked in the stuff. It also meant tracking the cauldron wouldn't be easy: there was no nice straight line from A to B for us to follow.

An idle thought crossed my mind: either the cauldron had left a trail of misery behind it as it traveled, or whoever was responsible for packing it up and moving it from one location to another had some kind of serious mojo going on. I said, "Remind me to talk to the shipping company," into my phone, and could almost hear Billy's puzzled look. "Never mind. Look, what I found isn't necessarily helpful—"

"What is it?"

I heard his voice both in the phone and behind me, and turned around. He hung up and quirked an eyebrow. I glanced back at the death shroud expanding over the city. "The cauldron's gone. I mean, we knew that, but it's out in the city somewhere, and it's not leaving an easy trail to follow. Either it's been broken into pieces—"

"Not a chance."

Billy's confidence made me feel all proud for having sussed that out myself. "Yeah, I didn't think so. The thing is…" I trailed off, putting thoughts together. Billy gave me about a minute before impatience started dancing through his aura in bright flashes. "Its aura's so filled with death it leaves marks everywhere it goes. The display area back there is just a big black smear, with the Sight. I'm sure this place has got loading docks, that they don't bring the exhibits in through the front door, so I know the cauldron's gone out the front door. The floor looks like a kid's been walking through tar."

"But?"

I held my breath, eyeing Billy. Of everyone I knew, he was least likely to give me hell if what I was about to suggest didn't work. "You, um. Want to try something?"

His eyebrow requirked itself. "Is this something that'll get me in trouble with Mel?"

Laughter took some of my nerves away. "No. I read this thing about how to give somebody the Sight temporarily. I think it wouldn't hurt for you to see what I do."

"You want me to stand on your feet and look over your left shoulder?"

My jaw dropped. "How'd you know?" He knew because I was the kid at the back of the class. "Does it work?"

"I don't know. Melinda can tap into auras, but she doesn't have the Sight like you do. I've never known anybody who does." He walked up and put his feet on mine, keeping his weight on his heels. "Let's give it a shot."

I put my hand on top of his head, which was part of the ritual I'd read about, and drew breath to chant the charm. "…this isn't going to work."

"Not with that attitu—"

"No, I mean, it didn't actually say, but I'm pretty sure you can't be touching the ground. I think you need to really stand on my feet."

Billy looked down. "I'll crush them."

"That possibility did occur to me. Will you please stand on them before somebody comes out here and finds us like this? Ow!" Billy weighed two-sixty if he weighed an ounce, and while my shoes were good solid clodhoppers, meant for stomping around all day in, they weren't especially meant to be stood on by a second party. He wobbled and we seized each other's waists, trying to keep balanced. Maybe I'd been wrong. Standing in parking lots clinging to coworkers might get him in trouble with Melinda after all. I blurted, "Between my hands and my feet, these things I do keep, to a warrior of light, I grant you the Sight!" and waited for my head to explode of embarrassment.

Billy, gratifyingly, said, "Oh, *wow.*"

My gaze jerked to his face, a couple inches away from my own. "It worked?"

His eyes were filmed with gold. Morrison and Thor had said mine had changed color when I'd used the Sight. I was pleased enough that I forgot having a two-hundred-and-sixty-pound man on my feet hurt, and let him stand there a while before I even thought to howl with pain. Just before I started to complain, he shook himself and stepped back, a broad, astonished smile on his face as gold drained out of his eyes and left them brown again.

"Is that what you always see?"

"God, no. I'd get a headache and keep trying to walk through walls if I saw them as translucent all the time." Flippant half truths were my friends. I was a little afraid I'd become more and more disconnected if I used the Sight all the time. I wanted to belong in the world, not float above it, and I worried that using too much magic might unhinge me. On the other hand, I said, "It's pretty, isn't it?" and meant it.

"It's amazing." Billy let that linger a moment, then slid me a crooked grin. "Warrior of light, huh?"

I groaned. I was pretty sure the charm I'd read had been less stupid than mine, but I couldn't remember all of its words. "I'm not a poet."

"There are worse things than being a warrior of light." His grin stayed in place a moment, before he brought himself back to the matter at hand. "The black film?"

"That's the cauldron. Billy, I had a thought."

He gave me a look that said "congratulations," and I made a face. "Yeah, yeah. No, listen. It's all over the city, that stuff. And the cauldron's supposed to be death magic, the kind that brings the dead back to life."

Billy thinned his lips. "So you're thinking maybe you don't have to throw a body in to the cauldron to bring them back."

I touched a finger to the tip of my nose. "What time did our cauldron go nuts at the party last night? Around eleven?"

"About that."

"Want to bet Jason's time of death is eleven o'clock?" We hadn't been told yet how long Chan had been dead, but I didn't really think I needed a professional assessment on that one. "How long ago did the security tapes start looping? And what about the other guard, Redding? Why isn't he dead?" I was mostly talking to myself, not really expecting answers, but Billy chuckled quietly.

"You're getting better at asking good questions, Walker. One of our tech guys will look at it and see if they can figure it out, but the security tape loop's got the right guards making the right rounds for the whole night. I don't know when it was filmed, but somebody did his homework. He had to cover four different guards for the whole weekend, and he got them all."

I sighed and looked out at the city. The Sight was gone, leaving Seattle overcast and dreary. It'd get worse, too, with the days getting shorter still over the next couple months. "How long's the exhibit been in town?"

"Since the beginning of the month, but it's been advertised for almost a year. Plenty of time to set up."

"Great. Have we got yesterday's guards in to talk yet?"

"They're on their way."

I nodded and ran my hands through my hair, fisting them there before letting go and turning to Billy. "I think Jason's death broke the wards, and that's what set off the ghosts last night."

"Why didn't they get charged up when it got to Seattle, then? Or any time in the month it's been sitting here?" Billy wasn't arguing, just making sure I'd thought my claim through.

"It was warded." I didn't know if I'd missed the warding—not that I had clue one about what wards might look like—or if it'd been obliterated when the cauldron was moved, but I was, for once, certain of myself. "I know it's the haunted time of year, but the ghosts and the cauldron—it's not coincidence, Billy."

He said, "Don't let yourself get so fixated you overlook other possibilities," but what I heard was agreement. He was right: I shouldn't cling too hard to my theory and maybe end up blinding myself to the truth, but at least he didn't think I was barking up the wrong tree. Or into the wrong cauldron, for that matter.

"I won't." I turned away from the city before voicing the other idea I suspected Billy shared: "So. Sandburg?"

"Oh, yeah." He nodded once. "I think so."

Thunder rumbled up above and fat blots of rain chased us back into the museum to pursue our case.

Sunday, October 29, 4:44 p.m.

Four months of detective work hadn't yet accustomed me to just how damn long it took to question everybody linked to a murder case. Meghan, the poor girl who'd found Chan's body, had to be tranquilized before she could answer questions, and then she spoke in a soft monotone, tears draining down her cheeks. I'd eat my hat if she had anything to do with the murder. The security guards who'd worked the day shift swore they'd seen nothing and that the cauldron had been safely in place when they'd done their last check at a quarter to six.

The Sight, it turned out, was a half-decent lie detector. It picked up on the same kinds of things a polygraph did: anxiety tended to spike pretty much the same way in everybody. Baseline emotions ran pretty high during questioning, but to the best of my ability to tell, everyone was telling the truth about what they had or hadn't seen.

What threw me off was Sandburg read as innocent, too. I wanted him to be guilty; it'd be easy. But until Chan's autopsy report came back, and maybe not even then, we didn't have anything to pin on him except access and timing. He didn't have an alibi for the sixteen hours prior to turning up at work. He'd eaten dinner out, and had a credit-card slip to back up that claim, and then had gone home, where he had no family to verify whether he'd been there or not. Arresting him would be tidy, quick and satisfying. But only if we were right, and his steady pale aura said we weren't.

Billy and I were both near staggering with exhaustion before we finished. I'd gotten a whole three hours of sleep before work, and he'd had to drive home, so couldn't have gotten more than two and a half at the outside. I pulled in at the Missing O, the coffee-and-doughnut shop down the street from the precinct building, without asking or being told. We had a dozen things to discuss about the case. Instead we hunkered down over enormous cardboard cups and tried to keep our chins from dipping in. After enough coffee had turned to acid in my belly, I shuffled over and ordered two apple fritters and two maple-covered pershings before asking Billy if he wanted anything.

He glowered at me, which was disproportionately funny, and I came back to the table, giggling as I handed over his share of the doughnuts. "I never did get lunch."

"So we're having doughnuts for dinner? Don't tell Melinda. I've gained twenty-eight pounds since she got pregnant and I'm supposed to be on a diet."

"You'll lose it after she has the baby. You did last time."

"Most of it." Billy looked at his fritter despondently, then shrugged and ate half of it in one bite. "Dunno why it didn't all come back off."

I grinned and slid down in my chair. The coffee—plain black this time, no flavorings to mess with the doughnuts— was starting to give me a false perkiness. "Did you get anything from Chan?" A lot of cops came to The O to do business, but not many did it so their coworkers wouldn't overhear them talking about discussions with the dead.

Billy sighed around a smaller bite of doughnut. "Not as much as I'd hoped. He didn't really know he was dead yet. Said he had a migraine when he came in. I checked his records, he had prescription medication for them. He got the light-sensitive kind, with halos and sparks, so he liked working nights. He said he had one, not enough to make him really off his game, but that he wasn't at his best. He thought the lights around the cauldron display'd set it off. Poor kid. In the end I told him to just go over to one of the quiet corners and sleep it off, that I'd clear it with Sandburg. With any luck he'll just fade out."

I licked maple frosting off my pershing while I listened. It was a disgusting habit, but I'd been eating doughnuts that way since I could remember. First maple sweetness, then cinnamony goodness beneath it, spiraled in a flat roll bigger than my palm. Yum. I had to wipe my mouth to ask, "That was it? Nothing else at all?"

Billy shook his head. "He said it was quiet, that Redding entertained him with stories about his family, but that was about it. He never saw what hit him. Usually they don't when it comes from behind."

"I don't remember seeing anything about Redding's family." I dropped my doughnut, appetite gone. "Do I need to talk to them?"

"No, Chan said they were killed in a wreck years ago. A wife and two little girls. Redding liked to talk about them, and never got married again. He still wears his wedding ring. Chan figured that was love."

"Oh." My appetite, fickle thing that it was, came back immediately upon realizing I didn't have to go break bad news to an unsuspecting wife. "That's too bad."

"Yeah. I hope we find him alive. I— Who *is* that guy?"

I turned to see Daniel Doherty opening the O's front door. I didn't think he could be looking for me specifically, unless somebody'd told him when Billy and I radioed to say we were heading back to the office, in which case I was going to pull someone's toenails out. Doherty's gaze roved over the café in the way that strangers in a strange land look: as if they know they're the wrong type to hang out there but that they're shy on choices, yet still willing to turn tail and run if the territory looks too unfriendly.

I did my best to look unfriendly.

His expression of surprise, then relief, told me that one, he hadn't been looking for me, and two, that he would now cling to me like a leech. Briefcase in hand, he scurried over to our table. "Detective Walker."

"Mr. Doherty." I had a pretty good growl when I wanted one, but it failed to deter him. He offered Billy a hand, saying, "Daniel Doherty, it's a pleasure to meet you. May I join you?"

Billy picked up on my subtle "no" signal—I was kicking him under the table—and said, "Yeah, sure, Mr. Doherty. We were just discussing a murder case. What do you do?"

I kicked him one more time. Doherty put his briefcase down, tugged the thighs of his pants up an inch and sat. "I'm in insurance. I was at your office today to talk to Detective Walker." He procured a rueful smile that was probably meant to be charming. "I've been waiting for her to come back, and someone was kind enough to tell me I could get a decent cup of coffee here."

"Why the hell are you here on a Sunday, anyway?" I demanded. "Don't you have a family to go home to?"

"Actually, no," he said pleasantly, "but I came in because I believe your schedule gives you the next two days off, and I didn't want to miss you in case you had plans that took you out of town for your weekend. Really, I won't be in your way, Detective. I'll just be an observer. I could have even done this without informing you, but that approach always makes me feel like something of a Peeping Tom. It's an unpleasant sensation."

Not nearly as unpleasant as my elbow breaking his nose was going to be. Billy looked back and forth between us like we were a Ping-Pong match. "Committing insurance fraud, Joanie?"

Of all the things he didn't need to say right then. I savaged what was left of my pershing. "It's about the vandalism Petite suffered earlier this year, you jackass. The insurance doesn't like that me and my nice neat driving record suddenly had a slew of claims even though that's exactly why I pay full coverage."

"Oh. Crap." Billy shifted uncomfortably. "Sorry. If I'd known it was Petite I wouldn't have cracked a joke."

Doherty's eyebrows went up. "Why not?"

"Because Walker has no sense of humor about her car. It's like making apartheid jokes to Nelson Mandela." Billy, coward that he was, stuffed most of his remaining doughnut into his mouth and choked it down with coffee. "I'm going to check out Redding's apartment, see if we luck out and he's home, or if anybody knows anything about enemies. See you at the office."

For a guy complaining about weight gain, he blew out of there like a race car, leaving me with Mr. Doherty. We stared at one another for a moment before he said, "I feel like we've gotten off on the wrong foot, Det—"

"There is no right foot. I gather that, short of pouring you into a concrete block and sinking you in Puget Sound, I'm not going to get rid of you. Fine. Go do your job from stalker distance. I don't want to see you again. And I swear to God, if there's one hint, one whisper, of raising my rates or not paying up, I'll have you and your company in court so fast it'll make your head spin." I didn't know if I had a leg to stand on. I didn't *care* if I had a leg to stand on. Threats made me feel better. "I have more important things to do than cater to your comfort level while you decide whether to give me the service I've been paying a premium for. Now, if you'll excuse me, my goddamn partner's not actually supposed to go visiting sites without backup, so I need to catch up with him and do my job."

I shoved away from the table and stomped out after Billy.

CHAPTER ELEVEN

Billy had the grace to look apologetic when I caught up to him. I muttered dire imprecations and we called it good without actually discussing anything, which was how I preferred to resolve temper tantrums.

Archibald Redding lived in Ballard, not particularly convenient to his job, but if he'd lived there more than a few years, it was probably right on the money for what I imagined a security guard's salary to be. There was no answer when we knocked on his door, but the building manager, a sturdy woman in her fifties, let us in without a warrant when Billy explained the situation.

The two-bedroom apartment was the epitome of a Felix bachelor's pad: tidy to the point of looking almost un-lived in. His bed was neatly made, his clothes were hung up or folded, and the bathroom sported a carefully rolled toothpaste tube and inexpensive aftershave with an inoffensive smell. A lone, clean pot in the kitchen sink and an old-fashioned teakettle on the stove suggested Redding's cooking skills were rudimentary, not that I had any room to point fingers. The building manager trailed along behind us, setting imagined wrongs to right as we went through the rooms. "He's a nice man. Always pays rent on time. Always stops to ask how you're doing. Oh, but that's what they always say, isn't it?" She put her hands over her mouth, eyes large. "'He was such a nice man.' And then you find body parts in the freezer."

Billy and I exchanged glances and I went back to pop the freezer open. It didn't even have TV dinners, much less body parts: there were carefully labeled packages of fish and chicken breasts, and bags of frozen vegetables. "He must have another freezer," I said, trying to sound cheerful and reassuring. Somehow it came out macabre, and the poor building manager made a sound of dismay. Billy gave me a look that I probably deserved, then escorted the woman toward the front door, plying her with questions: how long had Redding lived there? Did he have friends we could talk to? Had she known his family?

The opportunity for gossip snapped her right out of her worries. "Oh, no. They died a long time ago. Archie's been living here twenty years, longer than I've been managing, and it's always been just him. Seems like a real tragedy, such a nice man living on his own, but he says true love never dies, and tells stories about his little girls. We have a Tuesday-afternoon bingo game he joins us at, so I'd say all of us are friends. I can get you a list of all the names, if you like."

"That'd be great. We'll be right there." Billy smiled and the woman went hurrying off too quickly to see how his expression faded. I saw it, though, and sighed as I leaned on the frame of Archie Redding's front door.

"I guess it's romantic, but it's also kind of sad. That kind of attitude, I mean. I mean, the way Gary talks about his wife, I think she really was his true love, but he's talking about dating again. It seems like that's good. Being hung up on a life that ended twenty years ago…" I shook my head, then frowned at the sudden uncomfortable idea that I could easily be describing myself.

"Gary's dating?" Amusement danced around the edges of Billy's mouth, his own concerns dying for a moment. "How you feel about that, Joanie? I thought the old guy was your territory."

I summoned up every ounce of maturity at my disposal. "Pblthbth."

Billy laughed. "Glad we got that straightened out. What I don't get is how anybody can live in one place for two decades and not leave more mark on the space than this." He gestured back at the apartment and I turned to consider it.

"Maybe he's just waiting to die. To be back with his family. It's morbid, but why bother collecting a lot of stuff if that's all you're waiting on?"

"But no reminders of his family? No photos, no mementos? The closets were empty. There are no finger paintings or wedding pictures. It's like he's a monk."

I shrugged. "Photographs fade. Maybe it's worse to see them turning orange and sepia than to rely on the memories. I don't know. We'll ask the bingo…team. What do you call a bunch of bingo players, anyway?"

"Does there have to be a collective name for them?" We closed Redding's door and followed the building manager downstairs.

Tidy; kind; charming; sweet; not an enemy in the world: the handful of bingo players—mostly women—we were able to contact quickly all used the same words to describe Archie Redding. The other men in the group were variously out of town for the weekend, already in bed or hospitalized: Billy and I exchanged glances, decided to put off further questions until morning and retreated to the station, less defeated than simply tired.

The proverbial "They" say the first forty-eight hours are the most important in a murder case. As it happens, They're right, but we hadn't heard back from the coroner as to how long Chan'd been dead, and I was convinced we were running out of time faster than the clock read since his body'd been found. The ghosts had awakened almost eighteen hours earlier, and all I had was a suspect whose aura made him look innocent.

On the off chance that our ghosts had died the same way he did, I spent over an hour searching for bludgeoning deaths around Halloween. There were a few, but none unsolved. Billy finally got a call from the coroner reporting that Chan had died from a blunt blow to the head, probably between eleven and midnight the night before. I said, "No shit," and he spread his hands, shrugging. They were doing their best, and so were we.

His phone rang again and I muttered, "Don't tell me, they're calling back to say it might've been a sudden cessation of breathing that caused his death, too." Forensics hadn't turned up anything like a murder weapon, or even drops of blood outside the huge smear around the display area. Our killer had been tidy. Just like the missing Archie Redding. I wrote down his name and put a question mark beside it, then shook myself and tried to pay attention to Billy's report.

They *had* picked up faint streaks on the white floor, parallel and leading, more or less without breaking, to the museum's front doors. Analysis suggested they were from hard black rubber, like that which heeled the security guards' shoes, but for all I knew, they also could've been from dragging a dolly with reluctant wheels through the museum. I wasn't sure how they told the difference between one hard black rubber and another, especially on a floor that had hundreds of people tracking things over it on a daily basis. Jason's shoes had no wear along the backs of the heels, but that was inconclusive: a third party might have dragged Redding out and left the scuffs behind. I just didn't know why a hypothetical third party would kill one guard but take the other.

An unpleasant gurgle squished through my stomach. I was assuming Redding'd been alive when he'd been dragged out, if that was indeed the case. He might simply have been less of a mess, and easier to clean up after. The only way I could think to test the cauldron was to throw a dead body inside and see what happened. A security guard killed in the course of stealing it would be handier than murdering somebody else to find out if the magic worked.

I put my face in my hands, exerting enough pressure against my eyelids to hold my contacts in place while I rolled my eyes beneath them. Tears sprang up and leaked through my lashes, warning me the contacts had been in too long and my eyes were far too dry, but I didn't have spare glasses at the station. That wouldn't be a bad investment, for days like this that went on forever. I rubbed tears away and parted my fingers to look at Redding's name on the paper.

He could have looped the security tapes; he had access. And he was missing rather than proven dead. What I couldn't see was any kind of motivation. If his family had just recently died, their bodies still on hand, then maybe I could see a certain kind of madness hoping to raise them from the dead. But the accident had been more than twenty years ago, and I was pretty sure that even with modern burial techniques there wouldn't be much left to their bodies besides a few sticky smears, hardly enough to resurrect.

Which brought me back to the innocently auraed Sandburg. "Billy, is there some kind of—there's got to be. Some kind of black market in magical artifacts?" I looked up to see him put his phone against his shoulder. I'd forgotten he was on it.

"You busy tonight?"

"It *is* tonight. What time is it, like seven?" I glanced at my watch and my stomach rumbled. "If I say I'm not busy, do I get one of Melinda's home-cooked meals?"

"No. You get to meet a medium."

"I'd rather have dinner, but yeah, I can—wait, what time?"

"She likes ten o'clock."

"Really? I've always been partial to a quarter past anything." I curled my upper lip in what I hoped was an approximation of *she likes ten o'clock? what the hell is that supposed to mean?* but shrugged. "Yeah, I can do that. I've got a fencing lesson at eight, but it'll be long over by then." It might be long over by five past eight. I didn't know what I was going to say to Phoebe, which reminded me that I hadn't called Thor. My life was getting hard to keep track of.

"Arright." Billy got off the phone and reached for his coat. "I'm going to go home and kiss my wife before I stay out all night ghost hunting. I'll meet you back here at nine-thirty. Take a break and get some real food, Walker."

Granted a dispensation to stop working, I turned off my computer screen and leaned back in my chair. "Yeah. I will."

I didn't.

The morally superior thing to do would have been to follow up my own question about black-market magic. I, though, had never even pretended to be morally superior, and cut out of the office a few steps behind Billy.

Doherty was sitting in a green 1998 Mazda Miata a few spaces down from Petite when I left the precinct building. He reminded me of Laurie Corvallis, one of the local news station's reporters, who'd stalked me earlier in the year, sure she could get a story out of me. She'd been wrong, not because there was no story, but because she didn't have the eyes to see it. Much as she'd annoyed me, I'd almost felt sorry for her.

I didn't feel sorry for Doherty. I was tempted to take Petite out for a high-speed spin and lose him, but it was still raining. Besides, his entire purpose in existing, as far as I was concerned, was to prove I was a liar, a fraud artist and an unsafe driver. No way would I give him the satisfaction of being proven right. I patted Petite's dashboard as I climbed in, promising, "Another time, baby," and drove over to Thor's apartment. I figured I could earn good-girlfriend points by ordering Chinese and sacking out with him for part of an hour, even if I hadn't called like I said I would.

His monster truck wasn't in the parking lot, and the lights were out in his window. I pulled over to dig out my phone and laboriously punch in his number. My general loathing for cell phones had instilled in me an utter refusal to learn how to use them properly, although I was beginning to break down: this one asked every time if I wanted to save the number, and I knew one of these days I'd give in and do it. Not today, though. I peered up at Thor's apartment as his phone's voice mail invited me to leave a message. "Are you out having fun without me? I'm sorry I didn't call earlier. There was a murder, and…" And that was all he really needed to know to forgive me. "I'll probably be busy with it tomorrow, but if you want to have lunch, call me, okay? It's supposed to be my day off, so I can probably sneak out for an hour to eat with you. Okay. I'll talk to you later."

I hung up and looked in my rearview mirror. Doherty's Miata was idling half a block behind me. They were decent little cars, Miatas. They were certainly the right size for somebody of Doherty's build. I wondered if Petite reflected my build accurately, and was sure The Truck reflected Thor's. Amused by the idea, I drove home, changed into clothes that could both pass on a fencing strip and be wearable in public, and ate a Pop-Tart on my way out the door to the gym. I got there early, but went in anyway, pleased with the idea of leaving Doherty sitting in his car in the rain.

My next conscious thought was that my ankle hurt. I

peeled my eyes open to find Phoebe standing beside the bleachers I'd sacked out on, her foot drawn back to kick my ankle again. "Oh, you're awake. I guess that means you're not having another out-of-body experience."

"I dunno. You didn't try kicking me last time." I sat up and mooshed a hand over my face. "You showed up."

"So did you." Phoebe folded her arms. "Prove it."

"What, that I'm here?" I kicked her in the ankle, feeling as satisfied as a seven-year-old with the tactic. "Good enough?"

"Ow! Prove you're a shaman." She thrust her jaw out, glaring at me defiantly.

I sighed. "Got any hangnails?" She probably didn't. Phoebe kept her hands in beautiful condition, whereas I did well to remember to cut, not bite, my nails. "Chronic pain? Recent injury? Bad teeth?" She shook her head with each question, until I rolled my eyes. "I'm a shaman, Phoebe. Basically what I do is heal. I need to have something to heal before I can prove it."

She got a glint in her eye and headed for her fencing bag. I jumped up and ran after her, catching her shoulder. "Don't be an idiot. Hurting yourself to prove me wrong is stupid. What if I can't heal you?"

"Then you're full of shit." She pulled away and I let her go, not having much of an argument against that. "You're full of shit anyway," she said grumpily. "What kind of crap is that? Shamanism? You weren't insane yesterday."

"Yeah, I was. You just didn't know it." I went back to the bleachers and sat down, elbows on my knees and head dropped. "Look, I get it. I'm like one of those nice ladies in a long skirt with wildflowers in her floofy hair who prattles about magic and Mother Earth and spiritual guides and who are tolerated because they seem harmless enough in their obviously crazy way. Except I don't own any skirts and my hair's only floofy right when I get up. And that's more like a mohawk."

Phoebe stared at me. I suspected I wasn't helping myself. "Believe me, I was more comfortable being normal. I don't talk about it because I don't want people to look at me the way you're doing. I'm sorry I can't prove it. All I can say is for me it's real, and I'll try to keep it out of your hair if you still want to give me fencing lessons."

She echoed, "'For you it's real.' Jo, real is real. You don't get a different real than I do."

"Of course I do." I blinked, genuinely surprised. "You're five-four, I'm five-eleven and a half. We experience different realities based on that, never mind something as off the wall as shamanism. We have a lot of converging points in our realities, but you live in a reality where you need a stepladder to change a smoke alarm, and I live in one where the top shelf in the kitchen is a reasonable place to keep things I use regularly. From one perspective, me being a shaman isn't any weirder than you trying out for the Olympic fencing team."

"It's a *lot* weirder."

"Yeah?" I arched my eyebrows. "How many Olympic-class athletes do most people know?"

"How many *shamans* do most people know?"

"That's my point." I shrugged. "They're both extraordinary. I'll grant you that the difference is, if you tell people you tried out for the Olympic team, they're likely to say, 'Really? Cool,' and if I tell people I'm a shaman, they'll probably say, 'Oh, reaaalllyyy…' and be uncomfortable."

"Well, what'm I supposed to do?"

I let out a breath of semi-laughter. "I'd ignore it." I *had* ignored it, but that hadn't worked out so well for me. Phoebe, however, wasn't stuck living between my ears. "Write it off as 'oh my God, Joanne's lost her mind,' and don't worry about it any more than you'd worry about a friend who collected snow globes or something else you had no interest in. The nice thing about me is I'm not likely to regale you with stories about shamanism, whereas some of those collector types can't talk about anything else." I thought it was a very convincing argument. In fact, I sort of wondered why I hadn't thought of it before. Presumably I'd been too hung up with self-loathing and rejection. I bet this approach was much healthier.

Phoebe looked at me a long time, like if she scowled hard enough or long enough, she might worm her way inside my mind and get a better understanding of what'd gone wrong. Finally, though, she shook her head and said, "Yeah, okay, whatever," and picked up her gear bag. "Are we going to fence, or what?"

I met Billy back at the precinct building, damp with sweat but in a better humor. He said, "I guess it went okay with Pheeb," and tossed me the keys to an unmarked police cruiser. I wanted to take Petite, but with the cost of gas what it was, driving a police vehicle on police business just made the receipts easier. At least I got to drive. Not that I could remember Billy ever doing the driving since we'd been partnered.

In police academy, they'd impressed on us that there were two kinds of good drivers. One was the kind who followed all the rules, drove the speed limit, never double-parked and always wore their seat belts. I was usually that kind of driver.

But I'd also cut my driver's teeth on hairpin Appalachian roads with plunging cliffs on one side and sheer rock face on the other. I could jackass Petite around a forty-five-degree turn at speeds way above the limit without losing momentum, and I'd spent my share of time feeling like Wile E. Coyote, dangling in the air over a dark green valley when me and another driver'd met coming opposite directions on a road barely wide enough for one. Dancing a police car through road cones and driving with blown-out tires was nothing.

Suddenly, for the first time in my life, I missed North Carolina and Qualla Boundary. I said, "Huh," out loud, and Billy looked askance at me. "Nothing. Just an alarming display of internal emotional stability."

He said, "Good," dryly. "Sonata gets upset around unstable people, and I'd like her to be able to get these ghosts off me."

"Sonata? Like the musical piece? Did she name herself? Oh, God. She's a new-age hippie freak, isn't she?"

"I swear to God, Joanne, if you can't behave yourself I'm leaving you in the car."

Me and Doherty in the driveway, together but separate, leaped to mind. I shut my mouth and drove us to Sonata's house, up on Capitol Hill. It was one of those gorgeous old Victorians that requires either inheritance or obscene wealth to buy. Being a medium seemed ideal for "just happening" to come into such an inheritance.

The woman who opened the ornately windowed front door was, in fact, a long-haired hippie freak, one in her mid-sixties who'd probably never left the Woodstock era. She wore moccasins, gypsy skirts with beaded belts, and an inordinate number of rings on her thin fingers.

She also wore a black T-shirt emblazoned with a smiley face that had a splash of blood marring its cheerful yellow circle. It wasn't exactly a hippie vibe. I tried to rearrange my prejudices as she put her fists on her hips and inspected us.

Inspected me, more accurately. Billy obviously already had the all-clear, and I was just as obviously lacking. After a good long examination, she said, "Are you sure this is the one you were talking about, William? She's got skepticism written all over her."

I glanced at my hands to check, but they were, thankfully, unmarred by ink. Stranger things had happened. Billy, ruefully, said, "I'm sure. It's good to see you, Sonny." He kissed her cheek and she smiled, then offered me a hand.

"All right, come on in, unbeliever. I'm Sonata."

"I'm Joanne." I thought "Joanne" had a nicer ring than "unbeliever," but I wasn't sure Sonata would call me by it. She nodded and ushered us in.

Victorians were the ultimate houses for séances. Sonny's was brighter and more airily decorated than I expected, but it still had a sense of somber grandiosity. I hoped she'd bring us to a dark room with the requisite enormous wooden table, and was looking forward to searching it for knockers and strings, but we went into a well-lit, comfortable living room where a young man was drinking a glass of wine.

Disappointment must've shown on my face, because Sonata looked amused. "Dark corners and spooky rooms are for charlatans, Joanne. This is Patrick. He'd be my partner in crime, the one dripping cold water down gullible séance attendees' spines while I asked if they felt the icy touch of the grave, if you're trying to keep track of how I'd run my scam. Pat, this is Joanne Walker, and you know William."

"Sure. Nice to meet you, Joanne." Patrick was a little older than me and had the unaffected good looks of a California surfer boy. My opinion of what constituted a medium shifted rapidly. Not only did Sonata wear inappropriate T-shirts, but she apparently had a hot young thing to keep her company. Maybe growing up to be a hippie freak wouldn't be so bad.

The hippie freak gave me another amused smile. "I'll be turning the lights down. Spirits are more comfortable in dim lighting. But if what William says is true, you won't need light to see if what I do is real or not."

My ears got hot. "I don't know. Billy's aura doesn't change when he talks to ghosts, and I can't normally see them myself." I didn't like that I could see these ones. It suggested the cauldron—if that was the root cause—had some kind of back door into my own magic, and I had no idea how to face or even find it. "For all I know, the Sight won't show me anything with you."

Sonny tilted her head, interest piqued. "I have to go into a trance to speak with the spirits. That may be different enough to trigger your ability to detect magic." She turned a knob on the wall as she spoke, and the lights dimmed.

I yawned. Unless absolute catastrophe struck, I was going home and going to bed after this. Billy looked as if he was having similar thoughts. Sonata sat down cross-legged on a cushion, hands palms upward on her thighs, thumb and middle fingertips curved in loose circles to touch. Patrick knelt just behind her, close enough to touch, and bowed his head like a guardian angel.

The Sight winked on, lending a surreal depth to the room and making Sonata flare with yellow and red as bright as the face on her T-shirt. I wondered if she knew her aura tended toward those colors, or if it was a sort of cheery coincidence. Patrick, in comparison, glowed serene white, a bastion of calm. Sonata closed her eyes, slowing her breathing.

I turned the Sight on Billy, checking his aura and his general sense of well-being. His gray ghost cloak moved away as I watched, gathering itself in the middle of the room and quivering. For incorporeal spirits, it sure looked like they were jittery with excitement. A few tendrils still led back to Billy, as if the ghosts were anchored there, but it was clearly Sonata they were interested in now. All except one: it hung back, staying with him, and when I turned my gaze away, it teased me with the faintest shape of a child, pigtailed and open faced. She disappeared again when I looked back, and I rubbed my eyes, wondering if I was losing my mind.

Sonata said, "Restless spirits," in a vibrating deep tone completely unlike the voice she'd spoken in earlier. The ghosts snapped to attention, and so did the hairs on my arms. Even Billy jumped a bit, but Patrick remained calm and utterly steady. Presumably he'd heard the voice before, and had been expecting it. "You are welcome in my home from this moment until I bid you leave. If you would speak with us, you will agree that my voice and the words *restless spirits, begone* will send you from this place. Strike a hard surface thrice, if we're agreed."

I thought only poltergeists had the corner on making noise and pushing things over. The cyclone of ghosts spun around, then darted to the room's hearth. I heard nothing, and shot a glance at Billy, who shrugged one shoulder. Sonata, though, opened her eyes and focused on the gathering of ghosts with a satisfied nod. "We're agreed." Then dismay contorted her face and she breathed, "Oh."

Billy and I both tensed, trying to anticipate disaster. Sonata sat silent, looking at the blur of ghosts with sorrow deepening the lines in her face. I wished, briefly, that I could see what she did, and was equally glad I couldn't.

"They're children," she finally said. "So many of them are children. A girl in a pinafore, two boys in diapers, an older boy who threatens me with a slingshot, and one who's just on the childhood side of being a woman. She has the most rage in her, and anchors the others." Sonata put out a hand, an inviting gesture, and the cloud of ghosts swirled around it. She rocked back, letting go a soft sigh, and spoke again in a voice much lighter than her own: "My name is Matilda Whitehead. I will not go back into the dark."

I nearly bit my tongue in half as Sonata's colors bleached, then tinged an off-shade of green. Another face faded into existence over Sonata's, outlined in lime and making her hard to look at. I cut off a combination of a yell and a question with a strangled noise, and Billy gave me a quick look that both appreciated and approved of my rare silence. He slid to the floor so he could kneel in front of Matilda/Sonata. "There's light waiting for you, Matilda. Are you called Matilda?"

"My brothers call me Tilly, but it isn't a proper grown-up lady's name. I like Matilda."

Billy cast a brief smile at the floor, then straightened his expression before meeting Sonata's gaze again. "Matilda, then. When were you born, Matilda?"

"In the year 1887." A shadow passed over Sonata's face. "That was a very long time ago, wasn't it?"

"Yes," Billy said quietly. "Yes, it was. The others who are with you, do you know when they were born?"

Sonata turned her head to look toward the cloud of ghosts. "The twins are too little to say. Anne-Marie was born in the year 1846." Consternation creased her forehead. "Ricky says he was born in 1943, but I remember nothing but the darkness after the year 1900. There are others." Her gaze sharpened and she brought it back to Billy. "There are others with us here, but I care for the twins and Ricky and Anne-Marie. The others are not like us."

The others. Billy'd collected ghost riders of his own before he'd taken on the ones trapped in my garden. I slid a glance at him, not wanting to speak, but he understood Matilda as well as I did. "How are they different?"

"They're older." I got the sense she meant they'd died older, rather than having died earlier in terms of calendar dates. "They died in the wrong way. In the wrong times. They are not like us." Everything the girl said was delivered in a cool, precise tone, as though she disdained or mocked us. I hoped it was just a century of being dead, and that she hadn't been quite so horrible when she'd lived.

"Died the wrong way?" Billy asked diffidently. I'd seen him use the approach with his own children when they didn't want to confess to something they'd done wrong. Affected disinterest on Billy's part made admission on theirs less scary.

"They were not sacrificed." She said it with such disinterest I suddenly felt the rage behind her words. The little girl had been dead for decades. What Billy was really talking to was a fury so potent it had refused to cross over.

"Can you tell me what the sacrifice was?"

Sonata put her arms out, and a long thin line of red split each of her forearms. Then she stood, and another bloody line scoured her from throat to groin, and then again, splitting the muscles of her thighs. Magic roared to life inside me, sending me forward a few jerky inches before I realized the blood was tinged with ethereal green, and that beneath Matilda's ectoplasmic presence, Sonata's body was unharmed. She said, "Five cuts, such a pretty star," and bent forward at the waist, arms spread out to the sides. Blood dripped from her arms and torso, pooling beneath her. Then she lifted one leg, then the other, so she hung in mid-air as though she'd been lifted there on a glass plate, and blood poured from all five wounds, splashing to the floor.

To my eternal gratitude, Billy, and Patrick, who'd stood when Sonata did, looked as astounded as I felt. We all three just stared at the woman hanging in the air, none of us able to get beyond the blatantly abused laws of physics.

The blood had actually started to slow before Billy finally cranked his jaw up and said, "Thank you for showing me, Matilda. You could sit down again, if that would be more comfortable."

To everyone's relief, she did. The injuries and the blood faded away, leaving the cool-faced child to meet Billy's eyes again. He, cautiously, said, "A star has five points," and I understood what he meant: the cuts she'd shown us made four starlike points, but the fifth obvious one would be the throat, not the torso.

Matilda shrugged. "The throat is too quick. The star bleeds slow to make the potion potent." She sing-songed the words, as if they were a nursery rhyme long since committed to memory.

Billy nodded as though she hadn't said something horrifying. "And the others died in the wrong times, too," he reminded her. I couldn't have maintained the casual calm tone he used, and was two parts impressed and one part shocked that he could.

"Fifty, one hundred, fifty, one hundred." Matilda flicked her fingers dismissively, sounding suddenly bored. "There is something the woman who offered me her body should know."

Magic thumped inside me like a heartbeat, warning. I hadn't spoken in a while, and my throat was dry as I asked, "What?"

Matilda's eyes came to me, and her mouth turned to a predator's smile. "I said I would give it back. I lied."

CHAPTER TWELVE

I bolted forward, hands outstretched to—to I didn't know what, exactly, but I was by God going to try. Billy let out a yell and I dodged his grab, crashing to my knees at Sonata's side. Outraged healing power lit me up like a Christmas tree, making my flesh translucent to my own eyes. I caught Sonata's face in my hands, and beneath the quiet repose of her expression, Matilda flung her ghostly head back and shrieked with glee.

As a child, I'd gotten the idea that when I was in pain, if I could only stick a needle into the hurting part—whether it was a headache or a gassy tummy or a scraped knee—that I could draw the pain out with it and cast it away. I'd probably picked up the concept by reading about trepanation, but the point was that even as an adult, part of my brain thought it made sense.

Matilda, for all intents and purposes, became a needle pulling my pain out, except *my pain* in this case was actually my power, and I didn't want to let it go. My fingertips turned to ice against her skull, stuck like a kid who's licked a frozen pipe, and magic flowed out of me free as water. Her ichory color flushed to a healthier hue, green revitalized into a springtime shade. The other four ghosts suddenly came violently clear to me, brightening with yellow and orange and double spikes of blue for the twins. They surged forward, all eagerness to lay their hands on me. For a dizzying moment I felt myself fly apart, and doubted I'd ever come together again.

Patrick slapped his hand against my forehead, and against Sonata's, and began to shout in a language I didn't understand. Matilda laughed, a cold hard sound all wrong from a child's throat. Under the shouting, under the flood of magic rushing out of me, I heard Billy's voice, compassionate and stern: "Matilda, there's a way out for you, but this isn't it. Let us release you. We'll take what you've told us and do our best to find your murderers, but you deserve to rest now."

Her voice vaulted me out of my body, if I'd even been there anymore. I looked down at myself, feeling like I was a million miles away. A silver cord thrumming with power attached me to myself, though even as I watched, it contracted, losing cohesion as Matilda sucked magic out of me to strengthen her speech. "I don't want to rest. I want to live." For the first time she sounded like a child, full of desperation and fear. "I never had a chance to live."

"And you still won't," Billy said calmly. "This body isn't yours to take."

"She gave it to me!"

"And you agreed to leave it."

Her smile turned nasty again. "Only when she says the

words, and I won't let her. This one's power will let me keep her voice locked inside."

Gosh. Apparently there was a reason Billy'd told me not to let a vengeful spirit latch on to me. Patrick was still speaking, his voice gaining strength. I concentrated on that, trying to use it to get back to my body, but after a few seconds it occurred to me that I didn't even know the guy, and there was no reason he should be my guiding light. I wrapped my hands around the cord, which felt weak and watery even in my non-corporeal grip, and started pulling myself down.

Patrick stepped back to English and murmured, "This is your final chance, Matilda. Let us guide you through your pain and anger and into what waits beyond. It will be a better place, that much I promise you."

Sonata shuddered, as though Matilda was entrenching herself more deeply, and my body-attaching cord turned to mist. I gave a panicked yell and dived downward, slamming into my body with a sick thud. I tried shouting, "Tally ho!" because I thought it was funny, but instead I said, "Trk!" and was astonished how much effort even that much sound took.

It didn't matter. Patrick was making sound for me, a low steady murmur: *"In nomine Patris, et Filii, et Spiritus Sancti…"*

Matilda arched under his hand and gave what, under normal circumstances, I would call an unholy shriek. Right now that was too accurate, and therefore seemed inappropriate. I Saw magic release from each of the child-size ghosts, and it snapped back to me with the sting of giant rubber-band guns misfiring.

Patrick's voice rose, and then rose again, rolling over the little girl's swearing and bellowing with infinite compassion and inexorable resolve. She bucked and twisted, and while my Latin wasn't exactly fluent, even I could recognize that I was witnessing—hell, participating in—an exorcism in God's name. Billy'd told me to get a priest if he was possessed. I hadn't believed he'd really meant it until right now.

I guessed Patrick wasn't a boytoy after all.

The children winked out, leaving cold spaces where their ghosts had been. Not the coolness of dead flesh, but the absolute nothingness I'd encountered in the Dead Zone, which was so remote from the rest of the astral planes I didn't know if there was anything on its other side.

If there was, I didn't think they'd passed through to it.

Matilda tore away from Sonata's body, her aura losing the healthy color it'd stolen from me and turning discolored green again. It stretched and thinned like a snot toy flung against the wall, distorting her features until she became something alien and terrible. Her fingers turned to claws, tearing at Sonata's flesh, and finally, howling wordlessly, she boiled out of Sonata's body. Sonata collapsed into Patrick's arms, the spirit quite literally no longer moving her.

The last parts of Matilda dove forward, dissipating into me. I dove after her.

A song ran through my head: *Round and round and round she goes, where she stops, nobody knows.* I spun after Matilda without a hint of control and even less idea where we were going. If *we* were going anywhere: I had no sense of the dead girl's ghost, no feeling of her presence. For all I knew, she'd launched herself at me to give me a scare, and for all I could tell, that was all that had happened.

I broke through into the cold bleak space of the Dead Zone, and hung in its infinity with every cell in my body straining to hear or see or feel an intruder. What I got, in spades, was nothing. No ghosts. No vengeance. No giant snakes or dead shamans or spirit guides, though I'd have taken the first several gladly if I could have the last one back.

This place has much in common with dreams, Coyote'd told me. I hung on a few long seconds, forgetting about Matilda and just wishing, *wishing,* that my friend and mentor might step through the nothingness and snap his teeth at me one more time.

After what felt like forever and still no time at all, I let go, fleeing the Dead Zone and retreating to the garden at the center of my soul.

The door to the desert was closed tight, key still in place under a lump of moss. Aware I was probably risking too much, I put the key in the lock and turned it, opening the door to a sandblast of wind that came scraping down the crater my door made the inverse apex of. Magic waited at the ready, the ridiculous Trans Am all but making tire treads in the earthy floor. But no one came screaming through the door, not from either side, and I locked it again before studying my garden.

I usually looked at it with pretty normal eyes, not calling up the Sight. This time, though, I was searching for intruders, and for once in my life, put everything into it. I could taste the waterfall with my skin, hear the recovering soil with my gaze. It flowed through me, filtered by my blood and magic, and I encountered impurities by the dozens. By the thousands, but even so, I recognized them as my own. Such overblown pride, hiding uncertainty, and the same with arrogance and smart-ass commentary. Shining confidence in a few places, strong enough to become a different kind of arrogance; those were my mechanics skills, or, of all things, the ability to deconstruct a poem. There were a hundred cracks in my armor—flaws in the windshield, when I turned my metaphor to vehicular terms—but they were mine, and not streaked with Matilda's vitriolic hate.

Glad no one could see me, I folded my hands over my heart and knelt there at the southern end of my garden, hidden by mist, and called up the tiniest shield of magic possible, just a spark of blue-and-silver light starting in the core of me. It expanded with every heartbeat, slow deliberate press outward, until my arms were spread and the magic kept thrumming to greater and greater dimensions. I didn't know how long it took, encompassing the whole of my garden with that new shield, but in time I felt the new one touch the old. A thrill shot back from the melding shields, zapping into my fingertips and squirreling through my body with a joie de vivre of its own. I looked up and silver-blue shimmered overhead, shields melding like a sunset of negative colors. I thought—I hoped—nothing alien could have remained within me, not when I'd begun a new shield from something so small and close, and strengthened the old with it.

Still, it wouldn't hurt to have Sonata and Billy check me out. I stepped back into the real world.

Patrick had knelt, Sonata still cradled in his arms. My hands were fisted, something I only noticed because my nails cut into my palms. I needed to trim them. My fingernails, not my palms. I put my hands together in front of my stomach and uncurled the left with the still-knotted right hand, then made myself unfold the right fingers with my left. "What happened?"

Patrick's aura remained serene, but tempered itself toward gold, as if that was the color of his sorrow. "They've been destroyed completely. It's the worst fate I can imagine for a human soul."

"Worse than being angry ghosts for a hundred years?" My hands were cold. I was abruptly aware of how tired I was, though Patrick had done the heavy lifting in the last few minutes.

"Worse than that," he agreed quietly. "They might have found redemption, at the end, and instead chose a darker path."

"You think there's such a thing as redemption?" I wasn't sure I wanted an answer, though I didn't know what I was afraid of if he gave one. I did want an answer to, "What are you, anyway?"

"I do." Patrick was maybe the steadiest soul I'd ever laid eyes on. His voice didn't hold the richness that made some actors compelling, but his calm conviction had the same effect on me. I could listen to him read a phone book, as long as he did so with the resolution that he spoke with now. "I believe the worlds beyond ours are complex, and that we have almost no idea how we mortals interact with them. But I also believe the soul continues on, and that where spirit remains, hope resides."

Then he shrugged, becoming a little more ordinary again, and said, "I suppose I'm a theologian. I went to seminary, but I was never comfortable with some of the strictures, so I left and studied comparative religion at university instead. My mother and Sonata were great friends. I've been coming by for years when she does a séance, in case something goes wrong."

"Has it ever gone wrong before?"

"This is the second time." Patrick spread his fingers over Sonata's hair, and I finally shook myself loose from my physical stupor and came to kneel next to her. "The second I've been present for, at least. She's been doing this longer than I've been alive. Is she all right?"

Actually, aurawise, she looked fine. Tired: the yellows and reds weren't as bright, but they didn't look sickly, and Matilda's ghostly green had faded entirely. "She's just sleeping. Billy, am I clear to…?" I glanced his way, studying his aura for shadows and finding none.

"Sonny could tell you better than I can." Billy frowned at the sleeping medium. "I think they're gone."

I nodded, turning back to Sonata. Light and warmth balled in my hand, healing magic at its most simple and comforting. It dropped into Sonata's chest, and though her breathing hadn't been strained, it eased a little. She turned her face against Patrick's chest and settled in, like a child seeking protection. His aura flared, white going hard and bright. The Sight winked off, sparing me a headache. "She'll be fine. Give her a few minutes and you can wake her up."

"Thank you." It was effectively a dismissal. I got to my feet and went back to Billy, whose frown had deepened.

"I thought you couldn't see them."

"I can't. Usually. I think it's the cauldron." I pinched the bridge of my nose and wished I was wearing my glasses so I could take them off and clean them; anything that would give me something to do while I tried to sort my thoughts into language. "I think Matilda might have tried jumping into me. I didn't see her go through the Dead Zone, and I cleaned my garden as best I could and can't see her, but…"

Sonata inhaled a soft waking-up breath. Billy and I darted to Patrick's side, so we were all sort of hovering above Sonny when she opened her eyes. She looked from face to face, eyebrows rising. "That bad, was it?"

"Yoda she's become. In trouble we all are." The Sight came back on, assuring me that her colors were steady and strong. "You'll be okay."

"And will you?" Sonata's eyebrows rose and she gave me a curious glance that went on to become a careful study. "She leaped for you, didn't she? But I don't see any traces of her riding you. The exorcism may have worked. Did you learn anything from her?"

I exhaled, glad she'd given me an all-clear. "A little. We need to be looking for a murder or missing person in the year 2000. That'll give us..."

The truth was, I wasn't sure what it would give us, but I hoped it would be a tie to the cauldron. I'd feel like a prize fool if this wasn't all somehow intertwined.

"The captain's not going to be thrilled with us digging up cold cases when we've got a hot one on our hands." Billy offered Sonata a hand, but it was Patrick who helped her to her feet. She leaned on him and he kissed her temple, earning a brief, weary smile from the older woman. I re-revised my estimation of Patrick's position in Sonata's life. Exorcist, yes, boytoy, no, but they had something most people didn't manage to share with people of their own generation, much less with somebody three decades their senior or junior. The two of them made my nose all stuffy and my eyes sting, and reminded me I hadn't talked to Gary in a couple of days.

I rubbed my nose surreptitiously and cast a shrug in Billy's direction. "Maybe we'll get lucky and they'll have caught the guy. Maybe all we'll need to do is a jailhouse interview." Because the odds of having caught somebody who'd been murdering people every fifty years for at least the last two centuries were so high. I wondered what a two-hundred-year-old killer looked like. Maybe the murders were part of a fountain-of-youth ritual, but the idea of a wrinkly bag of bones slicing people up was both funnier and scarier.

Billy gave me a look that said more or less all those things, except maybe without the bag-of-bones part, then turned his attention back to the medium and her exorcist. "Are you going to be all right?"

"I'll be fine after a stiff drink or two." Sonata quirked a smile and stepped out of Patrick's embrace to give Billy a hug, then to shake my hand. "I'm sorry I wasn't more help. That doesn't happen very often."

"You not being helpful, or insane ghosts taking over your body?" Sometimes my mouth said things even my brain wished it didn't. I pulled my tongue back under control and added, "You were helpful. We know more than we did before. Thank you."

Sonata said, "You're welcome," with a hint of dryness that turned considering as she went on. "Neither happens often. Even angry spirits usually want resolution more than corporeal form, and offer all the information they can. This one…"

Her gaze went to Patrick, and he said, "Matilda," with the ease of long understanding. Sonata mouthed the name, then turned back to me.

"When the sessions are over all I remember are impressions. Usually I feel drained, like I've spilled my soul, and I'm left with a sense of relief and sometimes gratitude." She pressed a hand over her stomach, eyes closed, as if she reached for the memory of a dream. "I can feel fear and rage distantly now. From the exorcism, I think, but below that, further away… Matilda didn't have a need to share her troubles as most restless spirits do. There was too much control in her, and that…" Her eyes opened again, gaze frank and direct on mine. "That's not usual. That may well be something beyond her, controlling her. Be careful, Detective Walker."

I opened my mouth for a flippant "I always am," realized that wasn't true, and instead said, "I will be. Thanks," more subduedly than usual. Everybody exchanged a second round of goodbyes, and I got halfway out the door before my question from earlier popped into my head. I turned back to Sonata and Patrick, earning a mutter from Billy as I did so. "Sorry. One more thing. Do you guys know if there's such a thing as a magical-items black market?"

"Of course there is. The darker the art, the blacker the market." Sonata frowned. "Why do you ask?"

I lifted a finger, heading off her question with another of my own. "I know you do ghosts, not auras, but can an aura lie?"

Billy shouldered back in. "Mel'd say yes. That an aura can be tricked the same way a lie detector can be. With enough physical or emotional control, everything might read positive or negative on the polygraph, but you wouldn't be able to tell what parts of it were true or false because it all read the same. Why?"

I wiped my hand over my mouth, remembering Sandburg's steady, calm aura. "I was just thinking that if I was looking to move a big-ticket item on a black market, one way to distract from what I was doing would be to have a couple people turn up missing or dead. Sonata, do you know anybody who might deal in…?"

The medium drew herself up primly. "I don't associate with that kind of person." After a moment she relented, turning a palm skyward. "I can ask in a few places. Probably better for me to ask than to have police nosing around."

"Thank you." We did another round-robin of goodbyes, and this time got the door closed behind us before Billy said, "You're back to Sandburg, then?"

"Him or Redding, but out of the two, the cultural anthropologist fascinated by ancient legends of magic seems the more obvious option." I climbed into the car and Billy got in the other side, both of us sitting in silence for a moment. Eventually I said, "You take me to the nicest places. Murder scenes. Séances. And without even buying me dinner first."

He snorted and jerked a thumb over his shoulder, indicating we should get going. "I'll stop in the station and set up a search on unsolved cases from Y2K. Maybe we'll get a hit."

"Yeah." I had a thought I didn't like. It took the whole drive to nerve myself up to speaking. Even then, when we got back to the precinct building and I'd killed the ignition, I had to lean forward and hang on to the steering wheel before I could manage words. "Mugwitch's cauldron's been buried somewhere in Ireland for centuries, right?"

"Matholwch." Billy got out of the car, exasperated, and I followed him like a lonely puppy.

"Matholwch, Mugwitch, Mud-blood, whatever. The point is, it's been buried on the other side of the world. So if I'm right about the party ghosts being woken up by Mugwi—

Matholwch's—cauldron, we might be dealing with murders that took place in Ireland over the last several centuries."

It wasn't fair. I knew keeping things to myself was bad. From Billy's expression, I could tell voicing them wasn't exactly popular, either. He kept the hard look on his face all the way through saying, "I'm going to work with the assumption that these are local ghosts stirred up by the cauldron's presence."

"Why? Wouldn't it be better to have ritual murders linked to the cauldron? Some kind of appeasement or something?" I wasn't trying to be a smartass. I really wasn't. It just made sense to me: shake a death cauldron and ghosts come out, regardless of whether it's their home turf or not.

Billy sighed. "It'd be tidy, and I'd rather that than find out we've missed semi-centennial murders in Seattle, not that I know how we'd have caught them. It's not much of a pattern. But I don't have jurisdiction in Ireland, and neither do you. So we look where we know the territory."

I knew he was right. My mouth still went all droopy, like sugar in the rain. Billy sighed again, louder this time. "Okay, all right, fine. I'll add Interpol to the search. You're fixing the minivan for a year if it comes up dry."

It seemed like a bad time to point out I'd fix the minivan anyway. I beamed, said good-night and headed home, praying nothing would go wrong so I could get a full night's sleep.

CHAPTER THIRTEEN

Monday, October 31, 8:13 a.m.

I jolted out of bed with the conviction of a woman who's just heard the bell tolling for her. Thirty seconds later I was scrubbing shampoo out of my hair and reaching for a towel, having completed the fastest shower in human history. My heart raced from the unexpected wake up, adrenaline souring my stomach. My brain hadn't yet identified whatever noise had awakened me, but it didn't matter. I was late for work. Morrison would ride my ass and I'd deserve it. I couldn't believe I'd slept through the alarm.

I couldn't, in fact, believe that I'd gotten home and gone to bed uneventfully. My past experiences suggested I'd be up for three days straight while I tried to get the world sorted out, so I was grateful for small favors. I tore out of the bathroom and flung my clothes on, then sat down and put my forehead against my knees. I was due in at eight. In the grand scheme of things, Morrison wouldn't be any more pissed if I got in at 8:31 a.m. than at eight-thirty. Something had woken me up with a scare, and I knew by now that was a bad sign. Half a minute to figure it out wouldn't signal the end of the world. On the other hand, not taking that half minute might. Such was my life.

The panic faded from my chest, heart rate slowing. I'd been awake barely two minutes. Two minutes was a lot of time in terms of things going wrong, so whatever'd awakened me— a guttural snort, I suddenly remembered, like a wookelar from the old Tim Conway Disney film. The wookelar had been a flesh-eating monster of some kind. It was too early to deal with flesh-eating monsters. I looked for door number two.

It opened with a bolt of sunny revelation. Heat flashed up my face, reached the top of my head, got bored and rushed back down again toward my collarbone. There was no wookelar. Furthermore, I hadn't slept through the alarm. I'd turned it off because Mondays and Tuesdays were my days off.

And then I'd woken myself up with my own snoring.

Hands over my face, I toppled into my pillow and blushed until my head pounded. This was the sort of event that haunted a person through the years until she suddenly couldn't take it anymore and flung herself from a building top. Darwinian embarrassment, though in my case it was too late. I'd already passed on my genetic legacy. For a rare moment I let myself dwell on that, hoping the son I'd given up for adoption was more socially adroit than his biological mother.

Of course, Godzilla was smoother than I was. I crawled out

of bed and drank two glasses of water, trying to get the blood in my face to thin, and considered going back to bed. Starting all over again seemed like a better way to face the day than starting out by terrorizing myself with violent snoring.

Unfortunately for me, there was a fresh murder case and a whole series of stale ones to be dealt with. I was showered and dressed anyway. I shuffled into the kitchen to make myself a cup of coffee—just what my jumped-up heart rate and sour stomach needed—and shuffled out the door, coffee mug in hand, to walk into a big wall of a man with his hand raised to knock.

Actually, I narrowly missed walking into him. We froze a scant inch or two apart while the coffee sloshed and burned my fingers. I felt like a cartoon character, afraid to move for fear the ground would be gone from beneath my feet. I eased back onto my heels, finding the floor still nice and solid, then grinned and took a full step back into my doorway. "Gary."

I got a gleaming white smile in reply. "Happy Halloween, doll."

Gary Muldoon was probably the only man on earth I'd allow to call me "doll." Or "lady" or "broad," or any of the other gangster-era endearments he used, for that matter. He wasn't quite old enough to use them legitimately, at least not unless he had mafia connections he'd never mentioned, but with a name like Muldoon I didn't figure he did. On the other hand, even at seventy-three, he'd be a great piece of hired muscle: he was a bit taller than me, and still had the broad shoulders of his linebacker youth. We'd been friends since I'd jumped in his cab most of a year ago and demanded he drive me on a wild-goose chase. I'd ended up almost dead—not his fault—and the circumstances surrounding it made him decide I was interesting enough to hang with. Not that he'd used the phrase. I was just proving my street cred with it.

I lifted the hand that didn't have a coffee mug in it and mocked thwacking his shoulder. "Happy Halloween. You didn't come to my party!"

He took my coffee and slurped. "You shouldn't be drinking this stuff before we do a session. Did I miss anything? This needs milk."

I stared at my—his—coffee in dismay. "We're not doing a session this morning. I'm going to work. There was a murder."

Gary pushed past me in search of milk. I followed him and made another cup of coffee as I recounted the weekend's events. By the time I had a new mug curled protectively in my hands, Gary's craggy features had settled into an excellent approximation of a sullen child's. "And you didn't call me?"

"I thought you were coming to the party. And then it was four in the morning. Why didn't you come?" I sounded as childish as he looked. We made a great pair.

Guilt slid across Gary's face. "I was busy."

"Too busy to come to the first party I've ever hosted in my entire life? What'd you have, a hot date?"

Gary's ears turned a deep, rich red, making a brilliant contrast against white hair. I gasped, very ingenue-like, and set my coffee mug down so I could point at him accusingly. "You *did* have a date! You had a date and you didn't even tell me! Garrison Matthew Muldoon! How could you?! Who is she? Do you like her? How did it go? Are you going to see her again? Why didn't you bring her to the party? When do I get to meet her?" I was worse than somebody's mother, but

I couldn't shut up. Curious glee had my tongue and was trying for my feet. It was all I could do not to jump up and caper around.

Gary's ears turned redder. I'd never seen him blush. I hadn't known he could. He'd been the most rock-steady thing in my life the past year, and rocks weren't known for their ability to get embarrassed. Delight got the better of me and I *did* get up and dance around, waving my hands and cackling. As far as I was concerned, he deserved every chance at happiness the world could offer.

I got ahold of myself and sat back down. My cheeks hurt from laughing, and poor Gary looked discomfited. I was utterly unaccustomed to seeing him anything but ruggedly suave, and relished the change enough to reach across and pat his hand. "Never mind the third degree. You're forgiven for not coming to the party." My eyebrows waggled, entirely of their own accord. "And maybe you didn't want me calling you at four in the morning anyway. I'd hate to interrupt."

Gary hid a not-very-convincing scowl in his coffee. "I don't give you this kinda trouble over your love life."

My eyebrows, still acting on their own, shot toward my hairline. "Excuse me? Mr. I-rescued-the-phone-number-you-threw-out Muldoon doesn't mess with my love life? You must have you confused with somebody else."

He gave me another unconvincing glower. "So when're we doing your next session?"

"Way to subtly change the subject, Gar." I picked up my coffee again, studying it like it might have answers. "Probably not tomorrow, unless this thing wraps up before then. Next week, I guess."

My "sessions" had been going on for months. A couple mornings a week, Gary came over to drum me under, letting me explore the astral plane and the Middle World through shamanic eyes. I was a hell of a lot more confident in my ability to See and to heal than I'd been, and I'd scared up a lot of memories that had been buried in dreams. My spirit guide, Coyote, who turned out to be not so spirity after all, had impressed on a much younger me that one of the essential aspects of shamanism was *change*. It made sense; healing was a fundamental change, from illness to wellness. At the height of my power, when both myself and my patient fully believed in what I could do, my will alone should be able to affect a healing pretty much instantaneously. I hadn't pulled out that particular big gun since I'd finally come to understand it, but on a fundamental level, I knew I could.

The trouble was, healing was a one-shot kind of deal. It wasn't so much good against ghosts or black cauldrons. I had other rabbits in my hat: I'd learned to fight in the real world, and had armor that could travel with me to other worlds, psychic protection against battles that didn't take place on the physical plane. I could bend light around me so I became much harder to see, but even that came down on the side of parlor tricks when I was going up against ghosts.

I said, "You know," idly, half forgetting Gary was even there to answer. He grunted curiously in response and I focused on him, a little surprised. "Nothing, really. I'm just rolling around in irony. I step up, and I find out I'm still behind the eight ball. I've learned a lot, but I'm starting to think it's never going to be enough. Once, just once, I'd like to go in basically knowing what I was dealing with."

"Darlin', wouldn't we all." He stood up and leaned across the table to kiss my forehead. Coffee breath spilled down. I wrinkled my nose, but it turned into a smile as he straightened. "I'll get out of your hair so you can get to work, but you need me for anything, Jo, you call. Arright?"

"I will." I got up to hug him, and we walked down to the parking lot in companionable silence.

Billy looked as if he hadn't gotten enough sleep. I retreated from the precinct building to the Missing O, got coffee and doughnuts, and brought them over in hopes of perking him up. He took a doughnut, managing to be both grateful and imperious as he pointed it at my desk. "I didn't have to go to Interpol."

Good little automaton that I was, I went to look, and found three missing-persons reports on top of other paperwork. One was from October 29, 1950, for a Richard "Ricky" David Peterson, age seven, and the other was for twin boys born in August 1999 and reported missing fifteen months later, the day before Halloween. They were all from Seattle. I put my doughnut down, appetite lost, then picked it up and ate it anyway, because I needed more in my system than caffeine. "Anything on Matilda?"

"This is as much as we have on data file." Billy nodded toward a clock on the wall. "I'll get Jen in Missing Persons to go through the older records that aren't digital yet, once she gets in. Shouldn't take long, we've got a pretty clear window for death or disappearance. You could hit the archives and check the microfilm for news stories."

"Okay." I took my doughnut, my coffee and the missing persons files and went to Morrison's office, then stood outside it frowning at the doorknob. I was reasonably certain his office didn't have much in common with the archives, although the idea of a zillion rolls of microfilm cluttering up his tidy desk and neat bookshelves pleased me.

"Can I help you with something, Walker, or did you just want to stand around in the way all morning?" Morrison spoke from behind me, a droll note to what once would've been a wholly acerbic question. I flinched anyway and narrowly missed spilling hot liquid all over myself a second time. Too much coffee, too little food. I couldn't quite remember the last time I'd eaten something that wasn't in the doughnut family.

I said, "We have this case," somewhat inanely, and waved the papers at him. He rolled his eyes and gestured me into his office ahead of him. I went in and sat down; he came in, shrugging off the seaman's coat he usually wore in the winter, and hung it by the window. His hair was light brown, like he'd washed it six or eight times since Saturday night and the temporary coloring had almost, but not quite, let go its hold. I waved my fingers at it. "You're going to have to grow the rest of that out, you know. It's going to stay discolored."

"You never struck me as the type who knew a lot about haircoloring products, Walker." Morrison unbuttoned his suit jacket and sat down behind his desk, hands folded over his chest. He looked younger. Dark brown hair had been disconcerting and profoundly wrong, but light brown took five or six years off, turning him from an aging superhero to one in his prime. I could imagine him blond, now, and it kind of worked.

I was sure he'd be terribly relieved to hear that I'd decided his natural hair color was satisfactory. I sighed at myself and leaned forward to push the files at him. "These are part of the ruckus at the party. There was a murder yesterday at the—"

"Cultural Arts Museum. I know. Are they related?" He picked the papers up, but he watched me.

"I think so. I just don't have proof yet. And if I get any it probably won't be the kind you can present in court."

He gave a noncommittal grunt and glanced at the files. "This is from the fifties, Walker."

"And the other ones we're looking up are from the turn of the century—the last two centuries—and 1850."

I had to hand it to the man. He didn't bat an eyelash. I guessed he'd meant it when he'd assigned the weird and wacky cases to Billy and me. If we were looking up missing persons from a century ago, it seemed he trusted that was what we needed to do. All he said was, "Yesterday's security guard doesn't fit that pattern."

"Yeah." I pushed a hand through my hair and got up to go stare out his window. Morrison had a great office. Two walls were windowed, one looking over the parking lot and street, the other looking over the main precinct office area. Usually the latter was open, but he hadn't yet pulled the blinds, so we had a modicum of privacy. Or we would have, if I hadn't put myself at the outside window to show everybody I was there. Raindrops clung to his seaman's jacket, close and cool enough to make hairs rise on my arms. "I don't think there'll be another matching murder for another forty-whatever years."

"I'm all for preventing crime, Walker, but…"

"We might be able to nab two killers at once here," I said over him. "Chan's murder might lead us to the party cauldron ghosts' killer. Look, I—" I bit off my words and turned to face Morrison, frustrated. "How much explaining do you want, boss? Do you want to know how I think the knee bone connects to the thigh bone?"

Morrison lifted his eyebrows. In somebody else I might've thought the expression was hiding a laugh, but Morrison and a sense of humor about weird crap were unlikely companions. "Will it make any sense if you do?"

"If you accept the basic premise that the cauldron that's gone missing from the museum has the capability to disturb the dead, sure." Okay, I wasn't known for my sense of humor about the weird, either, but I was starting to smile by the time I got through with that. I sounded so rational, as long as I didn't listen to what I was actually saying.

Morrison's expression wiped my smile away. He just sat there, regarding me, until I figured what was left of my coffee was undrinkably cold. Then, in a voice that really did sound calm and rational, and not so much like how I'd sounded after all, he said, "What do you want from me here, Walker?"

"I want you to know I'm working on two cases," I said very quietly. "I guess I want permission. I just want you to know what's going on. I'm just trying to be…" A good cop, but that wasn't something I could say aloud to my boss. Not now, not ever. It sounded too much like I was trying to live up to his expectations of me. Which I was, but that wasn't the point. I folded my arms across my chest and found a corner to stare at, unable to meet Morrison's eyes any longer.

"Don't let the party investigation get in the way of solving Chan's murder."

"Sir." I drew myself up with something close to military precision, relieved and surprised. "I won't. Thank you."

He nodded and jerked his head toward the door all at once, effectively dismissing both me and my thanks. I collected my files and my cold coffee, and got almost all the way out the door before my body staged a coup and turned back. My voice was in on the revolution, because it said, "Captain?" very quietly, and without any noticeable input from my brain on whether it should be talking.

Morrison was already absorbed in paperwork and looked up at me with a glimmer of faint impatience and expectation. "Walker?"

My rebellious voice said, "Thank you," again, while my brain threw its hands up in exasperation. *After all,* it said, and for once I was very sure the snide little voice was a hundred percent me, and definitely something that'd been around before my powers woke up, *after all, repeating* thank-you *is going to have some kind of profound effect on the almighty Morrison. What the hell.* I didn't even know why I was repeating myself. There was probably some kind of meaningful undertone to it, but my brain and I hadn't been let in on the secret.

My boss, though, apparently had been. He looked at me a few seconds, then sighed, his shoulders dropping. "You're welcome. Now get to work, Detective."

I got.

CHAPTER FOURTEEN

The *Seattle Daily Times* archives for November 1, 1900, had a scrap of a story about Matilda Whitehead, a thirteen-year-old girl from a good family who'd gone missing the night before. A likeness had been drawn, and if I squinted just right I could see a resemblance between the ghostly green spirit and the solemn-faced child in the sketch. The paper labeled it a tragedy and warned young women of the dangers in the night.

Two days later a much more salacious story smeared itself across the front page of a Seattle broadsheet publication that had gone out of business in the 1930s. I printed the story off and took it, clenched in my fist, up to Jen in Missing Persons.

I hated the Missing Persons office. I hadn't liked it before I went all sensitive, and now just walking in there depressed me. The walls, the desks—even the floor, in places—were covered with photographs of the missing, with lists of names, descriptions, last sightings; all the things that made up lives without endings. Homicide was bad, but even the unsolved cases there had a certain finality to them. In the MPD, unsolved meant a whisper of hope, and that much hope unanswered burned a bleak mark across the department.

A tall woman—tall by most people's standards, not by mine; she was probably four inches shorter than me—with straight brown hair and a new pair of horn-rim glasses came around a file-cabinet-lined wall and said what she usually did when I came by: "Close the door, Joanne. You're letting in a draft."

"I don't think it's me. I think this whole office is just drafty by nature." I closed the door anyway, and shook Jennifer Gonzalez's hand. Jen always shook hands when she met someone, even if she'd seen them five minutes earlier. It was her way of sizing somebody up, and I'd come to suspect it had a psychic component to it. She'd been one of a very few who'd known how to offer me energy in a cohesive manner, back when I'd asked the police department to help me stop a god. We hadn't really talked about it, mostly because she was as nononsense and straight-forward as I liked to think I was, and psychic impressions weren't the sort of thing normal people discussed over coffee.

I stood there for a couple seconds trying to remember what normal people *did* discuss over coffee, then gave it up as a bad job. "I like the glasses. Didn't know you wore them."

"Thanks. I didn't used to. They make me self-conscious, but I've been wearing them three weeks, and you're only the second person who's noticed."

"At least nobody's calling you four-eyes." I tried to push my own glasses up, even though I wasn't wearing them. I didn't, usually. I'd had contacts since college, and I was always a little surprised by the leftover body language that kicked in when I thought about glasses. "Did Billy talk to you about the Whitehead case?"

"Yeah. Come on back." She led me through a maze of cabinets and paper trails to her desk, where she handed over a single-page file. "There's not much there. She went for a walk Halloween evening and disappeared off the street. Her mother swore she saw—"

"A cloaked figure snatch her up?" I gave Jen the broadsheet story in exchange. "I guess people in cloaks were probably more common in 1900 than they are now, but…"

But Edith Whitehead had described the cloaked figure as moving like an old person, too stiff and slow to possibly seize a child. She'd insisted there had been something wrong with the abductor, something inhuman and monstrous that gave it unnatural strength. The same words were on the missing-persons file, written dryly, but in the broadsheet story they carried the frantic pitch of her voice clearly enough that I could all but hear it through the century that separated us.

Both versions came to the same conclusion: Edith Whitehead was deranged, and if she'd seen her daughter's disappearance at all, it was probably because she'd had a hand in it. The police report had a note tagged on years later, relegating the Whitehead kidnapping to cold cases. I wondered if there was a similar coda to the newspaper story, writing off a family's loss as dramatics brought on by a feeble mind.

"It's all I've got," Jen said, bringing me out of my musings. "The other girl, Anne-Marie, if she died here in Seattle, it was either before there was a newspaper or law enforcement, or it didn't get reported."

"Both, probably." I frowned at the files, trying to tease a thought out of my brain. It clung stubbornly, not wanting to see the light of day. I blew a raspberry to drive off the intention of pursuing it, opened my mouth to thank Jen, and instead said, "The interesting thing is they're all white."

Ha. My brain thought it was so clever, but I could still outsmart it. I knew it'd had something to say. All I had to do was pretend I didn't care. Ha! Jen, fortunately oblivious to my internal monologue, but more or less following what I'd said, said, "Serial killers usually stay in their ethnic group, unless their actions are actually racially motivated. Which is it?"

I wobbled my head. "There pretty much weren't white people in Seattle before about 1850." Billy's history lessons were paying off. "So either we've got incoming whites, one of whom is a madman, or a local tribesman trying to scare off the incomers. I think it's the incomers."

Jen's eyebrows inched upward. "Buying into the noble savage, are we?"

I snorted. "More thinking that if you're trying to scare off newcomers, you probably wouldn't stop with murdering just one little girl. And hoping that we're lucky and our half-century killer started with Anne-Marie, so we don't have to look beyond the city for this pattern repeated." I thumped my knuckles on her desk, then dredged up a brief smile. "Thanks, Jen. I think that's probably all we need right now."

"A case file on somebody who's been missing a hundred years? Billy didn't tell me what you were working on."

My smile went all crooked and I shrugged as I headed for the door. "Ghost stories."

★ ★ ★

Halfway back to Homicide, my phone rang. I'd learned to expect bad news when it did that, so I answered cautiously, as if wrinkling my face could ward off whatever'd gone wrong. For once, though, it was a friendly voice with a friendly question: "So are you going to manage lunch today?"

"Thor! Where were you last night?" It didn't matter; I was just as glad he hadn't been sitting around waiting for me. That kind of thing never seemed like healthy-relationship material to me, not that I knew from healthy relationships. "You know what, I can do lunch. Are you at work?"

"Lemme think about that." I could envision him rolling up his sleeve to look at his watch. He wore one like mine, a big heavy Ironman plastic thing that was hard to damage. "It's ten forty-five on a Monday morning. Yep, I'm at work. Where else would I be? I got your message last night. You doing okay?" He sounded genuinely concerned, which I found charming.

"I'm good. Busy with this mess that fell in our laps. You?"

"Fine. I went out with some of the guys last night. Sorry I missed you."

"Yeah. How dare you go out and have a life without me, especially when I've forgotten to call." I grinned and ducked into the Homicide Department, where I had a whiteboard lying across my desk. It made me feel like my life was a cop drama, which had its ups, as well as its downs. On the upside, it gave me the inter-office romance storyline that usually dominated the emotional side of those shows. On the downside, it meant I was investigating murders, which sounded cooler in theory than in practice. I took a black pen and started writing on the board. "You missed out on Chinese takeaway and me, all for what, a couple beers and a game of bingo?"

Archie Redding hadn't yet been heard from. Jason Chan was dead. I drew an arrowhead between them and put Sandburg's name in between, then struck it out with a yellow pen. His aura had just been too damn clean. Thor said, "Darts, and I won seventy bucks on the game," cheerfully.

"You can buy lunch, then." I fell silent a minute, half listening to his good-natured protest as I wrote down the names of a bunch of long-dead kids on the other side of the board, and drew another arrowhead to "Shadowy Cloaked Figure." I wished the bad guys would turn up wearing meringue dresses and pompadours sometimes, instead of being so predictably dour.

Between them I drew a cauldron, complete with a zombie climbing out. Right since the very beginning of my new life, I'd been hoping there was no such thing as the undead. I figured ghosts didn't count, since they weren't corporeal. I didn't want zombies, though on a scale of one to ten, they were maybe a seven, with vampires holding the coveted ten-spot. I didn't know what went in between, but it didn't matter. I really didn't want vampires. I put the phone against my shoulder, muffling Thor's account of the darts game. "Billy, that cauldron doesn't make vampires, does it?"

He said, "No," as if I'd asked a perfectly reasonable question. "Just undead warriors. Nobody ever mentioned them being bloodsuckers."

"Good." I struck a line down the center of the whiteboard, cutting the cauldron in half, to remind myself these were two different cases. Then I circled the cauldron, because two cases or not, I was convinced it was the heart of it all. "Billy, I'm going up to the Space Needle. Want to take an early lunch?" The second part was to the phone, but Billy shook his head.

"I get indigestion from the room spinning. Oh. You weren't talking to me. So I get left behind to do the dirty work while you cost lunch to the department?"

Thor, in my ear, said, "Lemme ask Nick," and, in defiance of all the studies that said people aren't made for multitasking, I said, "Pretty much," to Billy. "I'm going to see if I can get a read on the cauldron from up there. It's a better vantage point than the museum."

"What're you going to do if you lock on?"

"Finish my salad, then call you and we can go storming in like superheroes to save Archie Redding, arrest the bad guy, retrieve the cauldron and rebind it so it stops waking up the dead." It sounded like an awesome plan. I was all for it.

"Any idea how we're going to do that last part?"

"Not a clue. Don't burst my bubble. We'll be done in time for you to take the kids trick-or-treating. What're you going to do in the meantime?"

"I'm going to see if I can connect Sandburg to any kind of black market, and maybe find some reliable backup and go talk to him again." Billy gave me a dour look that made me feel only slightly guilty. There weren't many other detectives who wouldn't snort laughter in their sleeves while Billy asked questions about a missing cauldron and a potential sale on a magical black market, but there were a couple, whereas there was literally nobody else who could do what I was planning. I was cobbling together an unconvincing apology, when Thor spoke in my ear, startling me.

"Nick says I'm cool. Think we can make it back by noon?"

For an instant I didn't know what he was talking about. So much for my amazing multitasking skills. Then I caught up with the secondary conversation and shook my head. "I think we'd be lucky to get downtown and parked, much less eat and be back here by noon." I was only exaggerating a little. "Maybe we better take separate cars. I don't think I'm coming back here after lunch, at least not right away."

"Will you reconsider if you get to drive The Truck?"

My knees went weak. I never let anybody else drive Petite, but Thor'd handed over the keys to The Truck a couple of times. Climbing up into that big tall cab was enough to set me aquiver. I'd even worn a miniskirt the second time I drove it. We'd gone to a monster-truck rally, and I figured there was nothing more awesome than looking like a real girl at a show like that. I'd gotten thunderous applause just for climbing out of the driver's seat. I still felt sexy just thinking about it, and sexy and I weren't that familiar with each other.

I groaned into the phone. If there hadn't been witnesses, I might've said I moaned, but that would've been indiscreet. "Meet me in the parking lot and we'll discuss it."

"That sounds promising." Thor hung up with an audible grin. I grabbed my coat and scurried out before anybody could give me hell about getting worked up over a truck.

Doherty's green Miata was parked next to Petite. I'd managed to forget about him, so seeing his car was almost enough to make me climb into Thor's truck and have my way with it right then and there. While I was wibbling, Thor came out of the precinct-building garage and jangled his keys, siren sound of seduction. "You know you want to."

I groaned again and caught the keys when he threw them,

but threw them back. "You're right. I do. But I can't promise to be back here by noon. I'm hoping to arrest bad guys for dessert."

"You have a bizarre idea of fun, Joanne Walker." Thor rattled the keys one more time, then swung up into The Truck's cab. Doherty leaned over his steering wheel, watching us both, and I barely restrained myself from flipping him the bird as I climbed into Petite. He smiled pleasantly and gestured for me to pull out in front of him. I did, then, swearing, drove the speed limit all the way downtown.

I found parking at the First Avenue North Garage, which, at eleven in the morning, was against all odds. Triumphant, I scampered out to leave Doherty behind. He drove around the lot once, and must've invoked some kind of higher power of parking, because by the time he got back to Petite, a late-'80s Chrysler sedan had pulled out of the spot beside her and given him room to pull in. I wanted parking karma like that, although if I had to be an insurance adjudicator to get it, I wasn't sure it was worth the cost.

At least my unwelcome shadow didn't seem inclined to follow me into buildings. He was only interested in what I did with my car. I left him behind to watch over Petite—it was my car under surveillance, so I could interpret things as I liked—and bought two tickets to the Space Needle's fiftieth-story observation-deck pinnacle. Thor met me at the elevators and a tour guide told us that the Needle was the height of eighteen hundred and fifteen Mars bars set end to end. I whispered, "When did Mars bars become a standard unit of measurement?" to Thor, and the guide gave us a dirty look when we began snickering. We couldn't help it. "Marsing" wasn't a common synonym for laughter, and she was the one who started talking in terms of candy.

The Sight washed out my normal vision as we stepped into the rotating restaurant. The food was decent but hugely overpriced, which I thought should somehow show up in astral terms, like flashing neon signs over every plate reading, *You're paying too much!* It didn't happen, though. Very disappointing. Auras ought to come with a sense of humor attached.

A pretty girl at the greeting desk said, "Two for lunch?" in a voice that did a wonderful job of belying how very bored she was. Her aura lay flat against her skin, occasionally popping, and I was fairly sure they were the aural equivalent of spit bubbles. Maybe auras had a sense of humor after all.

I said, "Yes, by the window, please," and Thor gave me a dismayed look, his own colors going flat. "You own a truck that takes a stepladder to get into, and you don't like heights?"

"The Truck is different. It's not a six-hundred-foot drop from the running board." He edged his way toward his seat when the hostess showed us to our table, and leaned toward the center of the room once he'd sat down. Blue and gray sucked up against his skin, like even his aura was nervous.

I tilted my head so I was in alignment with him. "Maybe you should ask for a seat somewhere else. I'll come find you when I'm done looking for…stuff." It wasn't that I didn't want to explain. I just didn't know how to summarize "looking for metaphysical evidence of a death cauldron's location" in ten words or less. Like that, I guess.

"Your eyes are gold." Thor spoke on top of my last few words, his aura suddenly bouncing back with interest. At least he dropped his voice to say, "You're doing magic, aren't you?"

"Yeah." I crossed my eyes like I could see their color, then blinked at him. "I needed to come up here to see if I could get a pinpoint on something, but I didn't know you were afraid of heights. If you want to move…"

"No, no, it's okay, I don't want to get in the way of your thing." His aura'd brightened right up. Apparently Joanne's Funky Eye Tricks trumped long drops. That was good to know. Wondering if he'd asked me out in the first place because I was weird was less good. Maybe he was the kind of guy who couldn't resist the strange, and dumped it once he'd figured it out.

On the positive side, I was so far from figuring myself out that presumably nobody else had a snowball's chance. I could be looking at the love of my life. "Tell me if there's anything good on the menu. I want to…" I made myself really look out the window for the first time since we'd come into the restaurant, and discovered I didn't *want to* at all.

On the Go Team Me side, I'd been right: the Needle gave a fantastic view of the city and let me see, far more clearly, the thin inky blackness spreading over it. On the not-so-great flip side, a glance was enough to tell me that the death shroud was pooling in places. I sat there, gaze bleak as the room slowly rotated to show me other stretches of city. Thor asked me something about the menu and I nodded, less than half-aware that he put in an order with the waitress a few moments later.

Areas in the city glowed with serenity. Some of those soft inviting places were parks, deliberate bastions of wilderness within Seattle's confines. Others were graveyards, and even there, bursts of light—animals, people, insects—whisked through the calm light, proving that life prevailed.

Cauldron murk clouded and gathered above the cemeteries. From the distance I was at, it looked like far-off rain clouds, seeping toward the earth without yet reaching it. Watching it set up tenterhooks under my skin, thin piercing discomfort that dug into the center of me and began pulling outward. Pulling toward the black rain, in fact, as if that was where I needed to go. That sick-stomach feeling had gotten me into the shamanic mess that was my life. Having it step up again, no longer integrated into the rest of my magic, promised all sorts of damage about to be unleashed.

I turned my wrist up like I wanted to check the time, but I already knew everything I needed to. It wasn't quite noon, a good six or eight hours before Halloween night arrived. Come sunset, the cauldron mist would touch the ground. I was sure of it. I was also pretty certain something like all hell would break loose.

"Edward?"

"Yeah?" Flashes of red came through his usual stormy colors, concern and protectiveness. He put his fork down— the waitress had brought our food, and I hadn't even noticed—to give me his full attention. Red turned orange and dulled, a visible-to-me effort to tamp down his worry. I pressed my eyes shut, as if doing so would convince the Sight to turn off and stay that way. It wouldn't work, but at least when I opened my eyes again it had left me for the moment. It made looking at him easier, although it didn't make what I had to say any smoother.

"When you get out of work tonight I want you to do me a favor. Stop at a store and get some rock salt, and then go home, lock the doors and line every window and outside door with it. If you've got any left, make paper-bag bombs with the rest, and don't answer the door for anybody until morning."

He stared at me a good long time, then cracked a grin. "Sure you don't want me to load my shotgun up?"

I wanted it to be funny. I really did. All the funny parts of me, though, shriveled up under how level my voice was: "If you've got one, do it. But don't answer the door."

Bit by bit, Thor's smile fell away. "You're freaking me out, Joanne. What are you talking about? Rock salt?"

"You should be freaked out." I was freaking myself out. I looked toward the city again, and didn't need the Sight to remember the slow black rain falling over the graveyards. My stomach jolted again. I closed my fingers against the edge of the table, afraid I might take a dive toward distant death and find that it was nearer and darker than I'd anticipated. "The books say rock salt is good against the undead."

Technically, they suggested salt was good against spirits, but it couldn't hurt to have it on hand against other things that went bump in the night. I'd be going back to the station to check out a shotgun myself, because I finally had a real clear short-term goal: do whatever it took to keep that mist from seeping into the graves. Otherwise, that small cold place in my stomach said, there would be dead men walking tonight.

CHAPTER FIFTEEN

I went back to the station primarily to check a shotgun out of the weapons locker. It took twenty minutes of paperwork and some deeply skeptical expressions when I explained I didn't need shot, just the gun, so I was still downstairs when Billy called. I put the gun down, promised I'd be back for it, and ran up to Homicide to talk to him in person.

Sonata was with him, looking more out of place in her gypsy skirts at the precinct than she had in her home. She gave me a brief smile that turned to a shake of her head. "There's hardly a soul in town with any hint or hope of the mystical who hasn't been by the museum to see that cauldron this month, Joanne, but I haven't been able to find even one person who was willing to risk stealing it. I talked to two people who had buyers make them an offer, and believe me when I say it wasn't the kind of money most people can resist. Numbers in the tens of millions."

"Christ, for that kind of money I'd steal it myself." I caught Billy's look and subsided. "So what's stopping them?"

"That depends on who I talked to." A grim note came into Sonata's voice and I had the sudden feeling her *I don't associate with that kind of person* had been far more for show than I'd realized. The genuine ability to communicate with the long-dead probably introduced her to some of what might be politely called the more unsavory elements of society. I wondered if she could scare up Jimmy Hoffa's ghost.

I bit down on that thought, too, gesturing for her to continue. She shook her head again, tiny motion that suggested she didn't even like talking about the topic. "People that I would consider good guys—" She gave me a sharp glance, like I was about to argue that anybody who stole anything wasn't a "good guy" to begin with. For once, I hadn't been going to say a word, and after an instant's silence she went on. "They wouldn't touch it because the cauldron's miasma was so deep. It's death magic, if not dark magic, and they wouldn't risk contamination."

"Can that happen?"

"Maybe. If you believe it can, maybe."

I nodded, uncomfortable with the idea. I'd brushed by enough darkness already. I didn't like the thought that some of it might latch on and corrupt me. "And the others?"

Billy folded his arms across his chest, making himself a wall. "This is the part I like. The guys who'd do it for the money and not care about the death magic wouldn't touch it because of the wards. They were too—"

"Bright," Sonata finished, when he broke off and glanced at her. "Whatever was holding the cauldron's magic under wraps was so strong it actually burned when someone with ill intent touched it. That kind of power is magnitudes beyond what most people can imagine, much less command or effect. It's like giving an infant a baseball bat. The baby can't even grasp the bat, much less wield it."

I looked between them. "So somebody who knew what they were doing wouldn't touch it, and somebody who didn't, couldn't?"

"In essence, yes. I wouldn't know how to begin breaking wards like the ones described."

"Described? I thought you said everybody in town with an inkling of magic had been by to see it."

Sonata gave me a strange little smile. "I work with the dead, Joanne. I don't care for the idea of even observing a monstrosity that's meant to tear them from their rest and force them to walk in the world again. There are those who would say we need to see evil to recognize it, but I don't feel there's any shame in turning my back on it. Sometimes denying a thing can make it lose its power."

My eyebrows shifted upward. "I guess." I'd spent too much time the past several months seeing how badly denial worked for me to agree with Sonata's choice, but it wasn't mine to make. "Well, okay, thank you. That's something, at least. The usual suspects aren't likely to be the right guys this time." Not that I had any idea, in Magic Seattle terms, who the usual suspects might *be*. It was probably something I should find out, although maybe not right now. I turned to Billy, eyebrows still elevated. "Anything on Sandburg?"

"No mystical connections I can find so far, but I'm on my way to see if I can shake anything loose in questioning. You want to come along? You're the aura reader."

I shook my head. "I can't. I've got to take care of something else. Call me as soon as you know anything, okay?"

"Yeah. You, too." Billy waved me off and I ran downstairs to get my gun.

Maybe it was the all-American good ol' boy in me, but I couldn't help feeling there was something especially sexy about a chick with a shotgun. I didn't by nature have a Southern drawl, though I defy anybody who's lived in the Carolinas for four years to come through it entirely unscathed. Even my father's accent hadn't really rubbed off on me, for all that he'd been the one who taught me to talk. I'd spent too much time on the road and heard too many different voices to sound like I was from anywhere in particular.

Walking out of the precinct building with the gun, though, made me want to roll around in being a languid, long tall drink of badass, and there was nothing better than some down-home vocal sugar to complete the picture. My personal sound track switched to a five-beat blues riff, and woe betide anybody who caused those last two da-dums to become the distinctive click of a shotgun cocking.

Plus, it made Daniel Doherty sit up and look nervous, which was a win all on its own. He didn't have to know the gun was currently unloaded, or that it would only be carrying rock salt when it was. I waved at him, which didn't seem to reassure him at all, and climbed into Petite, feeling like the sexiest damn thing on earth. Not even stopping at the supermarket to buy five pounds of rock salt was enough to undo my cool. I actually had a plan, and nothing could stop me. The fact that it wasn't a very good plan pretty much didn't bother me. It was all I had, so I was going to run with it. I got a squeeze-top bottle of water at the supermarket, too, and drank as much as I could before pouring the rest out Petite's window.

There was a new chapel outside Crown Hill Cemetery, an addition to what was essentially a neighborhood graveyard. I slipped in, refilled my bottle with water from the font and mumbled an apology to anybody who might be offended. I figured sixteen ounces of borrowed holy water was a much lesser offense than zombies lurching around Seattle.

Man, I was hung up on zombies. So far the cauldron had only stirred ghosts, but I had visions of the undead sluffing around the city, eating brains and dropping body parts as they went. I was willing to err on the side of overkill, having done too little, too late, far too often.

I walked into the cemetery with a shotgun on one hip and a plastic bottle of holy water in the other, and decided I really needed a better costume for this kind of thing than jeans and a sweater. Maybe not the warrior-princess outfit, but something involving a dramatic black coat, at the very least. Or maybe a white one, since I'd been bitching about bad guys skulking around in broody black. I'd hate to be mistaken for one of them.

Cauldron mist hung above the graveyard like soot, fine black particles drifting against one another with barely enough weight to pull them earthward. Looking at it with the Sight, it seemed like I shouldn't be able to breathe easily, but it didn't cling in my throat or chest. Not now, at least. I wasn't sure what happened when the sun went down and it became Halloween night, and I didn't much want to find out.

I found a patch of darkness, popped the top of my squeeze

bottle and spun around, spraying water in a circle around me. Heavy droplets spattered, gems of light against the black fog. Where they collided, the mist was absorbed and fell to the ground, nothing more than water, all the darkness washed away. Tiny threads of steam hissed up from the grass, then faded, leaving a smell of springtime, which was to say, rotted earth turning new again.

That was it, the sum total of my plan. Much like Richard Feynman, I'd felt it wiser to experiment without an audience before wowing the world with the shamanistic equivalent of a glass of ice water, an O-ring and my brilliance. I capered in a little dance and shook my shotgun at the sky, then sprayed another circle of holy water to watch the mist fail beneath it.

I didn't know whose belief made it work. I had theories, which had been enough to send me out to try. Holy water was new magic, which was to say it had been recently blessed, not that the idea of holy water was new. That meant it had the strength of youth, which didn't necessarily trump the treachery of old magic, but combined with my expectation of causing change, and maybe with the God in whose name the water had been blessed favoring life over death—it had been worth a shot, and whatever the reason, whatever the combination, it had worked.

Now all I needed to do was hose down every graveyard and morgue in Seattle with holy water before sunset. No problem. I had another plan. Ablaze with triumph, I sprayed the rest of the water around, then pulled my phone out of my pocket and laboriously dialed Billy's number. I had the phone to my ear and was drawing breath to make outlandish requests, when a semi-familiar girl's voice said, "Officer Walker?"

★ ★ ★

I very nearly jumped out of my skin, and given my particular talents and proclivities, that phrase could take on an unfortunate reality. Fortunately for both of us, I merely jolted around guiltily to see who'd caught me spraying a bottle of water over gravestones. I didn't think I could get nailed for vandalism, but I could certainly be run up a flagpole as a disgrace to the department. Morrison would love that.

The green-eyed girl standing a few yards away didn't look inclined to turn me in. In fact, she mostly looked lost, and maybe like she wasn't quite human, with her wraith-pale skin and wheat-colored hair. The sneakers and jeans and high-school letterman's jacket were all a bit more prosaic and grounding, but in fact, she wasn't quite human, and I knew it. My voice went up two registers. *"Suzanne?"*

Relief swept the girl's face and she ran forward to hug me, hanging on like I was the last lifeline on the *Titanic*. Bewildered, I dumped the shotgun and put my arms around her. "You're okay, Suzanne. I've got you. It's okay now."

I had no idea what was okay, and really, if she was here looking for me, it probably wasn't okay at all. That, however, didn't seem like the appropriate thing to say. Suzanne Quinley's parents had died horribly ten months earlier, and I'd been too late to save them. She'd almost had her soul stolen away by a vengeful demi-god herself, but I'd gotten there in time for that. The aftermath had sorted out that she was the granddaughter of a god, and even looking at her with ordinary eyes showed me an ethereal air. I had no idea what she would look like with the Sight, and wasn't ready to find out. I said, "You're okay," again, then carefully disengaged her from the hug and put her back a step, my hands on her shoulders. "What are you doing here, Suzy? You should be in Spokane. Is everything okay with your aunt?"

Suzy whispered, "Olympia," and I felt like a cad. One little girl mixed up with my first big encounter with the paranormal, and I couldn't even remember where she'd gone to live after her parents were murdered. "My aunt's okay. I came to find you."

"How come?" I didn't think of myself as especially good with kids, even if the kid in question was pushing adulthood. I nudged Suzy toward one of the graveyard benches and put my arm around her shoulders when we sat. "How did you find me? This isn't where I usually hang out."

"I knew you'd be here." The poor girl sounded as if she'd been crying for a week, all stuffed up and exhausted. I hugged her harder, and she thunked her head against my shoulder like I was some kind of reliable support. I put my chin on her head and tried to figure out what to say. I didn't want to shatter the illusion, but I also didn't like the sound of *I knew you'd be here*. Before I asked, she sighed miserably and said, "I know all kinds of stuff about what's going to happen now."

"Now. Since January. Since your birthday."

Suzy nodded and I bit my tongue against a thousand or so questions, instead staring across the graveyard. The Sight had turned off when Suzanne scared me, and the scene looked typical for any rainy October afternoon in a Seattle cemetery. Soft misty light with a few patches of brighter clouds in the sky taunted us with the possibility of sunshine, and headstones sat in innumerable rows, all of them looking quite fierce and protective of their unmoving charges. There was no hint of anything that said the world was other than what it appeared to be. Nothing, at least, except the presence of a fourteen-year-old girl who should've been in school sixty miles away. I said, "Okay," without especial enthusiasm, and the Sight slipped back on.

We sat on the edge of a messy circle of clean air, cauldron mist beaten down by my rainfall of holy water. Three minutes ago I'd been sure my clever trick had worked. Now I hoped I hadn't just hurried things along, though the rich warm colors of the earth around us didn't look like they were being in any way impugned upon by dark magic. The headstones *were* protective of their dead, imbued with their own rocky strength and purpose, but it wasn't the kind of presence that could fight back, if bodies should start rising. The earth could fight for itself if necessary, but people like me were supposed to come to the game on its behalf. Shamans had willpower; the earth didn't, exactly. It had an implacable sense of *being,* but it wasn't conscious the way animals were, and if something hurt it badly enough for it to fight back—well, we called those things acts of God, or climate change, and were little more than frantic parasites trying to stay alive under a planetary version of warfare.

It was a nice little philosophical consideration, and it let me not look at Suzy for a while. But that was what I'd called the Sight up for, so I sat back to take a good look at her.

I'd never really looked at her grandfather with the Sight. Doing so was rubbing grease on a fat pig's ass: he was so astonishing by nature that I imagined he'd burn my eyes out if viewed with magical vision. And if Suzanne was any indication, I was painfully right in that assessment.

She burned. Not like Sonata's friend Patrick, whose

serenity was a bastion of warmth and comfort, but like moonlight, bright enough to warn that she reflected a far greater glory. She was young, very young, and the brilliance would only grow as she aged. Loops and flares, like sunspots, already rippled across her aura. Rippled across her *skin,* in a way that auras didn't. Power was a part of her, but not like it was part of me. At the end of the day my magic, no matter how strong it might be, was only human. Suzanne's was tempered by her mortal blood, but its core was raw and chaotic. She was unbound by time, and I Saw spikes shooting off her, reaching into the future and snapping back again to give her the precognition that had brought her to me. They came as dreams and visions, interpreted by a mind that was, in most ways, only a girl's.

In most ways. Looking at her, I knew I could perhaps save the world, or at least parts of it, when I was at full power.

Suzanne Quinley could destroy it.

That seemed like a hell of a burden to lay on a kid. I put my arm around her shoulder again and tugged her back against me, my chin on her head once more. "Does everything you see come true?"

"Yeah. Everywhere." She slumped against me. "I thought I was going crazy. But then I had a dream about a soldier from Olympia dying, and two days later it was in the papers. I started checking Googe things, and then I…stopped."

"Oh, God. I would have, too." It was bad enough to be playing catch-up all the time. I couldn't imagine how much it would suck to see the future and be unable to stop what was going to happen. "I'm sorry, Suzy. I might be able to help."

There went my mouth, haring off making promises my

brain didn't know if it could keep. But really, even if she was of immortal descent, she was still a human girl, and human minds weren't meant to be unstuck in time. I might be able to heal that rift in her mind, or at least help her learn some control.

I was getting big for my britches. I barely had a handle on my own magic, and there I was thinking I could help other people learn to manage theirs. On the other hand, they said teaching is the best way to learn, so trying couldn't hurt. Much.

"Could you?" Hope spilled through her voice and I squeezed her shoulders.

"I can sure try." The promise ended with a loud rumble from my stomach. I'd had lunch at the Space Needle, but apparently all the acid caffeine had dissolved it. "But first things first. When did you eat last?"

"This morning." Suzy's tummy rumbled, too.

I pulled together a weak smile and tugged her to her feet. "There's a Denny's a few blocks away. Let me buy you lunch, and you can tell me what's been going on."

"I don't think that's a good idea." She looked up through a curtain of thin blond hair. "I don't think we have very much time. I came to find you because I've been having nightmares, Officer Walker. Nightmares about a, a—" She made a circle with her hands, uncertainty darkening her pale features. "A huge black barrel. But not a barrel, a—a something else, there's a name for it—"

I dropped my chin to my chest, eyes closed to summon the strength to say, "Cauldron?"

"Yeah! I couldn't think of the word." Suzanne lit up vocally and I glanced at her, but her pleasure slipped away as fast as it had arrived. "Nightmares about a cauldron, and about you dying in it."

After the third or fourth prediction of my death, it seemed like it should become old hat and that I wouldn't worry about it. It turned out it was still a brand-new hat, though, because even having survived my death several times now, cold slammed through my blood like an arctic wind. The breath ran out of me in a *huh,* and for a moment the world went dark, Suzanne the solitary pinpoint of light to guide me home again.

Truth was, she looked worse than I felt. I shoved a hand at my hair and clobbered myself on the head with my water bottle, which was sufficiently humiliating as to push away mindless terror with a high-pitched chuckle. I brought my voice back down to a more normal range. "I've heard that before, and I'm still standing. Don't worry, Suzy. It'll be okay."

"You don't believe me. Nobody does. I thought you would." The poor thing deflated. I'd have needed a bulldozer to make her any flatter. I put my hands on her shoulders again, trying to get her to look up. When she finally did, I pulled a smile from somewhere, and actually kind of bought into it myself.

"I do believe you. When the grandchildren of gods drop by to make dire predictions, I listen." Oh, lordy, if the me a year ago could've heard me now, she'd take the shotgun I'd abandoned and whack me over the head with it. I even had sympathy for that me wanting to do so. But at this point if a precognitive teenager turned up to tell me I was going to die, well, I was a slow learner, but not that slow. "This is probably the last question you want me to ask, but do you have any idea when?"

"Halloween," Suzanne whispered. "Today."

★ ★ ★

On the positive side, I'd gotten through more than half the hours allotted to Halloween already, and I wasn't dead yet. On the negative, that meant the next ten hours could be very hairy. I looked at my watch. The next ten hours, eleven minutes and twenty-eight seconds, to be exact. It struck me that I'd be better off wearing the copper bracelet my father'd given me than the watch. I wondered if I could to go home and get it, or if moving would alert the universe that I was now worthy of hunting. I sort of didn't want to, just in case.

Poor Suzanne's eyes filled with tears while I stood there chasing idiotic thoughts around in a circle in my mind. I sat back down and squeezed her shoulders. "It'll be okay. There's a lot of daylight left to burn. Was it nighttime in the vision?"

"Um." Her voice cracked on the single syllable, but she nodded. "It was—there were—" She dragged in a deep breath and straightened her spine. She was tall, though she probably wouldn't grow up to rival my height. Still, I sat up straighter, too, hoping it was for sorority and not machismo. "There are a lot of people in the vision. Most of them are shouting your name."

A trickle of curiosity slipped down my gullet and took up place in my diaphragm, cold and bright. "What name, exactly?"

"Joanne, Officer Walker, things like that. I don't really re-member. I just remember that you go into the cauldron."

"Ah." The spot of curiosity turned warm, as if satisfied, and I put my head in my hands. "That's okay, then. It'll be okay."

Relief broke Suzanne's voice: "It will be?"

I nodded into my hands. "Yeah. It will. I promise." Joanne

Walker could die in the cauldron, and all it would be was a shedding of another skin.

Because my name wasn't Joanne Walker.

Oh, I responded to it, certainly, the same way I responded to e-mail sent to petiteboss1969@gmail.com, but that didn't make it my name. My birth certificate read Siobhán Grainne MacNamarra Walkingstick, which was pronounced Shevaun Grania, not Seeohbawn Grainy. I'd looked up the pronunciations dozens of times and still didn't quite believe it. My father had taken one look at the Irish mess bestowed on me by my mother, and anglicized it as he saw fit. I'd been Joanne my entire life, and I'd changed my last name from Walkingstick to Walker the day I graduated high school and left my Cherokee heritage behind. Two people besides me knew my real name, and I hadn't talked to my father in years.

The other was—inevitably—Morrison. I'd confessed the truth once without meaning to, and later in far more detail while trying to save his life. Names—and truth, it turned out—had power. I'd managed to get Morrison out of trouble, but if I had to stand back and look at it, I could see how somebody might consider Joanne Walker to be a mask. She was a hell of a lot more real than Siobhán Walkingstick, who, as far as I was concerned, barely existed, but the shamanic world might well consider her to be a construct sheltering my core.

I really didn't want to give Joanne up, but part of me saw a big fat sign of inevitability hanging over my head. She could die and leave Siobhán in her place, and I suspected the result would be nothing more—or less—than my skill ratcheting up another notch. That was shamanism: that was change.

One thing was for sure, though. I didn't care how burned-down-to-essentials I got: I wasn't going to start using *Siobhán* in day-to-day life. Scary stuff happened when people got ahold of my real name, and no way was I signing up for that kind of grief on a daily basis.

I lifted my head, cheeks puffed out, and blew a raspberry at the graveyard. "Your visions, Suzy. Do you control them? Can you call one up when you want to?" I'd be impressed as hell if she could. Precognition wasn't one of my tricks, but if a fourteen-year-old me had been handed that particular bag, I'd have probably cowered under the bed until it went away.

Actually, that wasn't true. At fourteen, with Coyote's guidance in my dreams, I'd have jumped at it. I *had* jumped at the chance to become a shaman, albeit unknown to my waking self. I'd wanted to be special, and that wasn't a good place for a young shaman to start from. On the other hand, I'd needed the training. Getting it in the sleeping world had covered all the bases: it prevented me from taking the darker path my bratty teenage nature would've dictated, while also preparing me to grow into someone worthy of the power I'd been granted. It'd been working very well, right up to the point where my older self came along and stole my teenage version's studies for her own use. I had a lot to answer for, and much of it was to myself.

"You want me to see what else I can see, don't you." Suzy sounded very calm for a girl with tear tracks on her cheeks. "You want to know if I can see anything that'll help you win whatever it is you've got to fight."

"No." Somewhere in the few seconds she'd been speaking, I aged about a thousand years. "What I want is to buy you some lunch and drive you home to Olympia where you can go back to a normal life. I don't want to ask you to look to the future and watch people die."

"But you're going to anyway."

I turned my head to study the girl. Her gaze was steady, all green and full of fire, like her grandfather's. No fear, no anger, just the sort of resolution the young can cling to because they haven't yet experienced loss, and can't imagine it would ever happen to them.

Except Suzanne Quinley'd lost her whole family in one horrible afternoon, and had almost lost herself. It wasn't bravado I saw in her eyes. It was courage. More courage, I thought, than I'd ever experienced myself.

I finally nodded. "Yeah. Yeah, I am. I'm sorry, but can you See for me, Suzanne?"

"It's okay." She smiled, a sudden gentle thing, and put her hand over mine. "It's okay, Officer Walker. It's what I came here to do."

All the color spilled out of her eyes, leaving them hideous and bone white.

CHAPTER SIXTEEN

I didn't know what it was about magic that made people's eyes go funky. The first precognitive I'd known had done the same trick, and then color had bled back in, turning the irises black with hints of blue and gold around where the pupil ought to be. Suzanne's did that, too, only with green instead of blue. Mine apparently went gold when I used the Sight, and so had Billy's. Weirdly, I didn't remember the coven's collective eyes changing color when they called up earth magic. A half-formed idea that the power's source dictated the change settled in my brain and faded out. It hardly mattered right now. I could pursue it when I wasn't asking a teenager to see the future on my behalf.

The clever part of me thought it'd be safer not to use the Sight on a girl reaching for the future, especially one who burned as brightly as she did by nature. The less clever part gave over to it without much consideration. Maybe it was human curiosity; maybe it was the shaman in me, hoping I could somehow help or guide her. Either way, the Sight flickered on in the same breath that Suzanne's eyes went white, and for a little while, the whole universe stopped.

She blazed. My God, she blazed, emerald fire pouring off her so hot it turned white at its edges. The world bent toward her as though she'd become a gravity center, pulling everything askew. My breath, light stuff that it was, had no chance, and my heart began to ache as my lungs emptied. The sunspots and flares I'd seen earlier cut through time in all directions, lashing out and hauling fragments of—

Of not just the future, but possible futures. All of them, and all the possible pasts, with every decision made and every path not taken highlighted with chance and choice. Boundless chaos and unavoidable pattern tumbled together, overwhelming and inevitable all at once. Suzanne was concentrating on me, and I on her, and with both of us bound together by magic and intent, I Saw every life I might have ever led.

Moving forward from this moment, spilling literally no more than a few days into the future: Thor on his knee with a diamond ring and a nervous smile, accompanied by a rough "I thought I was going to lose you, Joanne. I'd rather not do that." Chance and choice rushed forward from there, brief examination of a surprisingly ordinary life filled with neither great regret nor great joy, making it an easy calm course to follow. A dozen similar futures splintered around that, some taking longer to come to fruition, but all of them gentle lives, quiet paths as I helped the people around me in small ways. Making a difference without risking myself: that

was the core of who I became in those worlds. I had someone to go home to, something to lose, and never strayed so
far as to lose him.

My heart twisted, longing for that comfort, but at the same
time those futures turned ephemeral, fading away. I'd already
chosen a harder road, and the ease of a tranquil family life
seemed very far away.

Backward, but not very far: Morrison standing under the
July sun in his T-shirt and dark shades, arms folded over his
chest as he asked, "Would you take a promotion?"

And that time, in that future-past, I whispered, "No,"
closing the door on an investigative position in the force and
opening one that let Captain Michael Morrison tug his shades
off, stare at me incredulously, then pull me into an abrupt hug
that felt as bewilderingly wrong as it did fundamentally right.

Sideways: a young man with my eyes and his father's straight
nose looked at me with utter exasperation, and that was a
future that sprang up no matter what path I followed. In one
branching past, I stayed in Qualla Boundary and raised my son;
in one splintering future I met him again, and either way, he
was a teen and I was his exasperating progenitor.

Back, back so far it wasn't about me anymore, but my parents. Sheila Anne MacNamarra brought a three-month-old
baby girl to Joseph Leroy Walkingstick, and her ruthless ability
to make hard choices melted under his quick warm smile. I
spirit-walked at four, in that future-past, and my imaginary
friends weren't; they were only invisible to most people. I
knew Coyote for what he was, then, and the laughing girl I
was got on a Greyhound bus to visit him in Nevada the summer I turned fifteen.

And some things were fated, it seemed, because that me got pregnant, too, but when her Coyote lover found out, he came east to Carolina and it was a cheerful pair of young idiots who got married at the winter solstice. They should have been broken, so badly broken, but instead when the twins came early, Ayita, the baby girl born first with so little strength, survived thanks to the healing magic that bloomed in both her parents. Aidan, always stronger, lived as well, and that future-past, in its way, came around to the exasperated teenage boy again. This time, though, he stood shoulder to shoulder with his equally exasperated sister.

Right there, right now, in the real world, fire scalded my cheeks, thin lines of heat and regret for a life I'd never so much as imagined. But then Morrison was there again, in another future I might never see, roaring like a bull as he stood his ground and fired his gun once, twice, again, until the clip emptied and he flipped it around to pistol-whip whatever was coming at him. Gary was there, too, a big old man with line-backer shoulders, crashing forward against a fog of darkness, and I knew that the woman I'd become wouldn't have wanted to miss those two, not for anything in this world, and maybe not even for anything in any other world, either.

I couldn't see far enough down any one path to know if the girl who'd married Coyote would've been there to fight Herne or stop a banshee. Maybe she just would've had different battles to face, and the lives I'd disrupted, failed, or saved here in Seattle would never have been bent out of shape. Maybe there were paths I could've taken, that my parents could've taken, that would've let everybody come out alive.

But maybe, just maybe, I was who and where and what I

needed to be. Maybe all the prices that had been paid were nothing more than part of the high cost of living. For all my bitching and complaining, my life was turning out okay. Too much time spent mourning what might have been seemed like a reliable way to let bad guys latch on to me and push me toward mistakes.

Another future-past whipped around me: a recognizable *me,* the Joanne Walker we all knew and loved, with almost all her same history in place, standing in Seattle's heart like she belonged there. Only one anomaly ran through her life, compared to mine: the boy was at her side, and always had been, not given up for adoption as I'd done. Magic snapped around me, blue and silver and brilliant, but the boy had his arms folded, boredom writ large through his body language.

I said, "Aidan," out loud, and with the sound of my voice the myriad futures and pasts shivered to a stop. I caught a glimpse of a classroom, and of a kid in a vampire costume bent over a school desk. He lifted his head when I spoke, curiosity filtering though his expression as he twisted around, as if he'd heard someone behind him speak his name.

Across bent space and time and three thousand miles, I met my eleven-year-old son's eyes and said, idiotically, "I really hope there's no such thing as vampires."

Aidan rolled his eyes, settling into that already-familiar look of exasperation, and went back to his schoolwork.

Suzanne whispered, "Here," with such concentration it pulled me away from regarding all my possibilities. They lashed away from me, whipcords coming unbound and cracking the air with uncontrolled sonic snaps. I flinched at each sound, but Suzy turned blind eyes on them, confidence in the set of her jaw, and a lifetime of maybes braided together into a bolt of white that struck a thin true line going forward. Chaos receded, a lesser thing than Suzanne's will, but despite the thread's brilliance, when I tried to follow it forward, I met resistance. More than resistance: I was simply forbidden that path.

True future, the usually snarky part of my brain whispered. Whatever lay on the other end of that bright line, I wasn't allowed to see it because it was my true future, and no one could walk that more than once. I didn't know where that piece of information had come from, but it was wreathed in certainty.

Suzanne, though, wasn't similarly constrained. For one, it wasn't her thread to follow. For two, I wasn't sure middling details like not being allowed to see your own future applied to the grandchildren of deities. "We're outdoors," she said in a shaking voice. "At a house. A home. There's a swimming pool with children's toys beside it. The moon is overhead, reflected in the water."

I shot a convulsive glance skyward. It'd been gray and drizzly for days, and the overcast sky gave no particular hint of wanting to clear. Even with the Sight turned to it, all I saw were heavy clouds ready to release another torrent of rain. Oddly enough, that cheered me. Maybe Suzy had the day wrong.

Because it was so easy to mistake Halloween, when people dressed up as monsters, for any other day of the year, when they mostly kept the monsters inside. For a few seconds I was tempted to go home and put on my silly leather costume. Everybody knew she was one of the good guys, and wearing a nice obvious tag like that seemed like a good idea.

"What else?" I spoke as much to guide myself as Suzy. She probably needed it less than I did, but she jolted regardless, as though she'd forgotten I was there. Maybe she had. After all, she was the one looking into a future that didn't yet exist. I'd think that could distract a person but good.

"Detective Holliday is shouting. Shouting at you. The cauldron is on fire—no, steaming, just steaming, and you—y'know," she said, suddenly sounding much more like an ordinary teenage girl. "It's really not much of a cauldron. It's just a big barrel."

The very pragmatic side of me said, "Well, you have to admit that 'Matholwch's Barrel' sounds a lot less impressive than 'Matholwch's Cauldron.' 'The Barrel of Death'? 'The Black Barrel'? One sounds like it'll just roll over you, and the other sounds like some kind of fairy tale." Of course, fairy tales didn't used to be for children. Before I said that last bit aloud, Suzy laughed, and the lancing brilliance faded from her aura to leave her with the sunspots and solar flares that were a natural part of who she was.

Pale hair curtained her face as she ducked her head, laughter fading into apology. "I lost it there at the end, when I looked at the barrel. I'm not very good at holding on."

"Good grief, kid. You gave me plenty to go on. Somebody with kids has stolen the cauldron." That seemed especially awful, somehow, and I sketched past it with a wink. "That, and this all goes down outdoors next to a swimming pool. So if I stay inside all night I should be fine."

"Then maybe we should go inside."

Retreating to an indoor sanctuary hadn't even occurred to me. Suzy was clearly much better at this whole Practical Applications of Saving the World than I was. I got up and collected my rock-salt shotgun, making certain it wasn't primed before putting it over my shoulder and turning back to Suzanne with a swagger. "Well, li'l lady, Ah reckon that thar's jist about the best ahdea Ah've heard awl day."

Suzy's giggle turned into an undignified snort that, in turn, became a blush. Ah, yes, being fourteen, when the most absurd things could haunt you to your grave. I had occasional moments of *if I only knew then what I know now,* but mostly trading in on those didn't seem worth having to be a teenager again.

All the memories of might-have-beens rushed up around me for a moment, throwing me off. Some of those possible pasts might have been worth taking a second run at it, especially if I did know then what I knew now. The happy me, the one who'd had an oddball but stable family, would have been worth it.

For an instant, that life flashed even further forward, so vivid and unexpected I didn't know if it was Suzanne's precognition showing me another splinter, or if it was my own imagination running amok. The future affected the past: Sheila MacNamarra wasn't dead in that world, and I'd never moved to Seattle. But I did come, on January third of this very year, and got into a taxi and asked the gray-eyed, white-toothed old driver to take me to a church on Aurora Boulevard. Marie d'Ambra lived in that world, as did so many others who'd been badly served by my incompetence in this one. That Joanne was so much better than I was. So much more in control, so much more centered and more stable.

And so when the battle was won and she walked around a corner near the police station to bump into a silvering, blue-eyed man of exactly her height, she knew so much more clearly what she'd lost. My hands hurt with the pulse of recognition at what she didn't have, physical ache cutting across alternate worlds to knife my breath away and take the strength from my legs.

I didn't imagine that that Joanne Walker, who called herself Siobhán Walkingstick, had ever told her Coyote husband how she'd kissed a stranger in the street and walked away from him with tears on her face. I did imagine that that Morrison wondered, time and again for the rest of his life, what the hell had happened that day. I knew, clear as if I'd lived it myself, that the Siobhán of that possible future-past spent many more long hours staring through a crack in time at the world I came from than I would spend reaching for hers. Happy was easy. Whatever I got out of my life, I was going to have to work for, and that made it all the more worth having.

God, I'd turned into Dostoyevsky. I liked the Russian writers, but that didn't mean I had to embrace their dour viewpoint. I shivered, trying to shake off the ache shared with a me from another world, and pulled together a lopsided smile for the still pink-cheeked Suzanne. Time was funny stuff, dragging you through a whole lifetime in the space of a teenager's blush.

Time was funny stuff, indeed. I drew breath to speak, and something incremental and almost unseeable happened in Suzy's face. I didn't have *time* to see it, not in any way that could be broken down and made sense of, but I saw it anyway: how the corners of her eyes, crinkled with embarrassment, widened fractionally; how the embarrassed smile just barely began to change shape. One of the articles we'd read in the academy talked about how the human face can telegraph tremendous emotion in such fine detail that our forebrains completely miss it. A few really good cops trust their hind brains, and can read the most minute expressions so well it might as well be telepathy.

I didn't know if I was a good cop or just getting to be a decent shaman. Either way, I swung away from Suzy long before even her aura started to shout alarm, and had the shotgun cocked and ready to blast before I knew what I was facing.

A cadaverous Matilda Whitehead stood before me.

No doubt attempting a dialogue would have been the morally superior course of action. Me, I went "AAAAGH!" and pulled the trigger a couple times, forgetting to re-cock the gun in between. Rock salt exploded out the first time, and nothing, of course, happened the second. I remembered to cock it again, but Matilda staggered back far enough that I didn't pull the trigger a third time. Instead I stood there panting, trying to figure out what the hell a ghost was doing in corporeal form, and how it'd snuck up on me. There weren't any freshly opened graves, and even if there had been, my rain of holy water should've done the trick. And even if there had been, again, Matilda Whitehead shouldn't have come out of one. She'd gone missing a century ago, the body never found. I seriously doubted I'd just happened on her grave site.

Her body was stitching itself back together, not in any human fashion, but with little sparks of brightness that zotted from one wound's edge to another, pulling flesh behind it. It was a special sort of awful, and I locked my knees to keep from staggering myself. I was pretty sure there were more impor-tant things to do than pass out, like wonder, once more, how a ghost had become corporeal. As far as I knew, that didn't happen. I mean, apparently it did, because it was, but it wasn't *supposed* to happen. Matilda Whitehead was not supposed to be standing in front of me, nasty lime aura overflowing a body too gaunt and inhuman to be recognizable as a specific person. Wherever she'd gotten the body, it was in lousy condition.

A layer of muscle and fat blopped out of the skeletal form as I thought that, making her a tiny bit less horrible to look on. Dizzying exhaustion swept me, and the instinctive part of my brain suggested I pull the shotgun trigger again. I did. Matilda screamed. More sparks flew, trying desperately to repair the damage I'd done. The books said salt banished ghosts. They didn't say anything about the ghosts hanging around to do a frantic patch-up job.

A piston fired way at the back of my brain. Morbid curiosity made me fire the gun again. Matilda collapsed to her knees.

So did I.

The phrase *fuck a duck* sprang to mind. I set the shotgun butt into the ground and leaned on it, trying like hell not to topple over as I dragged in a long slow breath through my nostrils. "Suzy, I think you'd better get out of here. Walk, please. Casually. I don't think that thing's fast, but I'd rather not have you running." *And looking like prey* was how that sentence finished, but I didn't want to put the idea into her head. Either "her," for that matter, just in case Matilda hadn't already decided Suzanne would be a nice tender juicy morsel.

I'd checked the garden. I'd checked the Dead Zone. Billy and Sonata had both cleared me. But it hadn't occurred to me that the last vestiges of a furious dying spirit might have managed to dive inside my magic, hiding in the very core of the healing power I had to offer. I hadn't looked there, and life magic had apparently been enough to shield her from Sonata's eyes.

Life magic, with enough outraged will behind it, was also apparently enough to create a thought-form body for a vengeful spirit to inhabit. I was goddamn lucky that the thing seemed to need active, not latent, power to feed on, or I might very well have woken up dead today.

Suzanne, bravely, if not wisely, didn't run. She screamed for help, which seemed like the other sensible option. Nobody would answer, but that didn't make it any less sensible. I might've joined her, if I'd had the breath to spare. Mine was all taken up with pushing myself to my feet again.

Fifteen feet away, Matilda did the same thing. I lifted the shotgun, but even doing so, knew it was a stopgap measure. I'd completely cut my access to my power once before, in order to keep a bad guy from gobbling up Morrison's life force. I was pretty certain I'd have to do the same thing in order to cut Matilda's lifeline. The problem—there was always a problem—was I didn't know how long she'd survive once she was cut off, and I didn't know how fast she could move. In her shoes—well, okay, in her bony rigid bare feet—I wouldn't go for me. I'd go after Suzy. So I didn't dare try it until Suzy was safe, and she, bless her pointy little head, was still screaming for help. I really didn't want to shoot Matilda again and suffer the knockback myself, but she started forward and I cocked the shotgun, not sure I'd have a choice. "Suzy, please, please, *please* get out of here. I can't fight this thing until I know you're out of reach."

She gulped her last scream and scurried away. Matilda's head snapped after the motion. Bloodless lips pulled back from gumless teeth, rictus of a smile, and she leaped toward Suzanne with all the speed I feared she might be hiding. I pulled the trigger and rock salt knocked her from the air.

Weariness lashed back at me, no physical injury, just another announcement that my power took a beating every time I blew holes in the living ghost. I managed to keep my feet that time and lurched forward, zombie-like myself, to stand over Matilda's healing body and prepare another shot.

Above me, the cloudy sky tore asunder with a rip of lightning and a roll of thunder. I flinched back a few steps, gaze yanked upward as thunder turned to the pounding of hooves, broken by the long cold call of a hunter's horn. Cawing rooks poured out of the wound in the sky, and a howling pack of white hounds, their ears tipped in red, gave chase. Finally, behind them all, thirteen riders, led by a child but commanded by a deity, crashed down toward us on a thin beam of sun.

Someone had answered Suzy after all.

CHAPTER SEVENTEEN

I had a problem with the Horned God of the Hunt: I quite simply couldn't take my eyes off him. I'd never been able to, not from the first moment he'd roared into my life, a living thing of liquid silver and burning green. Nothing had changed since then, not his anger, not his strength, not his beauty, and not my ability to be anything other than stunned by him, either.

He came at me like a flash flood, hugged close to his mercury-hued horse. They were larger than life, the pair of them, magical creatures poured from molds that humanity only dreamed of. Nearly all I could see of the god was his wildfire green eyes, blazing with intent that was wholly focused on me. Everything else about him was a blur, written in by my memory: the starlight-spattered brown hair, the terrible sharp widow's peak it fell back from and the distorted bone at his temples that would give birth to the magnificent antlers he was named for. His body was slender now, not yet changed to bear the weight of a too-heavy head, and his clothes were living silver, flowing and caressing. I'd seen otherworldly beauty time and again in the past year as I'd raced through one madcap adventure after another, but nothing held a candle to the Horned God. Like an idiot, I found myself smiling at his approach.

Cernunnos slammed by at top speed, twitching at the last second to knee me in the jaw.

From the outside it must've been fantastic to watch. I felt my whole body stretch out in slow motion, head thrown back with the impact. My hands flew up like a backstroker off the block, and for an instant my body traced a perfect arch in the air.

Then, as it was wont to do, gravity called me home with a vengeance.

I just barely broke my fall with my hands, and more or less crumpled down on myself like an accordion. Astonishment kept me in a lump on the ground; astonishment, and the distant idea that the moment I moved I was going to start hurting an awful lot. I was pretty sure I should be hurting already, but surprise held it at bay. Cernunnos and I had parted on good terms, if you called him kissing me until my knees went wobbly *good terms*. I certainly had. Maybe gods judged these things differently.

Hooves smashed around me and I coiled up with my hands over my head, yelling wordlessly. Yeah, that hurt: pain exploded through my skull in piercing shards. In fact, I thought it was likely my skull was indeed made up of piercing shards, and that all the king's doctors and all the king's men weren't going to put Jo back together again. Oh, God. That was worse than the banshee. It had been going to rhyme me to death. Now I was going to rhyme myself to death. That was so unfair.

Worse, I was clearly about a million mental miles away from the calm that might help me heal myself. I stopped yelling and just groaned, then gave that up as a bad job, too, and went right for pathetic whimpering. I hoped I'd at least chipped the bastard's kneecap with my thick head, but I was reasonably certain I'd gotten the raw end of the deal.

The hoofbeats had faded into the distance. The tiny part of me that wasn't busy being impressed with how my brain ricocheted around inside its casing informed me that they were now returning, and that I might want to do something about it. In a supreme effort of will, I rolled over in time to watch Cernunnos's stallion skid to a stop above me. It reared up, front feet pawing, and it was clear that for the second time in my life, the majestic beast had every intention of killing me.

It was probably a dumb-ass time to leave my body behind, but that's what I did.

My garden was mind-blowingly peaceful after the cacophony of the Hunt. My head didn't hurt any less, but the silence felt like a pillow around my bruises. It took a few seconds to pull myself together and tentatively probe my face. Astonishingly, there was nothing broken, just a point of swollen flesh that I bet would bleed like a stuck pig if I poked a pin in it. It was just as well I didn't have a pin. My brain thought gallons of blood squirting out of my jaw sounded kind of cool.

I wrested my mind away from that image and searched for

one that would help me fix my head. What leaped to mind were bubbles in the paint job, but I was hardly going to sand the bruise off my head and paint over it. My car metaphor didn't always work smoothly. Draining the oil would have to do, though that led back to the squirting. I gritted my teeth and imagined working a clog out of the oil filter so it could flow smoothly through the engine again. I didn't want blood clotting up my head. It needed to move away from the injury, get back into the rest of my system. *Then* I could do a touch-up on the paint job, bruise and swollen flesh smoothing away.

With the ache in my skull considerably reduced, I took the shielding I'd so poorly protected my garden with, and brought it back with me to the real world.

The stallion's hooves smashed down on shimmering silver-blue magic, clanging like steel on steel. I watched reverberations shoot up the poor animal's legs—how it had gone from *trying to kill me* to *poor animal,* I didn't know—and gave a relieved meep at not being crushed to death. The horse slipped off my shields to the ground and pranced uncomfortably. Cernunnos, about a thousand feet above me, bared his teeth and drew blade.

This was all starting to seem strangely familiar.

Sadly for me, last time I'd had a steel butterfly knife in hand, and all I had right now was a whole bunch of diddly and a big lump of squat. More, this time I had a passionate amount of really truly swear-to-God cross-my-heart hope-to-die *not wanting* to impale myself again. Or be impaled, for that matter, but there was a short sharp sword on its way down to do just that. I closed my eyes, put my hand out and hoped like hell that I was right about being able to pull a rapier through inconveniently intervening space when I needed it.

It was even money on who was more surprised, me or Cernunnos, when I did. The god's jaw dropped open in as human an expression as I'd ever seen on anything, and my face split with a relieved, foolish grin. The sword was *there,* as solidly, as reliably, as it had been in the astral plane. Moreover, my armor came with it: a copper bracelet on my wrist, silver necklace settling in the hollow of my throat and a small round shield decorating my arm. Those four items together spun a circle of brilliance around me, and their connection to one another quartered the circle with me in its center. The psychic shields I could build had nothing on what gifts of love and spoils of war offered. I knew I wasn't invincible, but in that armor, carrying that sword, I thought I might be the best me possible.

That other Joanne, the one who called herself Siobhán, could never have had all of these things because she'd never met Gary, not the way I knew him, and she never would have fought Cernunnos the way I did the first time I faced him.

Something very like joy surged through me, and I slammed my rapier into the god's sword, knocking it aside. Then, because I was an idiot and suddenly full of piss and vinegar, I scrambled to my feet. I didn't know what the hell his problem was, but he'd started it. That was fine. I'd finish it. I did the classic "c'mon, buster" hand thing, with my palm turned toward myself and my fingers crooking in invitation.

And the master of the Hunt, who wasn't any brighter than I was, drove his heels into the silver stallion's sides, accepting the challenge. The animal leaped at me with an outraged scream. I shrieked and flung myself to the side as Cernunnos's sword went whistling over my head. Next time I pick a fight with a god, remind me to make sure he gets off his horse first.

Cernunnos wheeled the stallion and charged at me again. There was no possible way I was anything other than totally screwed, but this time I did my best to stand my ground, letting his blow smash into my shield and send me spinning. On the full circle I lashed out at the stallion's flanks, feeling that it wasn't quite fair to pick on the horse, but that it was distinctly less fair to get trampled. Ol' Silver clearly wasn't accustomed to taking hits for the home team, because he bucked with a violence that surprised even Cernunnos. There was no chance the Horned God would come unseated, but it took long seconds for him to get the stallion back under control.

In the meantime, the child who led the Hunt, the pale boy Rider who was Cernunnos's only immortal son, who bound the god to a mortal cycle of life and death, and whose life I'd saved once upon a time, tapped me on the shoulder and offered me the reins to his own golden mare.

I said, "Oh *hell* yeah," and swung up on the gorgeous beast like I knew what I was doing. The young Rider stepped back with a smile on his face, the same feral thing his father could wear, then fell back farther still, to stand side by side with his niece. Suzanne's screams had long since fallen silent, and now she had both hands over her mouth and her eyes were wide and green with either astonishment or fear.

Behind her—behind them both—stood the Hunt, waiting restlessly for their master to finish his business. Men, each and every one, from the thick-shouldered bearded king whose name I knew and would never dare speak, to the slim blond archer whose longbow had driven arrows through Petite's sturdy steel body. I wondered if there were no women because women committed fewer crimes that would condemn them to an eternal ride, or if they were simply better at not getting caught.

The boy Rider flicked an eyebrow, and I stopped wondering about the sociological makeup of a mythical host of riders in order to face its leader in single combat. "Mano a mano," I said aloud, remembering.

Eager rage contorted Cernunnos's features, and we came together like goddamn Titans clashing. I saw silver peel off the edge of my rapier, a sizzling thread that fell to the ground and was smashed beneath dancing hooves. My arm wobbled with the hit, and for some reason I laughed, utterly thrilled with pitting myself against a god. I wheeled my mare around with nothing more than a lean and charged Cernunnos again, standing in the stirrups to add to my already considerable advantage in reach. He was my height, maybe even a little better than, but the sword he carried was much shorter than the rapier, and I sucked in my gut to make his passing slash a miss. He rode by, and for the first time I could remember, I twisted and shot a bolt of deep blue magic from my fingertips.

It surged out of me like a tidal wave, more draining than fighting Matilda had been. I learned two things right then: one, using my power as a weapon would probably kill me, and two, even when I was thinking in terms of weaponry, the magic itself was hard to corrupt. Light crashed into Cernunnos, knocking him from his horse, but he didn't get up again. I brought the mare around and slid from her back, sword at a god's throat.

"Do you yield?" Power danced over my skin, blue and silver

threads weaving to make a net. I could drag him all over the world if I needed to, but there was a hell of a lot of appeal in just sitting on his chest and pinning his arms down with my knees, if he seemed inclined to continue fighting.

Green fire spat through his eyes. "You've changed since we last met, little shaman."

My mouth said, "So have you," and my mind only caught up with that a few seconds later. Surprise washed through my magic, loosening it a little, and I stepped back a few inches. "You have changed, my lord master of the Hunt. Your horns are gone."

Not just gone. He'd said they grew with his power, erupting fully on the last day before he returned to Tir na nOg, the world from which he came. I expected them to be nothing more than subtle patterns against his temple now, so early in his ride. But nothing at all graced his forehead, no distortion or stretching of bone and skin. I crouched and slid my fingertips against his temple, taking victory as an excuse for intimacy, and found no rough malformation through touch, either. "Cernunnos, what happened to you? You're all wrong." Magic stirred under my skin, searching for a way to put a wild thing back together.

"We were called too early from our place beyond the stars, little shaman. This is why I came in such anger, and took you as my enemy." His wildfire gaze went to Suzanne and came back to me. "You can be a fool, Sio—"

I put my fingers over his lips. "You can call me Joanne."

Silence went on far longer than was strictly warranted. I removed my fingers, and the silence kept going, very loudly. Eventually the Horned God said, "You *are* a fool. Joanne Walk—"

"—er."

Another one of those silences happened. "C'mon," I said. "I don't go bandying your true name about. Leave mine in peace."

Green fire flashed again. "You do not know my true name."

"Totally beside the point. You're a fool, Joanne Walker. What comes next?"

The third time he drew out the silence I began to think he'd never break it again. I'd have given a great deal to know what was going on behind his brilliant gaze, but I couldn't read it any more than I could read a rock.

Actually, okay, truthfully, I could probably read quite a bit from a rock, if I turned the Sight on it. But looking at Suzy had damn near burned my eyes out, and I wasn't in a hurry to see Cernunnos in any more primal a visage than the one he presented by choice. "You're a fool, *gwyld,* but had we come through at our rightful hour, I wouldn't take you for one great enough to threaten a child of my blood. My weakness is to your benefit. Had I been at full strength…"

Gwyld. I hadn't heard that word in a while. Not since the last time I'd encountered the likes of a death god, in fact. It meant *wise man* or *shaman* in Irish, and therefore technically applied to me, though I wasn't very wise. "If you'd been at full strength you wouldn't have tried riding me down, and I wouldn't have been able to kick your ass nearly that easily." I stood up and offered Cernunnos a hand. To my eternal astonishment, he looked at it, then accepted it and let me pull him to his feet.

I'd mostly only touched him when we were trying to kill each other. He was tall and hit like a load of bricks, so I didn't expect his body weight to be negligible. I gave him a quick surprised nod, but he knotted his hand around mine and stepped in very close, gaze hot on mine. "I trust you would not have 'kicked my ass' at all, Siobhán Walkingstick."

I swallowed, trying to remember why it was I usually thought breathing was important. He smelled of the forest in autumn, rich and crackling and clean, and I thought he would taste of cold fresh water from the stream. A smile curved his mouth and he let me go, though his eyes on mine kept me as arrested as his hands might've. I was okay with that. I could happily drown in his blazing gaze. I even felt a stupid little smile start working its way into place.

A light of satisfaction flashed in Cernunnos's eyes. "Grand-daughter," he said then, and released me by looking toward Suzanne. My breath left me in a rush and I squeaked, reaching for the mare to lean against. She ignored me, ambling toward the boy Rider and Suzanne, then stood with her head between their shoulders, snuffling for treats. I was abandoned all around.

"Granddaughter," Cernunnos said again. "Why have you called me before my time?"

"And how," the boy Rider said dryly, but hushed himself when the god's glare fell on him.

Suzy ducked her head so hair curtained her face. I wanted to step forward and pull it back so I could see the three of them together, the two part-mortal descendants of the god, rude copies of his narrow elegance, and yet both fragile by human terms. She whispered, "I was scared," and looked up apologetically.

"Frightened enough to tear down walls between the worlds?" Cernunnos did what I wanted to, brushing her hair back with a light touch. His hair was ash with starlight, and hers wheat-pale, but they were of a kind. My heart twisted to see them together, a strange family torn apart by worlds and time. "What could unnerve the child of a god so badly?"

"That." Suzanne pointed beyond him, beyond me, to the thing I'd forgotten about. I turned, dismayed, to find Matilda Whitehead far less a thing of death, and much more a simulacrum of a living girl.

She might have been pretty, if her idea of herself was true. Not happy, but then, I wouldn't be happy if I was a hundred-plus years dead, either. She had a solemn face with large eyes, and dark hair tied in a neat braid and decorated with a fat, colorless bow. She was still far too thin, but no longer cadaverous; another few bursts of magic on my part, and she might work her way up to healthy, though she'd never be plump.

Cernunnos let go a breath cold enough to chill the air, and turned to me with a look of both disgust and cunning. "This is a thing that isn't meant to be, little shaman, and it's born of you and your magic."

"I know." Non-existent bugs crawled over my skin and I shuddered, trying to wipe them away. "I was trying to get rid of it when Suzy called for you."

"*Its* name is Matilda," the thought-formed ghost said in a thin voice. She watched me like I was her next and maybe only meal. Hairs stood up on my arms and I told myself—again—that there was no such thing as vampires. "I only want to live. You can give me life."

"You've been dead a hundred years. I can't do anything for

you. I'm sorry." I wasn't, very, but some bizarre form of deep-seated societal training made me say it.

"All I need is a little more of your power." She took a weak step toward me, thin body straining with effort. "Please?"

I considered it for about a nanosecond, then shot a look at Cernunnos. He was a god of death. He should know something about this sort of situation. "What happens if I do what she asks?"

To my surprise, he turned a palm up and offered an answer with the gesture. "You feed a wrongness in the worlds. Make no mistake, little *gwyld,* you and she cannot both survive. Give her what she requires, and you wipe away the years granted to you."

"Right." My voice shot up and broke on the single word. "How do I get rid of it? I can't fight it with magic."

"Ah." Fine lines appeared around the corners of his eyes, evidence of a wicked smile that barely touched his mouth. "Perhaps I can help you."

On a scale of one to ten, that was up there around vampires in its reassurance factor. My heart tried making a break for it, then, stymied by my ribs, decided squeezing down into an invisible knot would do the trick. I thumped a fist against my breastbone and coughed out a pathetic little burp before getting enough voice together to ask, "At what cost?"

"A bargain," Cernunnos offered. "You've done so well with those in the past. You cannot fight this creature, not here, not anywhere, but I can. Ride with me, Joanne Walker. Ride with the Hunt a third and final time, and I will take you so far from this place that your magic will stretch and thin, and leave nothing for your undead child to live on."

"And what do you get out of this?"

"You'll bear my mark." His eyes were brilliant, compelling green, and his smile full of delight. "You will become a part of the Hunt, and when your final day comes, you will choose to ride with me through eternity."

"I thought…" I wet my lips and tried again. "I thought I already did. Bear your mark."

"Marked for me is not the same as bearing my mark. Many mortal souls are marked for me, and I carry those souls beyond this world and into the next. Make no mistake, I shall come for thee and I shall have thee in such a way at the end of thy days, but this thing I offer now, Siobhán Walkingstick, is a thing all of its own."

I closed my eyes and murmured, "You're talking in my head again, aren't you? Thank you." He was a god. I probably couldn't stop him from flinging my name around if he wanted, but the echoing depth of his voice suggested he'd changed from spoken speech to silent. It was a gift, and I was inclined to consider it in his offer. I opened my eyes to look at him again, repeating his words in my mind. "'I'll choose to ride with you through eternity.' You mean I'd have a choice. Even if I ride with you now, when I die I'll have a choice. I could just go through the Dead Zone and on to whatever happens next. Reincarnation, if that's what's on the plate."

"You'll make the choice now, in exchange for this monster's destruction." Smooth voice, soft voice, speaking perfect reason. I put my face in my hands, then looked up over my fingertips.

"I can't. I can't make the choice now. I could lie to you, but

I won't do that. I don't know who I'm going to be when that day comes around, my lord master of the Hunt. I might need to come back around to this world more than I need to keep my promise to you. So I can't make the promise. I don't know how I'm going to get rid of this Matilda-thing, but I'm not going to lie to you to do it."

"Wise little *gwyld*." Cernunnos lifted a hand to trace the scar on my cheek. "But think on thy words, Joanne Walker. Dost thou know for certain that I mean the end of *this* mortal existence as thy final day? I would have all of you that I could, and yet even I cannot stand against the makers of the worlds."

I stared at him, heart sick and small in my chest. "What do I miss out on? If I say yes, am I walking away from…from Heaven? From some kind of end-days party that everybody else is going to be at? Do I miss out on eternity with…" *Morrison,* was how that sentence finished, but I just let it fade away.

To my surprise, amusement quirked the corner of Cernunnos's mouth. "I am neither born of your world nor of your flesh, little shaman. I have no answer for you." He inclined his head, eyes lidding to hide some of the fire in his gaze. "Choose."

I looked back at Matilda. At Suzanne and the boy Rider, and the Hunt and the world around and beyond them. The Sight washed over my vision, turning the world to a quiet haze of waiting, as though I'd stepped a little out of time. Matilda was a black streak in that, a wrongness, as Cernunnos had said; the boy Rider was more brilliant even than Suzanne.

And the god, the god himself, I finally dared turn my Sight on, and found him blazing with restraint and quiescence. There were no easy words for his colors; they were raw and hard edged, mixing and spilling together and over and under, raw chaos and primal life clinging to a slender alien form.

I put my hand in his, and joined the Hunt.

CHAPTER EIGHTEEN

The boy Rider lent me his mare again. I put my palm under her nose, an apology for not having apples or carrots. She huffed over it before dipping her head in agreement to let me ride her. I hadn't asked the first two times, and didn't know why it seemed important now. Maybe because three was a magic number. Once astride, I looked back to the graveyard and to Suzanne standing alone with the young Rider, and at Matilda staring them both down. "Are they going to be all right?"

I'd asked Cernunnos, but it was the boy who gave me another of his father's feral smiles. "I invite it to test me."

Maybe on a rational level, that wasn't the answer I should've been looking for, but on a purely emotional one, it was perfect. I guessed that, like Cernunnos, he was coming in to the height of his power. If Matilda wanted to tangle with him, I was pretty sure she'd be digging her own grave. She might not stay in it, but I had very little doubt the green-eyed boy would put her there, and hard.

In fact, I kinda wanted to stay and watch. Cernunnos swung up on his silver stallion, though, and the Hunt fell into place, hounds slinking under horse bellies and gray-beaked rooks winging overhead. "Where are we going?"

He lifted his hands, reins held loose in them, and made fists that wove and touched together and bumped apart again. "Your world," he said of one, and then of the other, "and mine."

The Hunt leaped forward, and left my world behind.

There were ways upon ways to travel between the worlds, and I was beginning to think the differences in scenery were at least partly imposed by my subconscious. Starscapes littered my idea of the space between Tir na nOg and the Middle World, which normal people would call "the earth." Those same diamond-cut lights had winked in the void between my world and Babylon, because if I was moving between worlds, there ought to by God be stars. I suspected, though, that I was traveling the Dead Zone when I crossed to different worlds, and that the differences I saw were merely cosmetic.

In either case, this place was as cold as the Dead Zone, too cold to feel heat from the infinite stars streaking by. I buried my fingers in the mare's mane and hunched against her neck as much for warmth as to simply hang on. Time, space, speed, all apparently meant very little to the Hunt, and I wasn't sure what would happen to me if I fell off out here in the far reaches of forever. I'd ridden this road before, but never in body.

My heart went into triple time when that thought came home. I'd actually physically gotten on an animal that could break through the barrier between one world and another, and had left my own world behind, all on the offer of a god who'd more than once tried to steal or seduce my soul.

I was a nice girl. Not too bright, but a nice girl.

Cernunnos, under the rush of hooves, murmured, "Home."

A recognizable longing sprang up in me. It came through the mare, or through the Hunt; came, anyway, from somewhere that lay deeper across time than I did. It clawed at my belly, sinking hooks into me, and drew an image that became more and more real as we rode toward it. A misty world of silver-barked trees with deep green leaves came into focus, and then the scent of good rich earth and clean sea air. Crystalline laughter broke on whispering wind, then died in surprise as the Hunt broke through and trotted into a courtyard shaped from living oak.

So far as I could tell, it had been the trees themselves sharing laughter. Stillness rippled out around us, quiet and comforting until I realized how complete it was. There were no birds twittering, no hum of insects, no crack of sticks or hiss of grass as animals passed through. There was only the mist, peaceful and silent, barely disturbed by the Hunt dismounting. Even the rooks went quiet, settling in trees, some to tuck beak under wing and nap, others to stare with black-eyed interest at the gathered group of demi-humans, gods and mortals. The hounds lay down, stretched out long over dew-ridden grass, and one by one the Riders faded away until I was alone in the courtyard with Cernunnos. "What happened here?"

Tragedy marred the silver god's face. "Mortals seek eternity. Immortals seek rest. It is the irony of our lives." He dismounted, the last to do so, save myself, and the stallion melted into the forest as had everyone and everything else. I stayed where I was, swaying in my saddle as he walked to a bower where twined oak reshaped itself to make a leafy seat. He loosed his sword from his hip, then sprawled in the seat, all silver and inhuman, with the sheathed blade across his thighs. "Come, let her go. We cannot do this with her here."

I put my hand on the mare's shoulder and asked what seemed like both an obvious and an idiotic question: "Who is she?"

A hint of cruel amusement curved his mouth. "Don't you know?"

All of a sudden, I did. I blanched and the mare danced, discomfited at my sudden tension. I slid off her back, trying to cobble calm back together, but she pranced away, then galloped into the forest while I stared after her. "Does he know?"

"The boy? He did once. Now?" Cernunnos shrugged, a ripple of quicksilver. "He may have bound me to time and taken my immortality for himself, but his mind is partly human. He forgets things, and in doing so saves his sanity."

"But she doesn't." I swallowed against a tight throat, glancing after the mare again. "That's why she lets me ride her. She remembers what it was to be human."

"More," Cernunnos said softly, "she remembers what it is to become entangled with one such as me. She might have taken your life that night we raced down your *highway*."

I looked back at him, strength and low certainty coming into my voice. "Not if she wanted me to rescue her son."

Cernunnos tilted his head in acknowledgment. I straightened my shoulders, trying to put the mare out of my thoughts. "Okay. So here we are. How do I take Matilda on?"

"Ah." The god slipped his sword from its sheath, dropping the latter to the side and rebalancing the short blade across his thighs, fingertips light against its broad side. "Tir na nOg is a dying world, little shaman. A dead world, perhaps, but I am its king. What magic left here is mine to command."

At least half of me listened, I swear it, but my mind hitched on the sword he'd laid across his lap. It had no crossguard worth mentioning, and the hilt was wrapped with silver wire that turned into a heavy pommel. Tir na nOg's magic being his to command was obviously important. I could see how that might affect both Matilda and myself in a battle of wits, or what have you. Instead of following that opening, though, I said, "That's a different sword."

Cernunnos turned a dry green gaze on me. For a moment I forgot about the sword, too, and just had a dizzying moment of breathlessness. He was a god and a monster who had changed his son's mother into a horse, trapping her as part of his Hunt for eternity, and yet my brain still short-circuited when he wanted it to. I needed therapy. In a voice as dry as his gaze, he said, "You stole mine, little shaman."

"Stole? You stuck it in me, not—" That wasn't actually true. I'd impaled myself, if you wanted to get technical about it. I bit my tongue to keep from getting technical, and tried another tack. "You had a broadsword at the Seattle Center in January. I thought you'd have that, or another rapier. That one's…" I had no intention of using the word that came to mind, for fear the Horned God would disapprove.

"Primitive?" he asked flatly, and since that was the word I hadn't been going to use, I gave a jerky nod. "I could not return to Tir na nOg to fetch this when you stole mine, and was obliged to use the broadsword as the only blade available to me in your world. As for this, Nuada of the Silver Hand is disinclined to present the careless with new gifts, and so this is the first sword he made for me, so long ago to name the number of years would be meaningless. The rapier was the second, fashioned at my plea for a weapon of more…"

"Elegance," I whispered. The rapier *was* elegant, and suited Cernunnos's clean, almost alien lines beautifully. So did the brutal short sword, but it made him a different manner of creature entirely. With the rapier and his silver horse, he was dangerous seduction; with the short sword, he was just dangerous, a wild god barely constrained by the shape of his calling.

I met his eyes again, found green fire burning there, and felt color suffuse my face. A smile curved his beautifully shaped mouth, and I knew all over again that it would be too easy to forget the world and join the Hunt forever. I could live in that fiery gaze, and never care that I'd have to die to do so. Seduction didn't have to be elegant to be effective.

Cernunnos lifted his fingertips from the blade and turned them up in a smooth, inviting curl. Another of Suzanne's futures flashed through my thoughts, a future where, reckless creature that I was, I stepped forward and put my hand in the god's. My power in that future rivaled his, taking me beyond humanity and the constraints put on me by my Makers. I was bound to my world just as Cernunnos was bound to Tir na nOg. Partnered together, we rode from his world to mine at will, sowing dissent like the agents of chaos we were. The Hunt rode with us, collecting the souls of those who followed old faith and older magic, and in time the child we made together battered down the walls between all the worlds. Then we were free indeed, riding to the end of the universe, hounds and rooks crying at our sides. It was beautiful, that future: beautiful and free and cold.

"Familiar temptation, my lord master of the Hunt." I took a step back, not without regret. "I'm sorry, but no."

He kept his hand extended, green fire in his eyes ablaze with undeterred hope. "A shaman is a trickster, Siobhán Walkingstick. Tricksters are things of chaos, as am I. Your path lies close to mine. Walk it with me."

"Order and learning and lessons come from trickster stories, Horned God." I wished I knew his real name, less to pull rank as to even the playing field. Honorifics were fine and well meant, but he had no compunction against pulling out *Siobhán* when there were no ears to overhear us. It only seemed fair that I should be able to return the favor.

Life, as it turned out, wasn't fair. "You ride and collect the souls of the dead. It's my job to make sure there are a few every year you don't get to take home just yet. It turned out differently in some other future, some other past. That's going to have to be your consolation prize. Now." I wet my lips. "I'm sure it's arrogant to make demands of a god, but can we stop dancing around and get to the main event?"

"So far from home, and still so bold." Cernunnos rose from his oaken throne and walked a lazy circle around me, taking in the necklace and bracelet and shield I wore. The latter had retreated to its natural form sometime during the wild ride to Tir na nOg, and was simply a purple heart medal pinned to my sweater. The rapier was on my hip, worn like it belonged there, and the god's gaze lingered on it. "I'll have that back from thee, shaman, should you lose this battle."

"If I lose I'll have bigger problems than you wanting your pointy stick back."

He quirked an ashy eyebrow and shrugged agreement. "Put these things aside, Siobhán. Here, in my home, in my court, you're far removed from the magic of your world, and the threads that bind you to your lifeless doll are thin. They must be severed, and that I cannot do when you carry tokens of battle."

My hand fell to the rapier's hilt and tightened there. "What exactly are you going to do?" That would've been a good question to ask before I joined the Hunt. Someday I'd learn to do these things in the right order. Today, however, was not that day.

Cernunnos made a broad circle with his sword, encompassing himself but clearly meaning me. "Cut a hole in this dying earth, and tear what little power it holds away. It will become a null place, a void, with you at its heart."

"That sounds…" My skin turned to ice and the cold sank inward, strangling my words. It took a couple of tries to manage, "That sounds incredibly dangerous."

Cernunnos smiled. His canines had been curved the first time I saw him, mark of the beast within. They weren't now, no more than subtle bone horn marred his temples. I wondered if this flawless figure was how he always appeared in Tir na nOg, or if having torn him out of time and place left its mark on his form even at the seat of his power. He leaned in, a silver creature of promise and threat, and breathed, "Not for me," by my ear. Then he straightened, more serious, and added, "It will be, but I know no other way to sever links between the undead and the living. Thou'rt a dead thing in thy world, *gwyld,* should you let these bonds remain."

"Why do you do that? Use thee and thou, I mean." I used the flippant question to hide my nerves as I palmed the bracelet, preparing to set it aside. Cernunnos opened his hand, and I fought the urge to refuse him and put my belongings in a tidy pile beside me. I was on his territory. It was a bad time to stop trusting him, if that's what I was doing.

He turned the bracelet in his hand, examining the ring of stylized animals that chased each other around it. "A gift from a man, but not a lover. Your father? Mortals." The last word turned sibilant, breathed out over a long while. "You put such stock and such strength into your blood ties, and are still so easily wounded by them."

"You should talk." I unclipped my necklace and handed it over with less reluctance. "Any esoteric commentary about this one?"

I wasn't even Looking at him, so to speak. The Sight had lain quiet since we'd left my world, and yet when he took the necklace, power and astonishment flared through him brightly enough to leave afterimages dancing through my vision. I rubbed one eye and blinked the other as Cernunnos gaped at the silver choker dangling from his fingers.

To the best of my ability to tell, it hadn't changed any. Tubes of silver slid over a short chain, held apart from one another by delicate triskelions. The pendant, a simple circle quartered by a cross, rocked between his fingers, like he'd let go for fear it would burn him. "It's just silver," I said in bewilderment. "It shouldn't hurt you."

"Just silver." Cernunnos lifted vivid green eyes to me, and that time I thought I saw a hint of curving canine in his smile. "It is 'just silver' no more than that rapier you carry is, no more than my own blade might be."

"Cernunnos, my *mother* gave it to m-m-muh. Me. Uh. Rapier?" My fingers drifted to the sword again. "You mean my mother gave me a necklace made by an elf king? How the hell did she get—"

"A question I, too, would like to learn the answer to." Cernunnos curved his fingers around the necklace like he'd been given something precious. I had an unholy urge to snatch it back, and, trying to quell the urge, handed over the rapier with a bit more ferocity than necessary.

"And the shield." Cernunnos extended his hand a last time, and I unpinned Gary's medal reluctantly. Of everything in my arsenal, it was the closest to my heart, both physically and emotionally. Cernunnos's fingers danced above it, then closed without touching it. "Iron. Thou has brought iron here, into my realm. Iron given to thee by one who should have died under my sword, almost a year since. Dost thou seek to outrage me, little shaman, or—"

"Oh, for pity's sake. Yes, that's exactly it, Cernunnos. Ooh, I thought, I know! I'll ride across a void between worlds, put myself entirely into the power of a god whose edges are made up of the beginnings of the universe, and then I'll *piss him off.* That was *exactly* my plan. I'm amazed it took you this long to figure it out." Somewhere in there I'd begun waving my arms with exasperation, and now I shook the medal under his nose. "Where the hell do you need me to put this thing? Is it going to burn the earth where it lies? Because if it is I'll,

I'll—" Struck by inspiration, I pulled my sweater off, planted the medal on top of nice soft wool, and dropped the whole bundle at Cernunnos's feet. "*Here,* already. For crying out loud."

Tir na nOg, it turned out, was kind of chilly. I was wearing a long-sleeved T-shirt under the sweater, but without the thick warm wool, I might as well have stripped to the skin. Cold and grumpy, I folded my arms under my breasts and glared at the god.

Who said, mildly, "I use thee and thou, little shaman, because thy scattered human mind thinks it intimate, and there is a certain delicious delight in conveying intimacies to thee."

Then he drew his sword and cut a swath of darkness around me.

Alone in the dark wasn't an entirely unfamiliar feeling. It was the stuff of nightmares, for one, and the stuff of too many clumsy spirit journeys and esoteric battles for two. That said, none of those encounters had been quite like this. Cernunnos's teasing still rang in my mind, but when it faded, not even my breath disturbed the black.

I had an uncontrollable urge to fire a magic missile at the dark, which only went to prove I spent way, way too many hours on the Internet. Lucky for me, or maybe not so lucky, *magic missile* wasn't in my repertoire, and besides, when I reached for my magic, it was gone.

Panic isn't pretty, not even when you can't actually see it taking place. I'd whined, bitched and complained about the gifts I'd been saddled with, but I was also kind of accustomed to them now, and finding a void inside me as black as the one surrounding me did nothing at all for my peace of mind. I bit back a scream, not wanting to feel it in my throat but be unable to hear it, and spun around in the darkness, trying to find any source of light or life.

And from a very far distance, something came. It was weak: fragile, even, crawling inch by inch toward me. I knew what it was long before it reached me, but misery and guilt and the human ability to look away kept me from going to it. I *didn't* look away; that much I could give myself credit for, but I didn't move, and wasn't sure if it was weakness or strength that kept me from doing so.

Matilda Whitehead's scrawny thought-form clawed its way through the dark, finally resting at my feet and twisting its neck to look up at me. It said, *I'm dying,* in words that only echoed in my ears, and I said, "I know," out loud, not knowing if either of us would hear it.

Help me.

"I can't." Can't, won't, what's the difference? The words tasted like ash in my mouth either way. "You're feeding off my energy. We can't both do that, and you're already dead. How did you get here? I thought Cernunnos cut me off from everything."

I'm part of you.

Presumably that was supposed to make sense. I looked down at the ghost-given-body, seeing her—its—scalp through too-thin hair. I was as exhausted standing over her as I'd been fighting her, but it was she who seemed to become smaller and more miserable as the minutes went on. After a while, that made sense. I closed my hands in loose fists, wishing I could undo all the things in the past few days that'd brought me to where I was right now. "So I'm basically burning up all my energy trying to stay alive in a place that doesn't allow life. And you're the most external part of my energy, so you're burning first. I'm sorry. All I'm trying to do is survive."

As am I!

God. I crouched, hands knotted more tightly. "You died a hundred years ago. I'm sorry, but you lost your chance. It's way past time to stop fighting." I didn't even know how the thing could *be* fighting. It was worse than cadaverous now. It was shrunken, all eyes and knobby joints and ill-fitting skin. "Even if you could come back, everything you know is long gone. You gave us everything you could to help solve your murder. It's time to let go, Matilda. It's time to rest."

No! The silent word bordered on a sob. I could be a hard case, but I wasn't anything like that hard. Consequences be damned, I reached for the pathetic little thing and pulled it into my arms. "Yes. Time to rest, sweetheart. Time to let go."

It—she—kicked and flailed and screamed, a thin sound with almost no strength to it. I felt every punch and twist in my gut, part of me sharing her fight more literally than I liked. She got smaller, energy fading, and I curled her against my chest, mouth lowered against her head while I murmured apologies for refusing to save a life that wasn't meant to be. I wasn't even sure the magic would let me if I could reach it; it hadn't let me heal Colin Johannsen, or even fix the thin cut on my cheek. Some things weren't meant to be made better. Weary tears slid down my cheeks as Matilda shrank away. She hadn't deserved to die a hundred years ago, and now she didn't deserve to live. Somebody was going to pay, even if I had to walk into that damn cauldron myself, and smash it from within.

I whispered, "I'm sorry," again at the last. Matilda winked out, and I was once more alone in the dark.

Only then did I wonder how Cernunnos would know it was time to free me.

CHAPTER NINETEEN

I was sitting with my arms looped around my knees, head lowered, when the light came back. It looked like a position of defeat, but I was thinking more in terms of least amount of energy expended. Being vewy vewy quiet while I waited for a god to drop in and perform a rescue seemed like the optimum choice. Besides, though I'd gotten a good night's sleep, there was something almost soothing about total sensory deprivation. As long as it didn't kill me, I kind of didn't mind drifting in it for a while.

Energy came rushing back with the light, making me feel like I'd drunk three cups of my beloved amaretto-flavored coffee. I popped to my feet, totally invigorated, and discovered I stood on a little island of earth that was completely separated from the world around it. I mean totally: it, and therefore I, was floating a few inches above the ground. It, and therefore I, wobbled precariously when I leaped to my feet, and I spread my arms to keep from falling. "Holy shit! What'd you do?"

"I cut you away from this world as much as I removed you from your own." My clod of earth thumped back down into place, and Cernunnos sank to the ground with it. He looked exhausted. As a god, he was ageless, but time had marked his face, drawing deep lines through sharp features. Even the stars in his hair seemed dimmer, making him grayer than ash, and the green fire in his eyes was dull, hardly even embers. "There was no other way to free you from your parasite."

My skin tingled with enthusiasm that my thoughts didn't share, power running at full tilt. I'd burned Matilda up, maybe, but that only meant she wasn't draining me dry. Without her using my fuel, I felt over-primed, suddenly sharp and alive and edgy. "What happened to you?"

"A deeper magic than yours lent that creature the false hope of life, little shaman. You sustained it, fed it, but your mortal depth, rich as it may be, could never have given birth to it." Cernunnos lifted his head as though it bore the full weight of his crown of horns. "I rule the Hunt, Siobhán Walkingstick. Death is my domain, and once, before the boy was born, I may have thought myself its master. I have learned better, and had never seen that which could force death to bend its knee."

I whispered, "But you're a god. What's greater than that? What happened, Cernunnos? You look…" I trailed off, then let myself choose a weak word, one that came nowhere near the truth of how he looked: "You look tired."

All around me, Tir na nOg reflected the state of its god. The mists were heavier, and green-leafed trees had turned to brown. The air smelled of dust and rotting earth, like a graveyard. I dropped to my knees and buried my fingers in the cracked dirt, much as I'd done very recently in my own garden, and wondered, half seriously, if this whole world was Cernunnos's garden.

"Stripping your power from your black rider bared its genesis to me." A glint of humor brightened his eyes, if only briefly. "Some things not even gods are meant to see, little shaman. Be glad it was I who cut you away from all the worlds, for if you'd tried it yourself, you would soon be buried here, in the soft damp earth of Tir na nOg."

"But the ground is dry." That seemed terribly important somehow, the bits of dirt that crumbled under the pressure from my fingers. This world's peace was in its misty shadows and whispering trees. The vitality shouldn't drain out of it like water through a sieve. "What did you see? The cauldron?"

"Its maker," Cernunnos said, "its master." He curled up on the yellowing grass, tucking his head around more like a deer than a man, as though seeking comfort and warmth from his own body. "The boy will take the lead in the Hunt, Siobhán Walkingstick, and it will, as ever, need its thirteenth to ride with it. Join them now, little shaman, thy life for mine."

I lowered my head, fingers knotting deeper in the earth. My first journeys into the astral plane had brought me through a wonderland of color and spirit, from snowy, white blossoming trees to pathways cutting through mountains. There had been a cave off to my left, always off to my left, as though it was connected to my heart, and within that cave was a presence. I didn't know who or what he was, only that he was infinitely powerful, and that he regarded me as an amusing trinket to be dealt with in some indeterminate future. His very existence compelled me to seek him out, though the first time I'd crossed through there I'd been just barely smart enough not to. The second time, my dead mother had utterly kicked my pansy ass to prevent me from going to him.

A banshee had named it the Master, right before I'd ripped its shrieky banshee head off. Since then, I'd barely encountered him in my astral travels, and nothing I'd faced had mentioned it. Not until now, anyway. Cernunnos hadn't made the word *master* a title like the banshee had, but it resonated through me like a plucked bowstring.

Something had made the cauldron, once upon a time. Something strong enough to kill a god, and the banshee's master was a thing of death magic, feeding on blood and fear. It fit. It fit very well, and it filled me with rage that surpassed crimson and spilled to silver-blue and white.

"I'm sorry, my lord master of the Hunt." My own voice sounded bewilderingly distant and hollow, as if it had been filtered through light and come out the other side stronger for its journey. "I'm sorry, but that's just not going to happen. Tell me something. This thing you saw. Where was it?"

For the second time I wished I knew the god's true name. The land was almost dead now, blackened and raw. All the trees were shadows of themselves, and the Hunt itself, dogs and Riders and rooks, stood amongst the thin stick forms, waiting on a changing of the guard. "Cernunnos, answer me!"

He caught a slow breath, the kind that spoke of unwelcome wakenings, then murmured, "Buried. Buried behind a wall of stone, and still a glance was enough to strip me down to this. I'm weary, little shaman. Let me rest."

I dug my fingernails into the ground until dirt pushed back, making the quick hurt, and grated, "Not on my watch."

All that lovely fresh revitalized power pulsed out of me in a heartbeat burst of oil-slick color. Once, then again, and again, every thump inside my chest pressing life back into dying soil. I didn't know how big this world was, if it disappeared into the mist a few yards away and melted into nothing, or if it hung between the stars like another earth. I could never pour enough into a planet to ensure its survival, so I didn't let myself think about it. My heartbeats started coming slower after a while, but the grass around my fingers grew deep, and the earth softened again.

I might very well have killed myself trying to rescue a world, if exhaustion hadn't put me to sleep first.

I woke up with a blade of grass tickling the inside of my nose and the green-eyed god of the Hunt standing above me with an expression of bemusement. "A patch," he said, while I tried twitching my nose enough to dislodge the grass and go back to sleep. "A patch of earth, this courtyard and nothing more, but vitality begets vitality, shaman. Tir na nOg is healing, and from perhaps more than the maker's pull."

I said, "Yay me," without really hearing him, and pulled the offending blade of grass out of the ground, throwing it away before rolling on my stomach. A new piece of grass stuck itself in my nose. I whimpered and rolled over further, rubbing my face like a tired baby. Cernunnos kept looking at me with bemusement. I could feel it. After a while what he'd said started to sink home, and I pinched the bridge of my nose, trying to sort it out. "You mean it worked. You're okay now."

"I am," Cernunnos said dryly, "as you say, 'okay.' And the mists are parting, shaman. The time to ride approaches."

I'd gotten an upgrade. I was no longer a *little* shaman. Bully for me. Grown-up or not, I sat up still feeling like a sullen three-year-old, and scrubbed my hands through my hair. "Time to ride where? Oh. My world."

Cernunnos nodded. "All Hallow's Eve approaches, and we have souls to collect."

"Well, I can't go with you. I've got to…well, I mean, I guess I have to go with you to get home, but I can't ride with you. I have to, like—" I waved a hand "—save the world."

It had to be a godly knack, the ability to do something as mundane as offer a hand up and make the entire gesture ironic. Cernunnos did just that, pulling me to my feet. The bone crown was finally beginning to distort his temples, and I forgot about whining in favor of smiling at the oncoming change. "You really are getting better."

"I am, and I owe thee a—"

I put my fingers over his mouth. "Stop that. The theeing and thouing. You're right. It gets right under my skin." And in a good way, but I didn't want to say that out loud. "Stick with being normal. As normal as you can be, anyway."

His lips curved under my touch and he took my hand away, folding my fingers over his own. "As you wish. I owe you a debt of thanks, a greater debt than can be easily repaid." He examined my hand over his, then lifted his gaze again with a flick of his ashy eyebrows. "You made a choice in riding with us to this place."

I'd already managed to forget that. Now, reminded, I pulled back, but the god held my hand more tightly. "That choice is unmade, for what you've done here. It will come again at the end of all your days, but you have no bargain to settle with me. Your soul is your own, *gwyld,* and I leave no marks on it."

"Oh." I managed to keep my feet, but I also managed, in one two-letter word, to stagger with relief. Amusement lit Cernunnos's eyes, and I dragged a crooked nervous smile up. "Thank you."

"You are welcome." He passed me back my belongings—including the rapier—and tipped his head. The Hunt drifted out of the mists, once more at full strength and beauty. "Now, Siobhán Walkingstick, shall we ride?"

I'd ridden with the Hunt quite a few times by now, what with dashing here and there and back again to Tir na nOg and Babylon, and being chased down highways, which may not have strictly been riding with them, but which I counted for effect's sake. Name dropper and drama queen, that was me: *Oh,* I'd say someday, all light and insignificant-like. *Oh, Cernunnos and the Wild Hunt? I rode with them, back in the day.* And then I'd give a brittle laugh to show what I thought of my careless youth, and how I was better and wiser now than I'd been when I'd done such foolish things. No one would believe me, of course; I wouldn't even believe myself, but by that time I'd be far too late to live fast, die young and leave a good-looking corpse.

It was just barely possible I'd been watching too many rockumentaries on MTV. I needed to get out more. Anyway, none of that mattered, because I couldn't imagine sipping bitter dredges at the memory of this thing lost. If I ever looked back on that last ride with Cernunnos with anything other than exhilaration, the truth was, I was already dead and just hadn't noticed yet.

The goddamn sky split open under our horses' hooves. There was nothing for their feet to impact against, but I felt every step like a bolt through my body, the air itself breaking and rumbling under the Hunt's weight. Wind tore tears from my eyes and froze in icy streaks along my temples. Speed flattened my hair against my head, and my ears, my face, my *teeth* ached with cold. I wore a grin I recognized from the inside, even though I'd only ever seen it from the outside. Drummers in rock bands got that grin: musicians given over completely to abandon and the beat and the spirit-bursting excess of joy that came from finding the edge of life and leaning way the hell over to see what was on the other side.

My throat ached from howls of joy, and I could barely hear myself in the cacophony. Everyone and everything around me let loose the same cries; hounds, Riders and rooks alike, warbling raw calls mixed with long baying tones and the deeper shouts of men. The same feral grins split everyone's faces, from the lord of the Hunt to the bearded king and the blond archer. As the youngest, as the Rider of the pale mare, I was meant to have the lead, but we jostled and crashed against one another, a mob of enthusiasm all trying to reach my world and three months of freedom first. There was a solemn duty to be done during those months, yes, but in the moment, that was unimportant. For now, it was about the first breath of earthy air, the first glimpse of a sky studded with familiar starlight. It was chaos made manifest, that factor of the universe which could never be predicted, and it was, without any question, how the Hunt was meant to make the journey from their world to mine.

We burst through the cloud cover, thundering down toward the cemetery from which Cernunnos had taken me. For an instant I saw it as an immortal might, patches of green grass and gray granite memorializing the dead. It was both fascinating and meaningless to one who wouldn't die: gods might understand ritual, but the connotation of permanent loss gave it all an unfathomable air.

Suzanne Quinley and the boy Rider sat together on a stone bench, two distant points of life bound together by blood. Matilda no longer haunted them, nor could I see any sign of her in the graveyard; Cernunnos had delivered on his promise.

The boy stood as we roared down toward them. Suzanne followed suit more slowly, and for all that I was certain my vision wasn't clear enough to see it, I still saw the boy offer her a sympathetic smile. He murmured something I didn't catch under the pounding hooves, then turned away and locked gazes with me.

I bent low over the mare's mane, thrusting my arm out as we approached the two children. With absolute flawless grace and even more perfect timing, the boy reached for me in turn.

Our arms slammed together, fingers gripping with every ounce of strength we had available. I clenched my stomach and heaved, guiding the boy onto the mare's back behind me. In very nearly the same motion, I dove off her other side, flinging myself under racing hooves and paws.

The Hunt angled skyward and careened over me, never breaking stride. I rolled through dirt and grass and came up against a gravestone, hooting with laughter. Suzy tore over to me, attention ricocheting between me and the disappearing Hunt. "That was the coolest thing I've ever seen!"

"That was the coolest thing I've ever done!" I scrambled to my feet, feeling like a superhero and in search of a handsome man to kiss. There weren't any around, so I snatched Suzy up and swung her around in circles until I stumbled from dizziness. Her legs tangled with mine at the sudden cessation of momentum, and we went down in a heap of elbows and knees and laughter.

"You were gone forever!" She whacked my shoulder and rolled away, gasping at the sky. "They're already gone!"

"I don't think they're constrained by details like the conservation of mass and energy." I dropped my elbow over my eyes, still grinning, then peeled it away again. "How long was I gone? The sun hasn't gone down—" I pushed up, looking for the horizon. Distant clouds were turning gold, harbinger of a perfect Halloween sunset of red and orange. "Oh, hell." Gaiety fled, I fumbled my phone out of my jeans pocket and punched in Billy's number. I hated cell phones, but I'd hate having to race through Seattle at rush hour to bear bad news even more.

"Yeah, Joanie, what is it? Where are you?"

"I'm at the Crown Hill Cemetery. You think you can pull off the impossible in the next half hour?"

"You're at..." I could hear all the questions he wanted to ask and discarded as not strictly relevant just then. "Depends on the impossible. What do you need?"

"Can you call up Sonny's friend Patrick and ask him to get some local priests to go around and bless the water in the lawn-sprinkler systems in all the graveyards in town? Before sunset? And get them all turned on," I added, in case it wasn't obvious.

Billy sounded like his tongue was having a throw-down

with his brain over what ought to be said first. "You want the city's irrigation system filled with holy water?" won.

I said, "Yes," then, worried, continued, "I mean, it works that way, right? You don't have to, like, cart in holy water from Jerusalem to mix with the rest of the water or anything, do you? It can just be blessed and be good to go, can't it?"

Billy's tongue was still trying to strangle him. I wished my phone had video capability so I could see what that looked like. It sure sounded awful. "Look, I've got this other thing to deal with, and I'm seriously not the person to coordinate a citywide holy-water brigade. You saw that black muck in the air. Even if I'm totally wrong about the cauldron disturbing the dead, getting rid of it has to be good. If I'm right, washing it away before sunset is critical. I really need you to do this."

I also really didn't want a man whose wife was about to give birth out chasing a death cauldron with me, but I didn't think that was an argument that would go over well with my partner, so I left it alone. Billy spent about five more seconds choking on his tongue before saying, "What other thing?"

"The cauldron," I said evasively. Mentioning premonitions of my death seemed like a bad idea. "If you cover the sprinkler thing, I can deal with the cauldron." I sounded very confident. I hoped I was right.

"As soon as I've got this sprinkler thing under way I'm calling back and you're telling me where to meet up. I mean it, Joanne. You're not facing this alone."

"You're a big damn hero, Billy Holliday. I'll talk to you soon." I hung up, all too aware I hadn't asked him how his interview with Sandburg had gone, but unwilling to draw the conversation out and maybe let slip that I was on a deadly timetable. For a couple of seconds I looked around, feeling a bit wild-eyed and hoping I'd find a priest or a holy hand grenade lying around waiting to be used.

Instead, I found Daniel Doherty standing at the cemetery gates, a hand to his forehead like he was staving off an ache, and a frown between his eyebrows that said he couldn't have seen what he'd just seen, but he hadn't yet figured out how to explain it away. I squared my shoulders, looking for a story that would suit him, and headed over to feed it to him.

Right then, the sun's shadow slipped away from the cemetery, and the zombies rose up.

CHAPTER TWENTY

I suppose I knew on an intellectual level that graves weren't especially made for getting out of. I mean, you start with a hermetically sealed casket and then you dump six feet of dirt on top of it. Over time the earth gets compacted, which can't make it any easier to dig through. So even if you're a very angry and determined zombie, you've kind of got your work cut out for you just escaping from the grave.

Which was, I suppose, why we got hit with an initial wave of zombie bugs, birds and rodents. I bet some people would say if you've never picked undead mosquitoes out of your teeth, you've never lived. Under that definition, I'd be just as happy to have not lived, thanks.

I drew my rapier, feeling its connection to my armor zot to life with a sound like a lightsaber. I was sure that had to be internal editing, that nobody else heard a funky *zwonk!* of power lighting up, but I kinda hoped they did. Even zombies ought to be smart enough not to mess with a chick wielding a lightsaber.

Well, human zombies, anyway. A half-rotted squirrel ran at my foot, chittering like mad. I let out a perfectly girlie scream and swatted it away with the tip of my sword. Some fencer I was. I skewered a rat, which was much better in fencing terms, and a lot more awful in real-world terms. It kept trying to get me, teeth clattering and scaly little feet scrabbling in the air. I let out another yell and flung it away, hoping a nice hard smash against a tree or gravestone might end its nasty little unlife.

Something bigger than my head dove at me. I shrieked yet again and ducked, not even trying to strike back. Whatever it was pulled up, rained molty feathers on me, then dived again, this time with an unearthly scree that sounded, well, like the dead crying aloud. I thought maybe it was a goshawk, but I was too busy cowering on the ground, hands over my head, to really get a good look.

Not that the ground was all that good a place to hide from the undead. Half-rotted squirmy things boiled up through the dirt, maybe drawn to my body heat, or maybe drawn to all the noise I was making. For a big tough girl like me, I sure sounded like a fifties housewife encountering a mouse. Worse, I felt like one. My heart was in palpitations and my hands were wet with sweat. I wanted to throw up, but I was afraid the doughnuts I'd been surviving on for the past two days would turn out to have an unlife of their own, too, and would turn on me in bilious disgustingness.

Mice and shrews and robins and worms and myriad other

small creatures that lived in city greens all squeaked and charged toward me, dropping tiny body parts and dragging tiny guts along with them. Tears leaked down my cheeks, and my chest filled up, like all the dead cells in my body were coming back to life and trying to suffocate me. Angry gods I could handle. Murderous banshees were fine. The living dead, it seemed, even in comparatively cute and harmless forms, were not my thing. I was going to be eaten alive by rodents of usual size, and the best I could do was sob and gibber about it.

Right beside me, I heard the distinctive double-click of a shotgun cocking. I didn't think that was fair. Zombies, particularly rat zombies, shouldn't be able to use shotguns. A blast of rock salt, even at short range, probably wouldn't kill me, but it would hurt like hell, and make lots of little holes for the zombies to start nibbling at. I wailed and wrapped my arms around my head more tightly. I'd dropped my sword and didn't even know when.

A huge blast of rock salt peppered the ground in front of me, tinging off my sword and breaking some of the tinier rodent zombies into bits. Suzanne Quinley said, "Get up," and cocked the shotgun again. "Get up, or next time I shoot you so I have time to run."

I peeked up through my arms to see her standing above me like a pale god, shotgun riding on one hip and her hair flying in the wind. Her gaze was implacably calm, not at all like a fourteen-year-old girl's. She was playing the role of grown-up because the actual adult in this scenario was blubbering like a baby. I had never in my whole life been so grateful for somebody else to have her shit together.

Suzy said, "Get up," one more time.

Stomach in knots, hands trembling, I reached for my sword and got up.

Suzy gave me a severe nod, then lifted the shotgun to indicate Daniel Doherty. "What do we do about him?"

"Let him get eaten." I didn't mean it, and being snarky didn't make my hands any steadier. "We rescue him."

"You're the boss." Suzy let fly another blast of rock salt, and the air cleared of small flying undead things. I watched them fall to the ground, and wondered why my feet weren't moving. Suzy crashed her hip into mine. "Move. Move!"

"I'm trying. I really am." A tiny panicked sliver of silver-blue magic shot down my legs, looking for roots growing up from dead trees and binding me to the earth. There weren't any. It was good old-fashioned panic holding me in place. "Maybe you better go ahead."

"All I do is see the future!" Suzanne Quinley, who had to weigh at least thirty-five pounds less than I did, grabbed my sweater in one fist and hauled me a step forward. "*You're* the one with the save-the-world magic! You're the one who kicks everybody's ass! I didn't come all the way from Olympia to get eaten by bugs! Come on! *Save me!*"

I couldn't even save myself. I had no idea how I was supposed to save her. All I had was a sword that wouldn't kill zombies and magic that fed the undead until they took corporeal form.

All of a sudden I wondered what happened if you infused a killing weapon with life magic.

Smacking Cernunnos with a bolt of blue magic had made it very clear that my power was not meant to be a straight-out weapon. I'd nearly passed out, and that was from just one hit. I had no doubt that sustained blasts would drain my magic and leave me for the worms. Warrior's path or not, there seemed to be things a shaman just didn't get to do. But pouring healing power into a weapon, now that was tricksy, and all the gods and creatures of chaos liked trickery. Besides, I was facing the undead. If there was a modicum of fairness in the world, it would agree that going up against hordes of zombie beasties who were trying to eat me wasn't at all in the same class as fighting a god who hadn't done anything worse than attack without provocation.

Juxtaposing those two things made it really clear, once more, how humans tended to think choices were between one good thing and one bad thing. In fact, choices could just pile up on the side of suck without any kind of apology for it. Another zombie rat ran at my foot, and all my frustration and disgust exploded in a thin blue line down the length of my rapier. I stabbed downward with a shout and skewered the nasty little thing.

It exploded.

Bits of blue-white-lit flesh erupted everywhere, like a tiny box of fireworks had gone off at our feet. I yelled. Suzanne yelled. Doherty yelled. The attacking hordes of zombie critters didn't yell, but they did stop their headlong rush and looked around, my sword's light glowing in their undead eyes. My yell turned into a triumphant shout and I leaped forward, convinced I could scare off our attackers with a show of strength.

Sadly, zombies are not well known for their brilliance, and me and my glowy stick made a nice bright target for them. I swatted at flying things and stabbed at crawling things in what could kindly be called a panicked flail, while Suzanne blasted the shotgun. We backed up a few steps at a time, pausing so Suzy could reload, and we didn't make it anywhere near the gates before the first human zombies crawled out of their graves.

I was not a horror-film buff. The thing about horror films, see, is that they're scary. Scary, or gross, and I didn't much like either of those things. Despite this, I'd grown up in America, and apparently there was a cinematic image of zombies lurching from their graves that was part of the überconsciousness, because in many ways, I'd seen the scene unfolding before me a dozen times before. Slow-moving cadavers in various stages of decay, their skin peeling back, their teeth exposed, their fingernails too long, their hair falling out, all oozed from the earth—it was more of an ooze than an erupt, since *eruption* connoted speed—and latched on to us with their rotting eyeballs and began slogging toward us in such stereotypical fashion that I actually glanced around for a camera crew and the pretty heroine who was about to get eaten.

Two things caught up with me at once: first, Suzy, Doherty and I were playing the part of the about-to-be-eaten leads, and second, that zombie movies simply could not in any way get across the *smell* that preceded our encroaching dance partners. Rotted meat and formaldehyde swept toward us on the cool night air, so ripe that tears burned my eyes. Doherty and Suzy both doubled over, retching, but I held sickness behind my teeth through one part willpower and one part practice from four months of homicide investigation. I whispered, "Get behind me," and tried not to think about climbing into Petite with vomit on my shoes.

The other thing zombie movies didn't get right was how *dirty* they were. Filthy, and not just with rot, but with ordinary mud and grit. I'd never tried digging my way through six feet of packed earth, but I could see it wasn't a tidy endeavor. The very newest corpses looked as if they'd been in a mud fight, nothing worse, but the oldest were little more than black stickiness clinging to disintegrating bone.

Morbid curiosity made me look again, this time with the Sight, and I wished I hadn't. There'd been something seductive in the dark, deathless—or deathly, I guess—quality of the cauldron. It'd offered a comforting cessation of everything, wrapping around to draw you into a silence that would never end.

Zombies were what happened to the bodies when it ended. Memories flickered around them like the auras they'd once had, but too far out of reach: fireflies teasing at the corners of their undead vision. Like reached for like, scattered memories reaching for the thoughts and recollections that living humans carried with them. That was what drove empty bodies: their hunger, not for flesh, but for all the moments and details and tribulations that made up a life.

Raging spirits like Matilda had a memory, however feeble, of what they'd been. The things crawling from their graves had less than that, only an echo of that memory. If the spirit world had stroke victims, zombies might qualify: they were empty, but they remembered they hadn't always been, and they had no idea how to become more again. Looking at them was looking into a black hole of desperation and loathing, so thick I could drown in it; so thick they could only move slowly as they struggled through it toward us. Worse, I could feel myself slowing as I watched, their deadly ichor reaching for me and drawing me down.

I shuddered and shoved the Sight away, trusting normal vision to hold out against their insidious encroachment longer than magical vision could. "On the count of three, Suzy, I want you to run like hell for Petite."

"For what?"

I bared my teeth at the zombies, not wanting to waste time turning to show Suzanne the expression. Besides, it wasn't her fault. Her set of vast psychic powers included future-tripping, not mind reading. I wondered if anybody actually could read minds, then dragged mine back to the topic at hand. "My car. The purple Mustang outside the gates." I dipped my hand into my front left pocket and dangled the keys behind me. "She's solid steel. Hopefully that'll keep the zombies out."

"Steel windows, too?" Suzy asked with more sarcasm than I thought a girl about to be eaten by zombies should be able to command. I growled and she cocked the shotgun again, then muttered, "Okay, okay."

"Bring Doherty with you."

"What are you going to do?"

"I'm going to cover your retreat."

"That," Suzanne announced disdainfully, "is a stupid plan. We should all run together."

"Suzy, I don't know if these things can move faster than they're doing right now. I'd really rather not find out by turning our backs on them. Don't you watch horror movies?" The fact that I didn't seemed supremely irrelevant. You didn't have to actually watch them to know you should never turn your back on the bad guys.

"Yes," she said acerbically, "and the first thing that happens is all the idiots in the movie split up so the monsters can pick them off one by one."

Shit. She was right. I shot a glance over my shoulder to meet her defiant glare, and groaned. "Okay, you win. All together. You've got the ranged weapon, though, so I'm staying in front."

"What about me?" Doherty asked.

I risked another glare over my shoulder. "You can cower and let the hot chicks with weaponry protect you, or you can play bait and run toward the zombies while we run for the car."

Doherty cowered. I muttered, "Thought so," and turned back to our opponents under the cover of Suzanne's scream and a blast from the shotgun.

Zombies, for the record, do not die from a face full of rock salt. They do, however, get blinded by it, which makes it a lot easier to stuff a glowing blue sword into their throats and rip their half-attached heads off. I wasn't sure if that would stop one for good, but the one who'd attacked fell down, and that was a good start. Better yet, one of the monsters immediately behind it fell on its…corpse, for lack of a better word. I knew better, but I let the Sight come back for a moment so I could watch and confirm my suspicions.

The second zombie snatched and gobbled at the flickering bits of memory that had taunted the first. Apparently they didn't care much where their psychic food came from, so if we could create even a feeble wall of dead zombies—that was a Department of Redundancy Department phrase if I'd ever heard one—we might win ourselves a little time to make good an escape.

We got busy. My rapier made an absolutely gorgeous slash of brilliance against the fading light, magic pouring through it and burning away any gook or gunk that might have been inclined to darken its glory. Suzy took one step back with every blast of the shotgun, and Doherty...

Well, Doherty screamed like a little girl every time the gun roared and every time another body fell, but honestly, I couldn't blame him. My own hands were slick with sweat and my stomach was roiling like I'd drunk half a gallon of seawater. The only reason I wasn't joining him in the histrionics was Suzy'd bitch-slap me but good. That didn't really make me feel any better about myself.

All of a sudden we'd made a little wall of zombie bodies, and those coming on from behind it were brawling, more eager for the scraps left by their fallen brethren than for us. Apparently the movies had gotten that right, too: zombies weren't known for their scintillating wit, or one of them would've realized we were much tastier tidbits. The three of us stood there, breathless with surprise and relief, for about a nanosecond. Then our own scintillating wit caught up and we turned and ran like hell.

A faceless zombie lurched toward us from the side, too far from the original emptied graves to be distracted by the half dozen we'd downed. Suzy screamed and blasted it, and I jumped on top of it to chop its head off. Rapiers weren't really meant for chopping, but I did a damn fine job even so. After a couple seconds I realized Suzy's screams had words in them: "Can't you *do* something about these things?"

Sheer mindless irrationality rose up in me and I flung my hands in the air. "I'm sorry! Somehow I forgot to pack the scarab launcher into Petite's trunk this morning!"

"The what?" Suzanne dropped the shotgun's barrels toward the ground and stared at me.

"The scarab launcher! You know! Scarabs eat flesh, zombies are flesh, so you fill a bazooka with scarabs and launch them and poof, no more zombies?" I sounded hysterical. Well, that stood to reason. I *was* hysterical. I was doing better than Doherty, though, who was crawling toward the gate, sobbing. Okay, now I felt sorry for the poor bastard. Not even an insurance adjudicator who was trying to screw me out of my claim deserved zombie attacks or the other peculiarities that were part of my life. I didn't envy him the upcoming therapy bills.

Suzy, on the other hand, came to a full stop and gaped at me, far from looking as if she needed therapy. In fact, she looked like a young Norse goddess of some kind, her hair all tangled around her face and real strength in her slim body. Her green eyes glowed with admiration, which seemed all wrong, under the circumstances. "Scarab launchers," she said with great sincerity. "That's the most awesome idea I've ever heard."

I said, "Thank you," breathlessly, and then, because for once I felt a little too honest for my own good, I added, "I read it on the Internet."

"I am *totally* getting a scarab launcher when we get out of here." She shot a look toward the zombies, then toward the gate, and said, "Which I kinda think we oughta do now."

I picked Doherty up by the belt, and we ran for the gates.

Doherty stayed in Petite's backseat where I threw him. Suzy, with whom I was growing more impressed by the moment, snatched up the bag of rock salt and poured it across the cemetery's gated entrance as I slammed the gate itself shut. "Iron and salt," she said with astonishing satisfaction. "That ought to keep them in."

I wailed, "What, you just *know* that? I had to study to learn that! Does everyone but me just come pre-programmed with weird esoteric knowledge?"

Suzy, grinning, jerked a thumb toward Petite and Doherty. "You're not the only one. He's doing a lot worse than you are."

Somehow that didn't make me feel much better. Trusting Suzy and her shotgun and the salt-lined iron gate, I ran back into the chapel to discover I'd left the water bottle somewhere on the wrong side of the gate. Feeling like a complete moron, I stuffed my rapier through a belt loop and sank my cupped hands into the font, scooping up as much water as I could hold. There wasn't much left by the time I raced back outside, but it was enough to throw through the gate and watch what happened to the zombies who'd made their way toward it.

Unfortunately, what happened was "absolutely nothing." Apparently holy water did the trick on the mist, but once the zombies were risen, they were happy to stay that way.

"Right," I said brightly. "Time to go."

"What if the salt and iron don't hold?"

I was certain there was a heroic answer to that, but instead of searching for it, I grabbed Suzanne's arm and hauled her back to Petite. "Then we'll be really, really glad we're gone."

She whispered, "Fair enough," and a minute later we peeled out of there, leaving a cemetery full of cranky zombies behind.

CHAPTER TWENTY-ONE

My cell phone rang before we got back to the precinct building. I dug it out of my pocket and flung it at Suzy: driving while talking on the phone was one of my major pet peeves, even if the state hadn't introduced a law against it. She fumbled the phone, surprised, and looked uncertainly at me.

"What," I said under my breath, "you didn't think I was giving it to *him,* did you?" "Him" was Doherty, who had graduated from screaming to making these thin, bubbly whines of terror that were now turning to disbelief. I hadn't yet figured out what to say to him, so I was doing my best to ignore the nasally tones from the backseat.

Suzanne looked over her shoulder and a complicated expression that more or less translated to "yeah, I see your point" danced over her pretty features. She answered the call with a surprisingly steady "Detective Joanne Walker's phone."

Billy's voice shot up loud enough to be heard through a crappy cell-phone receiver and over the rumble of Petite's engine: "Where the fuck is Detective Joanne Walker?"

"She's driving," Suzy said calmly.

Billy's response was a lot more subdued; I couldn't hear it. Suzy grinned and said, "That's okay," and then, "Suzanne Quinley. I'm—oh." She whispered, "He knows who I am," to me. I nodded and she went back to the conversation, reporting, "He says the holy-water brigade is under way, he wants to know where you are, he says to come back to the station and pick him up," in little bursts.

I glanced toward the west, where a last few glimmers of sunshine faded over the horizon. The zombies at Crown Hill hadn't waited for the actual sunset, only for the sun's rays to no longer be touching it. I hoped the holy-water brigade was in time. I hoped we were all in time. "Yeah," I finally said. "Tell him I'm coming back to the office because I gotta take five minutes and think. In the meantime…"

"In the meantime," Suzanne picked up briskly, "you should get police officers out to the cemeteries and have them ringed with salt. And issue a citywide warning to stay indoors. Detective Walker's sword can kill the zombies, but we don't know what else can, so if you can get people to stay inside it's better."

I did a double-take at her and she shrugged. "It's like a disaster movie. I'm just following the rules for survival."

"Man. Remind me to have you on my side when the zombie apocalypse comes." I squinted at the road. "That was funnier in my head."

Suzy grinned anyway. "I know what you mean."

"Oh, good." We made the rest of the drive in relative

silence, accompanied only by Doherty's hysterical whimpers. I wanted to throttle him as much as I felt sorry for him. I'd be just as happy to hide in the backseat sniveling, myself. I didn't like zombies. Of all the things I'd faced, zombies just creeped me out on a visceral level, and I'd have done pretty much anything not to have to deal with them. Sadly for me, the only way I'd be able not to deal with them was to deal with them so they'd be gone, so I stuffed my own whinging terror into a box and dragged Doherty out of Petite's backseat when we got to the precinct building. "Go home, Doherty. Go home and lock the doors."

"How? You left my car at the cemetery. Wh—" He was a little guy. It probably wasn't his fault he looked like a miserable hobbit from my perspective. Still, with tears welling up in his big blue eyes and those pretty, chiseled features, I couldn't help thinking he was turning it all on in hopes of securing a nomination for Best Supporting Actor. "What was all that?"

Half a dozen snide answers leaped to the fore. I mean, really, it seemed like a dumb-ass question, but a year ago I'd have been asking the same thing, because I wouldn't have let myself believe my eyes. I sighed and propelled him toward the precinct building. "What do you want, Mr. Doherty? Do you want the truth? If I tell you it's what you want it to be, an incredibly well-realized film production, are you going to go home and write up our madcap race out of there as a liability and refuse me my insurance claim?"

His jaw dropped. So did Suzy's, for that matter. Apparently when faced with zombie attacks, I wasn't supposed to be petty enough to worry about my insurance. Well, they weren't paying premiums on vehicles older than they were, and I'd done the end of the world a couple times already, so I got to choose my priorities. "I'll get you the Miata back tomorrow morning. If you want to stay at the precinct building overnight, that's probably safest. In the meantime, how about you sit and consider the trouble we might've been in if I wasn't driving a 1969 steel-frame race car?"

Doherty reeled out from under my hand and wobbled to a wall, which he slid down, and laced his fingers behind his head. I dropped my chin to my chest and sighed. "It was a film, Mr. Doherty. They asked me to play a bit part at a graveyard because Petite's such a great getaway car, but I won't let anyone else drive her. Look, I'm sure somebody around here's got a bottle of booze. Why don't you hunt it down, have a stiff drink, and tomorrow morning everything will be back to normal, okay?"

It'd be back to normal, or I'd be dead. Either way, I wouldn't have to worry about it anymore. Doherty lifted his head to stare at me, then gave a feeble nod and looked around like the Vodka Fairy might appear at any moment. I nudged Suzy inside and we left Doherty behind.

She managed to hold her tongue for ten whole steps. "Shouldn't you have told him the truth?"

"No. By next week he'll have talked himself out of the truth anyway. I might as well give him something to hang his hat on. Left here, then upstairs."

I prodded her toward Homicide—the department, not the act—and she gave me a dubious look, but took the stairs two at a time before stopping at the top and saying, "You should've told him the truth."

"Suze." I scrubbed a hand through my hair, then turned

what I hoped was an earnest but serious face on her. "Suzy, you're atypical. You went through a lot of weird and horrible crap in January, and you came out of it believing everything that had happened. I've spent most of the past year watching people rationalize away the things that happen when I'm around. Half my best friends aren't anymore, because they can't quite convince themselves that what they saw wasn't real, and it makes them afraid of me. Doherty's going to be happier thinking he got caught up in a movie production than he is thinking zombies are actually rising on Halloween night. Trust me on this."

She stuck her arms akimbo and thrust her jaw out. "So how come I believe it all?"

"Aside from the premonitions you can't shake?" I spread my hands. "I guess you're just happier knowing the truth. You're tough. A lot tougher than I am. C'mon, I need to talk to Billy and see if he's gotten anywhere on our murder case."

Suzy hung back, frowning. "I'm not tougher than you. You're a real hero. You saved me. You help people."

God save me from the faith of innocents. I looked at the granddaughter of a god and knew that even if she preferred knowing the truth, I stood in one of her blind spots.

What the hell. Everybody needs heroes. I pulled her into a rough hug, promised, "I'm trying, anyway," and only then did we brace ourselves and walk through the doors into chaos.

Monday, October 31, 5:57 p.m.

I'd have hated to be on emergency dispatch right then. Halloween night was always nutty, and the department put extra people on in preparation for that, but nobody'd been given a primer on what to do with dozens of calls reporting that poor dead Fido had risen from the backyard grave and was trying to get inside the house, or that Goldy the fish was working her way back up the toilet drain. Grim-faced detectives were responding to unsolved homicides in which the dead were returning home, and I bet Missing Persons was suffering from exactly the same kind of deluge. It wasn't the kind of scene anybody in their right mind would take a fourteen-year-old into, but I didn't have anywhere better to bring Suzanne, and she was rather literally the only thing standing between me and certain death. I had no intention at all of bringing her on the case with me tonight, but storing her somewhere safe where I could communicate with her seemed like a good idea.

My desk was in the middle of the uproar, though. Not exactly the most peaceful place to sit and wait out a zombie attack or a cauldron search. I picked up the receiver on my desk to phone Morrison, and Billy pushed the call button down with a thick finger. "Want to tell me why there's an insurance adjudicator downstairs gibbering about zombie movies?"

I put the phone over my collarbone and groaned. "Because the other explanation was too unpalatable. Do you think if he loses his mind they'll just give me my money?"

"Detective Walker's having a bad day." Suzanne inserted herself into the conversation with a bright smile and an offered hand. "I'm Suzanne Quinley. We talked on the phone. Hi."

Billy said, "Hi," and shook her hand sort of automatically, but he didn't take his gaze off me. "How bad?"

"My bad day doesn't really matter, Billy. Did you talk to Sandburg?" I couldn't believe it was still Monday. I hadn't even gotten up twelve hours ago, but the day had been going on forever. We were only about five hours short of the forty-eight hour mark since Jason Chan had died and the cauldron at my party had awakened. Time was running out, and that didn't even include Suzy's premonition.

"I brought him in for questioning. Completely rattled him. I think he would've confessed to anything if it meant getting out of there, but either I'm the worst judge of character in Seattle or he was genuinely offended at the idea he might be involved in trying to sell the cauldron. I ended up sending him home again. The guy's got no hint of being a runner." Billy hitched himself onto the edge of my desk, arms folded across his chest. "The flip side is our tech guys say the security-tape loops started Friday just after the close of business. Everything matches up with the loop from three weeks ago perfectly. That means somebody with fantastic hacking skills or easy access is probably responsible."

"Redding or Sandburg." I pressed my fingertips against my eyelids. "I have a question I'm going to regret asking. Could somebody be manipulating Sandburg through magic so he didn't even know he was involved in anything illegal?"

Billy stared at me a long moment. "Occam's razor says no. Could you do something like that?"

Creepy-crawlies ran over my skin, reminding me of the unpleasant shock of slamming weaponized magic into Cernunnos. "I don't think *I* could, but witchcraft might be able to. Faye Kirkland magicked Gary into a heart attack. Seems like if you can do that, you might be able to affect people's actions."

Billy tipped his head back and glared at the ceiling. I couldn't swear to it, but I was pretty sure he was counting to ten. When he reversed his gaze again, it was to fix it on me like I'd become a bug for collecting. "I don't know, Walker. My department is ghosts. Do you think it's a real possibility?"

"I still think the cultural anthropologist is more likely than the security guard. Redding's probably dead by now. If I were stealing a cauldron to bring somebody back to life, I'd want to do a test run first." My stomach, which didn't know a cue when it heard one, rumbled ferociously. I had no idea when I'd eaten last.

Suzy, voice small, said, "I could look and See."

"See?" Billy frowned at her. "See what?"

"If that man is dead. I can…" She faltered, looking at me.

"Suzy can see the future," I said matter-of-factly. "Ever since January and the thing with Herne and Cernunnos."

Now, if somebody'd said that to me, I'd have gotten all skeptical. Billy didn't even blink. "We've got some of his personal effects in the evidence lockers. Would that help?"

Suzanne's eyes widened, then lit up. "I don't know. I never tried. Do you think it might help me control it? Because that would be awesome."

Billy said, "Using tangible objects belonging to the subject is a time-honored way of honing focus," which I was pretty sure meant "yes." Two minutes later we were downstairs opening an evidence locker while a bored recruit looked on. I wondered if he'd get a flashy show that would wipe away his boredom, and couldn't decide if I thought that would be good or not.

Suzy fluttered her hands over the handful of things with

Redding's name sticky-taped to them: a glasses case, a pair of civilian shoes, a long raincoat and hat, and an ink sketch of his wife and children, "A. Redding" printed in small letters in the lower right-hand corner. It was a head-and-shoulders image of all of them, his daughters in pigtails and his wife's hair in an upswept Gibson-girl style. I saw women on the street occasionally who still wore their hair like that: members of a small church I didn't know the proper name of, but which I thought of as the Church of the Ladies with Hair. Those women usually wore long skirts and blouses, and Redding's wife had the slightly puffed sleeves I associated with that look. The building manager out in Ballard had mentioned the bingo group, but not a church. Then again, it wasn't like I knew whether my neighbors went to church, either.

Suzanne lifted the sketch with careful fingers. I was just as glad I wasn't watching with the Sight as her eyes went all creepy and white again. She shuddered from the core all the way out, until bumps stood up on her skin and her hair looked like it'd been rubbed through static. Color flooded back into her eyes, eating away the white, and she sounded sick as she whispered, "He's still alive, but he won't be in a few hours. He dies at the same time you do, Detective Walker."

"He *what?*" In Billy's defense, I was reasonably certain his eardrum-rupturing outrage was over the part of that statement where I died, but Suzanne and I both nearly teleported five feet away at his sheer volume. She shot me a panicked look. I waved her down, and tried to do the same to Billy.

"Suzy had a premonition about my death, too. It's why she came up here from Olympia, to warn me. It's all right. It's going to be fine." I turned to Suzy, pretending my voice of reason was such that it would drown out Billy's horror.

It didn't, of course. He repeated, "It's *what?*" and hauled me back around to face him.

Normally I'd object to being manhandled like that. Normally, though, I wasn't looking my death in the face, so I just kind of got a warm fuzzy over him being that worried. I'd give him shit later, if I lived. Which I intended to do.

But if I didn't, it was good to have a chance to see him again, and to say goodbye. He was going to have to pick up a lot of pieces if I got myself killed, and I kind of wanted to look him in the eye and say I was sorry, if it was coming to that. "It's going to be okay. I think I've got this one under control, Billy. Don't worry. I've been under a death sentence before and come through okay." I squeezed his arm, gave him what I hoped was a reassuring smile and turned back to Suzanne. "Did he die in the same place I do? At the house with the swimming pool and the toys?"

Poor Suzy, all big eyes and misery, nodded. I exhaled noisily. "That's actually kind of good. It means we're going to find him. Did you see anything else this time? Any other markers that would help us place the house?"

"It's *good* that you're going to die?" Billy demanded.

"If Redding and I are supposed to go out at the same time, that means if we can save one of us, we should both be okay. And me, I'm all for not letting anybody get thrown into a cauldron and resurrected, so I'm kind of planning for nobody to die, partner." I gave Billy a genuinely sunny smile. Apparently I thought my logic was infallible.

Beneath all of that, Suzy whispered, "I didn't see anything else. I'm sorry."

"It's fine, sweetie. We're going to find him. It'll be okay." I actually believed that, but Billy growled.

"Walker, if Suzanne's seeing your death, you need to stay the hell away from anything that looks at all like her premonitions."

"I don't think that'd work. I think I could lock myself in one of the cells and…" Okay, I had to admit that locking myself in a cell seemed like a pretty sure-fire way of not dying by a household swimming pool. "Look, it doesn't matter, Billy. I'm doing this."

"No. You're not." Billy set his jaw. "What you're going to do is go tell Morrison about the premonition, and he's going to decide whether you get to walk into a trap."

Somewhere in the big bad universe was a version of me who snorted, rolled her eyes and blew off Billy's demand. After all, she was an adult and a shaman and knew her own mind and what needed to be done. So, for that matter, did I.

Not terribly long ago I'd have done as Billy asked because I'd have figured Morrison would give me a way out. Going into a dangerous situation was one thing. Going into a situation where my death had been clearly predicted was something else, at least if you were willing to take it on faith that dire prophecy had any basis in reality, which I was. No police captain would order an officer into certain death. That was for the military.

Me, I knocked on my boss's door and went in knowing even if he forbade me from going forth and doing my thing, I'd go forth and do it anyway. I barely knew me anymore, but

I thought the new me was probably a distinct improvement over the old.

Morrison looked up and got the usual pained expression that came with finding me darkening his door. "Two office visits in one day, and you're not even supposed to be at work. What did I do to deserve this?"

"Sorry. Would you rather Billy and I left the Chan case to molder for two days?" I sat down without waiting for an invitation, figuring I'd be on my feet for the whole interview otherwise. "Remember Suzanne Quinley?"

"Pretty little blond girl whose parents were murdered in January," Morrison said, apparently without having to think about it. Given that it'd been both my first paranormal experience and my first murder case, I wasn't surprised he could pull it up that easily, but I was willing to bet he could do the same with an awful lot of far more mundane cases. Morrison was good at his job, and cared about his people. "What about her?"

"She's upstairs in Homicide. No, nobody's dead. Yet." I winced at the last word popping out. It wasn't going to help my cause. "She's been having visions in the aftermath of what happened in January. She came up from Olympia to tell me she's had a premonition of my death in the cauldron. Tonight."

Morrison's expression slipped into something worse than neutrality. Neutrality meant I'd just said something unbelievable to the point of exasperation and that he was trying to hide his irritation with me. I was used to that, and had gotten to where I drew a small degree of comfort from it.

Under no circumstances could I imagine gaining any comfort from a look of gut-level belief covered by a stoic refusal to let emotion through. What was I supposed to say, *Go me, the dread Morrison's finally on board?* I turned my face away, gaze fixed on a tall, slim glass clock on one of the captain's bookshelves. It read 6:17 p.m., which meant in the worst-case scenario I had five hours and forty-three minutes to live. The clock's tick and my heart both seemed very loud in the face of Morrison's silence, but I couldn't make myself look back at him.

The clock clicked over to 6:18 p.m. and quite a few seconds before Morrison finally spoke. "Why are you telling me this?"

I set my lips, looked back at him, and looked away again, then did it all a second time before managing to fix my eyes on the desk in front of him, if not on my boss himself. "Billy thought that the boss man should make the decision about whether I was going to go off and potentially get myself killed."

"Bullshit."

My gaze popped up to his. "No, really, that's why. I'd have just gone and done it without asking, otherwise."

Morrison spread his hands on his desk and leaned forward. He didn't get up, but he didn't have to: the whole effect was one of looming anyway. "And if I say no?"

"C'mon, Captain." My voice softened and I tilted my head, a sad smile creeping up from somewhere. "You're not going to say no. You know that as well as I do. Even if you did…" I shrugged. "I have to go anyway. It's my job."

"So I'm not going to say no and you wouldn't listen if I did. Why'd you bother?"

Because Billy told me to was clearly not going to cut it. The other obvious, if sticky, answer was one I'd closed the door on back in July when I'd taken the promotion to detective, and had maybe locked shut when I started dating Thor. Well, if it was locked, there was still a major draft blowing through the cracks. I wasn't sure there was anything to be done about that, or that I really wanted there to be. It made dating safer, knowing my heart was tangled up somewhere else.

Man, I was really a piece of work. Thor deserved better. I either had to break up with him or get over Morrison. Or get murdered by a cauldron, if the first two choices were too hard. And all that thinking about other things gave my mouth the opportunity to say, "I came to say goodbye," without checking in with my brain first. "Just in case."

The captain turned purple. "Y—"

"Morrison. You asked, okay? I don't know what's going to happen tonight. I personally think it's going to involve banishing the living dead, retrieving a stolen cauldron and hopefully solving a murder. But Suzanne's having visions about my death, so there's a non-zero possibility that I might not survive. I'm hard to kill. You know that. You've seen the tapes. But you wanted to know why I came to talk to you, and I'm telling you." I looked away, suddenly tired. "There aren't very many people I'd want to say goodbye to, in the event of. You're one of the few. So I'm saying it. You can give me shit later when I come through just fine."

"Walker…"

I sighed and got up. "Next time there's a death warrant on my head, we'll just let this stand as writ, okay? I've said my melodramatic little goodbye. No more fuss after this. Just me, getting out of your hair." I managed a tired little smile. "Your weird-colored hair."

If it'd been me, I'd have at least put a hand to my head. Morrison didn't. "Could I talk you out of going, if I tried?"

"Do you want to?"

"You're an officer under my command. I don't want you walking into a death trap."

I ducked my head and let go a soft breath of laughter. Somehow Morrison dancing around his own evident impulse to protect me made my own inability to face certain truths a little more palatable. I looked up, still smiling. "That didn't answer the question, boss."

Chagrin deepened the lines of his face. Apparently I wasn't supposed to call him on avoiding the topic, so instead of making him actually answer, I said, "You can't order me not to go, because I won't listen, and asking me not to go will just make it harder. Don't make it harder, okay?"

Morrison gave me a hard look that ended in an over-blown sigh. "You're a pain in the ass, Walker."

I'm almost certain that in no way should that have made an idiotic grin bloom across my face. I snapped a jaunty salute, said, "Yes, sir," with genuine cheer, and strutted off to face the next demon on my list.

CHAPTER TWENTY—TWO

The next demon didn't go over so well.

Thor was bigger than me, which I knew on an intellectual level. I also appreciated it on a sort of frothy-girl-likes-big-guy level which, prior to Thor—well, really prior to Mark Bragg, but never mind that—I'd never really considered, and which now kind of made me cringe with girl cooties if I thought too much about it. I mean, I knew other guys who were taller than me; Billy and Gary both were, for example, but I was still accustomed to being one of the tallest people in any given room. *Taller than me* got its own quirky mental box in my mind, and not many people fit in it.

It turned out that when Thor got his temper up, he didn't so much fit into it himself. He more popped out of it, à la the Incredible Hulk, albeit without the green and with a considerably better vocabulary. At least, it'd been better while I explained Suzy's premonition. After that it reduced to "No way are you—you are *not* going out there to—" interspersed with my "Yeah, I am, Edward. Edward, yes, I am—"

We were on round three, and the entire motor-pool crew had gathered around to watch. Even my old boss, Nick, who hadn't looked at me comfortably since things went wonky in January, was sitting on the hood of Rodridgez's patrol car—the axle was probably out of alignment again—watching us like we were the last match at Wimbledon. I felt strongly that someone should be selling popcorn and hot dogs.

"Look," I finally hissed. Don't tell me you can't hiss a word without an S. There's not a better name for that particular pitch, full of emotion and sharper than a whisper, but much too quiet to be a full voice. Besides, I had plenty of esses in the words that followed. "I appreciate you don't want me doing something dangerous, but this is my job. You don't get to tell me I can't do it."

"I—" He finally noticed our audience, and didn't quite catch my arm to haul me away from the gawkers. Just as well, too, because if he had I'd have been obliged to hit him. Instead, he clenched his fists and jerked his head toward the stairs, where we could continue our discussion with a modicum of privacy. Someone'd finally replaced the fluorescent light in the stairwell, so there was no longer a patch of semi-darkness to hide in, but at least the crew couldn't see us without coming around the foot of the stairs, which I thought might be a little too obvious, even for them.

Once we were half hidden, some of Thor's puffed-upedness ran out of him in a sigh. "What am I supposed to do, Joanie? I want to protect you."

"You can't." Man. I hadn't known so many emotions could fit into two small words. Regret, sorrow, resignation, and maybe most of all, implacability. "Thor—*Edward*—you can't protect me. God knows people've helped me out, and I've needed it. I'll no doubt need it again. But you can't actually protect me. When we're talking about the kind of thing I've been dealing with, there's literally nobody else who can do what I have to do. I might not get out of this thing alive tonight, but I've got a better shot at surviving than anyone else."

His hands turned into fists. "I can't accept that. I can't just let you go off—"

My heart tightened up as much as his hands had. "You have to. I need you to trust me. Trust that I'll be okay."

"I can't. I have to be able to do something, Joanie. I have to be able to help. I can't just stand back and wait to pick up the pieces. I can't be—"

"The soldier's partner? The one she comes home to?" I closed my eyes and tried to breathe around an ache so big it overflowed my chest. "Then this isn't going to work. Because I signed up to be a soldier, and I need a partner. Not a protector."

"Holliday's your partner. How the hell do I fit in to that?"

"Billy's my partner on the job. He's got the skill set to deal with at least some of what I deal with. I'm not talking about on the job, Edward. I'm talking about the rest of my life. I need somebody who trusts me to do my job and come home."

A bitter, crackling edge came into Thor's voice: "Would this conversation be different if you were talking to the captain?"

The ache in my chest burst, sending phantom pain through my whole body. My hands curled against emotional misery turned physical, and my calves cramped from trying to stay steady when all I wanted to do was curl up. "It *was* different when I talked to Morrison, Thor. He didn't tell me not to go." I was a big girl, and big girls weren't supposed to cry, but my throat was tight and my eyes hot as I whispered, "I'm sorry."

Thor didn't say anything else. He just stood there and looked at me, and after a minute I turned and ran from the garage.

A Joanne who really had her shit together would've breezed back into Homicide all calm, cool and collected, ready for action. Me, I bounced off the half-open door on my way through it, and kept my gaze locked on the floor, like that would keep everybody from noticing my face was red and puffy and blotched with tears. It obviously didn't: a cone of silence rippled around me as I made my way toward my desk. I grabbed a tissue, tried to blow my nose discreetly, and instead sounded like a beacon for every Canadian goose on the planet.

It also signaled everybody around me to suddenly get very busy, and the noise level suddenly shot back up where it belonged. Only Billy and Suzy were left looking at me worriedly, and neither of them seemed in the slightest bit convinced when I said, "It's nothing. Forget it. Billy, you think Chan's ghost might still be around?"

"Not if he's lucky. Why?"

I could see him not asking what'd brought on my crying jag. I was more grateful than I could say. "Because he's our only witness as to what happened to the cauldron and Redding, and I want to see if there's anything else he can remember. I don't know where else to start. Can you call Sonata and have her meet you at the museum to try a séance?" I pinched the bridge of my nose, which was still swollen with tears. "I mean, can mediums actually call spirits who've crossed over back again to talk? I know you can't, but—"

"Sonny's stronger than I am," Billy said without rancor. "She might be able to. I'll call and find out, but what do you mean, meet me? Where are you going?"

"I'm going to go get Gary and my drum. If Sonny can call Jason back as far as the Dead Zone, I ought to be able to talk to him there."

"What about me?" Suzanne's voice said she knew exactly what the answer was, but I gave her props for asking.

"You're staying here. It's not that I don't think you'd be helpful, Suzy, because you probably would be. But you're fourteen, and this is a kidnapping and murder case, and there are zombies out there."

"I'm old enou—"

"Yes. You are. You're old enough to take care of yourself. But you're also my responsibility right now, okay? You put yourself in my hands by coming up here. Let me try to keep you safe, Suzy. Please. I don't know what happens if I'm trying to watch out for you, as well as myself." I wondered if that argument would have gone over well with Thor. It didn't go over all that well with Suzanne, but her shoulders slumped in agreement anyway. I said, "Thank you," and meant it. "Call me if you get any more future flashes, okay?" I wrote down both Billy's and my cell numbers, and Suzy folded the paper into her hand.

"Be careful, Detective Walker."

"I will be." I gave her another quick hug and grabbed my belongings as I headed for the door. Billy fell into step behind me, catching my elbow at the door and pulling a bulletproof vest off the wall. "Zombies don't use guns, Billy. They chew you to death. Have you heard from Patrick? Did the holy-water brigade do any good?"

"Put it on anyway." Billy sealed a vest in place across his own broad chest. I struggled into mine on the way down the stairs while he dialed Patrick, though the sigh he let out at the end of the conversation didn't fill me with confidence. "It worked in a lot of places, but not everywhere. Sonata's out with a lot of the other talent in the city, trying to keep things calm. I'll call her from the car."

"Talent." I scraped a little snort of laughter. "Is that what we call ourselves? All the witches and mediums and shamans?"

"Oh my," Billy said a bit compulsively. "And, yeah, it is. Joanie." He touched my shoulder as we hit the parking lot, and I turned back to him with a frown. "What happened with Morrison?"

For a few seconds the question just didn't make sense. Then understanding flooded me, and color burned my face. "Nothing. Nothing. Morrison and I are fine. It's Thor. I—we—we just broke up."

Dismay made Billy's face long. "Oh. Oh, crap. I'm sorry, Joanne. I thought things were going pretty well for you two. What happened?"

I looked down at myself. I was wearing a bulletproof vest and a gun, and a still-glowing sword at my hip. I could see hints of light from my necklace and bracelet, and if I thought about it I could feel the weight of my esoteric shield on my left arm. The Sight washed on, making all of those things much clearer, and I lifted my gaze again to meet Billy's, knowing full well my eyes had gone gold and spooky. "What do you think happened?"

"Yeah," he said after a long minute. "Yeah, I guess I can see that. Sorry."

"Yeah." I pulled the rapier from my hip and tossed it into Petite's backseat. "So am I."

My apartment was only a five-minute drive from the precinct building. I ran up the stairs, noticing that the vest's extra weight didn't slow me down. It would have, not that long ago. I'd become studly sometime in the last year. I grabbed my drum and thudded back down five stories while phoning Gary. "You said you didn't want to miss out on any more fun stuff. Does fighting off hordes of undead sound like fun?"

"Lady, you got a weird idea of fun." Gary sounded thrilled. "Where're we meeting?"

"That depends on where you are."

"Home, but I can get into the city fast." Gary lived in a three-bedroom ranch-style house on the edge of Bellevue. It'd been paid off thirty years ago and recently renovated. I figured if he sold the place he'd be a millionaire.

"I'm in Petite. It'll be faster for me to come get you." That wasn't precisely true, but I no longer had Doherty on my tail and I had a serious urge to bury my sorrows in speed. The one danger in driving like a bat out of hell—aside from the inherent danger of driving like a bat out of hell, that is—was that Petite was a very recognizable car. There weren't that many liquid purple classic Mustangs out there, and only one of them had a license plate reading *PETITE*. Still, I'd yet to meet the cop car I couldn't outrun, and I might even get away with claiming police business if I did get caught. "I'll be there in fifteen minutes. If you've got a shotgun, bring it along."

"Fifteen? Since when do you have a transporter bea—"

I hung up and made it to Gary's house in eleven and a half minutes. He was waiting outside the front door, a sawed-off shotgun over one shoulder and an expression of disapproving delight marring his features. I didn't bother killing the engine, letting Petite grumble as Gary slid the gun into the backseat with my sword, then crawled in the passenger side to say, "What kept you?"

"The bridge slowed me down." At least there hadn't been any zombies on it, just ordinary traffic. I filled him in on the day as I sped back into Seattle proper, ending with, "So I want you to drum me under for the séance. If we can get anything from Chan, then we go monster hunting."

"What if we don't?" It was possible I was driving too fast. Classic Mustangs didn't have oh-shit handles, but Gary kept reaching for one. "And you think *I* drive by using the Force?"

"At least I look where I'm going." We spun out coming into the museum parking lot, though if it hadn't been empty I wouldn't have indulged. Look, driving fast cars was the next best thing to sex, and I'd just written off any hope of a sex life for the foreseeable future. I wanted my thrills where I could take them.

Gary let go a bellow that sounded one part terrified and two parts excited, then fell back in his seat, clutching his heart. "I had a heart attack four months ago, you crazy dame!"

I called up a handful of healing magic and thumped my hand over his, against his chest. It fluttered and sank in, and I smiled. "Yeah, and the doctor said you've now got the heart of a twenty-five-year-old. You can handle a joyride or two, Muldoon."

"You're dangerous, lady."

"You have no idea." I got out of the car not knowing why I'd said that, but it made me feel strong and confident, which, right then, I was glad of. Gary collected his gun and my drum. I put the rapier back on and looked up to find him frowning at me.

"The dye's smearing, Jo. Didja get it wet?" He tested the drum's surface just like I had two nights ago, and found it as taut and smooth as it had ever been.

"I don't know what's wrong. I think it's…" All my confidence drained away. "I dunno. I always thought that was a wolf, but now I'm wondering if it's a coyote and it's been ruined because he's gone."

"Aw, c'mon, Jo, that sounds…" I could see him struggling between a couple choices of words: *silly* was one, and *like magic* was the other. Both were true. It sounded silly and it sounded like magic. Gary shrugged his bushy gray eyebrows. "Guess that could be it, then."

"Yeah." We sat down together on the museum's front steps and I nerved myself up to take a look at the city with the Sight. I didn't think I could see holy water sprinkling down and washing the cauldron's black goo out of the air, but at least I should be able to see where the stuff had been washed away.

And in most places, it had been. There was a hint of light where the cemeteries were, residual water in the air, maybe. The clouds overhead were breaking up and moonlight lent more strength to the bright patches. I just didn't know if it was enough. Most graveyards closed their gates at sunset, so hopefully any undead who had risen were stuck behind iron, but it wasn't something I wanted to bet the farm on. I needed to find the cauldron and destroy it. I couldn't think of anything else—short of me going around and stabbing every dead man walking in Seattle—that would tear their unlife away from them. I'd do it if I had to, but breaking the source of their magic would be more efficient. "You know what I still don't get?"

"Legions of faithful fallin' at your feet?" Gary gave me a bright grin when I dredged up a glower for him. I'd never seen a man his age with such nice white teeth. They had to be false, but I couldn't imagine how to ask that politely.

"That either," I admitted, "but I was thinking about the cauldron. That thing is death on wheels, and I don't get why it hasn't done this everywhere it's been. Or, rather—" I flapped a hand "—I don't get why whoever warded it so it *wouldn't* do this hasn't just come and fixed the wards."

"I like how you say that. Warded it. Like it's normal." The funny thing was, I thought Gary actually *did* like how I said it. I think he considered it a good sign that I was talking about warding and magic spells like they were part of my everyday life. After all, they were.

I turned my gaze back on the city, looking for any trails the cauldron might have left now that its murk was largely drowned. There was nothing: the pools of black mist had gathered together, dissolving any trail even before the blessed water'd fallen on them. "I wonder if that kind of thing is in my repertoire. I can shield myself. I can even shield other people, at least for a while. I wonder if I can make a shield against a death cauldron leaking all over a city."

"Reckon you'll get a chance to find out." Headlights swung into the parking lot as Gary spoke. We both got to our feet, waving a greeting to Billy, then Sonata, as they got out of Billy's patrol car.

Billy muttered, "I don't even want to know how fast you drove to get here before us. Sandburg's on his way with the keys."

"Gary picks locks just fine. Maybe he can let us in."

"I can pick a lock, doll, not break into a state-of-the-art security system. Gary Muldoon." The last was to Sonata, and was accompanied by a roguish smile that I considered pretty high on the irresistible scale.

Sonata apparently thought so, too. Dimples appeared and she let Gary linger over her hand as she murmured, "Sonata Smith," in reply. "It's a pleasure to meet you."

"Pleasure's all mine, ma'am."

I grinned at my feet. Gary's Saturday-night date had competition. Once in a while, things went right in the world. I took my smile from them to the road, feeling it fade as minutes ticked by. It was after eight, and while being at the museum instead of at a home with a swimming pool boded well for my long-term survival, I thought our window for finding and breaking the cauldron was shrinking. The deepest part of the night wasn't all that far away, and it seemed likely that whoever had the cauldron would be calling up its full magic right around midnight. I wanted to find it before that happened.

Sandburg finally pulled in to the parking lot. His aura, still pale, twitched with concern as he got out of his car, but there were no sparks of off-colored resentment dancing from him. Evidently he understood that sometimes people close to a murder case got hauled off for questioning. Me, I wasn't sure I'd be all that understanding.

In fact, thinking that way made me try to deepen my perception of his aura. I had no idea what a compulsion spell might look like, but logic dictated it had to leave *some* kind of mark, if it was there.

A glimmer of greenery, pale as anything else I'd seen off Sandburg, washed up around me: just a hint of his garden; of the state of his soul. I held on to it, hardly daring to breathe as I searched for a hint of something wrong within him.

A raging deep river of green, of *greed,* slammed out of nowhere and dragged me into Sandburg's depths. Triumph and panic bloomed within me at equal rates: that kind of avarice could push a man to do almost anything—including drown a nosy shaman who went poking around in his soul uninvited. But I only needed to hold on a few seconds, just long enough to see where Sandburg's hunger brought us.

The river swept me into a library at the edge of a desert: monumental pillars under a hard blue sky. Within seconds it morphed around me, changing from the legendary library at Alexandria to a modern, recognizable Library of Congress. To, I realized with embarrassment, a representation of a repository of all knowledge. Greed wasn't necessarily for power, and what lay at Sandburg's core was a desire to *know* things. With that much passion driving him, I suddenly felt sorry for anybody who tried to trick or ensorcel him into doing something he didn't know he was doing. I jerked my gaze to the side in a silent apology as Sandburg bounded up the museum steps to join us.

"Have you found something?"

"We need to take another look around the murder scene," Billy said. "I'm afraid it's going to seem a little strange. If you could let us in, I'll explain while the others prepare."

"A little strange?" Sandburg unlocked the doors and reset

the electronics with his pass code. I could See the numbers he'd pressed, and the order in which they'd been chosen, fading from one end of the spectrum to the other. I filed that away under Handy Tricks, though I doubted it was a morally superior use of shamanic magic. "One of my guards is dead, another missing, and Matholwch's legendary cauldron has been stolen. How much stranger can anything be?"

"We're going to work under the assumption that the magic of the cauldron is real, and see if we can contact the dead to learn more about it." Billy spoke so reasonably that Sandburg nodded agreement before he'd fully grasped what had been said.

"We—you—what?"

"Mr. Sandburg, if you don't mind sitting down with the rest of us, your presence will be extremely calming to Jason Chan's spirit." Sonata tucked her arm through Sandburg's and walked him down the hall. "The familiar is very comforting to the dead, and I would be terribly appreciative of your help in this matter." She was wearing a white blouse instead of the dead-happy-face T-shirt, which I thought was probably a good choice for out-of-house calls. The blouse went better with her smile and gentle tone. Sandburg found himself agreeing all over again, though I could all but see his mind whirling and trying to make sense of what she was saying.

The cauldron's black smear had lessened considerably. It was, I thought, partly that I'd shaken off its effects once, and partly that it was losing the connection with the place it had rested. Either way, that had to be a good thing: I couldn't imagine that with the weight of death pulling at them, any ghost might survive long in its presence. Billy said, "Chan's gone," under his breath. "Poor kid went ahead and crossed over."

"I'm sorry we have to disturb him again."

Sonata got Sandburg settled down at the farthest point from the cauldron's empty space. "William, if you'll stand here…?" She pointed him to a place a few steps to Sandburg's right, and took up a place opposite Billy on Sandburg's left. I shuffled over to stand much closer to the cauldron's dais than I wanted to, and Gary, without being told, stood opposite me, so the five of us made a half circle around the display. "William explained your intentions to me, Joanne. The dead must have a desire to speak with the living for me to bring those who've crossed over all the way back to this world. If Jason Chan is reluctant—"

"As long as you can get him as far as the Dead Zone, I can talk to him." I sat down, folding my legs and plucking at the vest, but decided to leave it on. Easier than arguing with Billy, who gave me a stern look as he, too, sat down. The others did the same—sat, not frowned at me—and Sandburg, looking nervous, followed suit. I felt a surge of sympathy for the mild museum curator. A few months earlier, I'd have felt just as awkward and out of place as he did.

Now, though, I glanced at my friends, then nodded at Gary. "Let's do this thing."

The first beat of the drum shattered the cauldron's remaining death shroud from the air.

CHAPTER TWENTY-THREE

Everybody except Gary flinched, though I didn't know if the shared wince was because the drum was surprisingly loud or if everyone had a sense of the shroud falling. I thought it got distinctly easier to breathe. It was like being in Los Angeles after a rare rainstorm: all of a sudden you couldn't see the air anymore, and breathing instantly felt less labored.

It was a good sign, anyway. My drum and my magic were all tied up with one another. If the cauldron's murk could fall under a good thump of healing magic, maybe that meant the universe was on our side. I was all for that.

I was also procrastinating, in that I was allowing myself to be distracted by things that weren't actually the drum and an inward focus that would send me to the Dead Zone. On the other hand, while we were short on time, we were also trying a séance, and if Sonata could call Jason Chan to us without me tripping the light fantastic, that seemed like a better way to go. My track record for speaking with the dead wasn't what it could be, and Sonata's talents actually lay in that direction. I wondered suddenly where Patrick was, and whether it was safe to be conducting a séance without him.

Sonata's "Weary spirits" rolled through the room and earned another flinch from everybody except Gary, who was evidently completely at one with the drum. I envied him a bit, then tried to tuck away emotion and get ready to slip through the walls of the worlds if Jason didn't answer Sonata's call. "I beg forgiveness, spirits, for disturbing you. I come seeking knowledge, not about what lies beyond the veil, but about what has come to pass on this side of it. I have come to a place of sorrow and violence in hopes that one among you may have answers to share with me. Jason Chan," she said much more quietly. "I know you seek no vengeance, but your fading memories of this world may help us to save another life. Will you speak with me?"

All of us, even Gary, straightened up and peeked around, searching out ghosts. Sandburg looked both poleaxed and fascinated, like he didn't believe he was participating in a séance and at the same time wanted it to be real with all the strength of a child's hopeful imagination. Shots of pink zotted off his aura, fireworks-bright, and I had to think that if he was guilty, he wouldn't be nearly so excited about the prospect of a ghost coming to point a finger at him. Too bad. It would've been easy for him to be the killer.

"Jason Chan," Sonata repeated, then began a quiet, oddly respectful litany of the young man's history on earth. His full name, Jason Matthew, and his birth date, the nineteenth of

September. He'd been barely twenty-four. His family's names, the towns he'd lived—all information available from his work record, and all of it meant to draw a dead man closer to the living's world.

All of it meant to draw him closer to life, when there was an ancient, magical cauldron pouring warped vitality back into the dead, and when we already knew that it could help a ghost latch on to mortal magic and gain corporeal form.

Wow. I'd had some really bad ideas, but right then, this one was the prizewinner. I said, "Oh, *crap*" out loud, and let go of the real world as fast as I could, racing for the Dead Zone.

I wasn't at all sure it was safer for me to go traipsing around the Dead Zone than it was to call ghosts back from the dead, not when the cauldron was doing its thing. I was, though, very sure that letting Jason Chan or any other ghost get a foothold back in the real world was a mistake, and the only way I saw to have my cake and eat it, too, was to fling myself into another plane of existence and hope like hell it worked.

My general impression of the Dead Zone was a bit *Hitchhiker's Guide:* it was a tad smaller than incomprehensible infinity so the human mind could encompass just how really, really big it was. My few encounters with the dead—or anything else there, for that matter—had put me sort of in the middle of an impossibly large space, so that I could feel properly insignificant. It went on for-freaking-ever, and even when I moved around, it never let up with the hugeness factor, or gave me the impression of being *near* to anything.

Jason Chan stood right on the edge of infinity, about to dive over into the living world. Space and time and eternity spread out, all that enormous emptiness somehow unques-tionably behind him, and the only thing standing between him and a twisted unlife was me.

I sprang at him, catching him in the middle with my shoul-der, and we skidded halfway across the universe before coming to a stop. The edge of the Dead Zone disappeared, thankfully and familiarly an endless distance away. I flopped over, trying to calm a rabbit-fast heart.

Jason, upon whom I'd flopped, said, "Jesus Christ, lady, what the hell is your problem?" He flung me off in a tangle of elbows and knees, and I skittered onto my backside.

"Sorry. Sorry, I—"

"Are you crazy? What're you doing tackling people like that? Are you—" He broke off, panting for breath and staring at me. After a couple of seconds his ire faded, leaving him with a little grin. "Okay, so this isn't usually how I meet girls, and you're nuts, but maybe I shouldn't bitch if women are going to literally throw themselves at me." He offered a hand. "Jason Chan. You always tackle guys when you want to meet them?"

It probably said something about my life that I actually had to think about it before saying, "I don't think so," and shaking his hand. "I'm Joanne Walker. Sorry about that."

"Nothing to be sorry for." His grin broadened and we finished getting untangled from one another. "I've seen you before."

Dude. Even the dead used the worst pick-up line in history. I said, "Er, no, I don't think so," again, and he shook his head.

"Yeah, I have. You were at the museum yesterday with that cop who was asking me about the cauldron. You were the other cop!" He scooted back a few inches and looked me over.

"I didn't recognize you right away. You look better now, if you don't mind me saying so."

He'd been *dead* when I was at the museum yesterday. I opened my mouth to say that, then decided it wasn't the best way to keep a conversation going. I glanced at myself instead, discovering my astral self didn't feel a need for bulletproof vests, and that I wore knee-torn jeans and an oil-stained white tank top. Work clothes, in other words, though the job in question was mechanic, not detective. I guessed I knew how my subconscious continued to define me. "It's fine. You look better than you did yesterday, too."

Because yesterday he'd had his head bashed in, which hadn't been such a good look for him. Today his self-image was what he'd looked like alive: young, broad shouldered, short black hair, quick smile. He was cute, the kind of guy you'd bring home to Mom. "How's your head? Billy said you had a migraine."

"It's gone," he said with a mix of astonishment and satisfaction, then laughed. "The migraine's gone. My head's still here." He clapped both hands against it, making sure of that, and grinned again. "So, did you guys have any luck with the cauldron? The other detective said he'd clear my going home with Sandburg, but he's gotta be pissed. You'd think he'd given birth to that thing, or something."

"We're still looking for it. That's..." Ice crept over my arms and made me shiver. Jason Chan apparently had no idea he was dead. I didn't know what would happen if I pointed it out to him. "That's why I'm here. I hoped I could ask you a few more questions."

"Sure." He glanced around, then came back to me with a

smile. He smiled easily, this dead young man. I wondered if he had when he'd been alive. "Would it be unprofessional if I took you out for a drink while I answered your questions? This isn't the greatest place to get to know each other."

There were many aspects of my bizarre life that I was coming to accept. Getting hit on by a dead guy was not one I was eager to mark up as commonplace, or, in fact, as anything less than seriously creepy. "Maybe we'd better keep it professional. If you could concentrate on your surroundings, it might help you remember details that escaped you earlier due to your migraine."

"Oh, sure." Jason frowned, glancing around again. I had no idea what he saw, but I was pretty sure it wasn't the rolling endless gray of the Dead Zone. "Like I said to the other detective, I came in to work with a low-grade migraine. Seemed like I'd had one all month, so my focus wasn't at its best."

"I've only had a migraine once. I thought I probably had a brain tumor and was going to die." Embarrassingly enough, that was true. It certainly gave me sympathy for somebody who suffered them regularly.

Jason shot me a rueful look. "Yeah, basically. It wasn't that bad, but—you know, it was weird, but I swear it got worse around that cauldron. I always get a light show when a migraine comes on, but just looking at that thing was like staring at the sun."

The ice that had settled over my skin melted suddenly, turning to a trickle of interest down my spine. "Really? I know it sounds odd, but that might be important. Can you describe exactly what you saw?"

He hesitated, eyebrows drawing down. "I hadn't thought

about it, but now that you ask, it was always the same. That's not what usually happens. Usually the patterns change when I looked away from something. Anyway, usually it was—" He broke off with a sheepish laugh. "You're going to think this sounds stupid."

"You wouldn't believe some of the things I've heard, said and done in this job. Try me."

Chan rolled his eyes and looked away, then glanced back. "I said it was like looking at the sun, and it was. All kinds of flares and loops in really bright white and gold. But it was dark in the middle of it, like there was a black hole in the center of the sun. And the way the loops wove around it, moving all the time, it was like they were constantly retying themselves around the darkness in the middle."

"The warding spell." I dropped my face into my hands, rubbing a thumb over the scar on my cheek. Lots of people got migraines. I wondered how many of them were at least occasionally seeing, but not recognizing, auras or magic being done. Hoping Jason hadn't picked up on the spell comment, I looked up again. "Is that what it looked when you came in Saturday?"

"Shouldn't you be writing this stuff down?"

"Oh. Yeah. Thanks." I reached for my back pocket, where, in real life, I never carried a pad of paper. But this was the Dead Zone, an astral plane, and if I needed paper, it would be there. And so it was, a little spiral-bound blue notebook with a puffy Mustang sticker on the cover. My subconscious not only thought I was still employed as a mechanic, but also that I was nine years old. Great. At least there was a pen stuck through the spirals. "Sorry, go ahead."

"It's Jason Chan, C-H-A-N, and my number is 216—"

I laughed, cutting him off. "I have all your particulars back at the station, Jason."

He snapped with a melodramatic sweep of his arm. "Can't blame a guy for trying."

"I guess not." Too bad he hadn't had the opportunity to try when he was alive. "So, Saturday night?"

"There was nothing weird. Archie and I always trade off which wing we're doing. He did the special-exhibits wing first while I did the permanent wing, and then we'd switch. The place is so quiet we never thought we needed to stick together. We'd say hi when we crossed in the lobby, and if one of us was early—like we'd made it into the other wing before the other one was done—we'd give each other hell. Archie's a cool old guy. Is he okay?"

"We don't know yet. I'm sorry." Jason'd told Billy the same things, but I wrote everything down in my notebook. I wondered again what he'd think if he realized he was dead, but I didn't want to get into it. I'd thought avoiding the topic of the cauldron with Sandburg had been complicated. At least that hadn't made me want to apologize.

"So my head was hurting anyway, but now that you asked me to think about it, the lights I'd gotten used to seeing around the cauldron were different. It was like the black in the middle was getting bigger. I radioed Archie and said it was coming to life, like in that movie? I mean, it's that time of year and everything." He smiled suddenly. "I'm taking my little sisters trick-or-treating tonight. They're eleven and fourteen and they're dressing up as these anime characters. First time I saw them in their costumes I just about locked them in their rooms. My sisters aren't supposed to look that hot."

My answering smile didn't get anywhere near my eyes. I was pretty sure Jason's sisters weren't going trick-or-treating, and might never again, with all the associations Halloween would now have for them. "Anyway," he said, "Redding told me I was an idiot and I kept going on my rounds, but every time I came through there was less light than there'd been. I remember it must've been around ten-thirty or eleven that I stopped and really took a good look at it, because I'd never been able to without it making my head hurt more. Then—" A deep frown marred his forehead, and I wished there was a way to head him off. "Then I guess the lights flared up again, because my migraine got a hell of a lot worse. The next thing I really remember is talking to Detective Holliday, and…and then to you.

"Detective Walker, what happened to me?" Jason's voice got very small, the Dead Zone pulling him impossibly far away, until he was barely more than a dot in my perception. Sonata'd called him close to the living world, and now the dead one was taking him back.

"You were tricked, Jason." An image of Coyote, my mentor and one of the world's most famous tricksters, flashed behind my eyes. I'd given Jason a few minutes of real life again, whether I'd meant to or not, and the universe was reordering that, undoing what had been done. Tricksters weren't kind, but humans learned from them. Learned, or failed to learn at their peril.

If that was what I was on the road to becoming, I wasn't sure I wanted it. But that was the price I'd paid for my own life, and so if I was to become a trickster, I hoped I could at least manage to leave my fools a little dignity behind. "Something evil tricked you," I said very quietly. "And now I've done it again, to learn what I needed. I'm sorry, Jason Chan. I hope you can forgive me."

I never knew if he could. He winked out and a little girl of around ten or eleven took his place. She wore her hair in braids and had her arms folded over her chest, but a smile split her face when our gazes met. She waved, cheery little action, and then, like Jason, disappeared.

I spluttered a wordless question, but a gasp of raven wings burst around me, and I fell back into my own life, my own body and my own world.

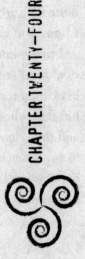

CHAPTER TWENTY-FOUR

The little girl's image danced behind my eyes as I shook off travel fatigue, or whatever it was called when a person goes zipping through different levels of reality. I'd never seen the girl before, but she'd felt familiar. An odd little hitch came into my breath as I frowned at where the cauldron used to be. *Somebody* had, at some point, put a warding on that thing, one that kept its power from leaking all over the world as it was moved from place to place. An eleven-year-old girl seemed unlikely, but I'd just finished telling Jason Chan about tricksters. Just because I was seeing a kid didn't mean that's what it really was.

She'd felt friendly. I decided to take blessings where I could find them, made a note to myself to look up creatures who could bind ancient evils and who liked presenting themselves as children, and turned my attention back to my audience. I didn't normally wake up to quite such a large one. Billy and Gary looked relieved I'd woken up, but Sonata's mouth was pursed. "You didn't need to interfere. He was willing to cross over."

The woman deserved an explanation. Intellectually, I understood that. She hadn't been there for the follow-up fiasco with Matilda. Still, explaining seemed like so damn much effort that my intellect threw up its metaphorical hands and stomped off in a fit of pique. Abandoned by it, all I could do was drop my face into my hands, exhale and eventually say, "I know. Sorry."

It took effort to lift my head again, and my gaze strayed to my watch when I did. A quarter to nine. If things went badly, I had a maximum of three hours and fifteen minutes to live. Not a cheering thought. "Jason's migraines got worse around the cauldron. I think he was seeing the binding spell that kept its magic from leaking out like it's done now. Billy, this isn't your field any more than it's mine, but who the hell can create something like that? A piece of tied-off magic that holds another magic inside? Would it be a kid?"

"Culturally speaking," Sandburg volunteered unexpectedly, "the cauldron would belong to one such as the Morrigan, the threefold goddess of war, knowledge and death. There are no stories of it being in her domain, but given her status in the Celtic cycle, I would consider it hers. Her antithesis would be Brigid, the goddess of healing, birth and learning. Anthropologically, I assume she would be one of the few to hold sufficient opposing magic to bind a death cauldron."

He glanced at the rest of us, who to a man sat silent with stupefaction, and wet his lips. "That is, assuming you were taking the myths and legends of old as writ, which under the circumstances, it seems you are."

My neck creaked as I glanced toward Gary. "Remind me to keep a cultural anthropologist handy for, you know. Everything." He waggled his eyebrows and I turned my attention back to Sandburg, trying not to stare. Trying not to stare at him, and trying not to stare at the museum's marble floor, where Jason Chan's lifeblood had been smeared in a circle around the cauldron. "Okay. Two more questions. One—could you in theory break down a ward put in place by somebody like Brigid by doing a blood sacrifice in someone else's name?"

Sandburg opened his mouth and closed it again, looking around at the rest of us like he was just realizing this wasn't a game. "I'd think a single sacrifice would lack the necessary power. Maybe a single willing sacrifice, because it's assumed willing sacrifices have more…"

"Mojo," I supplied into his silence. "I think we can trust Jason wasn't a willing sacrifice. So it'd take more than one?" I didn't want to say Redding's name aloud, as if doing so would spell his doom. Except Suzy said he wasn't dead yet, so he hadn't been sacrificed to free the cauldron.

"If I were participating in a ritual to break a goddess's binding, I would probably spend years building the groundwork." Sandburg spoke very carefully, an awareness that he was offering us the rope to hang him with in his words. "I would wait for an opportune date, one associated with my patron, and I would make repeated offerings in order to weaken the spell so that at the appropriate hour a final sacrifice would shatter it." His voice tensed, gaze jumping from me to Billy and back again. "*I,* though, would be acting and speaking metaphorically. You understand that, don't you? This is…hypothetical."

"Hypothetical but useful." I thought of the pigtailed little girl I'd seen once or twice, and drew a deep breath. "Second question. Would a goddess show herself in the form of a child? A little girl?"

"A maiden form is usually represented as older, a young woman rather than a little girl. That said…" Sandburg relaxed marginally as neither Billy nor I leaped up to slap cuffs on him. "Who's to stop a goddess from appearing any way she wants?"

A tiny surge of relief cleared my blood and my thoughts. "That's awesome. Anybody know how to summon a goddess and ask for her help in laying the smackdown on her enemy's cauldron?"

"Not her enemy." Sandburg regained a shred more equilibrium and sniffed a bit prissily. "Her opposite. Two beings at diametrical points of a power structure aren't inherently antagonistic. They can merely be balancing forces, one capable of growing too powerful without the other's influence. And no," he added as we all went back to staring at him, "I don't know how to summon Brigid. It appears that would be your domain." A small circle of his hand indicated he meant all of us when he said *your*.

"Right," I said after a minute. "I guess it is." The problem was, I only knew one person who did goddess-magic, and that was a witch for whom I'd almost ended the world a few months ago. She wasn't exactly high on my list of people I wanted to contact again, and even if I'd been willing, I didn't know if her goddess was the same as the one I needed here and now. I desperately wanted a handbook that cross-referenced things like worldwide names for the gods and goddesses whose domains were more or less the same. If there was any kind of justice in the world, they'd be different names for the same being, though I didn't know why there should start being justice at this late date. Cernunnos and Herne were the same guy by a lot of people's reckoning, but I had empirical evidence to the contrary. Still, as a research tool, it'd be very handy. Somebody'd probably written one. I'd have to search Amazon, assuming I lived through the next three hours and twelve minutes.

Out loud, and in an attempt to shut off the free association my brain had tumbled into, I said, "You're taking this well."

Sandburg gave me a small smile. "I'm really not."

Oh. Apparently my brain should've just kept going with the research thing. Billy, sounding like the voice of grim patience, said, "Did you get anything off Chan?"

"Only that his migraines got worse around the cauldron, right up until the night he died." I outlined what Jason'd told me about the encroaching darkness he'd noticed, then spread my hands. "Short of calling up a goddess, I don't know what to do. And I don't have 1-800-GODDESS preprogrammed into my phone."

I got a round of dry looks. Okay, okay, I guessed I didn't need it preprogrammed if I could spell *"goddess,"* but jeez, tough crowd. Billy, though, broke my discomfort by muttering, "Melinda does."

"You cannot seriously be suggesting we get your pregnant wife involved in a death-cauldron scenario." I spoke before thinking, but even if I'd thought, I'd have said it anyway. Melinda'd had a traumatic enough pregnancy, thanks to me. Adding more stress to the final week of waddling was the last thing I wanted to do, even if the rational part of me recognized it was Mel's choice. This was not about rationality. This was about Joanne Walker, Reluctant Shaman, getting all puffed up and out of sorts over the idea of her friends diving headlong into trouble just because she was in the middle of it herself.

In Billy's defense, he didn't look thrilled about the idea himself. On the other hand, that didn't stop him from saying, "Know anybody else on speaking terms with a goddess?"

"I don't," Gary said, "but if you're offerin' introductions, that's a social class I ain't familiar with."

I glowered at him. "You're not helping." He gave me a toothy white grin with no repentance in it at all. Sandburg watched the three of us like we were the final match in an exceedingly complex game of Ping-Pong. "Sonata, tell me you've got another solution. Any other solution."

She shook her head. "My strengths lie in communicating with the dead, Joanne. I have no special relationship with any god."

I could feel the enamel on my molars wearing thin. A Herculean effort unclenched them just far enough to grate, "This goddess Mel's on speaking terms with... Is she on speaking terms with her?" I nearly backed up to try vocally capitalizing the "she" in that sentence, then decided if Cernunnos didn't get a capital *H* when I referred to him as "he," then a goddess didn't get one, either. Not from me, anyway.

Besides, Billy followed my pronouns easily enough, shrugging a shoulder in response. "She says she does. I see dead people and my police partner heals with a touch. Who am I to argue?"

There was a certain logic to that. Not an irrefutable logic, perhaps, but I didn't think I had the moral high ground to refute it. Bizarrely, that reminded me of Morrison's dyed hair, and therefore of Morrison, and I spent a few seconds wondering what he'd do in my position.

Truth was, he'd do what he already had done: he'd use the resources available to him, whether he liked it or not. Billy and I lived eyeball deep in a paranormal world, so Morrison'd set us loose to play cop in that world because we were the only ones who could. If asking Melinda Holliday to chat up her patron goddess was the surest bead we had on finding the cauldron, then he'd already be halfway to their house and annoyed at me for wasting time.

Even in my hypothetical situations, he ended up annoyed with me. It was good there were some constants in the universe. Time flowed in one direction, light traveled at 9.46 trillion kilometers per year, and Captain Michael Morrison was always irritated with me. I sighed. "All right. Okay. You haven't installed a pool at your house, have you, Billy?"

He eyeballed me. "Since you came over three weeks ago? No."

"Just making sure." At least I wasn't going to bring down death and destruction on their home again. Suzy's premonition had been of somewhere else.

Gosh. What a relief.

I shoved the thought away by jamming my fingers through my hair. "Does Mel need advance notice? Should we call ahead?" I got to my feet as I spoke. Everyone else followed suit, Gary with my drum tucked carefully under his arm. Sandburg stole glances between all of us, and I wondered what he was thinking. Possibly that we were equal parts fascinating and alarming, which was a verdict even I could get behind.

Billy took his phone off his belt, nodding. "I'll let her know. Mr. Sandburg, thank you for grace under pressure, and I'm sorry if this was bewildering. I'll try to explain it sometime, if you like, but in the meantime, if Sonata doesn't mind, maybe you could drive her home?" He gave Sonny an apologetic look that she brushed off. Sandburg looked between him and Sonata, and then, evidently deducing he could be the heroic gentleman of the hour, offered the medium his arm. We all trooped out after them, Billy on the phone to Melinda as Sandburg locked up behind us. I hoped I'd never see the inside of the MoCA again, at least not as anything other than a tourist destination.

Some of my steam had bled off. I drove to Billy's house without breaking many speed limits or giving Gary another heart attack. Billy, presumably wise in the ways of neighborhood shortcuts, managed to get home just before us, so he was the one to initially greet Melinda. She stood in their doorway, arms akimbo to her enormous tummy, and nerves surged through me all over again. I didn't care if it was the only viable choice. I didn't like asking Mel to be searching out death magic when she was only a few days away from giving birth. It seemed like too much could go wrong.

"My goddess is not Brigid," she said softly, as soon as we were within earshot. "She may not be willing to help. She may not be able to. But the downstairs is ready. Eric wants you to come kiss him good-night," she added to Billy. My partner smiled and kissed her first, then went upstairs to look in on his kids while Melinda ushered Gary and me downstairs.

I'd been in the Hollidays' home dozens of times, and in the daylight basement half a dozen times, usually chasing the younger kids around the house in a madcap game of tag. It was fully the size of the rest of the house, with a laundry room adjacent to a large playroom. If I had four kids and Seattle's rainy winters, I'd have wanted a room that size to keep my children entertained in, too. Especially since there was a door at the top of the stairs that could be closed, isolating piercing shrieks from the rest of the house.

There were several other doors off the playroom, none of which I'd ever really thought about before. One stood open now, the scent of fresh paint emanating from it. I peeked in, then lifted a curious eyebrow at Melinda. "It'll be Robert's new room," she said with a degree of regret. "He's old enough not to have to share with Eric, and with the new baby we won't all fit upstairs anymore. Clara's agitating to move down here, too, now. They're growing up."

"You going to let her?"

"Oh, probably. It'll make Robert feel less alone, and she's not old enough to think of having boys sneak in through her window yet." Melinda made a face and opened a door at the opposite end of the playroom. "I hope. Come, this is my room."

Gary breathed, "Sure is," as he stepped in, and I couldn't help but agree with him. Dozens of low-burning candles sat on small tables, illuminating the room. The floor was concrete and littered with brightly colored pillows made out of fabric ranging from rough satin to raw cotton. Rosaries and Stars of

David hung from the walls, and a chalk drawing glowed on the concrete floor. I took a breath to comment, and instead inhaled a lungful of delicate sweet air. I'd never thought of Melinda having any particular scent, but the light perfume smelled like her, and was just enough to wash away the smell of candle wax and flame.

"Vallesia," she said. I blinked and she smiled. "People always ask what flower it is. It grows in Mexico. My grandmother loved it."

"Your grandma had good taste."

Amusement danced in Mel's eyes. "Or a good sense of smell."

Gary chortled. I made a face. Melinda, pleased, walked around the perimeter of the room, lighting a handful of candles that had been blown out when the door opened. I came farther in, stopping at the edge of the chalk outline. "I don't know what I expected," I said after a minute, "but this isn't it."

"You expected a pentagram," Melinda said amiably. "It's the only power circle anybody ever uses on television, but it's not the only one available to us. You should know that, Joanne."

I closed my hand over the necklace pendant at the hollow of my throat. "I guess I should."

The drawing inscribed on her temple floor—because that was the only word I could use for the room, *temple*—was the same quartered circle I wore. It was a symbol used by both sides of my disparate heritage: for the Cherokee it was a power circle, embodying the directions, the elements and the shape of the world. Actually, as far as I could tell, it represented exactly the same things for the Irish, though it had also been adopted as a particularly Celtic symbol of Christianity. My

C.E. MURPHY

mother's grave was marked with a Celtic cross, as were many others far older than hers. "What does it do?"

Melinda shrugged. "Protects. Captures. Honors. The same thing the pentagram does, really. They call the pentagram the devil's circle, but it's only a symbol. This one could be used for corruption, too. Anything can be, and almost nothing is so weighted by external perception that it leans toward good or evil on its own."

"Almost nothing?" That was Gary, asking the question I wanted to. I sort of felt like I should know this one.

"Traditional Christian crosses, Stars of David, the star and crescent." A smile flashed across Melinda's face. "Buddha statues. Even with so much religious strife and conflict in the world, those symbols are nearly impossible to use as focal points for wicked things. It's why they're reversed in so many hate rituals, the cross upside down, the star with its point toward the ground." She wobbled a hand. "Not that the Star of David can be reversed, but a true devil's circle puts the spire of a five-point star at the bottom. It's only by altering their aspects somehow that darker magics can gain a hold on them."

"What about people who do evil in the name of those symbols without reversing them? How can they do that without staining the original?" I had never thought about any of this. I was a little in awe that Melinda had.

"They can't." She shrugged. "But through the millennia, there have been more good people, with good hearts and good faith, who have stood beneath these shapes and put their trust in them, than there have been evil. Sometimes the balance comes very close. A token of peace can be corrupted in a single generation, if enough people come to see it as a representation of evil."

"The swastika," Gary said. Melinda nodded, and a sort of guilty surge of relief raced through me. That one, at least, I knew. It had been a symbol of healing, kind of an ancient Red Cross, and now it was the universally recognized sign of one of the worst evils man had ever done. If there was ever a symbol that needed rehabilitating, the swastika was it, but I wasn't sure it should be. Maybe it was better to have it always raise hairs on the arms and give a prickle of discomfort, to remind us of how badly we could go wrong.

Billy came down the stairs, surprisingly light-footed for a guy as heavy as he was. "Robert wheedled another half hour of reading time out of me. The rest of them are asleep."

"Robert would've read for another half hour whether you gave him permission or not." Melinda smiled and stood on her toes to kiss her husband, who grinned.

"I know, but now he feels like we've entered a conspiracy. It's a male-bonding thing."

Mel rolled her eyes in my direction, then tipped her head at the door. I shut it. The room warmed up noticeably within a few seconds. Maybe sweating was an important part of summoning a goddess, although that sent my mind down paths I didn't think it should follow. I mean, candlelight, sweat and deity-summoning all went together if you were summoning a particular sort of goddess, but Mel'd never mentioned being a disciple of Aphrodite. Of course, she'd never mentioned being anybody's disciple, so what the hell did I know?

"Since we have four of us, we might as well make use of

that. Two men and two women." Mel dimpled. "That works out well."

Gary and I exchanged glances. "I keep telling people it's not like that, but nobody believes me."

"I don't tell 'em any such thing. Who'm I to shatter their illusions, 'specially when their illusions set me up with a pretty girl?"

"You could do worse," Mel told me. "I mean, not that you've done badly with Edward."

The smile that'd come up at Gary's flattery fell away again while Billy made a small *no! stop!* gesture toward Mel that I probably wasn't supposed to see. She looked between us in bewilderment. I muttered, "Yeah, that thing with Thor didn't turn out so well in the end. We broke up tonight." Chasing ghosts and cauldrons was a pretty good distraction, but the reminder made me want to crawl in a hole and pull the earth over my head for a while.

Dismay washed over Melinda's face. "Oh, Joanne. I'm sorry. I didn't know. What happened?"

"It…" Pulling the world over my head wasn't going to work, and I had more important things to do than dwell. "It doesn't really matter very much right now. Let's deal with the zombie-producing cauldron first." I caught Gary's frown and exhaled in exasperation. "Look, teacher-man, I know you don't like me running away from problems, and I promise I'll get all maudlin and heartbroken tomorrow, okay? This is more important." While that was true, it didn't stop my head from stuffing up like somebody'd filled it with cotton bandages. I snorted snot into a thick murky sinus cavity and wiped my eyes with the back of my hand. Yeah, that was me, Joanne Walker, Tough Girl. "What do we need to do, Mel?"

She said, "Choose a direction," and while she was probably talking to all of us, I said, "North," without thinking about it, which made her smile. Defensive, I said, "What?" and her smile broadened.

"Nothing. It's just that north is the direction usually associated with finding wisdom."

Oh, God. My esoteric self was making Meaningful Choices in the midst of my minor emotional breakdown. I hoped the Maker of the world, or whoever'd mixed me up, found that kind of thing amusing, because I didn't. Melinda pointed to the bar of the circle that pointed north, and I stomped over to it and folded my arms like a sulking child. Which I was.

"East," Gary said, and I couldn't help notice that when we were both facing the center of the circle, that put him on my left, beside my heart. Apparently not even the universe believed it wasn't like that. Jeez.

Melinda was smiling again. "Sunrise, the opening of the ways, the opening of the heart. Bill, I think you'd better take west. It'll balance us man and woman, and you can be the guide to closing what Gary's opened." She stepped up to the circle directly across from me, and power danced over my skin as Billy took his place to my right.

"I thought we were going ask a goddess for help," I said uncomfortably. "How come this feels a little too much like it's about me?" I didn't think I was being egocentric, not when Melinda'd arranged the circle around my initial choice.

"You're the strongest of us." Somehow Melinda managed to be reassuring, placating and teasing all at once. "Besides, I could have come up with something equally impressive-sounding if Gary'd chosen somewhere else. Youth to age, if he'd taken the south, man to wife if Billy and I were facing each other. Want me to go on?"

A blush curdled my cheeks. "That's okay, thanks. What now?"

"We may as well sit down. This can take a while." Melinda did as she suggested, tugging a pillow beneath herself. Gary and Billy followed suit, but I froze halfway into my own crouch.

Light shimmered at the heart of Melinda's power circle before she even began speaking, so faint I called up the Sight in hopes of seeing more clearly. For long seconds nothing resolved, only scattered bits of brilliance, like the last rays of sunset on the water. Without really thinking, I knelt and put my fingertips on the chalk outline. Magic sparked as if I'd touched a live wire, a gentle shock that pulled silver-blue power from me. It bolted around the circle, hiccuping with recognition as it touched first Gary and Billy, then whisked around to greet Melinda and meet itself.

Silver shot up, crashing into the ceiling. I looked up for the first time, finding another circle inscribed above us, capturing the magic that poured out of me. A nattering little part of my mind thought I should be afraid: spilling power like that was usually a bad sign. This time, though, it felt more like healing; like it had when I'd tried to breathe life back into Cernunnos's forest, or like when I shared a bit of my own strength with Gary to shore up his weakened heart. Encouraged, I leaned in to it, pressing my fingers against the concrete.

Magic cracked, an audible sound of thunder, and slammed through the quartered cross. Hints of color that weren't mine danced in the silver and blue: fuchsia and orange, rose-pink and yellow, and a deeper silver that was somehow different from my own, carrying more weight and confidence with it.

The effect was a gorgeous cascade that made auroras pale by comparison.

And something at the heart of it was desperately trying to break through. The nattering voice at the back of my head cried another warning, but something familiar rippled through the encroaching presence: the cool touch of mist, the scent of rich earth, a soft crystalline laughter from an unearthly throat. I breathed, "It's okay. I've got you."

Power spiked, almost all of it my own, but bits and pieces fed in by my friends. Their trust burgeoned in me, and I lent that to the blazing circle, offering a safe refuge for the traveler.

The boy Rider appeared, pale and disheveled and without his mare. Without the Hunt, for that matter, and, as I frowned at him more carefully, it started to look like he was without mass or physical presence, either. He whispered, "We bring death where we ride, and now death itself has called us to it. Follow me, *gwyld*. Follow me if you can."

He winked out, leaving only a glimmer of starlight behind.

CHAPTER TWENTY-FIVE

Magic wiped itself clean behind him, all the power dropping back to the earth with the ripple of a digital system creating a visual representation of music playing. It hissed into nothingness, and silence wrapped around me as my friends turned curious gazes my way.

Gary broke it, saying, "Ain't seen him in a while."

Billy, released from silence, said, "Who—what—was that?"

"Rider of the Wild Hunt," Gary said when it was clear I wasn't going to answer. "Cernunnos's son. Jo here rescued him from oblivion, or somethin' like it, back in January. What's he doin' here, Jo?"

I didn't answer. I was afraid to blink, much less speak, because I wasn't sure the whisper of starlight the Rider had left would remain visible if I did. Instead, I got to my feet and was halfway to the door before Melinda snapped, "Where do you think you're going?" in a dangerous mommy-voice.

I winced and my eyes closed. To my relief, starlight remained streaked behind my eyelids, lingering when I opened
them again. "Just to save the Riders. I'll be right back."

"Not by yourself you're not." Steel came into Gary's voice,
answering my question as to where the other silver in the
aurora of power had been birthed from.

"Yeah, actually, I am." I kept my voice to a whisper, still
afraid I'd blow away my trace vision of the Rider.

I called magic, bent light around myself, and disappeared
in front of their eyes.

It was a dirty trick, and under normal circumstances I
wouldn't have been sure I could do it. I'd never rendered myself invisible with a bunch of people actively looking on, and
part of my brain thought I shouldn't be able to. Fortunately,
my need was far greater than my uncertainty just then. The
Rider's trail was fading, and I wasn't going to get out of that
particular discussion with anything less than a melodramatic
exit.

My friends' voices erupted in astonishment as I ran as
quietly as I could for the stairs, taking them two at a time. I
stopped at the head to grab the key off the top of the door
frame—that was where the Hollidays habitually kept keys,
though I bet by tomorrow afternoon they'd be in new hiding
places—and locked my friends in the basement. Between
Gary and Billy I figured the door would last about thirty
seconds, a minute if I was lucky, but that was time in which
Petite's big old engine could warm up and I could get the hell
out of Dodge. Or Aurora, as the case actually was.

They hadn't made it to the front door by the time I pulled

out of the driveway. I let my magic go, not wanting to find out what would happen if a cop saw a car driving itself, and focused on the Sight harder than I ever had in my life.

The starlight trail didn't, of course, lead tidily down streets and highways. It barely made a trail at all, really: it was more of a gut feeling, certainty buried under my breastbone and charging me to make a left here, a right there. I could've navigated with my eyes closed and I'd still have "seen" just as clearly where I was meant to go.

It was a long enough drive that regret had a chance to raise its ugly head. None of my friends would happily accept "Suzy's premonition had a bunch of people in it, so I figured I'd change the scenario by leaving you behind" as an excuse for me running out. As it happened, that was exactly the reason for my daring escape—the more I changed the details of Suzy's premonition, the more likely it was the whole scenario would change—but my friends wouldn't think it was very convincing. Neither would Billy be any too happy with "your wife is about to give birth, stay home with her, you idiot," which was every bit as valid a motivation for abandoning him.

Oh, well. They could only kill me if I survived.

The starlight pull turned to sharp white agony through my diaphragm, cutting my breath away. I pulled Petite into an illegal parking space in front of somebody's driveway and doubled over, hands cold on the steering wheel, then shoved myself straight and stared blindly down the block. I didn't know where I was, except half a city from where I'd been. The Sight glowed with trees overhanging the blue-black mark of the street, and moonlight cut through branches to turn them even more ghostly in magic vision.

Moonlight. Suzy'd said there'd been moonlight when I went into the cauldron. That was a good sign, for some perverse value of good; it meant things were aligning properly for me to find it. On the other hand, if I could've pulled a cloud cover over and sent the details of the premonition that much more askew, I'd have been happy to. I'd have to see if quick-fixing the weather was supposed to be in a shaman's repertoire.

Later. Later, assuming there *was* a later. I inhaled through my nose, trying to breathe away some of the pain slicing my stomach. This was a family neighborhood: the Sight showed me sparks of high-energy life in the houses along the road. I imagined a lot of them to be kids too wired on sugar to be sleeping yet, and some of the more sedentary spots to be parents willing to put up with a houseful of kids on a school night just to hold an appropriately spooky party.

Cernunnos had to be in there somewhere. Maybe not one of these houses specifically, but it'd been the boy who'd come to me, not the god. If the boy had been removed from the Hunt, if he was dead, as the sudden cessation of starlight from him suggested he might be, then Cernunnos was no longer bound to the mortal wheel of life and death. I'd nearly blinded myself looking on him with the Sight once. I wasn't sure what he'd look like unbound, but I bet I'd be able to see it blazing, no matter where he was in the city.

I'd gotten out of Petite and left her several steps behind without noticing it. My keys were in my hand, suggesting I'd locked her up safely, and either I'd be dead or I'd move her before anybody tried leaving the driveway I'd blocked. That, or a never-around-when-you-need-one cop would impound her while I was out fighting bad guys.

None of which really mattered. This was classic Joanne Walker–style dilly-dallying. I took a deep breath, held it until determined air sluiced away the rest of the cramps in my belly, and asked the Sight to find me a god.

Most of the world faded away. The black bands of human-built streets became translucent, then clear, and the purposeful rigid forms of buildings melted into mist and disappeared. Even natural things like trees and moonlight became cut-away simulacra of themselves, then bleached away. Only living things were left, sparks of brilliance that turned to dust as the Sight discarded them as insufficient to be a god. The smallest things went first, bugs and birds and squirrels. Their disappearance reminded me too much of the undead critters I'd fought, and for a few seconds my concentration wavered as I hoped there were no graveyards nearby.

If I lost my focus there would be zombies all over the damn place. My hands turned to fists and I leaned into my efforts, looking at a world growing increasingly dark, in hopes of finding a single point of radiance.

Cernunnos's wildfire green hit me between the eyes, and the cauldron's black mass took me down for the count.

Monday, October 31, 11:37 p.m.

All the blood in my body had come to live in my head. My skull was so swollen with it my eyes felt puffy and my nose was stuffed. I was pretty sure it was blood and not, say, a sudden-onset head cold, because of the throbbing in my temples and the general ferocious itching of my face. I'd dangled upside down often enough as a kid to recognize the symptoms. Furthermore, the rest of my body had the opposite kind of itch, the kind that comes on from being cold due to a lack of blood flow. My hands were pretty much numb, in fact. My brain sent signals that my fingers should wiggle, but didn't get any feedback on whether that was happening.

I really didn't want to open my eyes, but I had to try anyway. *Try* was the operative word: for some reason they wouldn't open, and my psyche was of two minds about what I thought of that. The first mind was just as happy, since it didn't really want to look around anyway. The second mind was reasonably certain not being able to open my eyes was bad. I had to agree with the second one, and for all that my body was already cold, its core temperature dropped another couple degrees as low-grade panic set in. My face became a sticky, sweaty mess and bile came to make friends with already-worn enamel. My heart jumped into triple time, which made my face itch more, which was the only reason my panic stayed low grade instead of racheting up to top level. I was just too damn physically uncomfortable to give terror more than its basic due.

Beyond the thudding in my ears I could hear a whisper of leaves, the lapping of water and a man's voice mumbling in a language I didn't know. It wasn't any of the easy ones I didn't know, like Russian or Spanish or Latin. I decided I needed a smaller repertoire of ignorance, and made a note to get right on that. As soon as I figured out what had happened to me.

Well, said my sarcastic little voice, *you* could *use the Sight to take a look around. Or would that be too easy?*

I was going to start therapy and get rid of that voice as soon as I got out of wherever I was. Before reducing my general ignorance, even. Because if I didn't, one of these days I was going to take a rock and bash my own head in so I didn't sarcasm myself to death.

There was, as usual, a flaw in my logic, but I didn't want anybody, not me and not my smart-ass back-talking brain, to point that out. Teeth set together against peanut-gallery commentary and bile, I reached for my magic, and had the sudden hideous idea that it wasn't going to respond.

For once sensationalism didn't win out. Brilliant, unearthly vision spilled through the darkness, and I came to terms with an ugly truth: there were probably more humiliating things than being a shaman who awakens to discover herself trussed up, blindfolded and hanging inverted over a death cauldron, but right then I really couldn't think of any.

The goddamn cauldron was enormous. I'd seen pictures, and I'd known how much space it took up at the museum, but that was a whole different perspective than staring into its deadly gaping maw. Intellectually I knew it couldn't be more than five or six feet deep, but looking into it with the Sight was worse than looking across the Dead Zone. There, I had a sense of perspective. Granted, it was a perspective that told me how very very small I was, but that was better than staring into the cauldron. It was full of empty nothingness, and it went on forever.

Black magic rolled out of it, seductive and cool. Black didn't mean evil, just black: that was its color, but it didn't feel dreadful and wrong. It felt inviting, and it was much, much more powerful than its remnants had been at the museum. It whispered that I could relax, give up my cares, be comfortable and quiet, undisturbed for eternity. All I had to do was accept that all life came to an end, and slip within its hungry mouth.

For all that being dangled like a worm on a line was mortifying, it was a hell of a lot better than being free to fall into the thing beneath me. I scrabbled for healing magic, slamming up a barrier between myself and the cauldron. Shale blue wrapped around me, all the silvers and blues mixed together to create the most cohesive shield I'd ever built, but it didn't release me from pig-squealing terror. The magic wasn't afraid of death, not in the least. What it did and what the cauldron offered were two sides of a coin.

In no way did that make me feel better. I clenched my eyes shut, even if they were, technically, already closed. I wanted to breathe through my teeth, slow tense breaths to calm my heartbeat, but trying made me realize a gag was stuffed between them. That wouldn't have been so bad, but noticing it also made me notice it tasted like the bile I'd spat up. I gagged again and tears leaked out from under my blindfold to trickle down my forehead. My face reminded me that it itched, then took the itch up to a whole new level, like rubbing poison ivy on chicken pox.

I'd been wrong. Writhing around, sobbing and trying to scratch my face with my shoulder while being suspended above a death cauldron trumped just being suspended above the cauldron any day. I had a miserable feeling I'd be adding to that list of mortification before I got out of there.

My watch, which regularly beeped on the quarter hour and which I was typically too habituated to notice, beeped. A single beep, which meant it was a quarter-hour notification, rather than the double-beep of an hour. I didn't know which quarter hour it was. It'd been pushing ten o'clock when I'd left Petite in front of somebody's driveway. In the worst-case scenario, I had fifteen minutes to get myself out of this. Except my watch was set seven minutes fast to prevent myself from being late, so in fact in the worst scenario I had twenty-two minutes to get myself out of this, and in the best I had over ninety. I thought I should probably go with the shorter time frame, just in case.

It turned out having an extremely short deadline, where the *dead* part was going to be depressingly literal, helped clarify my thoughts to a remarkable degree. I was a shaman. I could heal things. I could, therefore, presumably encourage my blood to ignore gravity and work its way back into my system instead of trying to all explode out of my skull.

This fell under the category of *easier said than done.* I ended up with this dreadful mental imagery mixed between reinflating a tire and a clown blowing up balloon animals, but it worked. It also caused screaming pain in my extremities as blood was reintroduced to them, but at least if I could get myself out of this trap I'd be able to catch myself before I fell into the cauldron. I hoped. I hadn't quite figured out how I was going to magically snap the ropes tying me in place, but I was working on it.

I rubbed my face against my shoulder again, relieved myself of residual itching. The movement knocked my blindfold loose and sent me swinging a slow circle as the piece of cloth fell into the cauldron below me.

Seeing: a bonus. What I was seeing: less of one. The sound of water was from a family-size swimming pool a few yards—the measurement, not the behind-the-house garden area—away. The pool water glowed with a peculiar colorlessness, as though it had been sterilized. A play set with swings, a slide and a sandbox filled the area beyond the pool, but the Sight showed them as gray and utilitarian. The same held true for a beach ball and other scattered toys: none of them had any life, like they'd all been purchased for show, not use. Creepy. Appropriate for Halloween, I guessed, but creepy. It was even more appropriate to the setting in which Suzanne described my forthcoming demise, which didn't even qualify as creepy. I didn't have a word for that, except maybe *augh*. *Augh* seemed like the right response to being hog-tied in the place I was supposed to die.

I swung away from the swimming pool on a slow turn, like a rotisserie chicken, and caught a glimpse of the pole holding me up. It belonged to a basketball backboard, and beyond it sat a picnic table. That was okay. It was gray with disuse, like the rest of the yard, but generally okay.

The freezer-burned female corpse sitting at the table was considerably less okay.

CHAPTER TWENTY-SIX

My brain wouldn't let me process more than the dead woman for a few seconds. She'd been blond once upon a time, and for a desiccated corpse she still had a lot of hair. It was piled in a loose bun that was beginning to fall around cadaverous cheekbones and sunken eyes. Her skin was mostly blue, with rough raw purply-red streaks marring her flesh where it was exposed under her dress. At a guess, I thought she'd been dead for over a hundred years. Not that I really knew from long-dead bodies, but her dress looked straight out of Laura Ingalls Wilder.

The two little dead girls sitting with her, which my eyes had been trying very hard not to see, wore equally old-fashioned clothes. Their hair, dull brown, was carefully braided, and the fragile lace on their collars looked as if it'd undergone an attempt at cleaning bloodstains and viscera from them.

All three of them were partially crushed, though their bodies were sitting in such a way as to almost disguise that. The woman, though, tipped to her left, like her hip couldn't bear weight, and there was a collapse to the left side of her torso that couldn't be accounted for by perspective. Her left ankle, booted in fading leather, seemed both whole and delicate, which made the rest of the mess that much worse.

The bigger girl was angled away from me, but once my vision adapted to her mother's misshapen form, I could see that the child's shoulder and rib cage were smashed in, and I thought her face was turned the other way to hide similar damage to her features. The littler girl was more broken in half, a childish smile on her dead face as she rested her head on her arms against the table. I suspected that was the only way she could sit up at all, given the flatness of her hips and waist. Even frozen solid, her body wouldn't have the integrity to remain upright.

I rotated another quarter circle or so, and Archie Redding stopped reading the foreign language to smile beatifically at me and say, "Hello," in perfectly comprehensible English.

I said, "You crazy motherfucker," except I had a gag in my mouth, so it came out something like *"Y'kavee moffaffuka,"* which, under the circumstances, I felt got the point across. Redding looked like somebody's genial grandfather with sparkling green eyes and a sweet old smile, just as he had in his museum security photograph, although he hadn't been wearing a long black hooded robe in that. "Wwava vuk iv wong wivvu?"

"I'm sorry," he said very earnestly. "I'm afraid I can't understand you. I'd remove the gag, but I can't allow you to start screaming, so we're going to have to do without clear communication. Don't worry, though. It won't last long. I'll be cutting your throat in about ten minutes. I need a test case for the cauldron, you see. My guide suggests that between midnight and the first minute after, it has the power to actually bring the dead fully back to life, rather than simply make undead warriors like these poor fellows." He gestured to one side, and I finished my rotation to discover ten silently screaming dead men standing in rank beside me.

I admit it. I'm not proud. I screamed like a little girl. The gag did a decent job of making me sound deeper and more rugged, but in my heart of hearts I knew that the sound that had erupted from my throat was up there with the most soprano of sopranos, a pure ripping sound of absolute terror.

I spent a good fifteen seconds at it before I realized the dead men weren't lurching to pull my flesh from my bones or eat my eyeballs out or anything else of equal disgustingness. Nor, at a second look, were any of them Cernunnos or his Riders, so I flung my weight sideways and rotated back to Redding. "Whevva vukivva *Hhnnt?*"

He shook his head with what looked like a genuine affectation of sympathy. "I do wish we could speak. I'd like to know what brought you here, and there's so little time." He brightened. "But if the cauldron works as my guide believes it will, then we'll be able to talk afterward."

Hopefully, I said, *"M mmnt hweem,"* and meant it. I'd gotten all my screaming out already. I was sure I could make better use of my time than screaming if he'd ungag me. Like biting his face off, or something.

Redding looked like he'd understood me that time, but it didn't make him remove the gag.

"Whovvavuk iv vrr *ghyyyv?*" I was getting better at talking through the gag. At least, I thought I was. Redding didn't seem impressed. What's a girl got to do? I ask you.

The obvious answer was keep him talking. If I could stretch my useless interrogation out to one minute past midnight, the dead family would stay dead, I would stay alive, and maybe I could jimmy myself off the basketball hoop and knock Redding out with my body weight as I tried to avoid head-diving into the cauldron. It was a plan. I ran with it. "Vvt hhvvnd voo vr fmmvy, Revving?" I *was* getting better at talking. My gag was loosening. Apparently Redding hadn't taken Kidnapping 101 before tying me up here.

Wherever the hell *here* was. We'd visited Redding's apartment, and I was pretty sure if there was other property listed in his name, we'd have visited there, too. Either this place wasn't on the books or we'd done some embarrassingly sloppy police work. Which reminded me unpleasantly of the little army of dead men at my side. Those people had gone missing from somewhere, and they didn't bear the Redding family's freezer burns. He hadn't been keeping them on ice to use for test runs in the cauldron.

The thought that they were, in fact, hordes of undead birthed straight from the cauldron, like in the movie, swept over me, and I swung back around to look more closely at the little army.

They carried short swords and wore leather armor over their cadaverous bodies, which lent credence to them being ancient warriors torn from the cauldron's heart. Either that, or Redding had murdered a bunch of soldiers from the Society of Creative Anachronism, which honestly seemed less likely than undead killers several centuries old.

"Vve cauvvron *vrks,*" I said in genuine astonishment. I didn't want it to, but a tiny part of my brain chalked up a functioning black cauldron as unexpectedly cool. "I vvoght vrr wavvnt an army invvide it. Vrr'd vey cmme frmm?"

Redding, to my dismay, checked his watch before answering. I wasn't fooling him into losing track of time. Evidently we had enough, though, because he said, "My master gave me the incantation to retrieve ancient souls held captive in the cauldron, warriors who would protect me while I completed the ritual for my family. More were born, but most were too weak after so much time. These are all that are left."

That suggested the undead could die. I actually relaxed into my bonds, slumping in relief. There was light at the end of the proverbial tunnel. I cast a thankful glance upward, except up was down and the tunnel below me was the cauldron. I said, "Crap," so softly that the gag couldn't distort it, and, more urgently, repeated, "Vvt *did* hhvvn voo yrr fmmly?" Keeping him talking could only benefit me.

He sighed, turning a page in his book and finding the text he wanted with a fingertip before answering me. "We ought not have been traveling in winter, but it had been mild, and we hoped we might push through the mountain passes and be in California by spring. We wanted to farm, you see. That was our dream, me and Ida and the girls." He fell silent again, cheery countenance darkened with old, maddening sorrow. "There was an avalanche. I was thrown clear, but Ida and the girls…their bodies were frozen by the time I retrieved them. Some of the others in the wagon train buried their dead there, but I could never do such a thing. I took them west, all the way west, praying for a miracle that would bring them back to me." His smile came back, beatific and terrible. "And before winter broke its hold, a miracle came to me."

"Vervuvvos?"

"A banshee," he corrected, though I couldn't tell if he'd understood me. It didn't matter. His answer stripped the strength from my muscles and I sagged toward the cauldron, eyes closed in something very close to defeat. More or less everybody knew banshees were Irish harbingers of death, that they came to cry on a porch the night someone was due to die.

The one I'd met did a whole lot more, too. Every thirty years or so, when the full moon and the winter equinoxes aligned, it came to kill in the name of its master. If it could do that, I had very little doubt it could do more, like answer the prayers of a desperate man willing to do anything to restore his family. Whatever price it demanded would be unspeakable, but I doubted very much that Redding had cared about or considered that angle of retrieving his family from the dead. Revulsion flowed through me, my power's answer to a hideous idea, but Redding's expression remained serene. "It told me how to preserve their bodies in salt and ice and blood, and gave me a charm to chant when I opened my own veins to offer the blood. It offered me an answer to my prayers."

"Rivvual murvur iv nevvar a good anver." I felt strongly that this was true. On the other hand, I was a few minutes from dying and very curious. Also, I intended to stage a fanastic rescue just as soon as I figured out how. I'd left the rapier in Petite's backseat, and I wasn't sure it'd do me much good for getting out of a hog-tie anyway.

On the other hand, it was a damn sight better than nothing.

I fixed my eyes on Redding, doing my best impression of listening hard, and took a long slow breath through my nostrils to steady my breathing. I'd drawn the rapier out of nowhere once before, when the circumstances hadn't been any more forgiving. If desperation counted for anything, it would materialize in my hand any second now. Redding glanced at his watch again, suggesting my *let me explain, Mr. Bond* tactic wasn't working as well as I hoped. He tapped the text he intended to read, checked his watch a third time, then turned his attention back to me. Apparently the timing had to be just perfect, and we were still a little ways out from my impending doom. "The blood had to be my own. Family to family. Nothing else would preserve them through time until they could rise again. But I was already aging, and so the banshee offered me a way to extend my own years so I could tend to my dear wife and children. The death of a child on the eve of the dead," he said solemnly, "at every fiftieth anniversary of the year of my birth. That was the least it would accept, to give me life long enought to see my family restored."

I kept my mouth shut that time, partly because I suspected what I had to say wouldn't be helpful: *killing somebody else's kid to bring back your own seemed like a good idea?* and partly because my heartbeat had slowed and the calming, serene confidence that I could bend space just enough to grab my sword was starting to come over me. Snarking at Redding seemed like a bad exchange for possibly saving my own neck.

He gave me another startlingly beatific smile. "And it was right. I've waited a hundred and sixty-seven years for this night, and you've come to help me assure it will be successful. Even if I only have enough time to resurrect you tonight, in another year I can awaken my children and their mother."

I had the unpleasant idea that my zombie would be his companion for the intervening year, and it turned out that vampires weren't actually at the top of my Very Bad Undead list. Me as one of the walking dead beat vampires hands down. Inspired by panic, I forgot about trying to be Zen and cool and one with the universe. I'd been trying to save my own life a few hours ago when I'd yanked it through the ether. There'd been no calm involved. Right now, I was all for terror-induced teleportation. One sword coming up, or one dead Joanne going down.

And time ran out. Redding drew his hood farther over his head, making himself a black mark against the night, and took a long slim knife from beneath his robe. A sudden vivid image of Sonata hanging in the air, ghostly blood draining from long cuts on her body, sprang to mind. I wasn't spread-eagle, and he'd probably cut my throat to make sure I was dead before midnight, but I had no doubt I'd be made victim to the same five-cut ritual Matilda and the others had died in. That was a hell of a way to go.

My fingers, cold as they were, had enough feeling in them to close around the rapier's haft. I put bursting into tears of relief on my list of things to do about an hour from now, and did my absolute best to whip myself in a circle and cut Redding's totally insane head off. I was pretty sure I'd seen a movie trailer with a martial-arts expert trussed up like I was. He'd managed to kick the bad guys' asses. It could be done.

Not, however, by me. I swung around in a lazy circle without anything like enough momentum to do damage. The rapier stuck out from behind my back at a ridiculous angle, enough to make Redding step back in surprise, but I didn't think I was going to surprise him to death. I swished around again, trying to shift the sword enough to saw through the ropes around my wrists. This was, by any reasonable expectation, impossible. I'd spent a lot of time with the impossible over the last year, though, so I wasn't quite ready to give up hope. In the worst scenario, I could arch into the ties and attack the rope holding my feet. A living body entering the cauldron was supposed to be what destroyed it. It wasn't top on my list of choices, but if I couldn't get free in the next few minutes, there were worse ways to go out.

Sadly, I had not anticipated the silent platoon of undead taking the sudden appearance of my sword as a threat.

Matilda Whitehead had never gotten her bony hands on me. I didn't know how grateful I was for that until half a dozen cadavers surged forward, grasping for me. The other four swept into place around Redding, making a…prophylactic or phalanx or something like that, of protection. In the *good news* department, he wasn't actually all that happy to be protected, since his window of opportunity for murdering me was rapidly coming to a close. Sharp, skinless phalanges digging into my skin fell under *less good news*. I screamed like a little girl again, and had the bare wittering presence of mind to slam my shields outward, making them into as defensive a weapon as I could.

Three of the warriors staggered back. Another one burst into blue flame, which astonished everyone, including me, enough to stop and gape for a couple of seconds. I recovered before they did, though the two I hadn't knocked away still had their claws in me. I twisted and bucked, actively trying now, to slice the rope around my ankles so I could fall into the cauldron. Better a willing sacrifice to end a run of evil than being chewed apart by undead soldiers. On my third or fourth flail, the rapier caught in the rope with a soft hiss that signaled parting threads. I said *"Shit"* as the rope frayed and I fell.

The dead men caught me.

Cold surged through my body as though life itself tried to flee from their unfeeling hands. My shields flared, and the one part of my mind that wasn't gibbering with fear shut them down. I was balanced precariously on rickety arms whose ropy black muscle held me out of the cauldron. The last thing I wanted to do was make those arms burst into flames.

They didn't speak, the dead, but they moved together. Three tiny sways, and then a good heave-ho sent me tumbling away from the cauldron and toward Redding's swimming pool. I hit the concrete edge with my face and tasted blood, but given that I'd been expecting to taste untimely doom, blood was pretty nice.

Behind me, the distinctive note of metal leaving leather hissed. I clenched every muscle in my body and tried to flip myself over, pissed off at the idea of being stabbed in the back at this late date. I almost made it, too, but a booted foot caught me in the back of my ribs and kept me on my stomach. A wordless yell broke from my throat, and for all that it was muffled by the gag, it at least felt like the kind of thing a fighter should go out on. It was angry, full of defiance, ready to face whatever the fates had in store.

It was also a completely inappropriate response to the ropes binding me being slashed apart by someone else's blade.

My hands flopped to the ground and my feet smashed downward, thunking into the lawn that bordered the swimming pool's patio. I'd pushed blood back into my system, but actual non-magically-assisted blood flow let me know just how inadequate my efforts had been. Good enough to let me grab the rapier, but not nearly good enough to keep pins and needles that felt like pitons and spikes from driving into my extremities. I lay there for a few seconds just gasping with pain, unable to even care that my back was exposed to a bunch of presumably murderous corpses.

Once that thought worked itself through my over-oxygenated brain, I rolled over on my back and lifted my rapier in a feeble defense. The five warriors who'd taken me down stood in a loose circle, and Redding was caught in the midst of his phalanx, shouting furiously. Apparently they didn't consider him their general, because they stayed where they were, watching their mates, who were watching me. Waiting for me to do something. After a while I realized what it was.

They wanted a fair fight.

I yanked the gag out of my mouth, spat bile and jumped to my feet. My feet protested this treatment with a shriek of agony, and I had a brief dazzling image of Petite's brake pads going. Replacing brakes took a while, time I didn't have, so I slammed the idea of a little extra brake lube through my system and the dancing anguish faded. I didn't really need new brakes. I just needed to not fall down while I took on undead warriors in man-to-man combat.

All five of the semi-circle of fighters moved forward at once, as one. I guessed they didn't want a *totally* fair fight. On the other hand, I'd torched one of them already, so maybe me against nine wasn't such bad odds. Especially since I only had to stay alive about six more minutes and the witching hour would be ended.

Teeth bared in a grin, rapier aglow with life magic, I fell into a fencing stance and for the second time that day, lifted a hand to say *bring it on*.

Archie Redding threw his sacrificial knife and caught me in the belly.

CHAPTER TWENTY-SEVEN

I had learned something during the break-neck three days in January when my shamanic talents had awakened from their slumber. Well, I'd learned quite a few things, but the relevant one right now was this:

Getting a knife in the gut really *hurts.* I'd done it twice then, both times in fights with Cernunnos. It turned out having a mortal, or semi-mortal, human being wielding the blade didn't make it hurt one little tiny bit less at all. My vision went black, because going white seemed like too much effort. It was already dark out, after all. Pain didn't have to go very far to turn everything to swimming, blinding darkness. It wasn't quite a mortal injury sort of darkness—I'd had those, and this was different—but it was very calm and very reassuring and very easy. Easier than I thought it should be, which I blamed on the presence of the cauldron. It took everything I had to draw in a breath, and even doing that brought a host of regrets.

The knife moved in my belly. I honestly couldn't decide if it would be better to take it out and start bleeding, or if I should leave it in and hope I didn't cut myself up more while I fought undead warriors. I was pretty certain that either way they weren't going to give me the time to heal myself. This was not a three-second repair job, not any more than rewelding a torn door or hood would be a quick fix.

I pulled the knife out before I let myself think about it anymore. While I was doing that, I realized I wasn't wearing my Kevlar vest anymore. Not that it mattered: it was meant to stop bullets, not knives. Edged weapons had a whole different manner of entry. Still, it wasn't the sort of thing I should've lost. Redding must've taken it off me before suspending me over the cauldron. I hoped I was right about zombies not using guns.

Focusing on the missing vest in no way stopped the world turning white and spinning violently. I supposed it always did the latter, but I wasn't usually intimately aware of it. I couldn't clear my vision, so I reached for the Sight, and found it more fragile and uncertain than I was accustomed to. Still, it gave me shadows, and that was more than I could see with my normal eyes.

Redding's face was split in another of those saintly smiles. He gave me an encouraging nod: encouraging me to die, I imagined, so he could throw me in the cauldron. His bodyguards didn't look happy, though I wasn't sure what happy looked like on a dead man. My five warriors were still standing there, though they'd lifted their swords now, and I was pretty sure I could either start fighting or just get cut down.

Fighting seemed better. I was Inigo Montoya. I wasn't going to let my guts spill out on the ground while the six-fingered man got away. I stuffed my left hand against my belly, admiring how the world swam red, and raised the rapier with my right. It wobbled, but at least it offered some kind of defense. I wished I had a wall to lean against, but I didn't think the swimming pool would suddenly become a solid vertical surface at my whim.

The cauldron warriors moved in, and did it like bats out of hell. None of this sluggish-zombie routine for them, oh no. They could move fast enough to keep me from falling into the cauldron, and they could sure as hell move fast enough to look like emaciated death swooping down on me. A sword glittered in my Sight, cutting the air on its way to doing the same to my neck. I made an absolutely pathetic parry and silver skittered away. A tiny wellspring of hope opened in my chest. Maybe I could beat them after all.

A much larger wellspring of blood opened in my left shoulder as one of the others drove his sword into it. A raw yell that was more surprise than pain tore my throat, and red film poured through my vision, blocking out the Sight. The pain in my gut faded, and my nerves never got a chance to tell me how much the wound in my shoulder hurt.

Glorious, savage power rushed into me like I was drawing it from the earth. My eyes cleared, though everything re-mained tainted a dangerous crimson. I whipped around, totally uncaring that I was exposing my back to half the undead soldiers, and shoved my rapier hilt deep into the one who'd stuck my shoulder. His jaw dropped open in a fair impression of astonishment, and I jerked upward with my sword, severing the monster's breastbone and continuing toward the sky.

I did not have the strength to do that. Don't get me wrong: I've got decent upper-body strength from working on cars, and I had a noticeable height advantage over the undead guy. Moreover, his bones were probably a little fragile, since death wasn't usually good for structural integrity. And the rapier, while basically a stabbing weapon, did have an edged blade all the way to the crossguard. Still, these things did not make for splitting a body from the sternum up.

It felt *awesome*. Blazing blue magic roared along my rapier and exploded into my opponent, shattering what little of his body wasn't already cut in half. Beneath the sound of ancient flesh ripping apart, I heard another whisper of sound, and twisted to slam my sword into another soldier's oncoming blow. My teeth bared themselves in a bloody grin, taste of iron burning my mouth. Intellectually I knew that couldn't be good, but what I thought of as my intellect had largely gone to cower in a corner while I went medieval on a bunch of zombie asses.

My opponent gave me a rictus of a grin in return, undead gaze flickering over my shoulder in a classic feint. I swept my blade around, knocking his aside, recovered from my lunge and flung my left hand behind me to catch an oncoming blow with my palm. It hurt. It *had* to hurt, but that was like saying the sky had to be blue above the clouds: I knew it was true, but when rain poured down from the heavens, it didn't matter. The soldier drew his blade back, destroying the muscle and tendons of my fingers along the way.

I hissed and decided the risk of using magic as a deliberate weapon was worth it just then. My sword burned with righteous healing power that meant a quick end to the zombie warriors, and showed no signs of petering. Maybe the magic just hadn't liked being used against a god. Or maybe I was about to make the last mistake of my life, but at least it'd be a good show.

The first soldier hadn't been disarmed, just knocked off balance. He came at me again. I ducked under his sword—no mean trick, given I had at least six inches on the guy—and came up inside his guard for another through-the-sternum hit. He exploded. I jerked around, raising my useless left hand and calling power that burst from my palm tinted red with rage.

My third opponent flew back across the swimming pool, into a hedge, and lit on fire. Interestingly—even in the blur of action and anger that propelled me, it was interesting—only he burned, not the sticky black branches that held him. And the silver-white magic filling me didn't burn away or leave me exhausted. It seemed there were things I could throw it at without suffering ill effects myself.

The last two of my set came at me from opposite sides. I ducked and swung around behind the one to my right, nailing him in the neck as he collided with his friend. It looked very Three Stooges, right up to and including my sword sticking in the one's spinal cord. Gooey flesh burned away under the blade's healing power, but not fast enough for me to shake it loose, even with the preternatural strength that washed through my veins. I howled frustration and let the sword go as the fifth and final of my attackers ran at me. My plan, such as it was, was to let him run the sword through me and throttle him when he tried to pull it out, but my body was smarter than my brain. At the last possible instant I took a small step to the side and thrust my arm in front of his chest, clotheslining him.

He went down with a surfeit of grace, sword flying in an elegant arc as his arms lifted toward the sky. I pounced on him, grabbed his throat with my one good hand and poured healing power into his desiccated shell. Like his brothers, he simply exploded, spattering bits of dried-up viscera all over the yard. I could get to like that. Triumphant, I jumped to my feet, snatched up my sword—and toppled as the entire world came rushing in at my head like a planet-bashing asteroid.

I stuffed the rapier into the ground so I had something to lean on. There were body parts all around me, black and smoking with their severed ends glowing silver-blue. Pride, and then mind-boggling agony, bloomed in my chest. I fumbled my utterly useless left hand toward the hole in my shoulder, which was way too much to ask of my injured body. I tried for the other hole, the one in my gut, and couldn't manage that, either. Stymied, I dropped to my knees, right hand wrapped around the rapier's pommel, and looked up.

I'd thought berserker rages were supposed to ignore all injury and wait until the battle was over to give way to hurting. Apparently mine hadn't gone to Berserker Rage Finishing School, because I had nothing, not one single goddamn thing, left. I couldn't even muster up a whimper: it took too much energy. Blasting Cernunnos had wiped me out, too. Maybe I was paying for using healing magic offensively, after all.

On the other hand, maybe I was just paying for having a bunch of holes in my previously unperforated body. My left hand was doing something worse than throbbing. Hot wetness drained from it without any particular surcease or increase as accorded by the beat of my heart. Blood leaked from my shoulder, too, a semi-enthusiastic drizzle that I doubted could keep up the enthusiasm much longer. Finding out what my belly was doing meant looking down. I was reasonably certain I would never look up again if I did that, so I kept my gaze resolutely fixed on Redding and his bodyguards.

The latter four stepped away from Redding and moved toward me, loosening their swords in their sheaths. A groan tried to break free, but gave it up as a bad job somewhere around my esophagus. If I didn't have the energy to groan, I was pretty sure I didn't have the strength to fight off four more undead warriors. I set my teeth together carefully, mimicry of a clenched jaw that I hoped would inspire resolution within me.

It didn't, really. It didn't even inspire a rally of healing magic, which was apparently as exhausted as I was. I held on to my sword, dug deep in my gut for power, and took the one choice I thought still lay open to me.

I waited until they were close enough to flash-fry with my shields, and let loose with everything I had left.

Magic made the *fssht!* sound of a candle being doused with water and collapsed inside of me without even the faintest external flare. I went after it in a slow luxurious fall, the rapier no longer enough to hold me up.

The last clear thing I saw was four blades rising to take my life, and the Wild Hunt, accompanied by Suzanne Quinley, Gary Muldoon, Billy Holliday and Captain Michael Morrison, pouring out of the sky to override Redding's backyard like a bunch of kids playing at cowboys.

When I stepped between planes of existence, the one I was in tended to be all-consuming, whether it was my garden or the Dead Zone or a visit to the Upper and Lower Worlds that made up the trifecta of which the earth was the center. I had, once or twice, stepped out of my body and remained in the normal world, but my consciousness had gone with the spiritual version of myself, rather than the physical. I hadn't ever learned to see in two versions of reality at once, maybe because it had never been necessary.

I learned real goddamn quick right then, because there was no *way* I was gonna miss this.

My garden was by far the clearer of the two realities I stood in. It was like the diner all over again, with my disembodied emotional self kneeling above a mangled idea of my body. I knew what I was doing this time, which was both good and awful: a girl shouldn't have to patch up god-awful wounds like the ones I'd sustained *once* in a lifetime, much less two or three times. We were talking major bodywork, and to my huge relief, the magic wasn't gone. It just apparently didn't think blasting zombies was as important as surviving. It responded easily to my garden-self's ministrations, and on a distant level I felt the screaming pain in my hand ease.

All of that was secondary in my interests to watching the home team kick the hell out of a zombie army.

Okay, it was a very small army, what with only four of them being left standing, but the Hunt itself wheeled away once it had deposited my friends across Redding's back lawn. Even though I thought it'd be helpful to have a god on Morrison's side, if Redding or that cauldron had drawn the Hunt in, I really couldn't blame them for getting out of there as fast as they could. We puny mortals would only lose a lifetime, if we were thrown in the cauldron. A god and his Riders would lose eternity. Even if I wanted Cernunnos to help my friends, I could easily see how that price would be too high.

Besides, it wasn't like I was in any condition to stop him.

Morrison had ridden with the god himself, both of them on the liquid-silver stallion and both of them wearing near-identical grins of fury. I couldn't for the life of me imagine what had convinced Morrison to ride with the Hunt, but he looked comfortable on the stallion right up until the moment he dived off its wide back. He hit the ground in a roll and came to his feet less than a yard from one of the zombies, his duty weapon at the fore. I saw six flashes of light from the gun's muzzle, though I didn't hear a thing, and the undead monster collapsed with a skull full of lead.

Gary'd ridden with the bearded king, and Billy with the archer. Suzy was with her uncle, the boy Rider, and all three of the mortal passengers flung themselves away from their inhuman hosts in the brief space of time it took Morrison to wipe out the warrior he'd faced. Gary smashed into another one with a flying tackle. This time I heard something: bone popping and cracking as his weight made a ruin of an already ancient body. He rolled to his feet as easily as Morrison had, breaking into a run, and skidded to a stop beside me.

Love and joy and all sorts of other gooshy things welled up in my chest. My God, I had good friends. I'd have never expected him to take time to check on me, not in the midst of chaotic battle. Tears blurred my already-poor vision and fell over the bridge of my nose to seep into the ground. I wanted to smile, but I was still too tired. That didn't matter: the upswell of emotion actually breathed new life into my power, and the garden version of myself sparked with relief and grim triumph. My breathing eased. I could still feel wrongness in my belly, but it wasn't as bad as it had been.

Gary, my savior, my friend, my hero and my protector, yanked my still-glowing rapier from the earth, thundered back to the zombie he'd broken and began hacking it to pieces.

Every drop of romanticism and foolhardy joy went flat and wry within me. I mean, I had to hand it to him, that was a smart move, but it shot the shit out of my sails. A snicker bubbled up from somewhere inside me, which seemed like a positive sign, and I moved my head a little to get a better view of the rest of the fight. That I could was an even better sign.

Billy'd gone the same route Morrison had: he'd emptied a clip into one of the zombies, and stood over it with his gun at the ready, daring the thing to move again. It was normal, it was human, it was the expected response.

It made Suzanne Quinley look all the more extraordinary.

Suzanne flung her head back, hair white and crackling in light born of magic. Wildfire green seared from her raised fingertips, dancing over the yard like a plasma lamp. It touched Morrison, touched Gary and Billy and me, all of us at once, with a quick cold shock that discerned, deliberated and discarded us in an instant. We were living. We were meant to be.

It touched the undead warrior, and the silent monster opened its jaws in a noiseless scream. Green magic hissed into its thin blackened body, embodying it, enfleshing it. Color came back into its skin, hair sprouted, its eyes came alive. Its scream turned audible, a man's voice torn from hell and spread across the night for examination.

Then it began to youthen, hair becoming fuller, its face losing the lines of age, its body growing stronger until it was in its prime. The scream continued, and so did its unaging: from man to teen, from teen to child, all the way back to a shriveled bit of nothing that winked out with a near-silent *pop* of sound.

An echo rolled over me, an echo of a life lived centuries ago and abruptly undone. Ripped wholly out of time, as if it had never been. The part of me given over to healing stopped, filled with horror, and I came together again, more or less whole in body and spirit, to stare at Suzanne and what she'd wrought.

That was wild magic. That was chaos magic, born from a child of immortal blood. She saw the future, but could unmake a man who'd become a monster so thoroughly that he'd never existed.

It was over in seconds.

Suzy collapsed, all the brilliant color of her magic fading away. I rolled to my hands and knees, determined to get to the girl's side and make certain she was all right.

Morrison said, "Walker," with unrestrained relief.

Archie Redding's living, breathing, screaming wife erupted from the cauldron.

CHAPTER TWENTY-EIGHT

Redding cried out with a disbelief echoed by every other living being in the yard. His daughters scrambled out of the cauldron behind their mother, screams torn from their throats, too. Newborn babies cried on entering the world, but this was something worse. The Sight whispered on, stronger now than it had been over the past few minutes, and I started to move before I really understood what I was seeing.

They were alive. They were honestly, truly, swear-to-God alive, full of vivid energy and surrounded by snapping auras. Their fractured bodies were healed. Better than healed: the Sight and my magic wound together and looked through them on a fundamental level. They bled new life, as though they *were* newborns, not a single flaw or strain in muscle or bone or skin.

They screamed because smoky-black monsters were trying to pull their freshly born souls from their bodies.

The monsters reminded me of the banshee, narrow things cloaked in death shrouds that did nothing to hide their emaciated form. Bony fingers clutched each of their heads, the Sight showing me how bruises were forming beneath the vicious grips. Each of the things—hell, for all I knew they *were* banshees, if not the specific hatchet-faced Blade I'd faced once before—each of the banshees brought its hooded face to its victim's, offering a bleak kiss that ripped at their very essence. They made me think of gas masks working in reverse, sucking up to the mouth and nose and forcing poison in instead of filtering it out. And Archie Redding, who had spent half a dozen lifetimes trying to bring his family back from the dead, was held by two more of the banshees, whose faces split in screaming laughter as he struggled to free himself and join his suffering wife and children.

Ida Redding hit the ground, writhing and clutching at her face. Scrapes appeared, only some of them from her own hands. The girls, especially the littlest, had less fight in them. The little one's aura sparked too much fear and confusion to understand what was happening at all: her breath simply wasn't there, and it didn't make sense.

It made a terrible sense to me.

"Banshees feed the Master," I said so quietly I wasn't sure my voice carried beyond my own ears. I felt detached from myself, moving with purpose but watching myself from the outside. Time had slowed down; it did that a lot in critical moments. "The Blade performed ritual murders under the winter moons, only we disrupted that, so the Master's got to be awfully hungry. This must be the next best thing, or maybe even better than the rituals. These are brand-new reborn souls, too weak to fight and totally innocent. I bet pure souls taste good." The banshees, the Master, weren't like the zombies, trying to snatch bits of memory from the living. They just wanted the essence of a human soul, a tender, sweet tidbit to snack on. "The Master's one nasty son of a bitch."

Morrison, predictably, said, "What the hell's the Master?"

To my surprise, I could smile, a soft gentle little thing. I turned it on Morrison in lieu of the hug I wanted to give him, just for being himself. "I think I can save them. Sorry, Morrison. Maybe you'll forgive me someday."

I crashed back into my body, no longer feeling distant or as though time was stretching, and ran like hell for the cauldron.

Two steps away from it, Billy Holliday caught my shoulder, spun me around and cold-cocked me.

Once upon a time getting hit in the jaw by a guy Billy's size would've laid me out. As it was, I still whipped around in a circle and staggered a few steps in the wrong direction while startled magic tried to steady my inner ear and reduce the ache in my jaw.

That was all the time it took for Billy to scramble up the aluminum stepladder leaning against the cauldron and dive in.

I said, "Oh, no, you fucking *don't*," and went in after him.

I lay on my back in tall grass, a straw hat knocked forward over my eyes and a hayseed, I kid you not, a hayseed, stuck between my teeth so I had something to gnaw on. Wind hissed around me, low and quiet and comforting as bees buzzed through it. I didn't have to look to know I wore my favorite oil-stained jeans and a tank top, or that heavy boots were on my feet. I was so comfortable that pushing the hat back and rising up on my elbows to look around took some convincing.

The overgrown dry grass I lay in got shorter a few yards away from me, flattening out into a big rambling lawn that ran up against an old farmhouse. It looked ramshackle at first glance, but a second look told me it was just old, the boards faded to a non-descript gray and curtains in the windows washed free of color, but left softer than silk. It was probably a hundred years old, and for all that it showed its age, it'd been kept in good repair through all the intervening years. I liked it instinctively: it was a home, comforting and inviting.

A shadow passed through my sunshine and I squinted at the sky. Non-threatening thick white clouds puffed over the sun and moved on, letting summer heat spill down to warm my grass bed and the house's dark shingles alike. I could smell tar on the roof and fruit from distant apple trees. A hand-built fence, grayed by time, marked off boundaries that only the handful of cows and horses beyond them might pay heed to. One of them worked its way to a stream and poked its nose in, slurping loudly enough to hear over the wind and the distant sound of laughter. There was no sound of traffic, no evidence of the peaceable holding being disturbed by anything from the outside.

It felt a lot like heaven.

Not my heaven, maybe. Mine would have a falling-down barn somewhere visible on the property: a place where I might find Petite, or a cousin to her, and where I could work on her for all the long hot daylight hours. But this was somebody's idyllic world, and if this is what people got for climbing into the cauldron, I might think a deathtime of servitude to a dark master would be worth it, too.

I got up, grateful for the hat that turned sunlight into speckles instead of a blinding wall, and discarded my grass stem for another one to nibble on as I followed the laughter. Tir na nOg had brought laughter forth from the trees and earth itself, but I thought I was hearing ordinary kids. Whoever's heaven this was, it didn't seem like the kind of place peopled by the ethereal. When I got close enough to the house, I shouted, "Hello?" and had a sudden bemused hope that I wasn't about to be greeted by a shotgun and a smile.

Three kids burst around the corner of the house instead, racing pell-mell after one another with the abandon of youth. The oldest was a boy of maybe fifteen, keeping well in the lead, with a girl of around eleven behind him and another boy, about eight years old, giving valiant chase to them both.

I knew the little girl.

She was the ghostly image who'd turned up in my garden a couple of days ago, so brief and unformed I hadn't recognized her when I'd gotten a clearer look in the Dead Zone. It was the same hint of a ghost I'd seen hanging back and staying at Billy's side during Sonata's séance. She was all braided pigtails and smiles, with big brown eyes and strong fast legs, and as I watched, she gave up any hope of catching the older boy by turning to bellow, "Come on, Billy, we've almost got him!"

All the pieces fell into place.

Her name was Caroline Holliday, and she was Billy's older sister. She'd died in a drowning accident when she was eleven, probably in the same creek I could hear burbling in the background. The red-cheeked little boy chasing her was Billy, and the older boy leading the game of tag was their officious big brother, Bradley, whom I'd met a few months earlier and had utterly failed to get along with.

This was Caroline's heaven, or maybe Billy's: a place and time when his family were all together, Caro safe and alive, Brad less uptight than the man he'd grown into being.

Brad skidded to a stop when he saw me, then spread his arms, keeping his younger siblings safe behind him as he thrust out his jaw in challenge. "Who're you? What're you doing here?"

"I came looking for Billy," I said with maybe a little too much honesty. "He's a friend of mine."

"You're a grown-up," Brad said suspiciously. "And I don't know you. How can you be his friend?"

Caroline crashed into Brad's back, and Billy caught up with both of them, smacking Brad's outstretched hand to yell, "You're it!" in triumph. Then he grabbed that same hand and stared at me. "Who's that?"

"She's a bad guy," Brad said with wonderful conviction.

"No," Caroline said, and I could see all the excitement die in her eyes. "No, she's not."

The world changed around us.

I stood in a cemetery, but not a city-run or official one. It was a family plot littered with wooden grave markers and homemade crosses. Wildflowers grew up all over the place, richest on the low heaps of earth abutting the markers. Some of them were so old as to be barely there anymore, only scraps of wood that hadn't quite melted back into the ground yet.

Others were much newer, shellacked and gleaming against the elements. A fence like the one near the house surrounded the little graveyard, making it private and sacred, but still open and part of the world. It was a good place to be buried, better than almost anywhere I could think of.

Billy, an adult now, looking very like the man I knew, knelt by the freshest grave. Caroline Holliday, still eleven years old, still in pigtails and a solemn look, sat on the grave marker with her knees drawn up and her arms wrapped around them. She shouldn't have been able to: it was headstone-shaped and too narrow for even a little girl to sit on like that, but the dead, I thought, didn't have to conform to quite the same laws the living did.

"Your friend's come to get you, Billy. See?" Caroline pushed a toe out and nudged Billy's shoulder so he would look around toward me. "She came to take you away. You're not supposed to be here yet."

Caroline could no more move an unwilling Billy than she could've moved the moon, but he shifted with her touch and looked over his shoulder at me. Dismay cut lines into his face. "You're not supposed to be here, Walker. The whole damn point of hitting you was to keep you out."

I shrugged. "I'm not so good at letting my friends make dramatic sacrifices. What the hell am I supposed to tell Mel, huh? So either we're both staying or we're both going. I'm not letting this happen."

"You have to. The only thing that'll destroy the cauldron is a living body entering it willingly."

"Yeah." I squinted at Caroline, then at the sun, then around the graveyard. "Yeah, the problem with that is it didn't break apart or anything when you jumped in, or I wouldn't have been able to follow. Besides—" I shook my head and sat down, leaning against one of the headstones "—I mean, I get why you dove in. You were trying to save me. Thank you, by the way. But, Billy…why the hell did you dive in?"

He gave me a familiarly exasperated look, which made me happy. If I could still annoy him, there was hope for bringing him back. "You're a hell of a lot more important in the grander scheme of things than I am. I wasn't going to—"

I cut him off with a wave of my hand. "Overlooking the fact that I fundamentally doubt that, it's not what I'm asking. It's a death cauldron, Bill, and you've got four kids and another one due in a couple of days. Why on God's little green earth would you do something like this?"

Silence rolled over the cemetery, Caroline looking between me and Billy and back again. It took a long time for him to say, with a note of uncertainty, "I had this idea it would be all right. That I could just…rest for a while. That it'd be comfortable." Another few seconds passed before he admitted, "That doesn't make any sense."

"It's the cauldron." I tipped my head against the headstone and looked toward the sky again. Clear and blue and reassuring, an unmitigatedly beautiful day. "Every time I've gotten near it I've started wanting to climb in. I don't know if it really offers peace, Billy, but it sure as hell talks a good game. The cauldron itself is seductive. It makes you want to get in it."

"Well, how can that be? If living people just want to climb in—" His mouth worked and while I was pretty sure it wasn't his original intention, his sentence ended with, "Shit."

"Yeah. So I don't know how we destroy it."

Caroline's foot thumped against her headstone. "You could ask the expert." She sounded more like Billy than I'd expect a little girl to. They used the same inflections, though her voice was a couple octaves higher.

"Billy is my expert. What he don't know, I don't know. Only I don't know a lot more than he don't know." I frowned and stopped talking, afraid I'd get myself stuck in a paradox or something.

"No," Caroline said patiently. "I meant, you could ask the dead girl."

She'd looked pretty normal, right up until then. She'd looked, you know. Alive. That trapping fell off, turning her into something unlike anything I'd ever seen. She was still generally little-girl shaped, still with braided pigtails and a solemn smile, but it was like the girl had been peeled away to reveal a pure bright soul beneath it. She wasn't alive. She hadn't been for a long time, but it hadn't left the kind of mark on her that it had on Matilda Whitehead. Love had kept her from moving on, not vengeance, and over the years that had just kept building up.

Billy's mortal form began to fall away, too. I didn't like that: it suggested too strongly that he was dead, and that me diving after him into the cauldron hadn't done any good, which was not an answer I was prepared to accept. But stripping away the human shell let me begin to understand just how tightly entwined his soul was with Caroline's; how much she'd been informed who Billy had become. They'd been best friends in life, the big sister protective and proud of her little brother, the younger brother awed and admiring of the older sister. I could hardly imagine the intensity of their bond surviving into adulthood had she lived, and at the same time desperately hoped would have.

But she hadn't lived. She'd drowned, and she'd been so worried for her baby brother that she hadn't gone on to wherever human spirits usually went. She'd stuck around, protective and protecting, and the place that had always belonged to her inside his own soul had made a little more room, accepting her there. He saw ghosts because part of him was one.

Unhappy certainty crawled up from within me and made me ask, "How do we break the cauldron, Caroline? If it's not a living body, what is it?" I knew the answer. I hadn't until now, but I knew the answer, and I wanted her to give me another one.

Radiance spilled from her as though the question made her glad. "An innocent spirit," she said lightly. "That's all it takes. An innocent spirit."

"Like you," I whispered. Like an eleven-year-old girl who'd never had much chance to live.

Caroline smiled. "Like me."

Billy's human form closed up over his spirit-self again, a growl contorting his voice. "Like hell."

Caroline turned to him, putting brilliant fingertips against his chest. "I'm so far overdue, Billy. I should've gone on years ago. You know that. Even Bradley knows it. It's why he hates all of this so much. It's long past time for me to let go, and if I do it now…" Her smile blossomed again. *Smile* didn't come close to what happened when she expressed happiness. The whole world around us lit up, grave markers casting white shadows and a sense of joy and excitement wiping out other emotion. It utterly lacked in artifice, but was wise enough about the world to make it achingly poignant.

"If I go now," Caroline said again, "I can help you. I can save that family. I can put all those restless dead back to sleep. It's a good time, Billy. This is a good time to go."

"Caro…" Billy's voice cracked.

I got up and jerked my head toward the world beyond the little graveyard. "I'll wait out there. Take your time." I walked out and closed the gate behind me, as though doing so could give them the privacy they deserved.

A few minutes later a supernova expelled us onto Archie Redding's lawn.

CHAPTER TWENTY-NINE

Tuesday, November 1, 12:01 a.m.

From my perspective, quite a lot of time had passed since I'd jumped into the cauldron. From the world's, it looked like very little time had passed at all, and yet what *had* passed was filled with bitter dredges.

There was no fight left in Ida Redding's body, nor in her daughters'. They were still relaxing, in fact, falling out of tormented arches and twisted shapes to collapse into stillness on the earth. A terrible stillness: one that spoke of life already spent and gone. I didn't need the Sight to tell me we'd broken the cauldron too late, but it washed over me anyway, lighting up the bodies of three people who should have been left in peace more than a century and a half ago.

Two things came blazingly clear, holding me in time and

letting the rest of the world fall back in irrelevance for just an instant. The Reddings' fresh-born souls still lingered, bewildered and injured but not ripped from their bodies; not swallowed by the banshees' hunger. I blinked in astonishment and my ability to see them faded; mine wasn't a talent for observing ghosts, and all I was left with was a layered look at the bodies they'd abandoned.

Between midnight and one minute after. That was the window Redding could revive his family in. What he hadn't known, what the banshees and the Master had never told him, was that those sixty seconds would be the only time in which life ran in their veins again. The bodies lying on the grass were tens of decades dead, burned with years of primitive preservation. It hadn't been only salt and ice that had kept them together, but magic, as well, and I could see that fading; could see the collapse of cellular structure. They would decompose by morning, finally gone to the ashes they should have been so many years ago. Exhaustion and sorrow closed my eyes for a moment, before I made myself look again at the chaos surrounding me.

Redding himself was on his knees with his forehead against the earth, hands folded over his head. I could hear his sobs, and thought, uncharitably, that he was doing nobody any good. Suzy was hidden behind Gary, who still had my blazing blue rapier in hand, though he'd flung his sword arm up as if in defense. Morrison looked as though he—

Actually, he looked like he was in the midst of cauldron-diving himself, only to rebound off an invisible barrier. He looked pissed, mostly, with a solid dash of confused added to the mix.

As for myself, I lay on a huge iron-bound oaken circle, shards of the cauldron blown to bits around me. In fact, iron bands were scattered all over the yard, and chunks of oak were floating in the pool. A half circle of slivers, some delicate and some massive, lay at Morrison's feet, like they'd hit something and slid off again. I shot another look at Gary and my sword. He lowered it and shrugged.

Belatedly, I realized I was technically lying on Billy, not on the cauldron's base at all, and that he wasn't breathing.

There was something in shamanism called *soul retrieval,* which was exactly what it sounded like: sometimes people get inexplicably sick and began to fade away. The shamanistic viewpoint on that was their souls somehow become dislodged from their bodies, which then begin to die, as the essential life force is no longer there to vitalize it. Soul retrieval was the moral equivalent of Shamanic Graduate School: it was not the sort of thing the half-trained and emotionally damaged should undertake.

Obviously, I undertook it. I rolled off Billy's chest bellowing, "CPR! CPR! Morrison, he needs CPR!" which, really, was not the calmest or most awesomely shamanistic way to approach the situation. The truth was, though, I didn't think I had the stuff to get Billy's breathing back in line and go chasing after his soul at the same time. I trusted my boss could handle restarting Billy's heart.

Me, I closed my eyes and ran for the Dead Zone.

I had one advantage. I *knew* Billy's soul had gotten lost. I wasn't working on conjecture. Caroline had wiped out the cauldron, and it could be read one of two ways. One, she'd taken too much of Billy with her. Two, and this was the one I thought more likely, he'd just flat-out refused to let go, and had been ripped away from the life she was trying to give back to him. If there was anything left to her now, she'd be trying to stop him from crossing over. I just needed to get there in time to give her a helping hand.

The Dead Zone refused to let me in.

Intellectually I knew why. I was too agitated, not centered enough, and hadn't been forcibly thrust into an alternate state of consciousness by, say, being clocked over the head. Shamans, I suspected, were supposed to be patient. Patience was a virtue. I was not especially virtuous. I felt Morrison crash down beside me on the cauldron's remnants and let go a silent shout at the inside of my head: Morrison was doing *his* part. I had to do mine so he wouldn't be disappointed. I had to do whatever it took to find Billy and stitch him back to his body. While I railed at myself, Gary picked me up and moved me from the cauldron, which was no small feat. A moment later I heard a whisper of breath being pressed out of Billy's lungs, like wings on the wind.

Raven wings had cut the air when I'd last left the Dead Zone.

I dropped my chin to my chest, throat going tight and eyes filling with hot tears. "Raven, Morrigan, Trickster, Maker. You guided me once before. You showed yourself to me when I sought a teacher. I don't do you the honor I should, I know that, but for what it's worth, it's because I'm an idiot, not because I don't trust you. I just don't…think about giving thanks and bringing baubles. I'm still not very good at this. I'm taking it more seriously, but I'm still not what anybody'd want me to be." I opened my eyes, turning a tear-stained face toward the cool distant moon. "I need your help, Raven. Protect my spirit. Protect my soul. Help me find my friend. Please."

Sleek black feathers enclosed me, and I fell backward into the Dead Zone.

I had never, not once, felt any degree of control in the Dead Zone. Sometimes I could slide from place to place, but mostly if I moved it was through my subconscious getting the better of me. Tackling Jason had been a by-product of my entrance: an object in motion tends to stay in motion.

The raven on my shoulder changed all of that.

I didn't know if it was because ravens were so strongly associated with death, or if it was that having a spirit guide in a dangerous part of the astral realm genuinely made it safer. Either way, the Dead Zone's near-infinite curve shrank to a definable space, one that I could look from end to end of. My vision was unusually sharp and clear, letting me see things I'd never seen before. Tens of thousands, maybe hundreds of thousands, of ghosts slipped through the emptiness. They were on a journey, and for a brief moment I saw all the paths they took. Thousands upon thousands of them traveled a river; thousands more walked hand in hand with a figure who shifted from the familiar cowled death's-head to a slender and effete being I thought of instantly as Morpheus. As many again rose upward, soaring to whatever lay beyond, and thousands sank down, all of them crossed the Dead Zone in search of another world.

I could have seen them all, if I'd wanted. Could have looked into their eyes, known them as the people they'd been. My vision was that clear, a raven-sharp consideration of a transition mortal eyes weren't quite allowed to see. Another time I might want to do that: to sit and consider, to sense fear or hope or a hundred other emotions, but not now. Not with Morrison trying to force breath back into Billy's body, and his spirit taking one of these innumerable tracks to a new aspect of existence.

"Help me find Billy?"

My raven companion leaped off my shoulder and winged its way through the starless void. The half shadows of passing mortality faded with its departure, leaving me alone in a zone grown smaller but no less mysterious.

What felt like a heartbeat later, but had to have been longer, given the distance the raven had traveled, it let forth an excited caw and spun around on a wingtip. I took a single step and joined it, trying not to gape at the space I'd crossed. It settled down on my shoulder again, and clarity washed over my vision again.

Billy rode on the river, one of many in a long flat boat poled by a man with coins for eyes. I caught his shoulders— Billy's, not the boatman's—and he turned an uninterested gaze on me. I swallowed, suddenly nervous. The raven dug its claws into my shoulder reassuringly, making me wince. "Ow. Hey. Hey, Billy. It's me, Joanie. Joanne," I corrected myself, then wrinkled my face and leaned forward to whisper in his ear.

"It's me, Joanne, except you kind of deserve better than that, don't you. My name's Siobhán Grainne MacNamarra Walkingstick, and you're my partner in defeating crime, and I'm hoping you don't really want to take this path just yet."

He stayed still, not responding. I sat back, lower lip in my teeth. "Come on, Billy. I can take you home. If you think this might not be your time, c'mon and listen to me. We'll get through this. Caroline didn't finally let go just to have you join her right away. You must know that."

His pupils dilated at his sister's name. Relieved laughter gasped through me. "Yeah. You remember Caro, Billy. She's been watching out for you all this time. You know what she's done to protect you. You know she didn't do it just so you could give up and die. Come on. Come home with me, Billy. You need to get back to Melinda and the kids. Remember them? Robert and Clara and Jackie and Eric? The new one on the way? You remember."

His gaze got clearer with every name. The raven's claws tightened again and it plucked a strand of my hair out, making me yelp. The sharp sound got an uncertain laugh from my partner, whose eyebrows drew down after a few seconds. "Joanie? Is that a raven on your shoulder?"

"Yeah," I said, back in the real world. Billy dragged in a sharp breath all on his own, sending Morrison and Gary back a few feet in relief and surprise. "Yeah," I said again. "It is. Welcome back to the world of the living, Detective Holliday. I think I'm gonna have to do a spirit quest for you, man. Find some kind of totem animal willing to keep you out of trouble when you're hanging around me."

Billy closed his eyes and lay there for a minute, looking and sounding like all he was doing was practicing breathing. Then he said, "That sounds like a good idea. Shouldn't I be dead?" in a very calm voice.

I knew that voice. It was the one I used when I was trying

really hard not to panic. "Not for lack of trying on your part. I took it up with the management." I put my hand over his heart, calling a whisper of healing magic to make certain of its steadiness. It felt tired, which I could certainly appreciate, but his aura was strong enough, and I slipped a bit of magic under his skin, hoping it would help.

His breathing got easier and he lay there another minute, staring at the sky. For a scene as chaotic as Redding's backyard had been a few minutes earlier, it was incredibly quiet now. The moonlight and water were peaceable, and not even Morrison had anything to say. Finally Billy said, "Thanks." Three sets of hands reached out to help him as he sat up. He said, "Thanks," again, and we all flinched back about five feet when his cell phone rang.

"It's five minutes past twelve," I said in astonishment. "Who's calling you?"

He found his phone, paled in its blue screenlight, said, "Mel," and answered with a hurried "Mel? Is everything— What? Right *now?* Oh, hell. No, I'm— No, Mel, this isn't a good—"

"Holliday," Morrison said in disbelief. "If that's your wife telling you she's giving birth, you had better not be about to tell her *this isn't a good time.*"

Billy's mouth snapped shut. His gaze shifted from me to Morrison to Gary, then back to the captain, and he cleared his throat. "Call an ambulance. I'll meet you at the hospital. I love you, Melinda." He hung up with a look of tortured apology that Morrison made another disbelieving sound at.

"Go. For God's sake, Holliday, go. Your wife is giving birth. If you're strong enough, get out of here. We can wrap this up without you."

Billy retained the apologetic look another few seconds. "I'm fine. I shouldn't be, but I'm fine."

"That happens a lot around Walker. Go on, Detective." An unexpected smile slipped over Morrison's face. "And congratulations."

Billy's expression faded from apologetic to shocked, then took a sharp right turn toward thrilled. "Thanks, Captain." He scrambled to his feet and tore out of Redding's yard like his tail was on fire.

I pursed my lips. "How's he going to get to the hospital? You didn't exactly come in on normal channels."

Morrison looked pained. "The department'll pick him up if he's got enough sense to call it in." He took his cell phone out and made the call himself, requesting a second squad car for himself. "Walker, do we have any concrete evidence on this guy?"

This guy was Redding, who'd crawled to his dead family and lay still among them. Very still: entirely too still, in fact. I jerked a few steps toward him, then ran the rest of the way, dropping to my knees to put a hand over his chest. Neither heartbeat nor breath stirred, and blue magic flared, instinctively rising to the challenge of forcing life back into a broken body.

I turned my gaze toward Morrison. "I think he's had a heart attack. Um. Should I...?"

"Can you?"

"Yes." Tired confidence filled me. "Yes. I can save him. He can stand trial for trying to kill me. For killing Jason Chan, probably. For—"

Suzy quietly said, "There are bodies buried beneath the swimming pool. I can see police officers digging them up. I can see—" She blanched and shivered. "I can see the rituals he tried to bring them back. I can see his anger, his despair. He needed the cauldron. Nothing else had the power, but he kept trying. He has a lot to answer for."

I rolled my lips in, then nodded. "There's your evidence, sir, and it'll go down a whole lot better than attempted murder when I don't have a scar on me to prove I was attacked. Or we could just…"

Morrison's silence didn't last that long: it couldn't, not when a man's life was in the balance and every second counted toward brain functionality. But it seemed like a long time indeed before my captain exhaled and said, "Do what you think's best, Walker. This one's your call." He turned away, deliberately leaving me to Redding and my own decision.

I looked down at the four bodies surrounding me. Three broke and shrank as I watched, and the fourth was achingly whole beside them. Whole, and yet what was inside him was more badly distorted than even the rapidly decaying family around him.

I could bring him back. Make him stand trial; make him answer for murders whose resolution might close heartbreaking chapters in strangers' lives. I could make him face a world in which he'd failed in a mission of such desperate love that it had taken him across centuries and driven him to commit horrendous crimes. I could force him to live with a broken heart, maybe with a broken mind, until death came to his door again. I could make him face the faces of those whose families he'd murdered, and could hope he would pay a price in guilt every day for the rest of his life.

I could not, in any way, see how doing that would make the world a better place.

The bodies below the pool would be identified. Answers would be brought to grieving families. They might be denied the catharsis of a trial, but they would be offered another, even more final solution to their hurt: the man who had done these things to their loved ones was dead.

Archie Redding had died knowing he'd lost. I couldn't imagine a heavier price for him to pay, and I had no stomach at all to prod him back to a life of nothing but sorrow. I closed my hand, healing magic subsiding within me, and got to my feet with tears sliding down my face.

"S'a good girl." Gary slipped his arm around my shoulders and pulled me against his chest. A sob broke in my throat and I made a fist against his chest, coughing tears. "S'a good girl," he said again, into my hair. "Right choice ain't always easy."

"Is it ever easy?" My voice shook like a kid's, and he squeezed me tighter.

"'Course. Looked like divin' into that cauldron was easy."

I snorfled against his shoulder and took a step back with a hoarse laugh. "Pretty much, yeah. What happened when I went in?"

"It exploded," he said with as much satisfaction as I'd felt at blowing up the undead warriors.

I sniffled again, but my smile got stronger. "That's what I hoped it would do. How come you didn't get blown up?"

He lifted my rapier, which he'd been holding away as he hugged me. "Guess this sword of yours tapped into the medal I gave you, 'cause it threw up a shield that kept us all from gettin' perforated." He said the last word like it was made of candy, rolling it around in his mouth. "Didja see our entrance, darlin'?"

"You mean you, the Wild Hunt and about a million pounds of kick-ass? Yeah. I caught that." Tears still spilled down my cheeks, but a grin worked its way across my face. I shouldn't be grinning. All sorts of things had gone badly tonight. I'd almost died. Billy'd almost died. The grin, though, wouldn't die. "How'd that happen? How'd you pull it off?"

Suzy stepped up, all but digging her toe in the earth. "I Saw the Hunt's terror. The cauldron was pulling them in, so I called them to me again. I guess blood's even stronger than death."

I glanced after Billy, thought of Caroline, and felt my smile go crooked. Happy, but crooked. "Yeah, I think sometimes it is. Good job, Suzy. Good job, everybody." I stuck the sword in the ground and dragged both of them into enormous hugs so I could mumble, "And thanks for saving my ass tonight. How'd you all *get* here? I mean, Suzy, if you called the Hunt, I can see them bringing you, but..."

She shrugged, characteristic teenage abrogation of responsibility. "Captain Morrison was there, and he told Grandfather that we needed to get Detective Holliday if any of us were going to come out of this alive."

I twisted to give Morrison's shoulders an astonished look. "Cernunnos listened to *Morrison?*"

"Well, I had to tell Grandfather he should, but then he did."

My grin turned, very briefly, into a giggle. Not even the Horned God of the Hunt could stand before the Mighty Morrison. I felt better about, well, everything. "Thank you," I said again. "Thank you all."

"S'what the good guys do." Gary squeezed me until I grunted, then guided Suzy out of the way as cops and forensics experts began pouring in.

Morrison left me to clean up the mess. Fortified by Gary and Suzanne making a coffee run, I stayed on until dawn, when Billy called and invited me over to the hospital.

Technically, Tuesday was the second day of my weekend. I passed supervisor duties over to somebody else, got Petite out of her illegal parking space and drove myself, Gary and Suzanne over to Northwest Hospital to meet the newest Holliday.

Melinda was asleep by the time we got there. Billy was waiting outside the maternity ward, holding a red-faced little bundle whose tiny eyes were squinched shut and showed off long eyelashes to great effect. All of us erupted in a spontaneous *awww* that made Billy look fit to pop with pride.

"We're thinking of calling her Joanne."

"Don't be silly." I bent over the baby and kissed the top of her head, marveling at the softness of her hair and skin. "Don't be silly, Billy. Call her Caroline. She should be Caroline."

They compromised. I had to ante up a whole lot of well-deserved explanation, but in the end, the name on her birth certificate went down as Caroline Siobhán Holliday.

I thought that was good.

★ ★ ★ ★ ★

Don't miss Book Five of the Walker Papers,
coming in 2010!

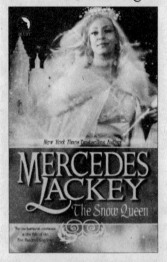

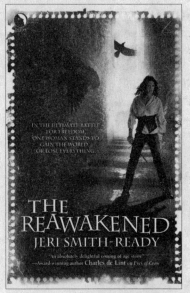

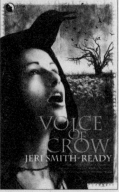